TERMS OF
ENLISTMENT

TERMS OF
ENLISTMENT

MARKO KLOOS

47NORTH

Revised edition: Text copyright © 2014 Marko Kloos
Originally published March 2013
All rights reserved.

Published by 47North, Seattle

www.apub.com

ISBN-13: 9781477809785
ISBN-10: 1477809783

Library of Congress Number: 2013948461

Cover Illustration: Marc Simonetti
Cover Design: Sam Dawson

Printed in the United States of America

For Robin: wife, best friend, and the most able person I know.

TERMS OF
ENLISTMENT

CHAPTER 1

FAREWELLS

"You should go see your father," my mom says from the kitchen.

I look up from my book reader and glance at her. She is putting a meal tray into the warming unit, so she can't see the smirk I'm giving her. I go back to reading about the destruction of the *Pequod*, which is a much more interesting subject right now.

"Did you hear me, Andrew?"

"I heard you, Mom. I'm just ignoring you."

"Don't be a smart-ass. Are you not going to go and say goodbye before shipping out?"

"Why the hell should I? He'll just be drugged out of his mind."

Mom takes the meal tray out of the food warmer. She walks over to the table and puts the tray in front of me, with emphasis.

"Put that thing away for dinner, please."

I let out a sigh—also with emphasis—and turn off the book reader.

"You'll be in training for months, Andrew. With the way his cancer is going, you'll probably never see him again."

"Good," I say.

Mom glares at me with an expression that's a blend of sadness and anger, and for a moment, I'm expecting her to slap me across the face, something that she hasn't done since I was ten. Then her glare softens, and she looks out of the window. Thick bands of rain are pouring down onto the concrete gerbil maze of our Public Residence Cluster. I hate rainy days—the moisture makes the smell worse. Piss and decaying garbage, the ever-present aroma of the welfare city.

"He's still your father," she says. "You'll never get another chance to speak to him again. If you don't go and see him, you'll regret it someday."

"You broke his *nose* when you left him," I remind her. "You weren't too broken up about the cancer. Why the hell should *I* care?"

"That was seven years ago," Mom says. She pulls out a chair and sits down at the table. "A lot of stuff has happened since then. He was proud of you when I told him about your acceptance letter, you know."

She looks at me, and I try to ignore her gaze as I peel off the seal on the meal tray. The flavor of the day is chicken and rice. There's not much you can do with the processed protein in the Basic Nutritional Allowance to make it appealing. I poke the fake chicken patty with my fork and look up to see that Mom is still looking at me with that dejected expression she has when she's trying to make me feel bad about something. I hold her gaze for a moment and then shrug.

"I'll go and see him," I say. "And if I get robbed and killed on the way over there, I hope you feel bad about it."

My room is just big enough for a bed, desk, and dresser. The furniture is made out of stainless steel, bolted to the floor so we can't dismantle it for scrap. The dresser is half empty. I don't own enough stuff to fill it up.

I open the top drawer, and toss the book reader onto the small pile of clothes inside. I traded a box of ancient rimfire ammunition for it last year, and the guy who traded with me thought I was a complete moron. The school property stickers are impossible to remove, but the public-housing police don't get excited about school hardware. When they do their sweeps, they only look for guns and drugs. I could keep the book reader hidden if I wanted, but the cops get suspicious when they find nothing illicit at all.

As I walk through the apartment to the front door, my mother sticks her head out of the kitchen nook.

"Andrew?"

"Yes, Mom?"

"It's Sunday. Are you going to stop by at the food station and pick up your allowance for the week?"

"I'm leaving for Basic tomorrow. I won't be around to eat it."

Mom just looks at me, and she almost looks like she's ashamed. Then I catch her drift, and I shrug.

"I'll pick up my allowance, Mom."

She opens her mouth to say something, but I turn around and close the door behind me, and her reply blends with the hollow clap of the door slamming shut.

The elevator in our wing of the building is out again. I pop the door of the staircase near the elevator, and listen. The stairs are a hangout for the various packs of apprentice hoodlums, who use the confined space to gang up on people. The public-housing police only show up in force when they do a drug-and-gun sweep. The rest of the time they stay well away from the tenements. We have security cameras on every floor, but most of them are broken. Nobody gives a shit about welfare rats.

Our apartment is on the twelfth floor of a thirty-floor building. I make my way down the stairs, taking three and four steps at a time, speed over stealth. At the bottom of the staircase, I pause again to listen. Then I open the door to the lobby and hurry out of the building to fetch my gun.

Guns are illegal in welfare housing, but just about everybody has one anyway. I don't keep mine in the house because of the random checks, and because Mom would have a fit if she found it. I hide it in a waterproof tube that's stuck into a crevice of the building's huge, mobile trash incinerator. It's a great hiding place—nobody ever checks there, and the container is always in the same spot—but it leaves me easy prey until I get out of the building. I check to make sure nobody is watching, and walk over to the trash container.

Every time I reach into the crevice, I expect to come up empty. Every time my hand closes around the cool metal of the magnetic storage cartridge, I let out a breath of relief. I open the lid and take out my gun. It's an ancient cartridge revolver, made over a century and a half ago. It holds only six rounds, but it works even with crummy ammunition, which is far more common than the good kind. Most of my meager ammo stash is hand-loaded from old brass cases and scrounged lead scraps. Revolvers are more popular than automatics because a dud doesn't tie up the gun.

I stick the revolver into my pants, right behind the hipbone, where the tension of the waistband holds the gun in place. It's risky to walk around with an illegal gun, but it's riskier still to walk around in the Public Residence Cluster unarmed.

There's one thing that's nice about the rain. It keeps most people indoors, even the predators. When it rains, the streets outside are almost peaceful. I pull up the hood of my jacket and walk out into the street.

I'm soaked to the bone within five minutes. You can stay mostly dry if you use the awnings and building overhangs as cover, but I'd rather get wet. Doorways and other dark places close to buildings are dangerous. You walk past one where a bunch of apprentice thugs loiter, and your journey is over. I almost got mugged twice last year, and I'm more careful than most.

My father's apartment building is almost at the other end of the PRC. There's a public-transit station nearby, but I can't enter without setting off the gun scanners at the entrance, so I walk.

This is the place where I grew up. I've never been outside the Boston metroplex. Tomorrow, I'll be off to Basic Training, and if I don't wash out, I'll never see this place again. I'm leaving behind everything I've ever known, and everyone who's ever known me, and I can't wait.

Dad opens the door after my third buzz. I last saw him over a year ago, and for a moment I am shocked at how much he has changed since then. His face is haggard. When he was younger, he was a very handsome man, but the cancer has eaten most of his substance. His teeth are horrible, enough to make me want to recoil when he opens his mouth to smile.

"Well, well," he says. "Come to say your good-byes, have you?"

"Mom sent me," I say.

"Of course she did."

We look at each other for a few heartbeats, and he turns around and walks back into the apartment.

"Well, come in, come in."

I step into the hallway of his apartment and close the door behind me. Dad walks over to the living room, where he drops onto the couch with a sigh. There's an enormous collection of medical supplies on the table in front of him. He catches my glance and shrugs.

"Pointless, all of it. The hack at the clinic says I'll be worm food in six months."

I want to give him a snide reply, but somehow I can't bring myself to do it. The room smells like sickness, and my father looks miserable. The cancer is eating him up from the inside, and he'll die in this place, where the stairwells smell like piss. There's nothing I can say or do that will make him feel worse than he does already, nothing that will make me feel any better.

When I was fourteen, I would have given anything for a chance to kill my dad, take revenge for all the beatings and humiliations. Now he's in front of me, weak enough that I wouldn't even need the gun tucked into my waistband, and I have no hate left for him.

"I thought your mother was lying to me," he says. "I didn't think you'd pass. You and your books."

"Yeah, maybe that had something to do with it," I say. "They do need people with brains, too."

"You'll be pushing buttons somewhere. No way they'll send you out to kill other people. You don't have it in you."

Why, because I never fought back when you used me as a punching bag?

His remark is the perfect excuse to hurl something back at him, but I realize that he's trying to provoke me, and I don't want to give him the satisfaction.

"We'll see about that," I say, and he flashes a faint smile. I look so much like him that it hurts. If I end up washing out, I'll be back here in the PRC, and then I'll end my life just like this someday, alone and afraid, confined to a few dozen square yards in the middle of a welfare city. PRC housing doesn't stand empty for long when someone dies. They throw out your stuff, hose the place out with a chemical cleaner, reset the access code for the door, and hand the apartment over to a new welfare tenant the very same day.

"When are you shipping out?"

"Tomorrow evening," I say. "I report to the processing station at eight."

"Keep your nose clean. If you get arrested, they'll fill your slot with someone on the waiting list."

"Don't worry about that," I say. "When in doubt, I'll just think of what *you* would do, and then do the opposite."

Dad just rasps a chuckle. When we were still living under one roof, that kind of belligerence would have gotten me a beating, but the cancer has sapped the passion out of him.

"You've turned into a little shithead," he says. "All full of yourself. I was just like that when I was your age, you know."

"I'm nothing like you, Dad. *Nothing* like you."

He watches, amused, as I turn to walk out of his apartment.

At the door, I turn around.

"Just go," he says as I open my mouth to say good-bye. "I'll see you again after you wash out."

I look back at him, the man who contributed half of my genetic code. I tell myself that this is going to be the last time I see him—that I should say something that will make me feel like I have closure. Instead, I just turn around and walk away.

I step into the dingy hallway outside and walk to the top of the staircase at the end. As I reach the stairs, I hear the door of my father's apartment closing softly.

———

On the way home I stop at the food station to pick up my weekly meals. They come in sealed, disposable trays, twenty-one to a box. Every welfare recipient gets a box per week, fourteen thousand calories of Basic Nutritional Allowance.

The stuff in the BNA rations is made of processed protein, enhanced with nutrients and vitamins and artificially flavored to make it palatable. They say it's deliberately designed to taste merely tolerable because it discourages excessive consumption, but I think that no scientific process can make BNA rations a culinary delight. In the end, it still tastes like they used ground-up feet and assholes for the raw protein, which is probably not too far from the truth. One of my friends in school claimed that BNA rations are partially made of reconstituted human shit from the public water-treatment plants, which is probably not too far from the truth, either. Public drinking water is recycled piss anyway, so it wouldn't be much of a stretch to complete the circle.

The rain is still coming down steadily. At the tenement high-rise next to ours, some guys are hanging out under the overhang by the entrance. They notice the box under my arm as I trot by, but none of them must like the idea of getting soaked to the bone for a few trays of badly flavored soy, because they all stay put.

As I walk up the stairs to the front door of our apartment building, I remember the gun on my hip.

There's one more thing left to do this evening.

Eddie and I meet in a dirty alley between two residence towers. Eddie buys and sells almost anything of value—guns, drugs, vouchers for the food stores outside the PRC, and fake ID cards that sometimes hold up to inspection.

"How much ammo do you have for this thing?"

"Eight factory rounds, and twenty-seven home-rolled," I say.

Eddie opens the cylinder and then spins it, something he has done three times already during our negotiation. It's almost painful to see my gun in the hands of someone else. I know that I'll never hold it again if the deal goes through.

"You're tossing that in, of course," he says.

"Of course. What am I going to do with the bullets without the gun?"

"Thirty-Eight Specials are common on the street," Eddie says. "You could sell the ammo to someone else."

"I'm joining the service tomorrow. No time to go shopping around. Call it a package deal."

"A package deal," Eddie repeats. "Okay."

He looks the gun over again, and nods to himself.

"Two commissary vouchers, and two ounces of Canada Dry. Last you for a week or more if you don't run around and share."

I shake my head.

"No go on the dope. If I test positive, they'll kick me out. Four commissary vouchers."

Eddie pinches his chin with thumb and forefinger in thought. I know he made up his mind on my offer the second it was on the table, but I let him go through the ritual anyway.

"Three vouchers, ten pills, regular meds, your pick of house stock."

I pretend to think about it.

"Three vouchers, fifteen pills," I say.

"Deal."

Eddie holds out his hand. We shake on the transaction, and my revolver disappears underneath one of the many layers of Eddie's clothing.

"What kind of pills do you have?"

"Let's see," he says. "Painkillers, antibiotics, blood-pressure stuff, uppers, a few downers."

"How good are the painkillers?"

"Headaches and stuff, not 'getting shot' kind of pain."

"Good enough," I say. "Let me have those."

Eddie reaches into his coat, gets out a tube of pills, and counts fifteen into my hand.

"These better be real," I say as I tuck the pain meds into my pocket.

"Of course they are," Eddie replies, mild offense in his voice. "I have a reputation, you know. People end up with fakes, they'll never buy from me again."

He reaches into one of his pockets again, and presents three commissary vouchers with a flourish, like a winning hand of cards.

"Appreciate the business," he says as I take the vouchers.

"I'll see you around, Eddie," I say, and know without a doubt that I won't.

———————

Mom looks up from her Network show when I walk back into the apartment.

"How was it?"

"Pointless," I say.

I walk over to the living room table and drop the handful of pills onto it. Mom eyes the meds and raises an eyebrow.

"Nothing illegal," I say. "Just some pain meds. I figured you could use 'em, with your toothaches."

She leans forward and scoops up the pills.

"Where did you get *those*, Andrew?"

"I traded some stuff."

I pull the commissary vouchers out of my pocket and place them on the table in front of Mom. She leans forward to inspect them, and claps her hands together in front of her mouth.

"*Andrew!* How did you get those?"

"I traded some stuff, Mom," I repeat.

She picks up the vouchers carefully, as if they are made of brittle paper. Each of those vouchers entitles the bearer to a hundred new dollars in goods at a food store outside the PRC. The government issues vouchers every month, and they hand them out from the safety of a concrete booth near the public-transit station on a lottery basis.

"Use 'em, or trade for something," I say. "Just don't let anyone cheat you out of those."

"Don't you worry about that," Mom says as she stacks up the vouchers and slips them into a pocket. "It's been a year and a half since we got a voucher. I'm dying for some bread and cheese."

I was fully prepared to feed my mother some nonsense about the stuff I traded for those vouchers, but she's so excited that she doesn't bother to dig any further.

"Good night," I say, and walk over to the door of my room. Mom smiles at me, the first one I've seen on her face in days.

Then she turns her attention back to the plasma panel on the wall, where some inane Network show is running on low volume.

"Andrew?" she says as I am at the door. I turn around, and she smiles at me again.

"I'll try and go over to the food store in the morning. Maybe we can have a decent lunch before you go."

"That would be nice, Mom."

I spend my final night in PRC Boston-7 reading the last fifty pages of *Moby-Dick*. Tomorrow I will have to leave the book reader behind. I've read the novel a dozen times or more, but I don't want to leave it unfinished now, forever bookmarked at the spot where the *Pequod* slips beneath the waves.

On the second day, a sail drew near, nearer, and picked me up at last. It was the devious-cruising Rachel, *that in her retracing search after her missing children, only found another orphan. . . .*

CHAPTER 2

INDUCTION

"Don't do it," the woman says.

I am an obvious target for the protesters that have gathered in front of the military processing station. I'm carrying a ratty travel bag, and I've saved the military the cost of a haircut by shaving the hair on my head down to an eighth of an inch.

"Excuse me?" I ask.

The woman has a kind face and long hair that is starting to go gray in places. There's a whole gaggle of people protesting out in front of the station, holding up signs and chanting antimilitary slogans. They stay well away from the doors of the station, where two soldiers in battle armor stand guard and check induction letters. The soldiers carry pistols and electric crowd-control sticks, and while they're not dignifying the protest with so much as a glance, none of the protesters ever comes within twenty feet of the yellow line that separates the public sidewalk from the processing station.

"Don't do it," she repeats. "They don't care about you. They just want a warm body. You'll die out there."

"Everyone dies," I say. That particular piece of wisdom sounds pompous even to my own ears. I'm twenty-one, she looks to be past sixty, and she probably knows much more about the subject of life and death than I do.

"Not at your age," the woman says. "They're going to dangle

that carrot in front of you, and all you'll get out of it is a flag-draped coffin. Don't do it. Nothing's worth your life."

"I signed up already."

"You know that you can back out at any time, right? You could walk away right now, and they couldn't do anything about it."

Right then, I know that she's never been within ten miles of a welfare tenement. Walk away, and go back to that place?

"I don't want to, ma'am. I made my choice."

She looks at me with sad eyes, and I feel just a little bit of shame when she smiles at me.

"Think about it," she says. "Don't throw your life away for a bank account."

She reaches out and gently puts her hand on my shoulder.

A heartbeat later, the elderly lady is on the ground, and the two soldiers from the entrance are kneeling on top of her. I never even saw them move away from their posts. She yells out in surprise and pain. Her comrades stop their chanting to shout in protest, but the soldiers don't even acknowledge their presence.

"Physically interfering with access to an in-processing station is a Class D felony," one of the soldiers says as he pulls out a set of flexible cuffs. They pry the woman off the dirty asphalt and haul her to her feet. One of them leads her inside, while the other soldier takes up position by the entrance again. The soldier leading the woman roughly by the arm is probably twice her mass in his bulky battle armor, and she looks very fragile next to him. She looks over her shoulder to flash that sad smile at me again, and I look away.

"The building is made of concrete and steel," the sergeant says. "It's extremely solid. You don't need to hold it up with your shoulder."

The guy next to me moves away from the wall against which he had been leaning, and gives the sergeant a smirk. She has already moved on, as if there is no point in wasting further time on the exchange.

We're standing in line in a hallway at the reception building. There's a folding table set up at the end of the hallway, and someone else is scanning the ID cards of the new recruits. The queue moves slowly. When I finally reach the head of the line, most of the evening is gone. I got here an hour before the eight o'clock deadline for reporting in, and now it's close to ten.

The sergeant behind the folding table holds out his hand for my ID card and the induction letter, and I hand them over.

"Grayson, Andrew," he says to the soldier next to him, who searches through an old-fashioned printout and then makes a check mark next to my name.

The sergeant takes my ID and sticks it into the card reader on his desk.

"Public college graduate, huh?" he says, equal measures of amusement and derision in his voice. "Academic overachiever. Maybe they'll make you an *officer* one day."

He chuckles to himself. Then he pulls my ID card out of the reader and flips it into a bucket beside the table, where it joins a pile of other IDs. The printer on his computer terminal hums, and spits out an unspectacular-looking slip of paper, which he hands to me.

"That's your assignment slip, professor. Don't lose it. Out that door, and find the gate listed on your slip. Report to the gate sergeant, and he'll get you onto the right shuttle. *Next.*"

The shuttle to my Basic Training station is filled to the last seat. The cushions are worn, the belts of the harnesses are frayed, and the carpet on the center aisle is a loose collection of fibers that have long lost any semblance of coherence or pattern. It seems they use the oldest equipment they can find, as if they want to avoid spending a dollar more than necessary on the new recruits.

The shuttle's engines send vibrations through the hull, and a few minutes later we lift off into the dirty evening sky. Some of the new recruits strain their necks to see out of the scuffed windows, but I don't bother. Even if you could make anything out, you'd only see precisely the kind of stuff everyone's itching to leave: identical-looking high-rises, all clumped together in a sprawling mass of concrete that resembles a rodent warren, except that it smells five times worse and isn't half as clean.

I've spent all of my life in the PRC we leave behind, and if the Sino-Russian Alliance nuked the place right this moment, and I saw the fireball light up the night sky behind the shuttle, I wouldn't feel a thing.

We arrive at the base at four o'clock in the morning.

The shuttle was airborne for four hours. We could be anywhere in the North American Commonwealth, from northern Canada to the Panama Canal. I don't particularly care. All that matters is that we're four flight hours away from PRC Boston-7.

When we step out of the shuttle, we are whisked off into a waiting hydrobus. As the bus leaves the shuttle station, I see that we're in an urban area, but there are no high-rise buildings anywhere, and I can see snowcapped mountains on the horizon behind the buildings of the city. This place looks clean, orderly, neat—all the things a PRC isn't. Out here, things are so different that it might as well be another planet.

The bus ride takes another two hours. We soon leave the clean streets of this unknown city behind, and the landscape outside is almost alien in its undeveloped state, like the surface of a strange and distant colony planet. I see low rocky hills and scrub-like vegetation that sparsely covers the hillsides.

Then we reach our destination.

The sudden transition into the military base is startling. One moment we're looking out onto the strangely barren landscape; the next moment we cross into a security lock that seems to have appeared out of nowhere. Just before the bus enters the lock, I can see miles of fencing stretching out into the distance.

We drive for another fifteen minutes, past rows of identical-looking buildings and artificial lawns. Finally, after many right-angle turns onto decreasingly busy side roads, we pull into a lot in front of a squat, unimpressive one-story building that looks like an oversized storage pod.

The doors of the bus open, and before any of us can contemplate whether we ought to stay in our seats or show initiative and get off, a soldier comes up the stairs at the front. He is wearing camouflage utility fatigues. His sleeves are rolled up neatly, with crisp edges in the folds, and the bottom of the sleeve is rolled back down over the fold so the camouflage pattern covers the lighter-colored liner of the fatigue jacket. There's a rank device on his collar, and there are many more chevrons and rockers on it than on the collar of the sergeant who accepted my enlistment papers back at the recruiting station. This soldier's expression is one of mild irritation, as if our arrival has interrupted some enjoyable activity.

"*Now*," he says. "You will smartly step off this bus in single file. There are yellow footprints on the concrete outside. Each of you will step onto a pair of those footprints. You will not talk, fidget, or scratch yourselves while you do this. If you have anything at all in your mouths, it will come out and be left in the trash receptacle of your seat. *Execute*," he adds with a tone of finality, and then he steps back out without looking back, as if there is no doubt that we will do exactly as he says.

We get out of our seats and file out onto the concrete lot. There are rows of yellow footprints on the ground, and we each find a spot. When we're all lined up in untidy rows, the soldier from the bus walks around to the front of our ragtag group, straightens out the front of his fatigues with a crisp tug, places his hands behind his back, and sets his feet a shoulders' width apart.

"I am Master Sergeant Gau. I am not one of your drill instructors, so don't get too used to my face. I am just here to guide you through the first two days while we process you and prepare you to meet your platoon drill instructors.

"*Now*," he says again, and the way he emphasizes that word makes it sound like he is ensuring more than just our attention, as if he wants to make sure we're mentally and physically in the present moment.

"You are among the ten percent of applicants accepted into the Armed Forces of the North American Commonwealth. You may think that this makes you special in some way. It does not.

"You may think that, because you made the initial cut, we will put in a lot of effort to shape you into soldiers, and help you overcome your individual weaknesses. We will not.

"You may think that boot camp is something like that stuff you've been watching on the Networks. It is not.

"We will not hit or mistreat you. You may choose to stop following orders and instructions at any time. If you fail to obey an order, you will wash out. If you fail to make a passing grade on any examination or skill test, you will wash out. If you strike a fellow recruit or a superior, you will wash out. If you steal, cheat, or display a bad attitude, you will wash out. Any of your instructors has the absolute right to wash you out for any reason.

"When you wash out, nothing will happen to you. You will merely be put on a shuttle home. You will not owe any money, nor suffer legal penalties. We will dissolve your contract, and you will be a civilian once more.

"We wash out fifty percent of recruits in Basic Training, and a quarter of you will get killed or maimed in your enlistment period without ever collecting your service certificate at the end. There are forty of you standing on this spot right now, and only twenty of you at most will graduate Basic Training. Only *fifteen* of you will muster out in five years.

"If you find those odds troublesome, you may turn around and board the bus behind you once more. It will take you back to the shuttle port, where you will go back to your in-processing station. If my speech has served to change your mind about being in the service, save yourself and your instructors the work and sweat, and step back onto the bus now."

Sergeant Gau pauses and looks at us in anticipation. There is some rustling and shuffling in the ranks, and three of our number step out of line and walk back to the bus. With the first few stepping out, the more timid find the encouragement to do likewise, and four more no-longer-recruits step out of formation and amble back to the bus with hanging shoulders. I notice that none of them look back.

"Thank you, people," Sergeant Gau calls after them. "And I mean that. It's good to see that some folks still have the smarts to see when they're about to grab the short end of the stick."

Then he turns back to us.

"The rest of you are dumber than an acre of fungus, and I mean that, too. Now go through that door, single file, find a desk in the room beyond, and quietly wait for further instruction. *Execute.*"

The room is empty except for several rows of creaky desk chairs. We each take a chair. I count the empty chairs after everyone is seated; there are precisely as many chairs in the room as there were people on the yellow footsteps outside before the end of Sergeant Gau's speech. There's nothing but a black marker on each of the desks. Some of the recruits take the black markers and uncap them, which displeases Sergeant Gau when he enters the room.

"I didn't say anything about picking up those markers. I said to find a desk and quietly wait."

The scolded recruits hastily replace the markers on their desks. Some of them look at Sergeant Gau as if they expect the offense to be grounds for a wash-out already.

"Now you will pick up your marker and uncap it."

We do as we are told.

"You will use the marker to write the following number onto the back of your left hand: one-zero-six-six."

I write the number "1066" onto the back of my hand.

"This is your platoon number. You are Basic Training Platoon 1066. You will commit your platoon number to memory."

Ten sixty-six was the year of the Battle of Hastings. I file the number of my platoon away in my brain. I briefly wonder if the platoon numbers are assigned consecutively, and when they started counting. Are we the 1,066th group of recruits this decade, this year, or this month? With a dropout rate of 50 percent, how many platoons have to cycle through boot camp in one year to keep the NAC forces staffed?

Sergeant Gau produces a stack of papers and drops it onto the desk of the recruit directly in front of him.

"You will take one form off the top of the stack, and then pass the stack to the recruit next to you. You will place the form on the table and leave it closed until I tell you to open it."

The stack of forms makes its way around the room. When it arrives at my desk, I peel off the top form, and pass the stack to the right. It feels strangely liberating to do precisely as instructed. I don't have to worry about displeasing the sergeant as long as I follow his orders exactly. For now, I resolve to not even scratch my nose unless I'm ordered by someone with chevrons on their collar.

"You will take your markers and fill out the forms in front of you. When you are finished, you will place the cap back on your marker and put it on top of the completed form. *Execute.*"

It's administrative paperwork, which seems redundant at this point. After I signed my application for enlistment back at the recruiting office, I spent many hours at the processing station filling out stacks of forms with all kinds of information. When you live in a Public Residence Cluster, the government knows everything about you, including your DNA profile by the time you're a month old, but the civil and military bureaucracies apparently don't talk to each other very much.

So I fill out the forms in front of me, entering the metrics of my existence for the thousandth time in my life.

The last page is a contract, five dense paragraphs of legal language, and I read over it briefly. It's the same information they gave us back at the recruiting office. Once upon a time, the job of the recruiter was to entice potential recruits into signing up for service by emphasizing the benefits and downplaying the drawbacks of military service, but that is no longer the case. Now they hardly talk about benefits at all. Everybody knows you'll get fed and that there's a real bank account and a certificate of service if you make it through your enlistment term. Now they try to discourage as many people as possible from signing up by describing all the drawbacks of service. I have no doubt that there's a monthly quota for turning away people before they sign an application for enlistment.

At the end of my term, the account will be activated, with the accrued balance of sixty-two paychecks available for withdrawal. If I die before the term of enlistment is up, all the money in my account flows back to the government, as reimbursement for the cost of my training and equipment.

I sign the contract. This is why I am here, after all—to get out of the PRC and have a shot at a real bank account. I don't care what they do with the money if I die. Until I have that certificate of service in my hand, that money is an abstraction anyway, just a bunch of numbers in a database.

When everyone is finished, Sergeant Gau has one of our number collect the forms and deposit them on the lectern at the front of the room.

"Congratulations," Sergeant Gau says. "As of this moment, you are officially members of the Armed Forces of the North American Commonwealth. Be advised that this status is probationary until you graduate from Basic Training."

There's no ceremony, no oath of service, no pomp or ritual. You sign a form, and you're a soldier. It's a bit of a letdown, but at least they're consistent in that respect.

CHAPTER 3

——HURRY UP AND WAIT——

We spend most of the first day standing around and waiting for stuff to happen. There's another medical inspection, a pair of doctors looking at an entire platoon, so it takes almost three hours for all of us to be examined. We get a quick scan and a blood check, to make sure we didn't engage in any last-minute chemical excesses. Then we get a series of shots, six different injectors that are administered in quick succession. I suppose I should be curious about the kind of stuff they're injecting into my system, but I find that I don't care. It's not like they'd let me refuse the shots anyway.

After the medical examination, Sergeant Gau leads us over to another building, where we stand in formation and watch other platoons filing into the door one by one. The other platoons are wearing uniforms, baggy fatigues in a mottled green-blue pattern that looks as if it would stick out just about anywhere.

"Mealtime," Sergeant Gau announces, and these words produce the first smiles I've seen on my fellow recruits since we got here early in the morning.

"We will enter the chow hall single file. You will grab a tray from the stack by the start of the chow line. You may help yourself to anything you see without asking permission. When you have finished loading up your tray, you will find a table and seat yourself. Once you are seated, you will eat your meal. You may converse with your fellow recruits while you are seated. When I call your platoon number, you will finish your meal, stop your conversations, return the trays to the collection racks by the door, and line up in front of the chow hall again."

Most of us haven't had anything to eat since we left for the in-processing stations back home. I'm hungry, and I can tell by the sudden eagerness in the ranks of the platoon that I'm not alone.

"A word to the wise," Sergeant Gau says before leading us into the chow hall. "Don't make it a habit to overeat. You'll end up puking your guts out once the physical conditioning starts. I advise you to keep that appetite in check."

The dining hall is already abuzz with muted conversation between the recruits who have claimed tables before Platoon 1066, but we keep our silence as we stand in line to fill our trays. Still, we can look around and make incredulous and excited faces at each other, and we do. There are big metal trays of food behind the glass partition between the chow hall and the kitchen, and I've never seen or smelled anything this good in my whole life.

The stuff on the trays in front of us is real. I can see mashed potatoes, sliced meat with gravy, noodles, and rice. I have to exert considerable self-control to not grab my tray and skip ahead to the end of the line, where I can see doughnuts, slices of pie, and some sort of fruit cobbler. It's probably just the sudden olfactory overload, but I am sure I can smell the chocolate frosting on the doughnuts all the way at the front of the line.

We all load up our trays with too much food. I take a salad, a bowl of soup that has vegetables and chunks of chicken floating in it, a heaping serving of mashed potatoes, and two pieces of meat. At the end of the chow line, I have to shift the food on my tray around to make space for a pair of doughnuts and a slice of apple pie. When I look back at the line behind me, I see very few trays that are loaded up less than mine.

I find a seat on one of the long tables in the chow hall and dig into my food as soon as my butt hits the chair. We're permitted to talk now, but for the first few minutes, we're all too busy filling our mouths with food.

"I could get used to this," one of the recruits at the table finally says. He's a reed-thin guy with acne scars and a scraggly chin beard.

"They'll make you shave that off," I say, indicating the location of his beard on my own chin, and he shrugs.

"They feed me like this every day, they can fucking shave off every hair on my body if they want."

There are four other recruits at our table, all engaged in trying to figure out how much food they can squeeze into their mouths without dislocating their jaws. Our table has gender parity—three guys, three girls—and when I look around at the other tables, it seems that the same gender ratio is reflected throughout the platoons.

"That's real meat," someone else at the table says, a tall girl with short, dark hair. "It's got texture and everything. I haven't had a real piece of meat since I moved out of my parents' place."

"Beef," her seat neighbor says, pointing at it with a fork. "That's a hundred-dollar piece of beef right there."

The girl slices off a healthy chunk of her beef and stuffs it into her mouth.

"There goes ten dollars," she says around the mouthful of food.

I'm sure they'll make us sweat for every bite later on, but right now I am resolved to enjoy my meal and stuff as many calories into myself as possible without throwing up. The food alone made the signing up worth the effort, and if all the meals in the military are like this, I'll cheerfully jump through whatever hoops they put up.

After lunch, Sergeant Gau walks us over to a warehouse full of military clothes and gear. The equipment issue works much like the chow line. We file past the issuing stations in a single column.

At the first station, the surly-looking attendant pulls a large rucksack and an even larger duffel bag from a stack and tosses them both onto the counter in front of me. There are scuff marks on the heavy canvas, the olive-drab color is faded in spots, and I can see the rectangular line of pulled-up stitching where the previous owner's name tag was removed from the outer flap of the rucksack.

The rest of the gear is used as well, ranging in condition from merely scuffed to nearly unserviceable. At one of the stations, they hand me a folding shovel and a utility knife. The blade of the knife shows the marks of hundreds of sharpenings. The folding shovel used to have a blade coated in olive-drab paint, but most of the paint has come off, and the edges of the shovel blade are nicked. It seems like they're issuing us mostly stuff that's good enough for one more issue cycle before being scrapped.

They measure us for our uniforms and then give each of us several sets of fatigues. Those are used as well, but I am happy to see that at least the underwear and socks seem to be brand new. I guess there are limits even to government frugality.

"Those are yours to keep," Sergeant Gau says when he sees me inspecting the new pairs of knee-high gray socks, checking them off on my "Received Equipment" list, and stowing them in my duffel bag.

"When you wash out, you get to take your socks and underwear with you. Nobody would want to wear them after you anyway. Consider those a souvenir of your short life in the military."

We spend the afternoon filling our rucksacks and duffel bags: uniforms, rain gear, equipment pouches, helmets, combat boots, chemical-warfare protection kits, running shoes, shower sandals, sewing kits, and a bunch of other articles of unknown purpose. When we finally clear the last station, it's late in the afternoon, and we are each weighed down with a rucksack and a bag that probably weigh a hundred pounds together. Some of the smaller members of our platoon are swaying under the load as we assemble again in front of the building. Marching us to our quarters with a hundred pounds of gear seems the perfect opportunity for a conditioning exercise, but Sergeant Gau has a bus waiting for us.

We are quartered in a large, flat-roofed building that stands in a long row of identical buildings. The only way to tell them apart is to look at the signs over each entrance, where a large screen lists the numbers of the platoons housed within. We share our building with five other platoons. The central staircase splits the building in half; each floor has a large room to each side of the staircase. When Sergeant Gau leads us into our platoon bay, we see two rows of bunk beds, one on each side of the room. There are two lockers in front of each bunk bed, facing out into the center aisle.

"There are name tags on your bunks," Sergeant Gau says as we file into the platoon bay. "You will find your bunk and place your equipment bags on top of the mattress. *Execute.*"

There's a bit of disorder as thirty-three recruits fan out to find their respective bunks, but we find that the order is alphabetical. There is a small stack of sheets, a blanket, and a pillow at the head of each bunk.

My bunkmate turns out to be the dark-haired girl from our lunch table. We give each other encouraging smiles as we haul our gear onto our beds. She has the top bunk, purely by alphabetic proximity—she's HALLEY D; I'm GRAYSON A.

We spend another hour unpacking our gear and putting everything into our lockers according to Sergeant Gau's direction. He stands in the middle of the platoon bay, with one recruit's bags emptied on the floor in front of him. He holds up one item at a time, calls out its designation, and waits for us to find the same item in our own piles of stuff. When he is satisfied that we're all holding up the same thing, he tells us where to place it in our lockers.

When all our gear is stowed, Sergeant Gau has us open our lockers again and take out our issue sweat suits and running shoes. We change into the suits, and for the first time the platoon looks uniform in appearance.

"Take your civilian clothes and stow them away in the bottom drawer on the right side of your locker. Most of you will need them again soon."

When all our equipment is stowed in our lockers, Sergeant Gau leads us to the chow hall. Dinner is no less overwhelming than lunch, and we eat ourselves into a stupor once more: grilled cheese sandwiches, beef stew, three different kinds of fruit.

After dinner we're back in our quarters, where we find personal data pads on our bunks. Each of them has a label above the top of the screen, bearing the last name of its new owner. The PDPs are of a kind I've never seen. They're large and clunky, with monochrome screens that look like a throwback to a bygone century. They have translucent polymer covers that fold over the screen for field use, and the whole thing is perfectly sized for the side pocket of the fatigues they issued us earlier today.

"Not exactly the latest technology," my bunkmate muses in a low voice as she inspects her own data pad. "I've had better stuff in elementary school."

"Those are your new companions," Sergeant Gau says from the center aisle of the platoon bay. "They may not look like much, but they're tough and reliable. Familiarize yourselves with your PDPs, and call up lesson 1.001, titled 'Enlisted and Officer Ranks.' "

We sit in two rows along the center aisle, calling up the lesson as directed, and Sergeant Gau has us repeat the rank structure of the armed forces from top to bottom. When we have prayed the litany a few dozen times, Sergeant Gau has us turn off our PDPs and repeat the process from memory another few dozen times. When he is satisfied that we have the rank structure memorized, he makes us stow our PDPs.

"Now," he says. "Let's see which one of you people actually listened to me earlier today. Assemble in front of the building, in three rows. *Execute.*"

We look at each other with budding dread. We've all stuffed ourselves at both lunch and dinner—more so at dinner, since we didn't have to exercise all day—and my stomach is still uncomfortably full. Just the thought of running or doing push-ups is making me nauseous.

"That means *now*, people," Sergeant Gau shouts, and we all rush to file out of the platoon bay.

———

When we're all assembled in three untidy rows, Sergeant Gau leads us down the road. We start out walking, but after a few steps Sergeant Gau falls into a trot.

"You want to keep up," he says. The way he words the statement makes clear that it's not a suggestion.

———

Sergeant Gau's pace is not particularly fast, but after ten minutes my sides are hurting and my stomach bounces up and down like a badly balanced counterweight. We're groaning and coughing as we try to keep pace with Sergeant Gau. He's running in fatigues and combat boots, and not even breathing hard.

After thirty minutes, the first members of the platoon stagger to the side of the road and puke out their dinners in hot chunks. I can feel the bile in the back of my throat as my stomach wants to follow suit, but I manage to keep a lid on things.

Then Sergeant Gau slows down to a walk once more. He gestures for the platoon to turn around, and then he has us gather around the three recruits who are now standing doubled over by the curb, straddling puddles of puke. The smell of fresh vomit triggers a new wave of nausea in my head, and I fall out to barf the contents of my stomach into the gutter.

As I finish retching, I notice that I wasn't the only one who couldn't take the smell. Half the platoon is busy adding to the stinking soup that's now filling the gutter by the side of the road.

"Lesson learned, I trust," Sergeant Gau says, without any mirth or malice.

Back in the platoon bay, Sergeant Gau has us stand at attention in front of our lockers once more. It's hard to look dignified with vomit on your clothing.

"Good enough for today," he says. "If you're wondering why none of you have washed out yet, the answer is simple. You have not begun your training yet, so we have not given you much of a chance to screw up. That will change tomorrow morning, precisely at 0430 hours. Right now, you have ten minutes for personal maintenance in the head at the end of the platoon bay. At precisely 2100 hours, you will line up before your lockers again, and you will be wearing your issued sleepwear. *Execute.*"

The bathroom is one large room, with toilets on one wall, shower bays on the other, and a circular arrangement of stainless steel sinks in the middle of the room. There isn't much space for privacy. Neither toilets nor showers have doors or partitions.

We wash up and change into our issue pajamas as ordered. The male and female versions look exactly alike, shapeless blue things that don't look martial at all. When everyone is assembled in the center aisle as directed by Sergeant Gau, we look like a bunch of overgrown orphans lining up for a bowl of soup.

"Rack time," Sergeant Gau announces after giving the platoon a cursory inspection. "You will climb into your bunks. There will be no conversation once the lights are out. If there is an emergency, one of you will knock on the door of the senior drill instructor, where I will be sleeping tonight instead of in my quarters with my wife. Don't bother me unless one of you is bleeding from the eyes."

When we're in our bunks, the scratchy military-issue blankets wrapped around us, the LEDs on the ceiling dim slowly until they are extinguished. The room is dark, and all I can hear is the breathing of my fellow recruits and the humming of the environmental system that keeps the room at sixty-eight degrees and filters out all the junk in the atmosphere. We're a long way from any of the metroplexes, but with Chicagoland, Los Angeles–San Diego–Tijuana, and Greater New York all topping fifty million these days, there are few parts of the country where you don't need environmental conditioning.

My bunkmate leans over the edge of her bed, and I can just barely see the outline of her head in the near-total darkness.

"This is not so bad," she whispers.

"Except for the puking part," I whisper back, and she chuckles softly.

The food was the best I've ever had, but the sleeping arrangements in the military aren't any better than what I've had in Mom's apartment in the PRC. The mattress feels like it was probably made in the same government factory as the one in my old bedroom.

As I try to go to sleep, I'm surprised to feel homesickness. As much as I was looking forward to getting out of the PRC, part of me doesn't want to be here, sleeping in a room with so many complete strangers, listening to their breathing and occasional coughing. At least at home I had privacy when I wanted it. Part of me wants the predictability of my old life back. When I woke up at home, I knew exactly what the day would bring. When I wake up tomorrow morning, I have no idea what's going to happen. It's liberating, but it's also scary as hell.

I wrap the thin foam pillow around the back of my head so it covers my ears. In the new silence, I finally drift off to sleep, my brain surrendering to my overtired body.

CHAPTER 4

——THE SWING OF THINGS——

At precisely 0430 hours, the ceiling LEDs turn on abruptly, and Sergeant Gau strides into the platoon bay.

"Out of bed, *now*," he shouts without preamble. "Do your business, wash up, and get dressed in your greens-and-blues. That's the kind of clothing with the spots on it. If you need help, check your PDP for 'UNIFORM, COMBAT, INDIVIDUAL.' Morning inspection is at 0455, so get a move on."

Twenty minutes later, we're all dressed and lined up in front of our lockers. If Sergeant Gau is pleased at all with the fact that we're ready five minutes ahead of time, he doesn't show it. There's a window set into the wall of the senior drill instructor's office, and I can see that he's fully aware of the platoon all lined up and waiting for inspection, but he doesn't come out of the office again until the clock at the head of the room says 04:55.

We march off to breakfast. It's only our third meal in the military, but the tables that were thrown together by coincidence on the first day are already coalescing into firm little groups. Our table of six has reconvened at every meal so far. There's me and my bunkmate Halley. There's Ricci, the thin kid with the acne-scarred face and the silly chin beard, and Hamilton, an athletic-looking girl with long blond hair. Then there's Cunningham, who is covered in tattoos, and who was wearing a buzz cut long before she decided to join up. Lastly, there's Garcia, a dark-eyed guy who never speaks unless you ask him a direct question. Halley is from SeaTacVan, Ricci from the Dallas–Fort Worth metroplex, and Hamilton from Utah. Cunningham signed up in some farm town in Tennessee, and Garcia merely shakes his head when you ask him about his hometown.

"What branch would you pick if you could?" Ricci asks us over scrambled eggs and toast.

"Shit," Halley laughs. "I'll be glad if I make it through Basic. They can post me into any branch they want."

"Come on," Ricci prods. "Everybody has a preference."

Halley shovels another forkful of eggs into her mouth and shrugs before answering.

"I don't know, honestly. They'll decide what we're good for at the end of Basic. I wouldn't mind something to drive or fly, though. Marine drop-ship pilot, maybe, or armor crewman."

"What about you?" I ask Ricci.

"I want navy," he says. "Coasting around in a starship. Not having to run around and get shot at. I'll do anything, seriously. Mop decks, clean toilets, whatever."

"You'll end up in the marines," Halley tells him. "Or worse, they'll put you into the army."

Our knowledge of the military branches is mostly limited to a number of self-contradictory shows on the Networks, and the promotional vids they played for us at the recruiting office when they were convinced that they couldn't talk us out of joining up.

The navy owns the heavy gear, the starships that jump between the colonies and provide the heavy firepower in territorial disputes, and the marines are the boots on the ground in the colonies. The navy is considered a choice assignment, with the candidates for fleet service going to Fleet School on Luna right after boot camp. With close to five hundred colonized worlds to garrison and defend, the marines have the most slots available, so that's where most of us are likely to end up.

The Territorial Army is for anyone who doesn't make the cut for the other two branches. Those are the grunts who keep civil order in the NAC on Earth itself, who slog it out with any of a hundred other nation-states. Army grunts don't get to travel in spaceships and defend colonies; they are the garbage haulers of the armed forces. The TA has to deal with the armies of all the belligerents on Earth, including the ones too poor or backward for colonial expansion. The TA is also the government's main tool to deal with violent strife in the NAC itself. It's dangerous to jump onto a new planet or defend a new colony settlement against an invasion of Sino-Russian marines, but it's a whole different level of danger to have your drop ship land you in the middle of a Public Residence Cluster in civil unrest, with five million people around you in various states of agitation and discontent.

"If they try to stick me in the army, I'll just walk away from the whole thing," Ricci says.

"Are you serious?" Cunningham asks. "After making it through Basic?"

"Hell, yeah," he replies. "I didn't join to get my head blown off. It's navy or nothing. Push comes to shove, I've had three months of real food, right?"

"What about you?" Halley asks me as we take our trays over to the collection racks at the end of breakfast time. "What do you want to be when you get out of Basic?"

I duplicate the shrug she gave Ricci earlier.

"Whatever," I say. "Anything's better than being back home." I think of washing out, and how smug and self-satisfied my father's face will be if I crawl back to the PRC without even having passed Basic. He would be delighted if his son didn't make it as long as his dishonorably discharged father. He would die knowing that he

34

wasn't the biggest fuck-up in the family, and I don't want to gift him even that minor pride.

I pause for a second as she steps in front of me to slide her breakfast tray into the collection rack.

"I do want to get into space," I add when it's my turn to discard my tray. "Get off this shitty rock, maybe breathe some unfiltered air on a colony somewhere."

Sergeant Gau gives us the evil eye from twenty feet away—conversation is to cease when we're away from the table—and we hurry to join the rest of our platoon assembling outside.

After breakfast we proceed to weapons issue.

The arms locker is in the basement of the company building. There are no windows, and a rather substantial steel door separates the room from the rest of the basement. Sergeant Gau has us line up in the basement hallway outside the arms room, and then takes a rifle from the attendant sergeant-at-arms. We all look at the weapon in his arms, a sinister piece of alloy and polymer that looks both sleek and bulky at the same time.

"This is the M-66T weapons system, and it will be your best friend for the remainder of your training here. The 'T' means this weapon is the training version of the one you will be issued in your service branch. It is identical to your future issue rifle in weight, balance, and operation, with only one difference."

The sergeant-at-arms hands him a square polymer box, and he flips it around and inserts it into a well at the bottom rear of the weapon.

"The difference is that this weapon does not fire live ammunition of any kind. It uses self-contained, disposable magazine packs like the service weapon, but the magazines of the training version only contain a bunch of circuits, weights, and a battery. The fired rounds are simulated and scored electronically."

Sergeant Gau removes the magazine from the weapon, cycles the action, and cradles the gun in his arms as he slowly walks down the line of recruits.

"The M-66 is a multipurpose personal weapon designed to defeat a wide range of battlefield threats. Its main component is an automatic impulse-operated fléchette rifle, feeding caseless three-millimeter fléchette cartridges from disposable 250-round magazines. The rifle operates in automatic, fully automatic, or user-controlled modes and can fire single shots or any combination of multiple-round salvos. The rate of fire in burst and automatic modes depends on threat profile and varies from two hundred to six thousand rounds per minute.

"The secondary component is the integrated forty-millimeter grenade launcher, which fires a variety of low-pressure grenades. Mission-specific munitions for the grenade launcher include high explosive, armor-piercing, fragmentation, buckshot, incendiary, thermobaric, chemical, and less-lethal ammunition. We call this a 'dial-a-pain' weapon. With just a change of grenades, you will be able to knock down a rioter or a reinforced one-story concrete building.

"You will each receive and sign for one M-66T weapons system. The serial number of the weapon will be linked to your service number and DNA profile. Let me be absolutely clear on this: If you aim your weapon at another person without authorization or instruction, you will wash out of Basic Training instantly. You will only handle your weapon when instructed. Once you receive your rifle, you are to sling it over your shoulder for the march back to your quarters. You will stow the weapon in your locker, and if you so much as touch it again between that point and the first day of weapons training, your status as recruit trainee will be terminated."

He looks at the line of recruits for a moment to gauge whether his words have had sufficient effect.

"Now you will approach the sergeant-at-arms one at a time and sign out your weapon. Once you have received your rifle, you will go back to the end of the line and re-form it. *Execute.*"

I watch as the recruits in front of me go and receive their rifles one by one. For the first time, it feels like we're really in the military. We are wearing camouflage fatigues, and now we are receiving weapons, even if those weapons are incapable of live fire. I look at the rifles slung over the shoulders of the recruits walking past my spot in the line. The rifles are clad in flat black polymer shells with lots of curves and few angles. They look almost organic in appearance.

Then it is my turn to sign out my rifle. The weapon is heavier than its compact shape suggests, and I reposition it on my shoulder briefly before starting my walk to the back of the line.

When we all have our weapons, Sergeant Gau lines the platoon up in front of the building again and then marches us back to our quarters.

"You will open your lockers and place your rifles in the holding clamps on the right side of the locker," he orders. "After you stow your rifle, you will not touch, look at, or think about it until being told to do so by a drill instructor."

There are padded clamps on the rear wall of each locker, and a polymer bracket on the floor that matches the shape of the rifle's butt end exactly. I secure my rifle, close my locker, and join the rest of my platoon to line up by the center aisle of the platoon bay. Sergeant Gau waits impassively at parade rest, his hands behind his back, until the entire platoon has fallen back in line.

"You now have all your issue equipment. You are now ready to begin your training. I will now hand you over to your drill instructors. Follow their orders, do exactly what you are told, and maybe I will see a few of you at graduation in twelve weeks."

He turns to face the door, and three sergeants enter the platoon bay in perfect lockstep. They've obviously waited just outside the door for Sergeant Gau to finish his speech. We watch with apprehension as they march up the center aisle and stop right in front of Sergeant Gau. All three are hard-faced and lean, without an excess ounce of fat between them. The lead sergeant has a rocker under the trio of chevrons on his collar, which makes him a staff sergeant. The other two just have the chevrons, which means they are plain sergeants. The senior drill instructor is also the shortest of the three. The other two are taller, but don't look half as mean. One is a hulking black man with a shaved head, and the other is a red-haired woman. She has a regulation high-and-tight haircut, her red hair shorn down to less than a quarter inch in length.

The senior drill instructor salutes Sergeant Gau, who returns the salute smartly. Then Sergeant Gau turns on his heels, walks around the row of recruits on the left side of the platoon bay, and leaves the room without another word. The short senior drill instructor looks at us like we're a boring little zoo exhibit.

"My name is Staff Sergeant Burke. These are Sergeants Riley and Harris. Our job is to send most of you back home and figure out what the rest of you are good for."

Sergeants Riley and Harris fan out behind the senior drill instructor and stand precisely one step behind him on either side.

"You will change into your issued sweat suits and running shoes. *Execute*," Sergeant Burke barks. We fall out to rush to our lockers. As we shed our fatigues and put on the blue sweat suits, Riley and Harris move over to the ends of the line of lockers, while

Sergeant Burke remains in his position in the middle of the room. All three drill instructors start counting down simultaneously.

"*Twenty. Nineteen. Eighteen. Seventeen. Sixteen.*"

I have no idea what will happen if I am not in my exercise outfit by the time they reach zero, and I have no particular desire to find out. By the time the drill instructors have counted down to seven, I have finished tying my shoes, and I am back on my spot at the center aisle when the count is four. All of us are in position in time, although two or three stragglers only manage to take their spots in the line just before the countdown expires.

"Most of you are out of shape," Sergeant Burke announces. "You have been sitting on your asses at home, watching the Networks and eating garbage. I have no clue how you can get fat from eating the shit they dole out to you people, but I see way too much flab in this room."

Sergeant Burke speaks in the same cadence as Sergeant Gau before him. Except for his slight Southern accent, he sounds just like the master sergeant. I wonder whether they teach a special drill instructor voice.

"We are going to run you through some physical exercises now. We need to find out which ones of you are in sufficient condition to even begin getting into shape."

He takes a step back, and the redheaded woman sergeant steps forward and takes his place. She gives us a glare that's hard as flint.

"Pla-*toon!*" she barks. "In front of the building, in double row, *fall in!*"

We rush out and file past the drill instructors, but I have a good idea that any speed at this point will be deemed insufficient by our drill instructors, even if we managed to teleport downstairs instantly.

"That means *now,* boys and girls!" she shouts. "You're not getting paid by the hour."

We trample down the stairs like a herd of panicked mountain goats. Outside, we re-form the platoon in a double line as ordered.

Our drill sergeants emerge from the building at a walk. Sergeant Burke once again steps in front of the platoon, while the red-haired female sergeant takes up position on the left end of our double row. The bald-headed black sergeant mirrors her position on our right side.

"We're going to play a game called 'Follow the Leader.' Sergeant Riley over there is the leader."

He nods towards the red-haired sergeant to our left.

"Sergeant Riley will lead the platoon on a little run. Your job is to stick with her. Sergeant Harris will bring up the rear. It is in your best interest to stay in front of Sergeant Harris and behind Sergeant Riley at all times."

Sergeant Riley looks like she could run a marathon, but I'm reasonably confident about my ability to keep pace with her. She's wearing fatigues and combat boots, we're wearing exercise clothes and running shoes, and I've been running the staircases back at our residence cluster for the last three months in preparation for military training.

We turn left to align the column as instructed, Sergeant Riley starts running, and the platoon follows.

After an hour, I'm not so confident about my stamina anymore.

I'm in the middle of the platoon, and Sergeant Riley is twenty yards in front of me. As far as I can tell, she's not even breathing hard. We've been running in one direction since we started, and I still can't see an end to this military base. Other platoons pass us in both directions, and all the recruits in those platoons run in perfect synchronicity. Platoon 1066, on the other hand, is a loose formation of coughing, wheezing, and gasping recruits in various states of misery. Sergeant Riley does not slow down. So far, nobody has dared to fall behind Sergeant Harris at the rear.

Finally, Sergeant Riley departs from the straight line she has been running for the last hour. There is a large vehicle park by the side of the road, and she veers onto it, skipping over the curb in a sickeningly light-footed fashion. The platoon follows, some of us only barely managing not to trip on the curb. Sergeant Riley slows down to a trot and comes to a halt when the bulk of the platoon is in the center of the square.

"Two rows, boys and girls. This is the military, not recess at school. Fall in!"

We shuffle around to line up as ordered.

"Leave plenty of space between yourself and the recruit in front of you," she instructs the back row, and I know what's coming next.

"Push-ups," she announces. "I count, you follow. Don't anyone work ahead of me, or we'll start back at one."

She drops into position on her hands, and looks at the platoon as we follow suit.

"One."

She lowers herself until her chin almost touches the ground. I take a glance sideways and notice that Sergeants Harris and Burke are doing push-ups as well, and both of them are watching the platoon as they follow Sergeant Riley's lead.

"I want to see good form here," Sergeant Riley shouts. "Noses touching the ground with every count."

"*One,*" she starts again. "*Two. Three. Four. Five.*"

We get to the midtwenties before the first recruits start wavering. As soon as it is obvious that some of us have begun to struggle, the two sergeants on either side of the platoon rise from their push-up positions and move in.

41

"If you can't do thirty little push-ups, there's really no point in sticking it out for the rest of the training," Sergeant Burke shouts at one of the recruits as he tries to keep up with Sergeant Riley on quivering arms. "Do yourself a favor and just drop on that gut of yours."

The recruit struggles through one more push-up on shaking arms, and lowers himself onto the ground with a groan. Sergeant Burke just snorts with disgust and moves on.

After a while, very few of us are still keeping pace with Sergeant Riley. I make it to forty-nine before my arms shake with weakness and I have to give up. I feel a little ashamed, but at this point most of the platoon are on their bellies, so my pride is only a little dented. Sergeant Riley keeps doing push-ups and watches as the still-active part of the platoon shrinks to four, then three, then two. The last recruit to remain on her hands and toes is Hamilton, the trim and lean girl from my mess table.

"Well," Sergeant Riley says as she stops mid-pushup and hops to her feet. "We're going to have to work on that. Only one of you is in decent shape."

She eyes Hamilton, who has remained in push-up position.

"Back on your feet," she orders, and Hamilton obeys.

"Platoon 1066, meet your platoon leader," Sergeant Burke says. "Recruit Hamilton here will lead our run back to the company building."

The smile that had briefly started to form on Hamilton's lips disappears again.

In the afternoon we learn the basics of moving like soldiers. It's called drill, and it involves our three instructors trying to get us to move in unison and respond to their movement commands at precisely the same moment. It's something the more advanced platoons have mastered to perfection, but it doesn't look so impressive when we try it for the first time.

"That sounds like shit," Sergeant Harris opines when we march across the space in front of the building, trying to maintain unison. "You people march like a herd of spastic goats. I want to hear every left heel hit the ground at once."

After two hours of loud and repetitive instruction, I find that drill works best when you switch off your brain entirely and just act like a voice-controlled robot. The rest of the platoon seems to have come to the same conclusion. We still suck, but much less than in the beginning.

It's a strange feeling to be walking in lockstep with a bunch of people dressed exactly alike. I feel like a cog in a machine, but that's one part of the military I don't mind. When you do exactly as you're told, and you're neither the best nor the worst at any task, you can disappear in the crowd and have a small measure of solitude. Graduation seems like an impossibly far-off goal at the moment, so I decide that I'll settle for a short-term one right now. I want to make it through the training session without getting yelled at or drawing extra push-ups. Then I can work on the next session, and maybe I'll make it through the whole day like that.

For the rest of the afternoon we sit in front of our lockers in the platoon bay again, listening to our instructors as they lecture us on subjects like the Uniform Code of Military Justice, the branches of the military, and our chain of command. Most of us are tired from the morning's exercise and the drill session after lunch, but when the first recruit nods off, we get a demonstration on the necessity of staying alert. Sergeant Burke suddenly stops his recitation of the history and mission of the Territorial Army, straightens up, and folds his hands behind his back.

"*Recruit Olafsson,*" he barks.

Olafsson, who sits right across the center aisle from me, suddenly jerks awake and looks around with a panicked expression.

"You seem to have a problem remaining conscious," Sergeant Burke says amicably. "I suspect it's a lack of oxygen. Get on your feet, now."

Recruit Olafsson obeys, clearly distraught about being the sudden center of attention.

"You will join Sergeant Riley on the quarterdeck," Sergeant Burke says, indicating the front of the platoon bay, where there's a generous amount of open space between the first row of bunks and the window to the senior drill instructor's office. Sergeant Riley is standing in the middle of the quarterdeck already, hands folded behind her back.

If the exercise on the quarterdeck under Sergeant Riley's tutelage is supposed to restore some oxygen to Olafsson's system, it seems to have the opposite effect. Fifteen minutes later, Sergeant Burke has finished his lecture on the Territorial Army, and Recruit Olafsson's face is a dark shade of red as he works through his sixth cycle of push-ups and sit-ups.

"Your attention is on *me*," Sergeant Burke barks when he catches a few of us glancing over to the quarterdeck. "I promise you that each and every one of you will have ample opportunity to spend time on the quarterdeck in the next twelve weeks."

He moves on to the history and mission of the navy, and Recruit Olafsson continues his efforts on the quarterdeck, with an impassive Sergeant Riley standing over him as he struggles through yet another set of push-ups.

Eleven weeks and five days to go, I tell myself. *Eighty-two days of running, getting yelled at, and doing punishment workouts on the quarterdeck.*

I briefly consider standing up and walking over to Sergeant Burke to announce that I want to quit, before I end up spending weeks sweating my ass off only to wash out anyway without anything to show for the work. Then I recall the PRC—the smell of piss and puke in the hallways and staircases, the garbage everywhere, the thugs rousting people just out of meanness and boredom—and I banish the thought. As much as I hate working out and getting bossed around, having to take a shuttle back to that place would be much worse. I'd end up just like Mom and Dad—not really living, just existing.

Hell, I think as Sergeant Burke drones on about the structure and organization of the Commonwealth Navy. *At least I'll be in great shape when I get out of here.*

CHAPTER 5

—INFANTRY KINDERGARTEN—

My battle armor is scuffed and beaten to hell, but I love it anyway. I love the rifle in my hands, too, more than a sane individual should love a mere object. Together, the rifle and the armor turn me into something different, something more advanced than the sum of myself and the technology in which I am wrapped.

We're in our seventh week of training, and squad-level combat training is the first thing I've done in the military that I wouldn't mind doing every day. We have spent the last few weeks getting to know our rifles and our gear and learning the basics of infantry combat: moving as squads and fire teams, assault, defense, the basic steps in the dance that is modern integrated ground warfare.

The first time we practiced squad movements with the help of the integrated tactical network, I felt like I'd been myopic all my life without knowing it and somebody finally slipped a set of prescription glasses in front of my eyes. The helmet has more computing power built into it than all the computers in my old high school classroom put together. On the inside of the eye shield, there's a sort of monocle over the left eye, and that's the truly magical part of the suit. It's the holographic projector linked to the suit's tactical computer. The computer analyzes everything I see, overlays my field of vision with tactical symbols over every friend or foe in the vicinity, and then transmits the data to the rest of the squad. Whatever I see, the rest of my squad can see as their computers integrate the feed coming in from mine. If one of us spots a new threat, their tactical computer automatically sends the new data to the other squad computers through the encrypted wireless network, and the entire squad is aware of the threat within a few milliseconds. We were only taught the use of the system two weeks ago, but I am already so used to the information feed that I feel blind and dumb when I am out of the battle armor.

The rifle is linked to the computer as well. It doesn't aim or sight itself, but it does everything else automatically. Whenever I aim the rifle at a target, the computer selects the right burst length and cadence for the threat. My rifle doesn't spit out any actual fléchettes, but there's a hydraulic feedback system built into the butt end that simulates the recoil of live firing. To make the illusion complete, there's a sound module that gives off a report.

Advancing with a squad and engaging other squads on the mock battlefields of the training facility is a strangely intoxicating experience. We're training for war, and I know that the enemy out in the real world is going to shoot high-density fléchettes and explosives at me instead of harmless beams, but so far it all feels like a very exciting sort of sporting competition. The squads square up against each other in training, and we win or lose matches, just like in high school. There's even the customary locker-room bragging in the showers after the training rounds, with gloating winners and sulking losers. Nobody dies, or gets hurt, except for a few bruises here and there. The battle armor gives off a bit of a zap when you're "hit" by enemy fire, but it's not really painful, just unpleasant, like brushing your hand against a stripped low-voltage wire.

We're just past the halfway point of Basic, and there are twenty-seven of us left. We have lost thirteen recruits in six and a half weeks. In the first week, it was just the linebacker who decided to quit in the middle of our first run, but since then, the pace of wash-outs has accelerated. Nine have left voluntarily, and the other four were ejected by our drill instructors for failure to follow orders or failure to meet standards. Our mess table has lost one member—Cunningham, the girl with the tattoos and the buzz cut. She made it to the third week and then decided that she'd had enough of Sergeant Riley singling her out for extra sessions on the quarterdeck. One evening in week three, she just tossed her PDP onto her bunk and walked out of the platoon bay. We went off to a class on chemical warfare, and when we returned to get ready for dinner, her bunk was stripped and her locker emptied out. They never empty a recruit's locker when the platoon is present, but they never wait long, either.

We're in the urban-warfare training facility, a mock-up of a generic East Asian city block. It's situated in the brushy desert on the outskirts of the base, and getting there is a training exercise in itself. We're on day three of our urban-warfare exercise, and every day we've been ready and in full battle gear by 0530. Every day, we've marched the twenty miles through the desert to the UWTF, encumbered with battle armor, rifles, fully stuffed backpacks, and three-gallon hydration bladders. The march to the UWTF takes two and a half hours at Sergeant Riley's pace, which is a march that's somewhere between a fast walk and a slow trot.

Our platoon is down to three squads of nine now. Every time we lose recruits, they shuffle the squads around to keep each squad at roughly the same headcount, and now we're too few to fill out a full platoon of four squads. On this exercise, I am the leader of my fire team of four recruits, and my squad leader is Ricci. We're one of the two attacking squads, and the defending squad is positioned in defensive spots up ahead in the "city." The squad leader of the defending squad is Halley, my bunkmate.

Ricci makes a lousy squad leader. Twice now our squad has been chewed up by the defending squad, and twice the instructors have reset the exercise and ordered us to do it again. Ricci does not deviate from his plan, which involves leapfrogging from doorway to doorway on the main road. Ricci doesn't want to play infantry, and it shows. He's aggressive where he should be cautious, and timid where he should charge ahead. We've wasted two hours on the setup and execution of his attack plan, only to get shot to bits by Halley's squad repeatedly, and I have no idea why the instructors aren't letting someone else drive the bus for a change.

"You need to get your team across the road faster," Ricci says as we come through the same alleyway for the third time, our squad taking up covering positions at the intersection with the main road. The illusion is almost perfect—there's trash everywhere, the walls are adorned with foreign graffiti and flecked with all kinds of bodily fluids, and there's warbly Chinese pop music coming from shops along the road. I've never been to the Far East, but the fake city looks just like the places I've seen in the news and war movies. The only thing missing is the population.

"It doesn't matter how fast we move," I tell Ricci. There's a modestly tall building overlooking the intersection at the end of the road, a hundred yards ahead, and the defending squad has at least a fire team in place up there. "You're having us charge a defended position, and they know we're coming. You can't outrun a freaking fléchette."

"Well, General Know-It-All, do you have a better idea?"

I bring up the tactical display on my monocle and study the overhead map of the block.

"Let's split the squad and go up those two side alleys, one team per side. When we're at the intersection, we pop smoke and then rush over from two sides. We can't go around the building because they'll shoot us in the ass from above if we do."

"Popping smoke, you might as well yell, 'Here we come!'" Ricci says.

"We don't make our own cover, we get shot to shit again. Your call, boss." I put just a little bit of acid into the last word, and Ricci flips me the bird.

"Two teams, then," he says. "I'll take mine up to the right, and you go left. You go ahead and pop smoke if you want. I'll use the diversion while you guys get fucked up."

"We'll see. At least we won't all get killed together in the middle of the intersection like the last two times."

Being on the attack is a crappy task. The defenders know you're coming, and you have to put yourself out into the open to come to where they are. You do, however, have the initiative.

We dash from house to house, using the cover of store awnings and doorways to mask our approach to the intersection. On my tactical display, I can see the other team making their way up the alley to our right.

We reach the intersection without any contact. I scan the top floor of the building across the intersection for movement, but the defending squad has it together. I know they have at least a fire team in that building—it's a natural chokepoint, and we can't go around it without exposing ourselves—but they are playing a good game of hide-and-seek.

I toggle the squad channel.

"Fire team Bravo, in position. Ready when you are."

"Go on three," Ricci says, and I pull a smoke grenade from the harness on the front of my battle armor.

"Wait for smoke," I say, but Ricci is already counting down.

"One . . . two . . ."

I let out a curse, pop the safety cap of the smoke grenade, and hurl it into the intersection.

". . . *three!*"

On my tactical display, I can see that Ricci's entire fire team has left cover. Then I hear the rasping of their rifles as they fire automatic bursts from the hip while running.

"Dumb fuck," I say, and give my team the signal to rush. The smoke grenade goes off with a muffled *pop*, and there's an instant cloud of thick chemical smoke over our side of the intersection.

"Go, go, *go!*"

We rush into the smoke, towards the building. It's only about fifty yards away, but that's an incredibly long distance when you know there are people with rifles and grenade launchers trying to keep you from reaching the finish line.

The training rifles emit no muzzle flashes, but I can hear the staccato of automatic fire coming from the building, on both sides of our advance. It looks like Halley has most of her squad in that building in anticipation of our dumb leader's third attempt at an offense. The tactical computers score individual kills, and so far our squad has chalked up a big, fat zero.

Over to our right, where Ricci's team is rushing across the intersection, I can hear cursing as the first recruits are hit by the virtual projectiles from the guns of Halley's squad. I rush through the cloud of artificial fog, listening to the chatter of at least two rifles from the part of the building in front of me, and my stomach turns in anticipation of that little electric jolt that signals a hit. When a recruit gets nailed by a virtual round, the tactical computer will assess the location of the hit and disable things based on the severity of the simulated injury. If you take a lethal hit, the computer turns off your comlink and tactical interface, so you won't be able to communicate or share data with the rest of your squad. It also turns off your rifle, so you can't cheat and fire back while you're dead.

Luckily, the defenders facing my fire team are merely firing blindly into the smoke, hoping to score hits by accident. My team makes it through the smoke and across the intersection.

When we're all lined up on the sidewall of the building, I check my tactical display for Ricci's half of the squad. Their symbols are blinking red, meaning there's no status information coming from their transmitters. I toggle the squad channel again, but I already know it's pointless.

"Squad leader, Bravo. You guys across?"

There's no response on the squad channel—they've all been mowed down by Halley's defending teams, and their computers have turned off their network links.

"Well, looks like we're on our own on this one," I tell my team members.

"Beats the hell out of being dead again," one of them says, and the others nod in agreement.

"Game's not over yet," I say.

There's a doorway on the side of the building. I signal my team to take up positions on either side. Halley has her shit together, so I don't want to just rush the team into the building. I take a grenade out of the harness on the front of my battle armor, and pop the safety cap off with my thumb.

"Ready?" I ask, and get three nods in response.

I activate the timer of the grenade by slapping the fuse button against the hard shell of my breastplate.

"Frag out!"

I toss the grenade into the doorway, aiming for the wall beyond the doorframe for a deflection shot into the hallway beyond. The grenade bounces against the concrete, and skitters onto the floor out of sight.

"*Fuck!*" I hear, and there's the sound of quick movement in the hallway, as someone scampers out of the way of the little black sphere with the pebbled outer skin.

Then the sound module in the grenade goes off with a muffled bang. The exercise grenade emits a bloom of simulated projectiles, beams reaching out in every direction, deflecting off hard surfaces and behaving much like their lethal counterparts.

"Go!"

We dash into the hallway in two pairs, by the book. There's nobody in the hallway beyond, but there is another doorway to our right, ten feet ahead. I see movement beyond, and rush up to the door, rifle at the ready. One of Halley's troops is scrambling to his feet just beyond the doorway, and I raise the rifle and shoot two bursts into his back just as he tries to bring his rifle around. There's another enemy in the room, still by the window, and he has his rifle trained on me. I know that he has beaten me to the punch, and I cringe in anticipation of the jolt that signals a hit, but when he pulls the trigger, his rifle remains silent. The recruit who paired up with me for the entry steps into the doorway, aims his rifle, and we both fire a burst into the second defender.

"Clear," I say into the helmet mike, and the other two members of my team come into the room, rifles at the ready.

"What the *fuck*?" the second one of Halley's troops asks, looking at his rifle in consternation.

"Musta taken a hit from that grenade," I say.

"That's bullshit. I was already through the door when that thing went off in the hallway."

"Computer says you're dead, so you're dead," my teammate says. "No point arguing."

"Stop the chatter," I say. "There's more rooms on this floor. Let's get busy."

Action beats reaction most of the time. We clear the floor in pairs, going room by room, sanitizing the rooms with grenades before going in and shooting everything wearing battle armor. We lose one of our teammates, who ends up getting tagged by a "wounded" enemy who tries playing possum, but at the end of the exercise, we have Halley's squad smoked out, with an attacking squad at only half strength. The rooms don't have any barriers to block the simulated shrapnel from the grenades we toss in, and Halley's squad can't find a counter against us quickly enough as we take them down pair by pair.

"Well done," Sergeant Burke says over the platoon channel when we have cleared the last room. "Gather your junk and form up in front of the building. Platoon, *execute*."

"What have we learned this morning?" Sergeant Burke asks us when we are gathered in front of the building for our exercise critique.

We've learned that Recruit Ricci sucks at infantry tactics, I think, but Sergeant Burke answers his own question before I can voice that thought.

"A strong position is your friend when you're in the defense, but it can also be turned against you," Sergeant Burke says. "The defending squad got a little too cocky on that third run. They were trapped in their own fighting positions because they didn't secure the back door, and because they didn't leave themselves a way out. The attacking squad kept the initiative and used the isolation between the defenders to take them down with local fire superiority. That means, Recruit Halley, that you had more guys in the defense but that it didn't matter because they were split up and dispersed too much. They were isolated and neutralized by the attackers in smaller chunks, which is exactly the way it's supposed to work when you do it right. The fight was four against ten in favor of your squad, but Recruit Grayson's team fought the whole thing with four against two in *his* favor. We call that a *defeat in detail*. Do you understand?"

"Yes, sir," Halley says.

"Well done," Sergeant Burke says in our direction, and my team stands up a little more straight. "If Recruit Ricci had managed to grow a brain and not get his team mopped up for the third time, it would have been no contest at all. Looks like some of you aren't completely retarded, after all."

Ricci looks at Sergeant Burke with an impassive face, but I know there'll be some trash talk at the dinner table tonight.

"Halley, you play attackers now. Form up your squad and move out to the staging point," Sergeant Burke orders. "Ricci, have your squad pick defensive positions. Let's see how you do on the defense."

We spend the day killing each other bloodlessly.

Being on the defense is easier and more difficult at the same time. We can prepare our fighting positions, make use of cover and concealment, but we also have to wait for the other team to begin the attack on their terms. We get wiped out once and beat the opposing team twice, getting our revenge for our earlier defeats at the hands of Halley's squad. At the end of the day, the score is even. One of Halley's fire team leaders takes first place on the individual kill board, with fourteen kills to his name. To my surprise, I come in second, despite our lack of kills in the first two rounds of the day. I scored killing shots on twelve of Halley's troops.

"Looks like you've found something you don't suck at, Grayson," Sergeant Burke remarks when he reviews the kill list with the platoon. "Just don't think you're a natural killing machine now. This shit ain't real combat, you know."

"You like that stuff too much," Halley says back in the platoon bay head as we shower off the sweat of the day. "You were having a good time out there."

"Maybe," I shrug, as I try not to be too obvious about studying her shapely backside as she turns to rinse the cleaning agent out of her hair.

"You don't watch out, they'll mark you for the Territorial Army," Ricci says from across the head.

"Is that why you sucked so much today?" Halley asks, and a few of the other recruits laugh.

"What do you think?" Ricci replies with a grin. "You think I want to give them a reason to mark me down as 'Good With a Rifle'? That way lies a TA billet."

"Well, you sucked at Land Navigation last week, too," I say. "And I think you were near the bottom of the list in Combat Control. You waiting for the Office Management instruction to show your true skills, or what?"

"Funny," Ricci says and hurls a container of liquid soap in my direction. I swat it back at him, and it clatters to the floor between the two rows of showers. Ricci gives me a sour look as he walks over to the middle of the head to retrieve it. Halley lets out a mocking wolf whistle when he bends over to pick up his soap. He holds his middle finger up without looking back at her.

"What a turd," Halley says under her breath.

I don't do so well in the next phase of the training.

Our "Air & Space Week," as Sergeant Burke calls it, begins with a day of instruction on aeronautics, cockpit systems, and the basic principles of atmosphere and space flight. I can understand the theory well enough, and I manage to receive good marks on the electronic exam at the end of the classroom part of the training, but somehow my brain can't translate that knowledge into practical ability very well. After the classroom instruction, we move on to simulator training, which takes place in a big room the size of our platoon bay. Every member of the platoon has their own soundproofed simulator capsule. From the outside it looks like a squashed egg with cables sticking out of its back, but when you sit in it, the inside of the shell turns into a giant display, and the seat and avionics in the capsule are exact replicas of those found in a standard Wasp-class attack drop ship. You take your seat, strap on your helmet, plug into the TacLink console, and the computer that runs the simulation does its best to make you believe you're flying the real thing. The whole thing sits on hydraulic actuators, which can spin the capsule through 360 degrees of movement. When I do my first practice drop from orbit into atmosphere, the imagery of the planet below combines with the movements of the capsule to give me a disconcerting sensation of vertigo.

The theory is simple enough. The stick on the right side of the cockpit moves the control surfaces on the wings and tail of the ship. The throttle on the left side controls engine thrust, and the hat switch on its side fires the maneuvering thrusters for extra-atmospheric flight. Pull on the stick, the nose comes up—push on the stick, the nose goes down. Tilt it left or right, the ship tilts in the same direction. The rudder pedals under my feet control the yaw.

Each control axis moves the ship around a different physical axis, and all the pilot has to do is coordinate his input on stick and throttle to move the ship where he wants it to go.

"A good drop-ship pilot can thread a needle with a Wasp. A great drop-ship pilot can do it with a fully loaded ship while under fire, with one engine and half a wing shot off," Sergeant Burke says when he introduces us to the simulators.

Apparently, I'm not a great drop-ship pilot. I'm not even a good one. After day two I'd settle for being mediocre, but so far I only manage to be abysmally bad. Somehow my spatial sense gets all messed up by the unfamiliar sense of weightlessness, and my brain refuses to synchronize my control input on all three axes properly. The exercises consist of following a flight path to a drop zone, and the helmet-mounted tactical display helpfully shows the right vectors and navigation cues directly in my field of vision as I release from the simulated attack carrier and tumble towards the atmosphere of the planet below.

Without the automatic landing feature, I can barely get my ship pointed the right way. The throttle accelerates the craft, but it keeps moving according to the laws of physics, which means that tilting the nose merely moves it away from the axis of travel, rather than changing direction. Before too long I end up flying sideways or backwards, and I can't figure out how to coordinate my controls to make the nose point forward again. Flying a drop ship requires constant adjustments in all dimensions, like trying to run while keeping a ball bearing centered on a dinner plate you balance on your fingertips. It's a skill that's beyond my mental abilities, and by the end of day three, I have burned up in the atmosphere on every one of my drops.

"Recruit Grayson has destroyed a total of nine hundred million Commonwealth dollars so far," Sergeant Burke says at the end of our third day, when he gives us his customary end-of-exercise critique. I feel my cheeks flush as some of the recruits laugh at his remark.

"Don't feel bad, Grayson," he tells me when he notices my embarrassment. "The rest of the platoon didn't fare much better. We don't expect anyone to actually land the ship, you know. We're just trying to figure out which of you even have the talent to *begin* proper flight training."

I don't have to wonder about that, at least.

"How did you do?" I ask Halley when we sit on my bunk after the evening shower. We get a little time to sit and check our PDPs before the lights are turned off, and Halley and I usually stick our heads together to vent to each other. She's unlike any of the girls I knew back home. Halley hardly ever talks about her own home, but I just know that she's never been within fifty miles of a PRC. Everything about her shouts "middle-class suburbs"—her straight and well-maintained teeth, the way she pays attention to her appearance even in the baggy uniforms we wear, the way she holds her cutlery in the mess hall.

"I landed the ship twice," she says in a low voice, and flashes a proud grin.

"No shit? Did Burke say anything?"

"He said I seem to have a hand for it."

"Looks that way," I say. "All I've done all day was to turn my drop ship into a comet."

"I'm just glad I'm good at *something*."

It occurs to me that our disparate talents mean we'll probably get posted to different services if we make it through Basic Training, and the idea of parting with Halley suddenly makes me depressed. I know it's irrational—there are so many different marine regiments and navy fleet units that we would almost certainly not be serving together even if we ended up in the same service branch—but I can't turn off the feeling. For a moment I consider aligning my results with hers, slacking off on the infantry training to not get ahead of Halley in that respect, but there's no way I could match her skill in the simulator, and I'm not even considering asking her to throw her results for my sake. Besides, the military being what it is, there's little method in the assignments anyway, and we may yet end up serving in proximity to each other.

Halley recalls her first successful simulated landing, and I listen to the story and watch the little dimples she gets on her cheeks when she smiles.

CHAPTER 6
───────GRADUATION───────

The last few weeks of Basic Training are a blur of PT—physical training, although we call it physical torture—classroom instruction, simulator sessions, meals, and private little get-togethers with Halley, carved out of our unceasingly busy schedules while dodging the near-constant supervision. At night the instructor on duty sleeps in the senior drill instructor's office, and by now we have learned which of our sergeants are light sleepers. Sergeant Riley practically sleeps with one eye open, Sergeant Burke stays up until the early hours doing paperwork and listening to the feed from the platoon bay's audio-monitoring system, but Sergeant Harris is usually fast asleep from lights-out to reveille. That means every third night is what we've come to call "date night," where Halley and I sneak off to the head in the middle of the night to get a little bit of time together, away from the eyes and ears of our fellow recruits.

Our arrangement is not exactly a secret. It only took so many people walking in on us in the head at two in the morning to make it common knowledge, and I suspect that word has gotten around to the instructors as well. For some reason, however, there are no enforcement measures to keep us from sneaking off to the head together two or three times a week, and the other recruits have entered into a sort of unwritten understanding with us. There aren't many of us left. Our platoon has shrunk to twelve members just before graduation week. Our chow hall table is still well represented, since we lost only Cunningham. Everyone else has made it through: Halley, Hamilton, Garcia, Ricci, and me. Hamilton is still platoon leader, and she will be carrying the guidon of the severely reduced Platoon 1066 at graduation.

When we march to our last communal dinner in the chow hall on the evening before graduation, we are every inch the last-weekers: fit and trim, with mirror-polished boots, marching in a precise cadence and at brisk speed. We march past newly arrived platoons, herds of bewildered-looking, long-haired kids in civilian garb, and they look at us just like we gazed at the last-weeker platoons almost three months ago.

On our last night, the sergeant on duty is Riley. Halley and I are already getting over the disappointment that we won't get to fool around in the head one last time when Sergeant Riley takes her PDP out of the senior drill instructor's office and turns off the light.

"This is your last night," she tells the assembled platoon, as we wait in front of our lockers for the order to hit the rack.

"You've made it this far. I trust none of you will be knuckle-headed enough to pull any stupid shit that'll get you kicked out just before graduation," she says, and gives us a little smile. It's more of a smirk, but it's the first time we've ever seen anything but her perpetual stern expression on her face.

"Have a bit of a party, if you want," Sergeant Riley tells us as we look at each other in disbelief. "Just keep it down, and make sure you're where you're supposed to be when reveille comes around."

She turns around, tucks her PDP into the side pocket of her trousers, and walks out of the room.

"Good night, platoon."

We grin at each other as she closes the hatch behind her.

"Well, how about that," Hamilton says with a chuckle. "I'd say let's break out the good stuff."

We've all brought back food from the chow hall before, despite the admonitions of our drill instructors. All the PT and quarter-decking has turned us lean and perpetually hungry, and the meal-times are simply spaced too far apart to keep our metabolisms going. Every time the chow hall serves a dessert that's easily portable, many recruits end up taking seconds, wrapping the contraband doughnuts or brownies into napkins, and tucking them into trouser pockets. The instructors aren't stupid, of course, but they turn a blind eye.

We pool our hidden food reserves on one of the empty bunks. They amount to a decent sampler of all the desserts served in the chow hall in the last week. We have a good variety of doughnuts and cookies, lots of fresh fruit, brownies, and even a few slightly smashed pieces of apple pie. There are no drinks, of course, but the water from the fountain in the head is cold and clean, and we're so elated about this unsupervised night and our impending graduation that it might as well be cold beer.

We eat the hoarded food, not minding the half-stale dough-nuts that date back to the beginning of the week, and toast each other with cold water, using our toothbrush cups as drinking vessels. With the restrictions lifted for the night, we talk and joke around like we're in the mess hall, only with less restraint. We've never had a chance to talk to our platoon mates without a drill instructor hovering nearby, and the experience is strange after twelve weeks of social hamstringing.

Later that evening, Halley and I retreat to one of the empty bunks by the back wall of the platoon bay. We have to endure some good-natured ribbing from the rest of the platoon as we fashion a sight barrier out of the scratchy issue blankets by hanging them from the frame of the top bunk. When we finish building our privacy booth, we slip into the bottom bunk, which is now shielded from view on three sides. Our ugly issue pajamas end up in front of the bed, and we finally have some time to enjoy each other on a real mattress, instead of coupling hurriedly in the corner of the head, listening for approaching footsteps in the platoon bay. There are some catcalls and comments from our platoon mates, but we're too busy with each other to pay attention, and after a while they go back to their business and leave us to ours.

"We'll stay in touch, right?" Halley asks later, as we lie on the thin mattress. I remember the original tenant of this bunk, a guy who washed out after three weeks for "failure to adjust."

"Of course," I say. "We'll write each other on the MilNet."

"Too bad Basic isn't about a month or two longer," she says, and I laugh.

"I thought you were eager to get out of here."

"Yeah, I am. But I wouldn't mind spending some more time with you, chowderhead. I'd even put up with a few more weeks of running and quarterdecking."

"Aww, that's so sweet," I reply, and we both laugh.

"Seriously," Halley says. "I'd love for it to happen, but I don't think there's a chance we'll both get posted to the same unit. I want to get mail from you every week, you hear? I want to know you didn't get your head shot off on some crummy colony world on the ass end of the known galaxy."

"Hey, they may not even post me to the marines. I may end up being a supply clerk on a carrier. I'll spend four years handing out towels and paper clips."

"Come on," she says. "Five hundred capital ships in the navy, and they're all so automated you could fly 'em with a crew of ten. Hundreds of colonized worlds, and each requires a marine garrison of at least company size. We'll all end up in the marines."

"I don't mind. Anything to get off Earth."

"Hey, I've grown kind of fond of the place. It's home, you know? I mean, smog and crime and all."

"Seriously?" I say. "You mean you'd not trade this place for a chance to breathe some fresh air on a colony somewhere? I hear there are colonies so small, they have a thousand people on the entire planet. Can you even imagine?"

"Yeah, I can." She looks down and smiles. "My uncle and his family made one of the colony ships a few years back. They won the ten-state lottery. Now they have five hundred acres on Laconia. They send pictures every now and then."

"Maybe we can pool our bonus money when we're out of the military."

"And what?" she laughs. "Buy a spot on a colony ship and farm a patch of dirt on the other end of the universe?"

"Sure. Why not? What else are you going to do when your time is up? Go back home and buy lots of crap, watch the Networks until your brain rots, and put on the mask whenever there's a bad air day?"

"Well," Halley chuckles. "I was going to do exactly that, but now that you put it like that . . ."

She looks at me again, her eyes finding mine, and her expression turns serious again.

"Fifty-seven months after today, Grayson. That's a long time. It's a longer time still in this kind of job." She puts a hand against my cheek and holds it there for a moment. "You try to make it through the next five years and we'll see, okay?"

I know we'll spend those five years in different corners of the universe. We both know that the military is not the place to be if you want to get or keep a mate. She'll probably shack up with some steel-jawed officer, or a succession of them, and I'll have my own flings. By the time our discharge date comes around, we'll most likely only be a faint and pleasant memory to each other. But the thought is nice, and we have the events of the last few weeks fresh in our memories right now, so I take the sentiment in the spirit in which it is presented.

"I'll see you after mustering out," I say. "Bring your bonus, and I'll bring mine."

Graduation day dawns with a cloudless sky.

We're up well before reveille, restoring the platoon bay to its sanctioned state and polishing our boots and belt buckles to a spotless shine one more time.

We march to the chow hall for our final meal of Basic Training. After breakfast we return to the platoon bay to shed our greens-and-blues and don the formal wear we've been issued just a few days ago. Sergeant Burke explained that the Class A uniforms aren't issued with the other stuff at the beginning of training because they are too expensive to waste on likely dropouts, and that recruits lose so much weight and gain so much muscle in Basic Training that the well-fitting uniform issued at the beginning would sit on its owner like a tent after twelve weeks.

We rehearsed for the ceremony in the weeks prior to graduation. Our platoon—what's left of it—is to march into the parade square behind the platoon guidon and move smartly to its assigned spot in the rows of graduating platoons. Then the commanding officer will hold a brief speech, we will all swear the oath of service, and there will be recognitions and merit promotions for excellent training performances. All in all, we'll be standing in the sun and listening to the brass talk for an hour, and then we'll be sent back to our platoon bays one last time to pack our gear and receive our final assignments for duty. Everyone wants to know their service branch and final job description, of course, so the whole pomp and circumstance is just largely pointless torture, but we have learned to shut up and execute, so we do.

Despite the rehearsals, we're not prepared for the sight of the main parade square as our platoon marches in, following Sergeant Burke and our platoon leader, Hamilton, behind the guidon.

The square is probably half a mile on each side, and it is packed with rows and rows of graduating platoons. There are hundreds and hundreds of platoon guidons flapping in the light morning breeze, making the square look like a multicolored cloth forest. We keep our pace up and our heads straight, but the sheer number of people on the square is a little shocking after twelve weeks of enforced segregation from other platoons.

We find our spot in the line, and the other two drill instructors, Sergeants Riley and Harris, are already waiting. We take our place in the formation, which is comprised of hundreds of platoons. When all the graduating recruits have filed into the square and shuffled into position, there are thousands of recruits lined up in front of the podium in the center of the square. We're all dressed in the Class A uniforms we're going to have to return right after the ceremony, and we all look lean and sharp.

There's a speech, of course. The commanding officer of the training depot addresses us for a mercifully brief period of time, talking about duty and commitment and the challenges that await us out there among the stars. It's all a bunch of fluffy crap, of course, and everyone knows it, but by now we know how to stand at attention and listen.

Then we swear our oath of service. There's something almost mystical about a few thousand voices chanting the same words in unison.

"I solemnly swear and affirm to loyally serve the North American Commonwealth, and to bravely defend its laws and the freedom of its citizens."

Then we're sworn in, active soldiers in the Armed Forces of the North American Commonwealth, graduates of Basic Training, the ten-percenters that have made it through twelve weeks of endless PT, lectures, physical and mental exams, and stress-test scenarios. We're ready to be let loose on the universe, to fight and die for the Commonwealth. There's only one thing left to do, and that's to find out what exactly the military has deemed to be our best use.

Back in the platoon bay, our lockers are already emptied and our duffel bags and rucksacks packed with our gear. Our instructors are standing in the middle of the bay, and we file into the room intent on taking our usual positions of attention in front of our lockers, but Sergeant Burke waves us off.

"At ease, people. Basic Training ended thirty minutes ago. Gather 'round to get your assignments."

Sergeant Harris hands him a stack of printed forms, and he goes through them top to bottom. We all cluster around him in anticipation. They've determined our final assignments, and now we will learn where and how we will spend the next fifty-seven months of our service careers.

"Garcia—*marines*. Second Battalion, Fifth Marines. You're going to tank school after marine induction."

Garcia accepts the form with a grin, and Sergeant Burke shakes his hand.

"Well done. Kennedy—*marines*. First Battalion, Seventh Marines. Infantry School."

Kennedy accepts his orders, shakes the sergeant's hand, and steps out of the cluster of remaining recruits to gather his junk.

"Halley—*navy*."

The rest of us cheer. Navy is the brass ring everyone's secretly aiming for. I grin as she steps forward to receive her orders. Sergeant Burke takes out another form and puts it on top of Halley's orders before handing her both.

"You'll be a drop-ship jock. You're also promoted to E-2 as of this moment. You managed the highest aggregate test scores. That's quite an accomplishment. I haven't had a graduate get a navy slot in three Basic Training cycles."

"Thank you, sir," Halley says, her face radiant with excitement. I feel a stab of envy—she'll be reporting to Fleet School right away, and she'll probably get to see Earth from space before the end of the week.

"Ricci—*marines*. Third Battalion, Third Marines. Mobile field artillery. You'll be a cannon cocker."

I had expected him to react to a marine assignment by making good on his promise and resigning his contract on the spot, but he merely takes the orders from Sergeant Burke and gives him a sharp salute before stepping out of line.

"Grayson," Sergeant Burke says, and my stomach twists as I await the final word on my fate.

"*Territorial Army*. Congratulations—you're staying Earthside."

Twelve recruits left in Platoon 1066, and eleven of them are going into space. I'm the only one who will get to serve on Earth, doing the shittiest job in the armed forces: domestic garbage hauler for the NAC.

I stay impassive when I hear Sergeant Burke's words, but my first instinct is to punch him in the face. *Congratulations?* I don't think I've given him any reason to dislike me, at least no more or less than the other recruits, but that word makes it sound like he's mocking me.

I gather my gear without enthusiasm, my head still spinning with the revelation that I won't be going into space after all. Still, I made it through Basic, I want the bank account, and I don't want to waste all the sweat I've put into this career already, so I suppress the urge to throw the printout with my orders at Sergeant Burke's feet. The alternative is a shuttle back to the Public Residence Cluster, and whatever the TA has in store for me, there's nothing that can be worse than that.

"Grayson," Sergeant Burke says as I shoulder my duffel bag.

"Sir." I slide the bag off my shoulder to stand at attention, but he waves his hand in dismissal.

"At ease. You don't seem too happy with your assignment."

"No, sir," I say, trying to not look dejected.

"There's not a thing wrong with the Territorial Army. I was TA myself before I was assigned a drill instructor slot."

"I was looking forward to going into space, sir. TA gets all the shit jobs."

Sergeant Burke looks at me and shakes his head with a snort.

"TA is the *real* military," he says. "Let me tell you something about the spaceborne careers. The navy guys spend their service mopping decks in windowless metal tubes. The marines get to go play battle kabuki with the SRA, one company against another, arranged like a fucking sporting event. That's not soldiering; that's jerking off. They're so convinced they're the sharp tip of the spear, but you know what? Any TA company I've ever served with could mop the floor with any marine company. You know why TA gets all the shit jobs? Because nobody else could *handle* 'em, that's why.

"Go and get on the bus," he says, nodding toward the door. "Don't listen to those future space bus drivers and garrison troops about how fucking lucky they are. They don't know shit about shit yet, and neither do you. Now get out of here, and forget about what you were 'looking forward to.' This is the military, and nobody gives a shit about what *we* want. We take what we're served, and we ask for seconds, and that's the way it goes."

There's a bus waiting to take us to the shuttle port. The ride into the base three months ago was a solitary experience, scared and anxious recruits sitting by themselves. The ride out is much more of a social event, as we take the opportunity to talk to our platoon mates one last time.

"You going to be okay?" Halley asks me as she watches me reading over my printed orders. I am to report to my Territorial Army unit at Fort Shughart in Ohio. She'll be reporting to navy induction at Great Lakes.

"Yeah," I say. "I'll be fine. It's not like I was expecting five years of milk and cookies anyway."

"Just keep your head low, you hear? I want to get mail from you every week."

"You'll be on a navy ship," I say. "You might be out of network for weeks, you know."

"You'll still send those messages," Halley says. "I'll check the time stamps. And if you get yourself killed, you'll be in deep shit with me."

"Noted," I grin. "And likewise."

At the shuttle port, we say our final good-byes to each other. The future marines are all on the same shuttle to Camp Puller, where all the new marines from east of the Mississippi are trained. Halley and I are on separate shuttles.

"Take care," she says.

"You, too."

We kiss one last time, this time more like brother and sister. I watch as she walks to her gate, duffel bag over her shoulder.

And just like that, I'm right back where I was when I boarded the shuttle at the processing station twelve weeks ago: alone, anxious, and clueless about what the next few days will bring.

CHAPTER 7

—WELCOME TO BATTALION—

My new unit is B Company, 365th Autonomous Infantry Battalion, Third Infantry Division. The 365th is stationed at Fort Shughart, a massive base on the outskirts of the Dayton metroplex. The TA seems ruthlessly efficient—I am expecting a repeat of the administrative snail trail from the first day of my service career, but I am directed to my company building, assigned to a squad, and given a locker and bunk in one of the squad rooms not thirty minutes after my arrival on the military bus from the Dayton shuttle port.

In Basic, there was one big room for the entire platoon. Here at B Company, the squads are quartered in rooms. The officers and noncoms get their private rooms, but the enlisted have to share, four troops to a room. There are two double bunk beds, four lockers, and a table with four chairs to every room. The building is old, but well maintained—the paint is fading, and the polymer coating on the floors is worn, but everything is clean. There's a communal head on each floor, and the toilets and showers have actual stalls built around them.

When I walk into my assigned squad room, my squad mates are gathered around the table, playing a game of cards. They all turn around to look at me, and I wave a hand in greeting. Two of my new roommates are guys, and one is a very pretty girl.

"Grayson," I say. "Fresh out of Basic. I guess I'm your new squad mate."

"Come on in," one of them says.

They all study me with curiosity, undoubtedly sizing me up.

"Your locker's over there." One of the male troopers points to his left, where a row of lockers stands lined up against a wall of the room. "It's the one closest to the window."

"Thanks."

I walk over to the locker and open the door. There's issue clothing already hanging on the rack, and the locker is dressed to boot camp perfection, with brand-new pairs of boots neatly lined up on the bottom shelf.

"This one's taken already," I say, and my new squad mates chuckle in unison.

"It's your new gear. Supply got your data as soon as they assigned you to the battalion. They stock your locker for you ahead of time."

"Well, *that's* handy."

The lockers are laid out just like the ones we had in Basic. I put my meager pile of personal clothing and gear into the only empty drawer in the locker. There's a lockable compartment for valuables, and it contains a PDP, a much smaller and sleeker model than the one they issued in Basic. I take the PDP out and turn it on to find that it already has my personal login on the main screen. It also has options on the main screen that weren't there before—the standard-issue PDP is fully network enabled, unlike the hobbled models in Basic that would only let us communicate with our instructors and fellow platoon members.

"We're off duty already," one of my new squad mates says behind me. "You can take your time stowing your stuff. Chow hall is going to be open for another forty-five minutes, if you want to grab something."

"Thanks."

My fellow squad mates are wearing the TA version of Individual Combat Uniforms. The camouflage patterns are different for each service: The marines have a polychromatic pattern that changes depending on the environment, and the navy likes a blue-and-gray pattern that looks like a geometry illustration. The Territorial Army issues a digital pattern that's black, gray, and washed-out green, the noncolors of the urban battlefield. Of all the issue patterns, it's the most sinister and business-looking one. I change into the ICUs to match the rest of my squad. The new boots fit well, but they have the annoying squeakiness of unissued footwear. It took me the better part of twelve weeks to get my issue boots in Basic to conform to my feet, and now I have to start the process all over again.

"So where'd you go to Basic?" someone asks, and gestures to an empty chair. I walk over to the table and sit down with the rest of my roommates.

"You know what? I have no idea. They never told us, and I never asked."

"Swampland, brushy desert, or nothing but cornfields?"

"Brushy desert," I reply.

"NACRD Orem," another soldier says. "I went there, too. Not too bad. You don't have the bugs and the humidity the poor fuckers at NACRD Charleston have to deal with."

All of my roommates have chevrons on their collars. One is an E-2, with a single chevron, and one is an E-3, a private first class, a chevron with a rocker underneath. People don't usually make E-2 right out of Basic unless they were top flight in their training battalion like Halley, and E-3 promotions don't ever happen before a year of active service. The third trooper in the room is an E-4, a corporal.

"Am I the only new guy in this squad?" I ask.

"Yep," one of them confirms. "Our platoon got four this cycle, I think, including you. They trickle the new guys in like that, so you can learn on the job. Grayson, is it?"

"Yeah."

The soldier across the table from me extends his hand, and I shake it.

"I'm Baker. The cheating fuck over there trying to look at my cards is Priest, and the one with the ponytail is Hansen."

I nod at each of them in turn.

"You're in luck, Grayson. You're in the squad with the best squad leader in the entire battalion."

"In the entire brigade," Hansen corrects. She has almond-shaped eyes and very white and even teeth, evidence of better dental care than you can get anywhere within ten miles of a Public Residence Cluster.

"Oh, yeah? What's his name?"

"*Her* name." Priest gives up his attempt to sneak a peek at Baker's cards, and leans back in his chair. "Staff Sergeant Fallon. She used to be a first sergeant, but they busted her down for striking an officer."

"I thought they kicked you out of the service for hitting a superior," I say, smelling a military fish tale.

"Oh, they do," Hansen says. "That's unless you're a Medal of Honor winner. They don't get rid of certified heroes. It would be bad PR."

"Medal of *Honor*?" I ask, and the disbelief in my face makes my three roommates grin with delight. "You are joking, right?"

The Medal of Honor is the highest military award for bravery, always awarded by the president of the Commonwealth personally. From what Sergeant Burke in boot camp told us, nine out of ten times the president puts it on a flag-draped coffin.

"No word of a joke. She got it when the NAC did that excursion into mainland China a few years back, at the Battle of Dalian.

You get the medal, you can ask for any assignment anywhere in the service, and she went right back to her old unit once she was out of the hospital."

"That's pretty wild. Is she a complete hard-ass?"

"Not at all. She's got no patience for slackers, but as long as you pull your weight and don't look like you're clueless, she's hands-off."

"That doesn't sound too bad," I say. "I was expecting . . . hell, I have no idea what I was expecting, actually."

"You were expecting some sort of penal colony," Baker says amicably. "You thought you pulled the shittiest card in the deck when they told you that you're going TA, right?"

There's no point denying it, so I nod.

"That's what everyone thinks at first. We all did. But this is a good outfit. Our sergeants know their shit, and our officers mostly leave us alone. We get the job done, and we look after each other. I've been TA for almost two years, and I wouldn't take a garrison post on a colony if you paid me double."

The others at the table nod in agreement.

I'm still disappointed about not going into space, and I have no idea whether I'll feel the same way about the TA in two years. For better or for worse, however, this place will be my home until my service time is up, so I decide that I might as well make the best of it.

"You play cards, Grayson?" Hansen asks.

"Sure," I say, and pull my chair up to the table.

Reveille in the morning is a low-key affair. The wake-up call comes over the ceiling speakers and all the PDPs at 0545, which is almost an hour later than our wake-up call in Basic Training. At first call, I drop out of bed and grab my personal hygiene kit out of the locker to file out to the head, but my roommates don't seem to be in a hurry.

"Take your time," Baker says as he climbs out of bed. "Nobody'll check on us or anything. Chow hall is open at six, and orders are at seven. They don't hold your hand and rush you through shit like in Basic."

"The TA assumes that you can figure out for yourself how to get squared away in the mornings," Priest says from the bunk above mine. "Just don't miss orders out in front of the building at 0700, or you're in deep shit."

"Got it," I say.

It's an odd experience to be left alone in the morning. Back home I never got out of bed before nine or ten o'clock, but twelve weeks of boot camp have turned me into an early riser. There was no freedom in Basic Training—with twice as many recruits as sinks, toilets, and showerheads, nobody had much time for leisure in the mornings—but there was also a certain sense of purpose. You could simply turn off your brain and follow the pack, and there was comfort to the predictability of the routine. Now I have to check the clock and take charge of my schedule once more, and as much as I like being able to take my time in front of the sink or in the toilet stall, I find that I miss the rigid structure of Basic a little.

So I do what I've been doing since I got off the bus at NACRD Orem—I follow the pack.

My squad mates don't seem to mind when I tag along with the group to the chow hall. I fall back a little on purpose as we enter the chow hall, so I'll be behind the others in the breakfast line, which will spare me from having to pick a table and then ending up sitting by myself. I watch the others with one eye as I load up my breakfast tray, and then follow them to their table.

There are other soldiers sitting at the table as well, people I don't know yet, and for just a moment I consider peeling off and picking my own table after all. Then Hansen catches my eye, and she waves me over.

"Don't be shy, now. Have a seat, and I'll introduce you to the rest of the squad."

She pulls out a chair, and I put my tray onto the table before sitting down.

"Guys and girls, this is Private Grayson. He's the new guy for this quarter. Grayson, this is the whole squad. These four clowns are in the room next to ours."

The other members of the squad size me up just like my roommates did yesterday, and I nod at them.

"Thank God," one of them says. "That means I'm officially no longer the FNG. Thank you, Grayson."

"My pleasure," I say. "Just make sure you pass along the handbook, okay?"

"Oh, there's not much to it. Just keep the fridge in the room stocked, and make sure everyone's boots are shiny every morning."

"Don't listen to Phillips," Hansen says. "If the job required being good at anything, he would have been fired on day two."

Hansen introduces the rest of the squad to me one by one. Phillips is a tall, freckle-faced guy with wiry red hair and glasses with little circular lenses. Jackson is an equally tall and thin black girl. She wears interesting tattoos under her eyes, some sort of tribal pattern. Stratton is a steel-jawed recruiting poster model who would look terribly intimidating in his perfection if he wasn't the shortest member of the squad by half a head. Lastly, there's Paterson, whose buzz cut doesn't quite conceal the fact that he's going bald already. Jackson is a corporal, Stratton and Paterson are privates first class, and Phillips is a one-chevron private. I am the only member of the squad without a rank device on the collar.

"This is not a training unit," I say. "I was sort of expecting some more advanced training. The other recruits in my platoon all went on to schools of some kind."

"Nope, this is a field battalion," Jackson replies. "TA infantry doesn't need to send people off to school. You got the skills in Basic, and infantry business is just some more of that, only with live ammo. You'll learn on the job with us, in the field."

"We're a pretty active battalion," Stratton says. "We have one or two live calls a month. You'll probably see combat before you have a chance to wear in those new boots."

I chuckle at this, but none of the soldiers at the breakfast table seem to think Stratton is joking, and my chuckle just kind of dies in my throat when I realize that he isn't.

"So you're the new guy," Staff Sergeant Fallon says when she enters our squad room. She's a short woman, with dark hair that she wears in a ponytail, and she looks hard enough to beat up half the squad without much trouble. She wears her ICU sleeves rolled up like the drill instructors in Basic did, and the muscles on her arms look like steel cables.

"Yes, ma'am," I say, and stand at attention, only to be waved off almost instantly.

"At ease," Sergeant Fallon says. "Jesus, don't those instructors over at the depot remove the corn cobs before they send you off into real life?"

"I don't remember having been issued any sort of vegetables, Staff Sergeant," I reply, and Sergeant Fallon chuckles.

"A smart ass. As if we didn't have enough of those already. I think you'll fit in just fine."

The duty schedule in a field regiment of light infantry is pretty simple, at least for the grunts whose main job is to pull a trigger. When your job is to kill people and blow up stuff, you either learn about how to do your job better, or you practice the skills you've already learned. We spend as much time out in the field as we do on manuals and classroom instruction. Fort Shughart has its own urban-combat training facility, of course, and every platoon gets to spend some time there every week practicing attack and defense, much like in Basic. There's a live-fire range, too, and Sergeant Fallon has me qualify on the M-66 rifle in my first week.

My issue rifle feels different from the training version somehow, even though it weighs the same and operates in exactly the same fashion. Maybe it's the knowledge that this weapon actually fires live rounds, fléchettes that can pierce armor and flesh instead of harmless beams that merely trigger a computer protocol, but somehow I have a lot more respect for this weapon. We don't practice with live ammo—the issue rifles fire blanks on the urban-combat course, and training adapters on the muzzle supply the simulated projectiles—but at the firing range there's nothing virtual about the fléchettes that leave the muzzle of my M 66.

The qualification course of fire for infantry soldiers consists of a hundred pop-up targets at random intervals and distances. I engage them all in turn, centering the reticle of my M-66 on the target and letting the computer determine the rate of fire. The rifle burps short streams of fléchettes at each target, and most of the time they fall down. The moving targets give me a bit of trouble at first, especially the ones that are moving laterally, but after a few missed silhouettes, I figure out the correct amount of lead, and my score improves.

"Not bad at all for a guy fresh out of Basic," Sergeant Fallon says when I finish the course and unload my weapon for safety inspection. "That's a seventy-nine. Marksman score. One more hit and you would have scored Sharpshooter. You can let it stand, or try for Sharpshooter or Expert."

"I'll try again," I say, and Sergeant Fallon nods with approval.

"Marksman's a good score for cooks and filing clerks, but the Expert badge looks better on an infantry Class A," she says. "Not that it matters in the end, mind you. What really counts is how well you can shoot when your targets are shooting back."

CHAPTER 8

——THE BATTLE OF THE——
EMBASSY

Two weeks after my arrival, we have a combat deployment. My boots aren't even close to worn in yet.

"Don't bother packing spare socks," Sergeant Fallon says as we get geared up in our squad rooms. "We're going light. Basic load only. We'll probably be home for dinner."

"Where are we headed, Sarge?" Stratton asks.

"Some milk run to the Balkans. Someone's declared independence again, and they've aligned with the Sino-Russians. We're just dashing over there in the drop ships to do an embassy evac."

"Back for dinner," Stratton says. "I don't mind a milk run for a change."

"We go skids up in forty-five minutes," Sergeant Fallon says. "Put on your party clothes, grab your guns from the armory, and hop on the bus. You know the drill, so let's get busy."

We help each other into our battle armor and check our latches and seals. Then we go downstairs to the company armory, where the sergeant-at-arms and his helpers are standing by to hand us our weapons. There are other squads lined up in front of the armory already, but the armory staff is efficient, and nobody spends more than ten seconds trading rack tags for issue weapons.

When we're all armed, we file out of the building to the waiting bus that will take us to the drop ships.

Our autonomous battalion has a squadron of Hornet attack drop ships. They're not the space-going version the marines use, only atmosphere craft, but they carry more armor plating and weapons than the marine version, because they don't need to dedicate any space or weight allowance to all the junk needed for space flight. Each drop ship can carry an entire platoon of troops, or a single battle tank. On this mission, we go light—command has determined that we won't need heavy armor, so we'll only use four out of twelve ships and load them up with one of the battalion's light infantry companies—Bravo Company.

Four platoons of TA soldiers carry a lot of firepower, even without the tanks and artillery. The Hornet drop ships don't just ferry us into battle; they serve as close air support and command-and-control units as well. When we pull up to the airfield, the four ships are already lined up, engines running, navigation lights flashing, and rear cargo ramps extended. They're squat and mean-looking craft, all angles and edges, with stubby wings that hold lots of fuel tanks and ordnance.

"Let's go for a ride," Sergeant Fallon says as she gets out of her seat, and everybody on the bus whoops and hollers like we're about to ride out to the stadium for a Commonwealth League football game.

The ride is a bit bumpy. Military drop ships skimp on the creature comforts. There are two rows of seats along the sides of the hull in the cargo bay, and they're merely fabric nets with lap belts that look like they were installed as an afterthought.

Somewhere over the eastern Mediterranean, the platoon

sergeant gets out of his seat and starts handing out ammunition containers to the squad leaders. Sergeant Fallon grabs two of the containers and brings them back to us. She pops the airtight seal on the crates, and the lid comes open to reveal neatly stacked rows of M-66 magazines and grenades.

"Five rifle mags per head," she says to us, undoubtedly for my benefit. "Four in the mag pouches, one in the rifle. Don't work that charging handle until we're on the ground and I give the go-ahead."

Two of my squad mates also receive a pair of launcher tubes. I recognize them from Basic—they're Sarissa antiarmor missiles. Everybody takes turns reaching into the ammo crate and filling up the magazine pouches and grenade loops attached to their battle armor, and I follow suit.

"Put on your helmets, and we'll check the TacLink. Mission briefing in five."

"What if we get into a mess and need more ammo?" I ask.

Sergeant Fallon merely points to the front of the cargo bay. "Drop ship has extra ammo storage. We get stranded somewhere, we have enough ordnance with us to keep us shooting for days."

We don our helmets, and lower the eyepieces. The tactical uplink activates, and I see the familiar diamond-shaped symbols marking individual squad and platoon members in my field of vision.

"Commo check," Sergeant Fallon says on the squad channel. We all check in by squad. Today, I'm Alpha-4, fourth member of fire team Alpha. Each squad is split into two fire teams of four soldiers each. Our squad leader is tied into the platoon channel, and the platoon leaders in turn are tied into the company channel. That way, the higher-level channels aren't cluttered with the battle chatter of every soldier in the company.

"Here's the scoop," our platoon leader says as our computers bring up little overhead maps of the target area.

"We're doing an embassy evacuation of NAC personnel. They got their eviction notice via rocket-propelled grenades this morning. Local defense crew is holding out, but they could really use some hardcore grunts on the ground."

One of the maps resolves into a three-dimensional representation of the embassy complex, and our platoon leader overlays deployment vectors as he continues.

"Once the ships are on the ground, First and Second Platoons will establish a perimeter defense to augment the embassy security team. First Platoon gets the front gate and the east wall. The guys from Second Platoon will cover the west wall and the back. They have two hundred personnel and civilian refugees to be flown out, so we'll have to ferry them in two trips with the drop ships. Third and Fourth Platoons are riding herd on the civvies. The drop ships come back, we load up the second batch of civilians, we do an orderly exfil, and then meet up with the other half of Bravo Company at the destination. We hang around until the transports come to pick up the civvies, and then we'll hop back into the drop ships and head home. Should be a cakewalk."

"Ain't it always," my seat neighbor murmurs.

"You heard the man," Sergeant Fallon takes over. "We're covering the front gate, together with Second Squad. Third and Fourth Squads cover the east wall. If the natives get restless, the shit will probably hit the fan at the gate, so we're the trip wire for the rest of the platoon."

"Rules of engagement?" Corporal Jackson asks. She looks sinister in her gray battle armor, her helmet covering everything but the tattooed area around her eyes.

"Anyone who points a weapon at us or tries to enter the embassy grounds is fair game. Lethal force is authorized. Use your judgment, as always."

"Copy that," Jackson says.

"Remember, the embassy is sovereign NAC territory by international law. Anyone shoots at us from the outside, light 'em up. Now let's go over the map for a second and straighten out the fire team deployment."

"Buckle in, folks," we hear over the ship comm channel a half hour later. "Descending into target area, ETA ten minutes. We're doing a combat landing, so hold on to your lunches, boys and girls."

My platoon mates groan at this, and I raise a questioning eyebrow at Stratton, who sits to my right.

"Combat landing. Corkscrew descent at high speed, to throw off targeting solutions. They go in at full throttle and hit the brakes, like, five seconds before the skids touch down."

He buckles in and tightens his seat belt firmly before placing his rifle into the holding clamps by the side of his seat. I quickly follow suit.

The engines of the drop ship increase power, and then the ship banks to the left and starts sinking at a rather alarming rate. My seat is on the left side, so the tight left-hand turn has me pressed back against the armor liner of the hull. Across the cargo bay, the members of Third and Fourth Squad are hanging in their seats, only restrained by their lap belts. I briefly wonder what will happen if the lap belt of the soldier directly across the bay from me breaks, and two hundred and fifty pounds of armored trooper come hurtling across the bay toward me.

The descent is harrowing, but mercifully brief. When the ship straightens itself out for the final descent into the target area, I'm only moderately nauseated. The drop ship has no windows in the side of the hull, so we can't see what we're getting into until the skids touch down and the cargo ramp lowers. The drop ship settles on the ground almost gently, and the squad leaders are out of their seats before the ramp is even a quarter of the way down.

"Lock and load," Sergeant Fallon shouts.

We get up and charge our weapons. The bolt of my rifle slams home, shoving a live fléchette round into the chamber. This is not the first time I've loaded real ammunition, but it's the first time I may be shooting those fléchettes at people instead of gel-filled polymer silhouettes.

The ramp hits the ground. Outside, I see a manicured lawn and a collection of low buildings beyond. It's night on this side of the Atlantic, and the helmet camera of my armor automatically turns on the low-light augmentation.

"Let's go, people!"

We exit the drop ship at a run, weapons at the ready. Our tactical displays show us the deployment vectors for the individual squads, so we don't need anyone to lead the way. Stratton is ahead of me, and I follow him across the lawn toward the front gate of the complex. Behind me, First and Second Squads follow, sixteen little blue diamond carets on the tactical map overlaid into my field of vision by the helmet display.

"Fire Team Alpha, let's find some cover by those planters on the left side of that gate," Corporal Baker says over the team channel.

There are two embassy guards in riot gear hunkered down by the guardhouse on the traffic island in front of the gate. The gate itself is a cast iron latticework, intended more for decoration than for use as a real barrier. I chuckle when I see that the guards have lowered the red and white arms of the traffic barriers as well, as if those ceremonial pieces of striped plastic will offer some additional resistance if someone decides to break through the gate.

We take up position behind the heavy concrete planters fifty yards behind the guardhouse, and the guards come rushing over, running with their heads drawn in like a pair of turtles. They wear impact plates, but those are nothing like our battle armor, just chest and back plates joined by quick-release fasteners. They're armed with short-barreled PDWs, little automatic submachine guns that are better than a pistol, but nowhere near as useful as a rifle.

"Glad to see you guys," one of the guardsmen says. "We're ready to get the hell out of here."

"Any trouble with the locals?" Corporal Baker asks.

"You could say that. We got some grenade fire into the central building this morning, and ever since then it's been small-arms fire here and there. The locals must have raided an armory or something. We keep getting drive-bys. Thank God they can't shoot. They just sort of drive up and spray a magazine into our general direction."

"Well, the next round is on us," Baker says. "You guys stay in the back a bit."

"No argument," the other guardsman says, and both of them rush off to find cover somewhere.

"Bravo One-One, first fire team is in position," Baker says into his helmet mike.

"I know, nimrod. We're thirty yards to your right. I can see you," Sergeant Fallon's reply comes back over the squad channel, and we all chuckle.

"Listen to that shit," Hansen says. There's a steady crackling of gunfire coming from the city beyond the gates of the embassy. I can see empty streets, illuminated by yellow streetlights. The area around the embassy looks like a business zone, shuttered shops and deactivated marquees.

"Wonder if they have any good bars around here," I say.

"Wanna go out and look for one? I got my universal credit card right here." Stratton hefts his rifle.

I open my mouth for a smart-ass reply, but now we hear engine sounds from the end of the street beyond the embassy gate, and everybody gets back to the business of finding cover. The distant noise sounds like an old combustion engine, the kind they used to put on heavy equipment. I can feel the pavement vibrate with the low drumming of the far-off engine.

"This can't be good," Hansen says.

"The drop ships are loading up the civilians right now," Sergeant Fallon says. "Anything comes around that corner that looks more dangerous than a street sweeper, you take it the fuck out."

There's activity at the far end of the street. The blunt snout of an armored vehicle appears, and we watch as it turns the corner, taking out a trash container and a shop marquee in the process. It's a battle tank, one of the old models that run on tracks. It stands much higher than a modern tank, and instead of a modular weapons mount, it has a round armored turret that looks like a frying pan turned upside down, and a cannon that's almost as long as the tank itself. It's a rolling antique, but if they have ammo for that big gun, it can still dish out a world of hurt.

"Fuck me," Baker says. "Get out of line of sight, people."

We don't need the encouragement. The planters are good protection against small-arms fire, but not against a tank cannon.

"Priest, get the antiarmor missiles up here."

There's more engine noise coming from the end of the street. Another tank turns the corner in a cloud of diesel smoke. A third one follows, and it has soldiers in uniforms and body armor following in its wake. The tanks fan out in a line across the width of the street, and then a fourth tank rumbles around the corner and takes its place in the formation.

"Super, a whole freakin' tank platoon. Sarge, we need some more AT guys up here."

"On the way," Sergeant Fallon says.

Priest swaps his rifle for the antiarmor launcher and takes the dust caps off his launcher tube.

"Grayson, cover Priest. Make me some scrap metal."

Priest dashes off to the front wall, and I follow, rifle at the ready. He follows the protection of the wall until he's at the gate, and then peers around the corner to gauge the advance of the hostile armor platoon. As his computer parses the information, we see four red icons on our map overlays where Priest spots the enemy tanks.

Priest flicks the launch-button cover with his thumb, and winks at me. Then he steps back from the wall and aims the launcher tube into the air. There's a muffled *pop* as the expeller charge ejects the missile from the tube, and then the missile's own motor kicks in with an undramatic hiss that sounds like Priest is firing a really big bottle rocket. The missile shoots up into the night sky.

"One Mississippi, two Mississippi . . ." Priest says, and then there's an earth-shattering *bang* on the other side of the wall. One of the red tank icons on my screen blinks out of existence. Priest peeks around the corner again, and hastily pulls his head back.

"*Uh-oh.* That pissed 'em off, I think."

The tanks open up with machine guns. There are chips of concrete flying as their bullets hit the corner where Priest fired his missile, and we retreat along the wall, away from the gate.

We're twenty yards from the gate when the wall of the embassy shakes, and part of it comes bursting into the compound in a cloud of concrete dust. The earphones in my helmet automatically filter the sound of the explosion, but even with the electronic noise filter, the explosion is almost deafening. When I look over my shoulder, there's a hole in the wall that's only slightly smaller than a garage door.

"Figures that we get here just before the shit hits the fan," I shout to Priest, who laughs as he readies his second antiarmor rocket.

"That's what we *do*, man. We're the fire brigade."

Then he fires his second missile into the sky, and a few heart-beats later there's another explosion, this one closer than the first one. Another red tank icon flashes and disappears from the tactical map. A few hundred feet to our right, where Fire Team Bravo and Sergeant Fallon have taken up position, someone fires another missile. I watch as the missile, barely longer than my arm, swiftly rises into the sky on a thin jet of brightly burning propellant.

A third tank explodes with a thunderclap. This explosion is practically on the other side of the wall now. The fourth tank guns its engine, and I can see its headlights illuminating the pavement on our side of the gate.

"One coming through the gate," I shout into the TacLink. Out of the corner of my eye, I see the muted flashes of two more missile launches from the area where Third and Fourth Squads have taken up position.

The gate comes out of its hinges with a bang as fifty tons of armor crash into it. The red-and-white traffic barrier sails through the air, tumbling end over end. The tank roars into the compound, machine gun blazing away at nothing in particular. From behind, Priest grabs my battle harness and pulls me back into cover.

"Watch out," he says.

The tank veers slightly to the right to avoid running over the guardhouse and getting itself entangled. The turret starts turning in our direction.

Then a flash lights up the night sky a few hundred feet above the tank, and I can see the warheads of the incoming Sarissas streak down. They tear into the roof of the tank, right behind the turret, and the tank disintegrates.

The explosion shakes the ground beneath my boots and knocks me off my feet, back into Priest. There are chunks of armor pelting the concrete traffic barrier that serves as our cover. All over the gate plaza, I can hear bits and pieces raining down onto the pavement. The cannon of the tank bounces off the wall of a nearby building and tumbles back onto the street with a loud metallic clatter.

When the steel rain has stopped, I peer over the top of our cover. There's not much left of the enemy tank—just the bottom part of the chassis, a few road wheels, and a length of broken tread. Amazingly, the explosion that ripped the tank into shrapnel didn't even scratch the road beneath.

"We have incoming infantry," Sergeant Fallon shouts over the squad link. "To the wall, and find a cozy spot."

My team rushes back to the hole in the wall left by the one tank shell the enemy armor column managed to get off. I go prone behind a low piece of the wall, and peer over the lip. Instantly, the TacLink updates with at least two dozen red symbols marking enemy infantry. The closest group of them is charging the gate at a run, and they're less than twenty yards away. I raise the muzzle of my rifle and draw a bead on the last soldier in the column.

"Engaging."

I press the trigger, and my rifle spits out a half dozen armor-piercing fléchettes. My salvo hits the trailing soldier in the mid-section, and he drops instantly. I can see little puffs of material where my fléchettes tear through his outdated body armor. I've been in fights in the PRC before, even hurt people badly a few times, but this is the first time I know for sure I've killed a fellow human being. I don't have time for reflection, because there are dozens of soldiers still advancing, and they aren't here to talk things out with us. I shift my aim to the next soldier, but before I can pull the trigger, Priest and Hansen open up next to me with short bursts, and the enemy soldier goes down.

Then the lead group of attackers is in the dead spot to my right, where the wall blocks my line of sight as they continue toward the gate. I duck behind the concrete ledge of the broken wall as incoming fire is spraying chips of concrete into my face.

Hansen and Priest duck as well, but not before Priest takes two rounds to his battle armor that knock him off balance. He crashes to the ground, rolls onto his back, and scrambles away from the wall opening.

"Sons of bitches can actually shoot," he says. I can see two gray smears on the chest of his armor where the enemy rifle rounds disintegrated on the hard shell.

Baker takes a grenade from his battle harness, pops the safety cover, and chucks the grenade through the wall opening.

"Flashbang out!" he shouts.

Flashbang grenades are not very effective against troopers in modern battle armor. The noise from the explosion gets filtered out by our helmet-mounted earphones, and the visors of our helmets automatically shield us from the flash. To troops without modern gear, however, a flashbang explosion is like looking into a nuclear detonation while getting ice picks rammed into the eardrums.

The grenade on the other side of the wall goes off with a crash that makes the earlier firing of the tank main gun sound like someone lit a wet firecracker. The flash momentarily turns the area in front of the embassy into the surface of the sun, millions of candlepower units burning out every unprotected retina in a thousand-yard radius. The firing from the enemy soldiers ceases instantly.

"Up and at 'em," Baker says. He steps back to the hole in the wall, raises his rifle, and starts picking off targets.

We join in.

Over at the gate, Second Squad is doing likewise. There's an entire infantry platoon deployed in front of the embassy, but they're mostly blind and deaf now, and we have eighteen TA troopers on the line, all networked with each other, sharing target data and threat vectors. The road in front of the embassy turns into the Seventh Circle of Hell as thousands of fléchettes from computer-controlled rifles sweep it clear of any living presence. Some of the enemy soldiers are behind good shelter, parked vehicles and metal refuse containers, but a few rifle grenades turn cover and covered alike into smoking ruins.

This is not a fight—it's a rout. The enemy soldiers are so far out of their league that it feels like we're a bunch of professional boxers beating up a schoolyard full of asthmatic grade-school kids. Behind us, two drop ships ascend into the night sky with their engines at full thrust. A few moments later, the other two ships follow.

"Drop ships are skids up," Sergeant Fallon shouts. "The clock is ticking. Fifteen minutes round-trip."

"We'll try to hang on, Sarge," Stratton replies.

After a few minutes there's nothing left to shoot at out there. The street is littered with bodies and wrecked vehicles. Little fires are flickering where grenades have set stuff ablaze. There's an acrid smell in the air, the burned propellant of thousands of caseless rounds.

"Cease fire, top off those rifles, and watch your zones."

I pull the partially expended magazine out of my rifle and check my magazine pouches for a fresh one. There are four pouches on the front of my harness, and each held a 250-round magazine when I stepped out of the drop ship. I don't recall reloading my rifle during the fight, but now two of my pouches are empty. I've blown through more than half my combat load in just five minutes of frenzied shooting, over seven hundred rounds of ammo. The hand guards of the rifle are hot to the touch.

"Fucking shooting gallery," Priest says, rubbing the spot on his battle armor where the enemy rifle rounds left their marks. "Dumb as hell, waltzing down the road like they're on fucking review or something."

"I'll take 'em dumb." Hansen shrugs as she reloads her rifle with a smooth and practiced motion.

I know that the soldiers we just killed had capable weapons of their own, and that any of their shots could have scored a lucky hit and switched my lights off for good. Still, the whole engagement felt little different from a range exercise, pop-up targets that just drop without a fuss when you drill them with a salvo.

The sound of a rifle shot rolls across the street, a deep boom that sounds nothing like the hoarse cough of our fléchette rifles. Over by the gate, where Second Squad has taken up position, one of the TA soldiers falls. We all take cover once more.

"Sniper!" one of the guys from Second Squad calls out. "Shop window at the end of the street."

A new tactical symbol appears on my TacLink screen. In my field of vision, I can see the red diamond shape projected onto the location of the enemy sniper, even though there's a solid wall between us. The enemy rifle booms again, and the bullet punches a hole into the wall of the guardhouse, where a Second Squad trooper has taken cover.

"That's a hell of a caliber," Priest observes. Next to him, Hansen readies her grenade launcher, and I decide to follow suit. I open the breech of the grenade launcher, take a grenade out of my harness, and stuff it into the launcher tube.

We both step away from the wall to give our launcher muzzles some clearance, and then line up the launcher sights with the red diamond marker showing the enemy sniper's location.

"Fire in the hole!" Hansen shouts, and we both pull our triggers.

The recoil from the launcher is brisk, and I have to take a quick step back to keep my balance. The report from the launcher is muffled, like hitting a pillow with a wooden bat. Our grenades arc over the wall and toward the sniper's position.

Hansen's grenade hits first. It kicks up dust and debris as the high-explosive warhead of the grenade goes off. Then my grenade follows, landing just inside the broken shop window.

The explosion from my grenade is only very slightly less noisy than the detonation of the flashbang earlier. The entire front of the store erupts into the street, and a moment later the front of the building collapses with a roar.

There's a moment of shocked silence, and then a few of the Second Squad troopers whoop in triumph. Next to me, Stratton laughs.

"That's one way to do it, I suppose. *Sniper down.*"

"You're supposed to save those thermobaric grenades for special occasions," Baker says to me over the team channel. "Those are expensive."

"Save 'em for *what*? I'm a few weeks out of Basic," I reply. "Snipers shooting at me is a pretty special occasion right now."

It's only when my whole squad erupts into laughter that I realize I toggled my response into the squad channel.

The rest of the mission is rather anticlimactic. The drop ships return empty, and Second Platoon loads up the last of the civilians while First Platoon stands watch. The indigenous revolutionaries have apparently lost the nerve for another brawl after the mauling they received in front of the embassy gates, because we don't see another living soul out on the street for the remainder of our brief stay.

Then the drop ships are ready to dust off, and First Platoon retreats to the embassy gardens in bounding overwatch, one half of the platoon covering the asses of the other half at all times. This is the most vulnerable phase of the mission, and any tactician worth his salt would have waited until now to bring in the heavy armor to shoot at the fully loaded drop ships, but the locals seem to have used up all their courage, and we board the drop ships and depart unscathed.

Soon after takeoff, the drop ships bank and circle back around. I can feel the thumping of an ordnance release, and a few moments later the drop ship is buffeted by the shock wave from a series of explosions on the ground.

"Did we just bomb our own embassy?" I ask Sergeant Fallon, who is sitting two seats away.

"Yep," she confirms. "We're going to be out a few million bucks, we might as well blow it up ourselves, right?"

"Right," I say. "Kind of a waste, though, isn't it?"

She looks at me with an amused expression.

"*War's* a waste, you know. We just broke a shitload of property down there. Never mind the poor slobs we killed. Just keep in mind that *they* started the shit. I would have been just as happy to stay home tonight and have a beer at the noncommissioned officers' club."

———

Bravo Company suffered no casualties. One of the troopers from Second Squad, Harrison, got knocked on his ass by the first round from the sniper, but his armor stopped the .50-caliber round. That kind of round is powerful enough to go through the visors of our helmets, and if the sniper had aimed about eight inches higher, Harrison would have been dead instantly. As things stand, he only has a bruise on his sternum, and the sniper is now finely dispersed organic matter.

There's no guesswork in modern warfare, no chance for anyone to talk up their exploits and claim imaginary accomplishments. The TacLink computers recorded the battle from the perspective of every single soldier in the company, tallied the kills, and analyzed our performance. Sergeant Fallon goes through the squad's kill sheet, and it shows that I shot three enemy soldiers with my rifle, in addition to the sniper I flushed out with the thermobaric grenade from my launcher. The credit for the sniper is split 25/75 between Hansen and me, according to the damage estimates of the computer. Once more, killing real people boils down to a number on a tally sheet, but these kills won't dust themselves off and take a turn at defense next round. Tonight I have ended the lives of four people, added a final period to their life stories with a pull of the trigger.

I guess I should be dwelling on that fact, and wonder how much those enemy soldiers were like me—trying to survive their service time to collect their money in the end—but I don't. They came to kill us, and we killed them instead, and I don't feel any remorse about that. In a way, it was a business transaction—nothing personal, just two groups of employees doing their jobs. I don't feel anger, or hate, or sadness towards those soldiers. All I feel is a kind of exhilaration. We went up against someone else's varsity team and gave them a drubbing. I am still breathing, and a day closer to my discharge date, and that's not bad at all.

CHAPTER 9

——LIFE AT SHUGHART——

Fort Shughart is its own little city. Everything we need is available to us within the safety of the base. We have our own movie theaters, clubs, sports facilities, and swimming pools. There's even a park in a quiet corner near the edge of the base, complete with duck pond, walking trails, and benches.

When we're in garrison, the workday ends at five o'clock in the afternoon. During the weekdays, we train in the field, we go to the shooting range, we sit in classrooms and listen to lectures, or we do weapons and equipment maintenance, but at five in the afternoon, the day officially ends, and we're off until seven in the morning. Most of us have dinner in the chow hall and then hang out at the enlisted club, catch a movie, or play some softball out in the well-maintained domed ball fields beyond the vehicle parks. The married soldiers go home to their families and their on-base housing in the residential section, which looks like any other generic suburban neighborhood outside a PRC, but most of us junior enlisted are single, and we're quartered in our squad rooms. It feels a bit like high school, only with guns and uniforms, and instead of learning trigonometry or North American history, we learn better ways to kill people and blow up their stuff.

I like my squad mates. First Squad tries harder, works better together, and has more fun than all the other squads. It seems that some of the luster of Sergeant Fallon's Medal of Honor is rubbing off on the squad, creating a sort of unspoken obligation to meet a higher standard. Most of my squad mates are funny and personable, the kind of people I would have wanted to befriend back home. Here, people aren't constantly trying to fuck you over for BNA rations or black market pills. Only Corporal Jackson, Fire Team Bravo's leader, mostly keeps to herself. She rarely joins in when we go for a game of pool and a few drinks over at the enlisted club, and she doesn't often laugh at other people's jokes or crack her own. There's something intimidating about her, and it's not just her usually stern expression or the tattoos around her eyes. She seems even more dedicated to honing her edge than the rest of us, and as far as I can tell, she spends most of her free time running, practicing drills, or studying field manuals on her PDP.

The other members of my squad are more approachable. Stratton is the joker of the group, Baker is thoughtful and laid back, Priest is a poker fiend and a skirt chaser, and Paterson is a big, dumb, good-natured jock. Phillips is a bit of a chevron sniffer, which is what they call the guys who try to buddy up to the senior NCOs, but he's competent and always willing to switch crap jobs with others, so nobody minds it too much. Hansen is the prettiest girl in the company, and virtually all the guys—and some of the girls—have a crush on her. She's also deadly efficient at hand-to-hand combat training, which is why her admirers content themselves with looking rather than touching. I can't deny that Hansen is easy on the eyes, but my mind is still fresh with memories of Halley.

Halley.

We're in touch through the MilNet, and we message each other almost every day. Her training schedule at Fleet School is packed, but she still manages to send one reply to every three messages I send her way. She hates the cramming sessions for astrophysics and calculus, and loves the weightlessness training, where all the navy trainees get their first taste of the peculiarities of spaceborne duty. The navy's ships all have artificial gravity, of course, but trainees still have to learn how to function in a zero-gravity environment, just like the sailors in the old waterborne navy had to be able to swim. After Fleet School she's going on to three months of drop-ship-pilot school, and then she'll get a copilot slot in one of the navy's many combat-aviation squadrons, where she'll ride in the left seat of a Wasp-class drop ship for a year before getting command of her own Wasp. I am more than just a little envious of her career path, which is pretty much the top job for a five-year enlistee. Halley will spend most of her first service year in training, but she'll be a junior officer by the end of that year, and she'll be dropping marines and flying attack missions on far-off colony planets in a three-hundred-ton war machine. I'll be slugging it out with belligerents on good old Terra, and the only things I'll be commanding after a year will be my own pair of boots and the rifle slung across my chest. At the end of our service time, she'll be a lieutenant junior grade, the equivalent of a TA first lieutenant, and I'll be a corporal at best, eight pay grades and a whole stack of social layers below her.

Strangely enough, it's Halley who professes to be jealous of my job. When I send her a long and detailed message with the story of our embassy evac—my first combat mission—she replies just a little while later.

That's fucking awesome. I wish I could have been there.

Are you serious? I reply. Real bullets and shit. There were two dozen guys out there trying to kill us.

Yeah, I'm serious. I've spent all month in a classroom, or in my quarters reading training books. The room is about as big as a broom closet, and I'm sharing it with a girl who snores like a fucking dockworker.

I feel an entirely irrational twinge of relief at the revelation that she's bunking with a girl and not a male trainee.

Well, hang in there. Pretty soon you'll be dodging ground fire on a drop mission to some barely terraformed ball of mud in the Outer Rim.

Ah, hell. If you gotta go out, might as well make a pretty comet, right?

I laugh at her reply, but part of me is keenly aware that many drop-ship jocks have met their fate in exactly that fashion. The drop ships don't just deliver marines; they also serve as close air support, and the SRA marines have drop ships and sophisticated antiair missiles of their own. No craft in the military arsenal is invincible, not even the huge new attack carriers that carry swarms of fighters and enough nukes to turn a fair-sized planet into a ball of glowing slag. A Wasp is a tough machine, but even a lowly rifle grenade can score a lucky hit on a critical part and bring the whole thing down in a fireball.

Gotta run—next class is in five. More later.

I turn off my PDP and stare at the blank screen for a moment, trying to imagine Halley up on Luna, attending classes and bouncing around in zero-gravity training. She's where I wanted to be, and I'm ashamed to be jealous of her, but what stings even more is the knowledge that I'll probably never see her again.

The military is tribal to the core. Fort Shughart is a massive base, and the 365th Autonomous Infantry Battalion is just one of many units stationed here. We share the base with a composite air wing, a transport wing, a military police battalion, a Special Forces group, and a half dozen other battalions with various specialties. Nominally, we even have a missile regiment of the Strategic Nuclear Command on the base as well, but the missile silos with their ordnance are a hundred miles away in Indiana, and the only part of the regiment actually present at Fort Shughart is a staff company building.

Any branch of the TA sees itself as superior to all the other branches, of course, so there is much competition between the units, both sanctioned and unofficial. There are base-wide sporting events, annual shooting competitions, and weekly brawls in the enlisted and NCO clubs. Infantry soldiers consider combat engineers dumb dirt chuckers, and combat engineers think infantry grunts are overly eager to get killed. The tribalism continues within the battalions, where companies compete against each other, and the companies, where platoons form their own little clans. Within the platoons, the good-natured rivalries extend all the way down to the squad level, and to the teams that make up each squad. Your battalion or regiment is your clan, your company is your extended family, your platoon is your immediate family, and your squad is your household. Like every family, we have our internal quarrels, but when some outsider picks a fight with one of us, we close ranks.

"Will you look at that?"

We're gathered around a table in the chow hall, picking at our dinners, when Jackson nods toward the door.

"Looks like we have dinner guests on base."

I turn around to face the door. There's a group of soldiers in unfamiliar uniforms walking through the door, and it takes me a moment to recognize the patterns.

"Holy shit, those are *marines*. Space apes. What the hell are they doing here?"

The marines don't look like super-soldiers. In fact, they look like any other grunt in the TA's infantry battalions: high-and-tight haircuts, no body fat, well-defined arms sticking out of the rolled-up sleeves of their ICUs. The pattern isn't the only thing different about marine uniforms—they fold their sleeves so that the lighter inner liner of the ICU jacket shows, whereas TA troopers roll up the sleeves and then fold the last four inches of outer camouflage pattern over the rolled-up part.

The marines walk into the chow hall with a bit of a swagger, fully aware of the stir their appearance is causing among the TA soldiers. We hardly ever see members of other military branches. Sometimes, a flight of navy drop ships or shuttles will stop by on the way to a manufacturer refit, but space-going craft are flown by officers, and those don't mingle with the enlisted grunts in the mess hall.

We watch as the marines walk over to the food counter. They each pull a tray from the stack to the left of the counter, and insert themselves into the line, cutting in front of the TA troopers lined up for chow. There's some grumbling in the ranks, but there are only ten or twelve TA troopers in the line, and the marines are at least two squads strong.

"I don't know about you guys," Jackson says, "but all of a sudden, I really feel like having some dessert."

We grin at each other.

"Right there with you," Stratton says. "Let's go grab some pie or something."

We all push back our chairs and get up.

All around us, fellow TA troopers catch on, and get out of their seats as well. Jackson strides to the head of the line, her meal tray in both hands. As she passes the line of marines, some of them size her up. Jackson is tall and wiry, and she looks more like a soccer coach than a combat grunt. She cuts in front of the lead marine just as he's about to put a dessert plate onto his tray, and then snatches the plate out of his hands. The marine stares at her, dumbfounded, as she puts the plate onto her own tray.

"TA ain't done eating yet," she informs the marine. "The lesser services don't eat 'til the *real* soldiers are finished."

The marine snorts in disbelief and turns around to share an incredulous look with the others. Jackson picks up a fork and takes a bite of the dessert, seemingly unconcerned that she's blocking the chow line in front of twenty marines.

With dozens of combat grunts from two different service branches watching, the marine doesn't have a choice but to accept the challenge. He turns back to Jackson and smirks. She's a tall girl, but he's almost a head taller, and probably half again as heavy. He reaches out and puts a palm on her collarbone to shove her away from the chow counter.

Jackson drops her fork, grabs the marine's wrist with her right hand, and drives her left elbow into his ribs. He recoils in pain, and she sweeps her foot and takes him down at the ankles. The marine crashes to the floor of the chow hall with an embarrassing lack of grace.

Just like that, the chow hall is transformed into a hand-to-hand combat training pitch. We rush to Jackson's side, where the marines closest to her are trying to make a better showing than their comrade, and soon every member of our squad is tangling with a marine or two. They outnumber us by more than two to one, but TA troopers from other platoons are jumping into the fray. I grab a marine by the front of his ICUs and shove him into the chow counter, where he bounces off the sneeze guard over the mashed potatoes. One of his buddies throws a punch that hits me on the side of the face, but then Stratton is by my side, and he clocks the second marine with a textbook jab right to the tip of the chin. To my left, two marines try to tackle Hansen, whose ponytail bounces as she sidesteps one of them gracefully before kneeing the second marine in the groin. As I watch, another marine tackles me from behind, and we both go down.

The next few minutes are a blur of punching, kicking, and shoving, marine and TA camouflage patterns all blending in a flurry of skirmishes. The marines hold their own, and they're very good fighters, but we have the numbers on them, and our hand-to-hand combat training is just as good as theirs.

Then the doors of the chow hall fly open, and a whole bunch of military police in full riot gear come flooding in. They all carry electric crowd-control sticks.

"Break it up! Break it up!" someone yells over a helmet mike. The MPs don't waste much time waiting for compliance. They start applying their buzz sticks to the nearest brawlers. I hear shouts of pain, and marines and TA troopers alike fall to the ground, immobilized by fifty-thousand-volt shocks. All around me, the fighting ebbs.

The marine who had me pinned to the ground releases his hold on my collar. Then he stands up, and extends a hand.

"Party poopers," he says as he pulls me up, and we exchange grins. My jaw hurts on both sides, my nose is bleeding profusely, and I know I'll have a bitch of a headache later tonight, but this has been one of the most entertaining dinners in months.

When we step out of the building for orders the next morning, we have a surprise waiting: Command Sergeant Major Graciano, the battalion's senior noncommissioned officer, is standing next to our company sergeant. I have a good idea why the CSM is present, and from the looks on the faces of many of my platoon mates, so do they.

"Sergeants, step out and tend to your shops," CSM Graciano begins. "This one is for junior enlisted ears only."

The squad leaders and platoon sergeants step out of the back of the formation and head back to the building. They have their own chow hall, and none of them were present last night when we redecorated ours with marines.

"Funny thing happened yesterday," the sergeant major says after the last of the sergeants disappears in the company building. "The sergeant of the guard called me up last night to tell me some fairy tale about a bunch of my troopers hassling some marines in the enlisted chow hall at dinner."

He walks along the front rank, hands clasped behind his back, pausing to look at those of us who bear particularly obvious marks of last night's dinner-hall fracas.

"I told him that he must have been mistaken, because I know that none of you knuckleheads would start a fight with members of our esteemed sister services."

He walks back to the center of the formation. The CSM is a short man, built like a bar brawler, and even though his military high-and-tight hair is snow white, he looks like he could take most of us in a fight. The CSM wears a lot of stripes, and there are a lot of colorful ribbons on his Class A shirt. When he says "jump," the entire battalion is usually in midair before asking for an altitude parameter.

"Now," he says. "I want to see everyone's hands. Master Sergeant Rogers and I are going to check and see who here has recent unexplained injuries."

We all hold out our hands in front of us, like a bunch of kindergartners being checked for cleanliness before lunch. CSM Graciano and Master Sergeant Rogers walk the line, and everyone with bruised knuckles or scrapes on the face receives a stern glance and a growled "*You.*"

When the sergeants have finished checking the company, CSM Graciano parks himself front and center once more.

"Everyone we've pointed out—fall out and make a new line over there." He points to the curb behind him.

My knuckles are bruised, and I have a fat lip, so I fall out as ordered. My entire squad walks over to line up behind the command sergeant major. We're joined by most of Second Squad, and a fair chunk of Third and Fourth Squads.

"Now, everyone who wasn't in the chow hall at the time, step out and go to your duty stations. You're dismissed."

About half of the remaining troops of Bravo Company file back into the building, relief on their faces.

"That means the rest of you were present, and did not participate in the alleged fight," the CSM says. Then he turns to us. "And you misfits decided to take on half a platoon of marines, huh?"

We don't say anything. Speaking without permission is a grave offense during orders. We just stand and await our fate.

"Well, I told the MP and the battalion commander that I'd investigate the whole thing and dish out punishment as required. Therefore, your weekend leave is cancelled. You will have an extra training session on Saturday, and one on Sunday."

He waits for a moment to let the news sink in, and gives us a grim smile.

"We'll be doing some supplemental close-combat training in the gym. That was a *disgraceful* performance. You should have been able to mop up that herd of space apes before the MP even got to the mess hall."

Then he turns around to face the remaining section of the company.

"And you people can kiss your weekend leave good-bye as well. The vehicle park needs a scrub-down, and I'm going to volunteer all of you to Master Sergeant Blauser for the job."

The expressions on the faces of the remaining troopers change from smugness and relief to distress.

"The next time your comrades get into a fight, you jump in and help out, you understand? If they can't count on you when they're getting pushed around by a bunch of jarheads, they won't be able to count on you when they're under fire."

CSM Graciano turns on his heel, clasps his hands behind his back once more, and shakes his head.

"*Dismissed*, all of you. Don't make me come back out here real soon, you understand?"

"That was fucking awesome," Stratton says as we file back in. "The best ass-chewing I've ever gotten. The old grunt has his head on straight, that's for sure."

"Yeah, he does," I say. "I thought for sure our goose was cooked."

"Don't be too chipper," Hansen throws in as she comes up behind us. "You know the CSM. He'll invite those same marines over for the extra-close-combat sessions and have them gang up on us two to one."

"We have the best fucking job in the world," Stratton says with a grin. "Playing with guns, blowing up stuff, picking fights, and getting paid for it. They can keep the space services. I can't even believe I ever wanted to be in the fucking *navy*."

At this point, my mind has fused the words *navy* and *Halley*. Last night, while I was nursing a fat lip in the squad room, my data pad chirped to let me know I had an incoming message, and it was from Halley—a picture of herself in a brand-new zero-g combat flight suit, ready for drop-ship-pilot training. There was no comment with the picture, and none was needed. She looked proud enough to burst, and just looking at the picture on my screen made my heart ache much worse than that bloody lip. If someone walked up to me right now and offered a slot in Fleet School, I'd take it without a second thought.

Nobody is going to do that, however, and I know that I'll be a TA grunt for the duration of my enlistment. I like my buddies here, and I'll try to be the kind of squad mate everyone wants at their side in a crunch. I'll even pick fights to defend the honor of my new family.

Still, I'd go navy in a flash.

CHAPTER 10
WELFARE RIOT

"The shit has hit the fan, friends and neighbors."

Sergeant Fallon is already in full battle armor when she strides into the squad room, where we're all scrambling to get ready. The alarm is still trilling in the hallway outside, and the red light from the overhead LEDs is backlighting our squad leader ominously.

"What's the deal, Sarge?" Hansen asks, and we all cease our noisy activities briefly to hear Sergeant Fallon's answer.

"Welfare riot," she says. "One of the PRCs up in Detroit."

The mood in the room instantly goes from excitement to anxiety. It feels like a polar breeze has just entered through the open door with Sergeant Fallon.

"Fuck me," Hansen mutters. My other squad mates murmur their assent.

I've seen a welfare riot before—not the riot itself, but the aftermath. When I was ten or eleven, we had one in our PRC, when an unholy alliance of street rats, hoodlums, fringe lunatics, and wannabe revolutionaries tried to torch every government installation in sight. The government did what it always does when the local police force can't keep a lid on things. They sent in the military—two full battalions of TA, complete with armor and air support. Even with the overwhelming technological advantage of the TA soldiers, the fighting lasted for two days. My mother kept me home from school for a week, which was fantastic, and kept me from going outside for that whole week, which was less so. When I finally emerged from our apartment three days after the fighting had stopped, there were TA troopers on every street corner, and the streets had not been cleared of all the rubble and the burned vehicles yet.

"Get geared up, kids. Light combat kit. Don't bother with the tents and toiletries—this one's just down the road."

Of all the metroplexes in the country, Detroit is the worst. The center of the city is ringed by no fewer than twenty-four PRCs, and over 80 percent of the metroplex residents are on the dole. Thirteen million people in Greater Detroit, and ten million of them are crammed into concrete shoeboxes stacked a hundred high. The place makes my old homestead look like a tropical vacation resort.

We suit up and help each other into our battle armor. There is no joking this time. Everyone seems tense and anxious.

"Been to a PRC before, Grayson?" Priest asks as I fix the quick-release locks on his battle armor for him.

"I grew up in one," I say. "Don't really care to go back to one."

"Yeah, well, this time you'll have a rifle, and a drop ship hovering overhead. It's still a shit job, though."

"Shittiest in the book," Hansen agrees.

"At least they won't have tanks," I say.

"Yeah, well, there's going to be a lot of 'em, and they'll all be pissed. If we have to start shooting, you better hope they run out of courage before we run out of ammo."

The drop ships are warming up their engines when we get off the bus.

"Make sure you have your boarding passes ready," the drop ship's loadmaster says as we trudge up the ramp.

"You're funny as shit, Atkins," Sergeant Fallon says from the rear of our little column. "Just remember, extra sugar, extra cream for me."

We strap in, secure our weapons, and watch as the rest of the platoon does likewise. The summer night is hot and humid, and the air smells of fuel.

"First Platoon, listen up," we hear over the all-platoon channel.

"We'll only be airborne for thirty minutes, so we're going to skip the formalities and the top-down briefings today. Our target is the civil administration center in PRC Detroit-7. We're dropping in with Second Platoon."

The tactical displays in our helmet sights activate, and Lieutenant Weaving runs us through the specifics of our mission. The target building looks like every other civil center I've seen, a squat, five-story building with small windows and reinforced concrete walls.

"Second Platoon will land on the roof and do a top-down sweep of the building to secure it. Our mission is to drop on the outside and then establish a defensive perimeter. We're deploying one squad on every corner of the building. The other platoons are securing other locations in the area, so it's just Second Platoon and us. We secure the building and all government property within. Anyone tries to get near the place, you strongly discourage them."

"What if we get mobbed, LT?" one of the squad leaders asks.

"Take whatever self-defense measures you consider necessary," Lieutenant Weaving says. "The drop ships will be overhead, and squad leaders are authorized to call in air support. Just don't mow down a bunch of kids and puppies, because that makes us look bad on the evening news."

"Ain't no kids or puppies in a riot zone," Corporal Jackson says. She pats the hilt of her combat knife as she says this. We all wear our knives in polymer sheaths on our left legs, but Jackson has hers attached to the harness of her battle armor, with the hilt pointing down. I've watched her sharpen that knife to a fine edge many times, and there's no doubt in my mind that she knows how to use it.

She catches my gaze as I look at her from across the cargo bay of the drop ship, and amazingly, she winks at me.

The drop ship descends into Detroit the conventional way—not the white-knuckle ride of a combat landing, but an almost casual ride that feels like a landing back home at the base. The skids of the ship touch down, and the rear cargo doors fold out as we get out of our seats and gather our weapons.

The scene outside looks like something out of a disaster movie. We step out onto the big square in front of the civil administration center and immediately lower our visors to seal our helmets against the acrid smoke of dozens of fires. The riot was probably in full swing when we arrived overhead. In the distance, we can see people running for cover, wisely yielding the square to the drop ship bristling with ordnance. They leave behind a wasteland of burning junk and torched hydrocars. The front of the administration building has scorch marks, and half the windows on the first floor have been shattered. I see shell casings from old-fashioned brass-cased ammunition everywhere.

"Let's move out," Sergeant Fallon says over the squad channel. "We have the northwest corner. Find some cover and watch your sectors."

The platoon splits up as directed. First Squad moves to the front left corner of the building at a run. Overhead, Second Platoon's drop ship makes a noisy landing on the roof of the administration building, and I can hear the hydraulic whining of the cargo ramp all the way down at street level with the enhanced audio pickup of my helmet speakers. Behind us, our drop ship disgorges the last members of Third and Fourth Squads. I look back over my shoulder as the hatch on our ship closes, and the pilot immediately goes gear-up. Drop ships are most vulnerable on the ground, where they are sitting ducks to incoming fire, and their pilots don't like to spend one moment longer than necessary with the skids on the dirt.

"There's shit for cover here, Sarge," Baker says over the squad channel.

"Use those pillars over there," Sergeant Fallon orders, and our helmet displays briefly flash a target marker overlay. The administration building has a second floor that overhangs the first one just a little. There are concrete pillars holding up the overhang in regular intervals. We hunker down behind the pillars near our assigned building corner and scan the area for threats.

The neighborhood around a civil center is usually the cleanest and safest patch of real estate in the PRC. If that is true here in Detroit-7, then the rest of the place must be a complete dump, because the street in front of us looks worse than the nastiest part of my old neighborhood. The buildings are all dilapidated, most of the windows are boarded up, and there are gaps in the rows of houses where old buildings have been partially stripped and torn down for raw materials. Most of the streetlights are out, and if it wasn't for the infrared-enhanced feed from the sensors mounted on my helmet, I wouldn't be able to see much in the late evening darkness.

"Where the fuck is everybody?" I ask.

"Waiting until the drop ships are out of sight," Hansen responds tersely.

Overhead, Second Platoon's drop ship lifts off and roars into the dirty night sky. There's the bang of a breaching charge as

Second Platoon blows the rooftop access door. Everything is going like clockwork once more.

"Uh-oh," somebody says over the squad channel.

My tactical display lights up with hundreds of red diamond symbols as the rioters come out of cover and stream back towards the administration building. I have no idea how those back alleys and dark lots could have held so many people just out of sight, but now they're streaming back into the street, first in pairs, then dozens, and finally hundreds. I check the tactical map, and over to our left the same scene is repeating itself on the plaza where Fourth Squad keeps watch.

"Be advised, we have incoming," Lieutenant Weaving says over the platoon channel. He sounds as calm as if he's telling us that the chow hall will be serving meat loaf and mashed potatoes tonight.

"No shit," Sergeant Fallon replies. "Put some gas rounds into those launchers," she orders over the squad channel.

The loops on the front of my battle armor hold a dozen grenades for my rifle's launcher. Four of them are rubber rounds, two are buckshot rounds, and the remaining six are chemical crowd-control munitions, the kind the military calls "less lethal," which is technically a true designation. For truth in advertising, the term should be "very slightly less lethal." They're filled with a particularly unpleasant chemical agent that will creep through any sort of mask or filter short of sealed battle armor. In Basic, we all had to endure ten seconds of exposure to the riot gas in the chemical warfare portion of our training, and I know that the stuff in those grenades makes anyone on the receiving end wish they had been shot with live ammunition instead.

I pluck a gas grenade from my harness, and stuff it into the grenade launcher. To my right, my squad mates are following suit. I scan the gathering crowd for weapons, and I'm unsettled to see that just about everyone out there carries something suitable for clubbing, stabbing, or shooting. A year ago, I would have been part of that mob, using the chaos as a convenient excuse to break stuff and steal things, but now I'm on the other side of the line, and I feel no guilt as I sight in on the advancing crowd.

"DO NOT APPROACH," Sergeant Fallon bellows at the rioters. Our commo kits have a public-address function, which we rarely ever use outside of playing pranks on platoon mates.

"DISPERSE AT ONCE, OR WE WILL OPEN FIRE."

The crowd responds with angry shouts, and by now the first rioters are close enough to throw stuff at us, which they do with enthusiasm.

"Let 'em have it," Sergeant Fallon says. "Launchers free, riot rounds only. Live ammo only in self-defense."

We're nine TA troopers, and the crowd surging towards us numbers in the hundreds. We're outnumbered fifty to one, and if they overrun our position, they'll beat or stab us to death. That makes this event a self-defense scenario by definition in my book, but I obey and keep my finger away from the trigger of the rifle. Next to me, my squad mates are sighting in their launchers, and I join in, aiming at the middle of the advancing crowd.

The rifle bucks in my hands as I lob my gas grenade into the first row of rioters. The grenade explodes with a muffled crack, and suddenly there's a cloud of white crowd-control agent expanding from the impact point. Between our nine grenades, the entire width of the street in front of us is blanketed in white smoke. The gas barrage has stopped the momentum of the surging crowd instantly, and I watch as a hundred of their number gasp for breath on their hands and knees.

"Give 'em another round, further back," Baker says.

I load another grenade, and lob it over the heads of the front row of rioters, into the crowd that is now scattering to avoid the spreading cloud of noxious white gas. To our left, gunshots are crackling across the plaza in front of the administration building, where Fourth Squad is holding the line. The gunfire doesn't sound like the hoarse, high-pitched report from our service rifles. A few moments later, Fourth Squad returns fire—first one rifle, then two, firing short bursts of fléchette rounds in response. It looks like things are swiftly sliding downhill.

"Mind your sectors," Sergeant Fallon says. "Anyone shoots live rounds, you shoot right the hell back."

"And that concludes the nonlethal portion of tonight's program," Stratton says in a mock Network announcer voice, and Hansen lets out a chuckle.

The crowd is now mostly in disarray, but it looks like some of them still have a fight on their minds. There's a burst of gunfire from the edge of the riot, the sharp staccato of an automatic weapon. To my right, Baker yells as several rounds hit his battle armor. He stumbles, regains his footing, and then scurries behind cover, like a man trying to get out of a sudden hailstorm. The first burst of live fire from the crowd means that the gloves are coming off, and I flick off the safety catch in front of the rifle's trigger with my index finger. When the shooter fires another burst, the thermal bloom from the muzzle of his weapon shows up on my helmet sight like a signal flare. I aim my rifle at the rioter and squeeze the trigger. The shooter drops in a cloud of concrete dust.

Now there are shots ringing out all over the street in front of us. Some of the rioters scatter out of the line of fire, and others regain their courage and come surging back toward us, hurling objects and shouting decidedly unfriendly words. The ones with the firearms are using the crowd as cover, which is smart, because we couldn't shoot everyone in the street even if we wanted. I duck behind a concrete column as the bullets from the incoming fire smack into the building behind us. The overhang is the only cover in front of the administration building, but it's also a shot trap, a box of concrete enclosed on three sides, which makes it a bad spot to be right now. Emboldened by the fact that we're all seeking cover from the incoming fire, the crowd advances on the building once more. I peek around the corner of my cover, and the fear gives my stomach a good squeeze when I see that the first line of rioters is now just a few dozen yards from our position.

I fumble for one of the buckshot grenades on my harness and stuff it into the launcher tube with clumsy fingers. We didn't receive permission to use lethal grenade munitions yet, but the point will be moot in another ten seconds. To my right, Hansen and Baker extend the crowd the courtesy of warning shots, firing short bursts of rifle fire into the ground in front of the surging crowd, but the report of their rifles is all but inaudible over the roar of the crowd and the cracks of gunfire from the armed rioters. Just in front of me, one of the rioters raises an old-fashioned shotgun and aims it in my direction. From ten yards away, the muzzle of the old scattergun looks like the business end of a howitzer, and I have no desire to find out whether my helmet's face shield can withstand whatever is about to come out of that muzzle. I level my rifle and fire the grenade launcher from the hip, touching off my own very large shotgun shell.

The launcher's bark drowns out the crowd for a brief moment. In the confines of the building's concrete overhang, it's loud enough for my helmet's audio filter to kick in and turn me temporarily deaf to save my hearing. In front of me, there's a sudden gap in the ranks of the charging crowd. There's nobody left standing within thirty yards of the grenade launcher's muzzle.

I open the launcher and reload with another buckshot grenade, my fingers performing the action seemingly on autopilot. The crowd directly in front of me scatters to get out of my line of fire, streaming to the left and right, and presses in on my squad mates instead.

Hansen and Stratton follow my lead and fire buckshot gre
nades as well, and the street in front of us turns into a madhouse.
The crowd is now close enough for the lead rioters to reach out
and grab our rifles, which some of them try to do. Someone tries
to seize Baker's M-66 and gets a five-round burst in return. I watch
in morbid fascination as the armor-piercing fléchette rounds pass
through the unlucky rioter and into the man behind him. Both of
them go down, but there are more coming, and the mass of people
in front of us is simply overwhelming.

To my left, a group of shouting rioters come around the concrete pillar I'm using for cover. One of them carries a clunky-look-
ing handgun. He sees me and raises his gun just as I bring the rifle
up to my shoulder and press the trigger.

There's a mighty shove coming from my right, and suddenly
I find myself on my back and skidding across the pavement. I
bring my rifle up and turn to face my attackers. Someone seizes
the muzzle of my M 66. As I feel the rifle getting wrenched out of
my hands, I trigger the grenade launcher with the buckshot round
in it. The attacker lets go of my rifle as he catches the full blast of
the grenade, four thousand spherical pieces of shrapnel that are
spread out to a merely fist-sized group at this range. His midsec-
tion erupts into a bloody mush, splattering blood and tissue onto
the face shield of my helmet.

Around me, there's the stuttering of fire from multiple M-66
rifles in fully automatic mode. Next to me, three or four people are
on top of Corporal Baker. One of them has seized Baker's rifle, and
the rioter swings it around to bring the muzzle to bear on Stratton,
who is struggling with his own pack of rioters a few feet away. I
aim my own rifle without thinking and shoot the rifle-wielding
rioter in the back. The rest of Baker's attackers are busy trying to
pin the corporal to the ground, and I pluck them off his back with

single shots one by one. Baker scrambles to his feet, looks around, and then picks up his weapon.

"Who's firing live rounds? *Who's firing live rounds?*"

The shout comes over the all-platoon channel. It sounds like our platoon leader, who is holding down one of the not-so-busy corners on the other side of the building with Third or Fourth Squad.

"Bravo One, we need you over here," Sergeant Fallon toggles back. "We're getting our asses kicked, in case you haven't noticed."

The tactical display is lousy with red carets. We are surrounded by a few hundred very pissed-off rioters. I'm out of buckshot grenades, and the magazine in my rifle is almost empty. I eject the disposable magazine block and pull another one out of the pouch on my harness with clumsy fingers. It takes me three tries to line up the new magazine with the well at the bottom rear of my rifle. In training, my reloads are always smooth, but right now it feels like threading a needle with winter gloves. I slap the magazine home and smack the bolt release with my palm. The bolt of the rifle snaps forward and chambers a fresh round, and the little counter on the lower left corner of my tactical display changes from "31" to "249." The computer keeps track of my rifle's ammunition status to let me know when it's time to reload and to tell my squad leader through the TacLink when I'm running low. What it doesn't monitor is how scared I am, how many times my armor has been struck, how much I feel like puking, and how badly I want to be back at the base right about now.

I pick out a new target, sight my rifle, and shoot. Then again, and again. There's no shortage of targets out there. I have stopped thinking of them as people. They're just silhouettes in my gun sight now, one squeeze of the trigger each. Our squad is huddled together in a cluster, everybody covering a sector in front, just like in training. For a few moments, all I hear is the steady chatter of our rifles, spitting out death at a few thousand rounds per minute. We fire our rifles methodically, steadily, like we're in a live-fire exercise at the base range at Fort Shughart.

And then the natives have had enough.

The remaining rioters must have changed their minds about the odds, because the forward surge of the crowd suddenly dissipates, and with it all the angry energy that has motivated the leading ranks to charge soldiers in modern battle armor with nothing but ancient small arms and homemade hand grenades. The formerly amorphous mass of people turns into hundreds of individuals scattering in as many different directions, anywhere but toward the muzzles of our rifles.

I take a ragged breath. It feels like I haven't filled my lungs properly since the shooting started. I look around to see all of my squad mates still standing, weapons at the ready, and scores of bodies on the street before us. There's a layer of white stuff in front of our position that looks like a dusting of snow on the ground, and it takes me a moment to realize that those are the discarded plastic sabots of our fléchette rounds, stripped from the tungsten darts after leaving the barrels.

Ten yards to our right, the grunts from Third Squad come around the corner of the building at a run, with the platoon leader in front. Lieutenant Weaving takes one look around and flips up the visor on his helmet.

"Holy shit, people. That's going to look awful on the Network news."

Sergeant Fallon starts a response on the squad channel, then catches herself, and walks over to Lieutenant Weaving. When she's in front of him, she flips up her helmet visor as well.

"Something wrong with your TacLink, Lieutenant?"

"Negative," he replies.

"Well, you may want to get it checked out when we get back,

seeing how it failed to show you the five hundred people trying to overrun us."

Lieutenant Weaving's posture tenses, but then there's a sound like a piece of hail hitting a tin roof, and he stumbles sideways and falls over. A sharp crack rolls across the street, the report of a high-powered rifle.

"Sniper!" three or four of us call out at the same time over the squad channel, and everybody ducks for cover. Sergeant Fallon bends over and grabs Lieutenant Weaving by the arm to drag him to safety.

"Little help here," she says. I leave the relative safety of my concrete pillar, dash over to her position, and grab the lieutenant's other arm. Together, we drag his limp bulk over to another concrete pillar.

"LT is down," Sergeant Fallon toggles into the platoon channel. "Valkyrie Six-One, this is Bravo One-One. Get your ship down in front of the building for a medevac, pronto."

"Valkyrie Six-One, copy. ETA two minutes," I hear in response. Valkyrie is the call sign for our drop-ship flight, and Six-One is our platoon's ship.

"Pop me some smoke, and find that sniper," Sergeant Fallon orders. Priest and Paterson pull smoke grenades out of their harnesses and throw them into the street in front of our position.

The distant rifle cracks again. There's a puff of concrete dust as it smacks into the pillar in front of us.

"Shoot the fuck back already," Sergeant Fallon says.

The smoke grenades explode with a muffled pop, covering the area in front of us in thick white smoke. The sniper is undeterred. He fires again, and the bullet strikes one of the windows behind us with a slap. Finally, someone gets a computer fix on the most likely trajectory of the sniper's rounds. The TacLink updates everyone's displays, superimposing a faint target caret over the sniper's suspected position a few hundred yards down the street, and the two squads around me open up with their rifles.

"Grayson, with me. Sergeant Ellis, mind the shop for a minute. Grayson and I are going to carry the LT back to the square and get him onto the bird. The rest of you, cover our asses."

"Affirmative," Sergeant Ellis replies. He's the squad leader of Third Squad and nominally equal in seniority to Sergeant Fallon at this point, but our squad leader is so high in the company's pecking order that any NCO lower than the company sergeant usually defers to her.

The lieutenant is out cold. The bullet tore the partially raised visor from his helmet and then nailed him in the forehead at an angle. His face is covered in blood, and his forehead looks like someone's given him a glancing blow with an axe, but he's still breathing, and the round doesn't seem to have penetrated the bone. Sergeant Fallon removes his helmet, drops it on the ground next to her, and then holds out her hand.

"Give me a trauma pack, Grayson."

I reach into the side pocket of my ICU pants and pull out a bandage packet. I pull open the plastic seal, shake out the bandage, and hand it to Sergeant Fallon. She places it on the lieutenant's forehead. The thermal bandage instantly adheres to his wound, sealing the gash in his head.

"He'll live to collect his Purple Heart," Sergeant Fallon pronounces. "Help me get him over to the ship."

We each grab one of Lieutenant Weaving's arms to haul up his bulk, which is considerable. He's a tall guy, 190 pounds at least, and the battle armor weighs another thirty pounds on top of that.

"Grab his rifle, too," the sergeant says. I stoop down to pick up the lieutenant's M-66. I notice that he still has four full magazine pouches, and my computer informs me that his rifle is still loaded with 250 rounds.

"Valkyrie Six-One, ETA one minute," I hear over the platoon channel. "Keep your heads low down there."

We head to the main entrance of the building at an awkward short-step run, with Lieutenant Weaving's inert mass hanging between us. There are still rioters all over the place, but they're mostly busy avoiding us, now that we've demonstrated that we're willing to use our live rounds.

Overhead, I hear the engines of the descending drop ship. They're coming in at high speed, a combat landing with emphasis. As we turn the corner to the main civic plaza, I flinch at the sight of more bodies on the ground, easily twice as many as there are in front of First Squad's position. Second Squad didn't hold back.

"Bravo One-One, this is Bravo One-Two. We have three casualties that need to go out on your ship."

"Copy that, Bravo One-Two. Bring 'em up, and don't dawdle," Sergeant Fallon responds.

The drop ship makes a dramatic entry. It breaks out of the low clouds, banked in a tight final turn. For a moment, a primal fear grips me at the sight of that huge, lethal-looking war machine. Whoever designed the Hornet drop ship didn't spend a moment considering aesthetics. It's all angles and facets, bristling with multibarreled cannons and ordnance pods. It looks like someone's fever-induced idea of a cross between a hornet and a dragonfly, blown up to massive size and clad in laminate armor.

As I watch, the landing gear of the drop ship extends, and the ship slows down for a vertical touchdown. At the last moment, the pilot turns the Hornet to make the tail and loading ramp face the administration building, and the weapons arrays point in the direction of the threat. I can see the cannon in the nose turret swinging side to side as the gun system automatically scans for targets. Then the main gear touches down, and the Hornet settles in a low crouch. The cargo ramp at the rear opens with a hydraulic whine.

"There's your ride," Sergeant Fallon tells the unconscious Lieutenant Weaving.

We carry the lieutenant into the plaza. The tail of the drop ship is a few dozen yards from the building. The crew chief steps out onto the ramp formed by the lower half of the cargo door and waves us on.

We're thirty feet from the ramp when the thunder of heavy automatic-weapon fire rolls across the plaza. I look around for a threat, thinking that the chin turret of the drop ship is engaging a target. Then I see that the tracers are coming in rather than going out.

"Hit the deck," Sergeant Fallon shouts, and we do, taking Lieutenant Weaving down to the ground with us.

Ahead of us, there's a noise like hail on a metal roof as the drop ship starts taking hits.

"Where the fuck is that coming from?" someone shouts over the platoon channel.

"The rooftops," someone else replies. "They got guns on the rooftops, right and center."

Ahead of us, the drop-ship pilot gooses the engines and picks the ship off the ground. The crew chief in the hatch holds on for balance and then retreats back into his armored ship. I wonder why the chin turret isn't firing back. The streams of tracers come from the rooftops of two tenement buildings, one on the right side of the plaza, and one at the far side, directly opposite the civil building. Both buildings are standard welfare shoebox stacks, thirty floors high, and I realize that the gun turret of the drop ship can't deflect that high.

The guns on the rooftops fire in bursts, maybe twenty rounds at a time. Sergeant Fallon and I are in the open, between the relative safety of the building and that of the armored ship. The hatch of the drop ship is much closer than the concrete overhang of the civil building, but the drop ship is already three feet off the ground, and it doesn't look like the crew feels like waiting around while their ship is getting sprayed with incoming fire.

"Where the fuck did these people get heavy machine guns?" Sergeant Fallon asks. She pulls a smoke grenade out of her harness and motions for me to do the same. We chuck our grenades out into the plaza, and a few moments later our position is obscured in thick smoke.

"Let's get the hell out of here," Sergeant Fallon suggests. We seize the still unconscious lieutenant by the arms once more and start our dash back to the building. Behind us, the machine-gun rounds keep hitting the armor of the drop ship in a steady staccato.

Suddenly, the pitch of the engines changes, and I can hear right away that something essential just broke. The steady howl of the turbines turns into a tortured shriek. I look over my shoulder and see smoke pouring out of the starboard engine. Another stream of tracers comes down onto the drop ship, which is now fifty feet above the plaza. As they impact the armor, they throw up red and yellow sparks, the telltale signature of armor-piercing rounds hitting a hard surface.

"Don't stop to sightsee, moron," Sergeant Fallon yells. We finish our dash to the safety of the overhang in front of the building.

Some of the troopers from Second Squad are crouching at the edge of the overhang. They're aiming their rifles skyward, firing bursts at the source of the tracer rounds raking our drop ship. Whoever set up those machine guns knows the capabilities of a Hornet. The ship is most vulnerable sitting on the ground, and the machine guns are high up on rooftops, out of reach of the Hornet's chin turret and its rapid-fire cannon. The position of the guns is either incredibly fortuitous or shrewdly planned. I set down the lieutenant, sling his rifle across my chest armor, and then check the loading status of my own weapon. The grenades in my harness are all nonlethal munitions, nothing that could do more than irritate the enemy machine-gun crews. In any case, there's nothing in my assortment of launcher munitions that can reach all the way up to the roof of a thirty-story building.

"Fuckers know what they're doing," Sergeant Fallon says, in a tone that's almost respectful. We watch as the drop ship swerves to the side and swings its tail around, the pilot doing her best to keep the cockpit and the remaining good engine away from the tracers. She tries to lift her ship out of what is now a concrete shot trap, but with one engine damaged, the Hornet is slow on the ascent. The machine guns keep hammering, and the path of the tracers follows the ship. Both streams converge at the cockpit.

The drop ship is a hundred feet above the plaza when it lurches to the side with alarming suddenness. Then the pilot catches the ship, and she swings the tail around and dips the nose down to gain speed. She's decided to abandon the vertical takeoff and get out of the kill zone at low level. Her path takes her right past one of the machine-gun nests, and the gun stops firing as the drop ship roars past well below rooftop level. The other gun never ceases its steady stream of bursts, and the tracers from the second machine gun follow the Hornet all the way out of the plaza.

Above, a squad or two from Second Platoon have taken up position on the roof of the civil administration building. I can hear the chatter of their rifles as they engage the machine-gun nests on the rooftops. The civil building only has five floors, so the machine guns still have the high ground. After a few moments of getting shot at by the TA troopers on the roof above us, the people manning the heavy machine guns decide to take advantage of their position and return the favor. One of the machine guns, the one on the opposite side of the plaza, starts firing again, and this time the streams of tracers reach out to our building.

"Bravo One, this is Valkyrie Six-One."

Our drop-ship pilot is calling the lieutenant on the platoon channel. She sounds like she's talking through clenched teeth.

"Valkyrie Six-One, this is Bravo One-One. The LT is down. What's the word on the ride?" Sergeant Fallon replies.

"Ship's busted," the pilot says. "My right-seater is dead, and I can't raise my crew chief on comms. Right engine is shot out, and half the shit in my cockpit is blown away. I'm making for . . . hold on."

In the distance, the sound from the Hornet's remaining engine rises sharply, and then cuts out with an ominous finality.

"Valkyrie Six-One, going down," the pilot matter-of-factly announces over the platoon channel. She sounds as calm and detached as if she's telling us about next week's weather forecast.

We can hear the crash of the ship from half a mile away. There's no explosion, just a monstrous racket, like someone dropping a giant bag of screws and bolts onto a hard deck. After a few moments, the noise stops.

For a few heartbeats, there is dead silence on the squad and platoon channels. Even the machine guns and rifles overhead have stopped firing.

"Well, *fuck*," Sergeant Fallon exclaims. Then she toggles into the platoon channel. "We have a drop ship down, people. Valkyrie Six-One is down in the PRC."

CHAPTER 11

——— DROP SHIP DOWN ———

Overhead, the tracers from the heavy machine gun rake the roof, where the Second Platoon grunts have taken up position. We're not tied into their comms, but I can tell from the yelling and shouting drifting down that things aren't going so well.

Sergeant Fallon peeks out from underneath the overhang and looks into the night sky, where the tracers from the machine guns reach out to our building like swarms of very angry fireflies.

"Getting our asses kicked by a bunch of welfare rats," she mutters. Then she toggles the comm switch and talks into her helmet mike. I don't hear anything on the platoon or squad channels, which means she's tied into Company.

"Valkyrie Six-Four, this is Bravo One-One. Valkyrie Six-One is down, a three-quarter klick to the east of our position. We have heavy guns on the rooftops, and they're kicking the shit out of Second Platoon. I suggest you clear off those roof positions, and then see what you can see at the crash site, over."

She listens to Valkyrie Six-Four's response, and switches to the platoon channel once more.

"Second Platoon's bird is making an attack run, people. Keep your heads down."

Valkyrie Six-Four doesn't waste any time. The first evidence of their attack run is a streak of cannon fire from above, and the distant

131

roaring of the Hornet's multibarreled pod cannons. The rooftop of the building on the other side of the plaza erupts in a shower of sparks as the cannon rounds rake the position of the heavy machine gun. The machine gun falls silent, and a moment later the drop ship appears overhead, thundering over the plaza nearly at rooftop level as it pulls up from its strafing run. I notice that some of the cannon fire missed the rooftop ledge and hit the apartments directly below. Several windows on the thirtieth floor are blown out, and a few cannon rounds have torn huge holes into the concrete sheets that make up the outer wall of the tenement high-rise. Chunks of window plastics and concrete are raining down onto the plaza.

"Bravo One-One, Valkyrie Six-One," comes the voice of the drop-ship pilot over the platoon channel. I can hear cockpit alarms blaring in the background of the transmission.

"I read you, Six-One. What's your status?" Sergeant Fallon replies.

"The ship is fucked. I'm right side up in the middle of the fucking street. Avionics and comms have power, but my chin turret's out. My crew chief and right-seater are dead, I think. I could really use a hand here."

"Six-One, sit tight. We're going to come out and fetch you. Keep those hatches sealed. You're in a shitty neighborhood."

"Copy that. I'm not going anywhere."

"We have you on TacLink," Sergeant Fallon says. "We'll be there shortly."

I stare at Sergeant Fallon as she cuts the comm link. *She wants to go out there, on foot?*

"We'll leave the LT with Third Squad," she says to me. "Grab his ammo. We're going to go for a little walk."

"First Squad, form up on me," she calls into the squad channel. I remove Lieutenant Weaving's magazines from their pouches and fill up the empty pouch on my harness before stuffing the rest of the ammunition into the side pockets of my leg armor.

"Nobody's ever been in a firefight and complained about having too many bullets with them," Sergeant Fallon says to me.

"I guess not," I reply, and close the flap on the magazine pouch with an unsteady hand. The last thing I want to do right now is to go out into the streets of the PRC, away from the rest of the platoon.

The rest of First Squad comes up at a run—Stratton and Hansen in the lead, then Jackson, Priest, Baker, and finally Paterson and Phillips.

"What's the plan, Sarge?" Baker asks as the squad gathers around us.

"Our ride is less than a klick that way," Sergeant Fallon says, marking the route on our TacLink displays as she speaks. "We have at least one pilot alive, so we're going to go out there, fetch our crew, and activate the demo charge on the drop ship. We're not leaving all that ordnance for the locals to pick up."

"A night out on the town," Stratton says. "See, Grayson? And you were complaining they never let us out of the base."

"Yeah, well, forget I ever opened my mouth," I reply with a grin. Stratton's cheery mood seems to be indestructible, but I find that his levity has a calming effect on me.

"Let's get it done," Sergeant Fallon says. She checks the loading status of her rifle and steps out into the plaza.

"Stagger it loosely, people, and watch your sectors. If in doubt, you shoot first and apologize later. And toss those rubber rounds. Anyone out on the street after this fireworks show, they're out to get a piece of us."

———

We move out into the streets of the PRC. The authorities have finally gotten around to shutting off the power grid to the rebellious welfare clusters, so the streetlights are all out. There are, however, plenty of burning vehicles and trash containers all over the place. Our helmet imaging sensors automatically provide us with optimal visuals—low-light magnification, thermal imaging, and about three dozen other filters. The people we're up against don't have the luxury of military-grade sensors, but for some reason they have a pretty good idea of where we are. We see small groups of rioters dashing across streets and into alleyways up ahead. They keep well away from us, and nobody's pointing weapons, but for some reason I feel like I'm back at the urban-warfare center in Basic and we're walking into a staged exercise.

PRC Detroit is a complete shithole. The area around the civil center was a showcase neighborhood compared to the dilapidation of the streets beyond. Back home in Boston, our buildings were ugly, but mostly intact. Here in Detroit, the welfare tenements are twice as ugly, and half of them are in various states of ruin. One or two lots out of every block are just foundations, or demolished buildings that have a floor and a half of crumbling structure remaining, like broken teeth in an already unhealthy jawline. There's nobody in those empty lots as we trot by, weapons at the ready, but the burning trash cans and scatterings of food boxes are evidence that the residents of those ruins aren't far away.

"Bravo One-One, Valkyrie Six-Four. We're circling overhead, and we have you guys on Tactical. Be advised, you have a group of IPs shadowing you on the street parallel to yours, on your four o'clock."

Our TacLink displays update with dozens of red carets, clustered in the street to our right and keeping pace with our squad.

"Copy," Sergeant Fallon responds. "How's the crash site look, Six-Four?"

"It's clear right now, but there's a bunch of the local rabble converging on the site, from the looks of it. I suggest you don't take your time down there."

"You can bet your ass on that, Six-Four."

"What the hell are they doing?" Paterson asks. "First they run into our rifles to get a piece of us, and now they're backing off."

"They're not backing off, dummy," Corporal Jackson says. "They're waiting until we're all the way in the bag. They know where we're going."

"Stop the chitchat, and keep formation," Sergeant Fallon says. "We're half a klick out. Double time, people. Let's hoof it before the welfare rats get a hold of the armory on that boat."

The drop ship is right in the middle of a major intersection, which is bad news, because it's out in the open and vulnerable from all four sides. The starboard engine is still smoking, its armored nacelle showing multiple holes from armor-piercing rounds. The port engine is running on idle, emitting a low droning sound. A half dozen locals have beaten us to the site, and they're banging on the side hatch and jumping up and down on the cockpit roof, oblivious of our approach in the darkness.

Sergeant Fallon makes our presence known by aiming her rifle and firing a single round without breaking stride. The rioter on top of the drop ship falls off the cockpit roof and then hits the pavement below without any attempt to catch his fall. The others hear the rifle shot and scatter like roaches at the sound of a light switch. We let them run off, and then rush up to the wounded drop ship.

"Six-One, we're right outside. Open the side hatch, if you can."

"Stand by," the pilot says. "I have a few broken bones here."

I walk up to the right side of the cockpit and look inside. The right-seater is slumped over in his armored chair, and the untidy hole in the side of his flight helmet leaves no doubt about his condition. The right cockpit side has taken a beating from the large-caliber machine-gun rounds, and one of them finally weakened the polycarbonate enough to let a round or two into the cockpit. Valkyrie Six-One's copilot had the misfortune to sit right in the trajectory.

I watch as the pilot undoes her harness latches and then tries to get out of her seat. The scream that follows is loud enough to reach my ears through the armored canopy.

"Sarge, her legs are broken. Hang on." I tap on the side of the cockpit.

"Six-One, can you blow the emergency jettison on the canopy?"

The pilot gives me a weak nod and an even weaker thumbs-up and then reaches for the red-and-yellow handle on her side of the cockpit.

"You folks may want to stand back," she says. "Like, way back."

We retreat to the side of the street, well away from the canopy panels.

"Go ahead, Six-One. We're clear."

The panels of the drop ship's canopy detach with a muffled crack. We rush up to the cockpit, and Jackson hands her rifle to Paterson before climbing over the side and into the now open pilot station.

"Someone come in here and give me a hand," Jackson says. I hand my rifle off to the rear and climb up to help.

The pilot is in bad shape. Both her legs are broken, and her right arm is bloody, the flight suit sleeve in shreds. The cockpit stinks of blood, fried electronics, and chemical propellant. She looks up at us through the clear shield of her helmet visor. I smile at her as I try to maneuver into position to heave her out of the chair with Jackson.

"Hang on there. We'll have you out of this thing in a flash."

"Watch out," somebody shouts outside, and there's a sudden fusillade of gunshots coming from the other side of the intersection.

"First Squad, you have lots of hostiles converging on your position," Valkyrie Six-Four announces with sudden urgency.

"Yeah, no shit," someone replies.

"Jackson and Grayson, get the pilot in the back and open that fucking hatch for us," Sergeant Fallon orders. The squad is firing back now, and the loud reports of the rioters' guns mix with the hoarse chattering of the TA rifles.

Jackson and I haul the pilot out of her seat with renewed urgency. She cries out as we drag her to the cockpit door, a small armored hatch three feet behind the pilot seats. The cockpit is too small for three people and a corpse, and anyone firing into the now unprotected space is bound to hit one of us. Jackson and I are wearing full combat armor, but the pilot only has a chest plate over her flight suit, and we shield her with our bodies as much as we can while Jackson yanks on the latch for the cockpit door. It slides open, and we stumble through the narrow hatch, the pilot between us. Outside, the rifle fire increases in volume. I can hear rounds smacking into the bulkhead to my right as I squeeze my armored bulk into the passageway beyond the cockpit door. My instincts tell me to duck and run, make for the safety of the cargo bay, but I stop and turn around to pull the latch on the inside of the door. The armored hatch slides out once more and seals the opening with an inch and a half of laminate armor plating.

We stumble through the narrow passage that leads from the drop ship's cockpit to the cargo hold. The pilot is half pulled by Jackson, half pushed by me. Finally, we reach the cargo space, and we put the pilot down on the rubberized floor, well away from the side entry hatch. The crew chief is splayed out on the floor by the tail ramp, facedown and motionless.

Jackson rushes over to the side hatch and pulls the emergency latch. Unlike the cockpit door, the side hatch is mounted on a hinge that opens to the inside of the craft. As soon as the door starts swinging into the ship, First Platoon's grunts start piling into the opening. Outside, the rifle fire is a steady cacophony. The hull of the drop ship is getting peppered with small-arms fire. It sounds like rocks against a polycarb window.

The squad comes stumbling into the drop ship. The last one in is Sergeant Fallon. She fires her rifle through the open hatch with one hand while she pulls on the door latch with the other, and she only lets off the trigger when the closing door is about to swing past her muzzle. Sergeant Fallon stumbles back as the hatch seals into place, and toggles into the company channel.

"Valkyrie Six-Four, Bravo One-One. Our location is crawling with hostiles. We're all buttoned down in the ship. What say you drop some ordnance around us?"

"Bravo One-One, Valkyrie Six-Four. We can't drop stuff in a civilian area, but we can give you a pass with the cannons."

"Try to miss the drop ship, Six-Four. We're all holed up in the cargo hold."

"Copy that, One-One. Stand by."

My TacLink display shows the drop ship surrounded by a sea of red carets. There are no windows in the sidewalls of the cargo hold, but the banging all over the exterior of the Hornet makes it clear that the locals have us cornered. The armor of the ship is thick enough to filter out most of the yelling, but the gunfire on the other side of the laminate plating is very audible.

"Where's my rifle?" I ask, and Stratton shrugs.

"I ran it dry and dropped it outside. Sorry."

"Well, fuck. What the hell am I supposed to shoot with now?"

"Get another one from the arms locker up front," Sergeant Fallon says. "Restock your ammo while you're at it. Baker and

Jackson, go with him and grab ammo for your teams. Take every-thing you can carry. I think we're in for a long evening."

———————

The arms locker is behind the cockpit, right next to the chem-ical toilet and the galley closet. It's like a small walk-in closet, loaded to the roof with spare weapons and ammunition. The small arms are lined up in rows along the back wall of the locker, and the ammunition is stacked in sealed boxes underneath the arms racks. I grab a pair of boxes labeled "MAGAZINE, RIFLE, M-66, 45EA" and hand them back to Baker and Jackson, who are stand-ing in the passageway behind me.

"Get some rifle grenades, too," Baker says.

I reach into the storage rack again and pull out several differ-ent hard plastic boxes full of forty-millimeter grenades. Jackson and Baker take them and toss the boxes to the rear, where the rest of the squad is busy reloading rifles and restocking ammunition pouches.

The weapons on the rack are mostly M-66 rifles, standard issue for most of us. There are several Sarissas lined up to the right of the rifles, which are not terribly useful to us right now, and half a dozen MARS launchers, which are. The multipurpose assault rocket system is a stubby little tube that fires a large vari-ety of stubby little rockets. It does the same job as the grenade launchers integrated into our rifles, but the bore of the MARS is twice as big, the range is twice as long, and the bang is four times as loud. I take an M-66 out of the rack, charge it with a fresh magazine, and sling it over my shoulder. On an impulse, I also grab one of the pistols and stick it into one of the empty grenade loops on my armor. Finally, I pull one of the MARS launchers out of the storage clamps. The cartridges for the launcher are neatly lined up on the rack underneath, their color-coded safety caps denoting their lethal flavors. Half the colors are unfamiliar to me, despite the fact that I paid attention in Basic when we were familiarized with the MARS. I do know the color codes for high-explosive dual purpose (red), and thermobaric (yellow and black). I take one of each, load one cartridge into the rear of the launcher, and sling the other cartridge tube over my shoulder, where it clanks against the rifle.

"Got any big plans for tonight, Grayson?" Sergeant Fallon asks when I get back to the cargo hold, the MARS launcher in the crook of my arm.

"Just making sure we bring enough bang, Sarge."

Outside, the banging stops. Then we hear a series of rapid-fire explosions outside, like someone's lighting off the biggest string of firecrackers ever made. A moment later, Valkyrie Six-Four roars by over our heads.

"Bravo One-One, you have 'em running for cover. We're making another pass."

"Copy, Six-Four, and thanks a bunch," Sergeant Fallon replies.

"Grab your gear, and get ready to bail," she tells us over the squad channel.

"We hit the side alley here." She marks the spot in question on our TacLink displays. "Make sure you get way the fuck away from this boat. When the demo charge goes off, this thing will be the world's biggest hand grenade."

"Someone check on my crew chief," the pilot says. Her voice is a slow drawl—Paterson, our squad medic, has injected her with the standard painkiller cocktail from the trauma kit, and that stuff is good enough to let you forget even a few broken bones for a while. She won't be able to feel anything below her waist for a few hours, but it's not like she would have been able to do sprints on those broken legs anyway.

"He's out cold, but he's alive," Paterson replies. "Knocked himself out good."

"Paterson and Baker, grab the chief," Sergeant Fallon orders. "Phillips and Priest, you take the pilot. Let's blow this joint before the crowd gets their courage back."

"Bravo One-One, this is Valkyrie Six-Four. We're ordered to evac Second Platoon's casualties. You're on your own for a while. Six-Two and Six-Five are en route from Shughart, ETA nineteen minutes."

"Super," Sergeant Fallon says. "That is just superior timing, Six-Four."

"Take it up with Company," Six-Four's pilot replies. "We're just doing as we're told."

"Don't sweat it, Six-Four. You are Second Platoon's boat, after all."

"So what's the plan now, Sarge?" Jackson asks.

"I'll check with Company," Sergeant Fallon replies, and toggles over to the company circuit. After a few moments of terse conversation, she shakes her head and comes back on the squad channel.

"Battalion is sending in Alpha Company and one of the armor platoons. Second Platoon's got a bunch of casualties. We're to hoof it back to the civil center and hole up with the rest of First and Second Platoons until the cavalry arrives."

"Sounds like a sensible plan," Baker replies. "Too bad they didn't send those tanks in right away."

"They almost never drag out armor for domestics, Baker. It looks too warlike or something."

It certainly looks like a war out there to me, I think. People are shooting at us, we're shooting back, and the ones that are hit don't get up again. Those are citizens of the NAC out there, the people whose rights we vowed to protect when we swore our service oaths, but civil rights are not exactly the first thing on your mind when someone fires a gun in your direction. Right now there's our small tribe of scared and tired troops, holed up in the wrecked drop ship, and then there's everybody else, and there's not a soldier in our squad who wouldn't shoot any number of Them to save one of Us.

"Let's bail," Sergeant Fallon says. "Rear hatch, everyone. Remember to stay clear of this ship. There'll be shit flying everywhere. Stratton, stay with me while I make the charge hot. The rest of you, get a move on."

We gather our junk and congregate at the rear of the drop ship. The conscious pilot and her unconscious crew chief are suspended between two pairs of TA troopers. I'm glad to only be encumbered with the MARS launcher—the four of us carrying the crew members will have a hard time shooting at anything. Jackson signals for me to cover the rear with Hansen.

"I'll take point," she says. "You two bring up the tail."

She reaches over to throw the lever for the ramp mechanism, and the cargo hatch opens as the inside light in the bay goes out. My helmet-mounted display flickers briefly, adjusting to the changing light. The bottom of the ramp hasn't yet touched the street when Jackson jumps out of the hatch and starts running for the alley.

"Go, go, go!"

The tail end is a disconcertingly exposed position. I can't overtake the two pairs of squad mates carrying the drop-ship crew, since I'm supposed to be shielding them. That makes me just as slow as they are. We run over to the mouth of the alley designated by Sergeant Fallon, most of us encumbered in some way.

The alley is a hundred yards from the stranded drop ship. It takes our gaggle of armor-clad troopers and entourage thirty seconds to cover the distance. When we reach the mouth of the alley, I look back over my shoulder. Sergeant Fallon and Stratton are dashing out of the rear hatch, and I drop to one knee and exchange the MARS launcher for the rifle to cover their run. Next to me, Hansen crouches down, rifle pointed downrange. Beyond the drop ship, on the other side of the intersection, there's some movement in the shadows of the building overhangs as the local crowd advances on the drop ship again, more cautious than before. Our air support is gone, off to play air ambulance for Second Platoon's wounded, but we have a little bit of time before the natives figure out that we're on our own. I see an outline as someone advances down the street in the distance, and my low-light imaging sensors clearly show the outline of a rifle. I take aim, and squeeze off three quick shots. The silhouette flinches back behind cover.

Sergeant Fallon and Stratton dash past, rifles clattering against hard battle armor.

"Get your asses behind cover, *now!*" the sergeant yells without bothering to toggle into the radio channel. We back-step into the alley in a hurry, rifles aimed and ready to engage threats until the last possible moment as we round the corner. Then we turn and run, away from the danger zone. Our squad mates have set up a hasty perimeter near a pair of huge trash containers. We catch up with the rest of the squad, and pause to catch our breath.

For a moment, it's eerily quiet—no gunfire, no shouting, no engine noise overhead, just the heavy breathing of nine TA troopers who just covered a hundred-yard dash in forty pounds of weapons and armor.

"Where's the *kaboom*?" Stratton says into the silence. "There was supposed to be an earth-shattering *kaboom*."

Sergeant Fallon starts a reply, but then there's a strange sound in the distance, like someone opening a huge container of carbonated soda, and the filters built into my helmet cut the audio feed completely.

Even with the active efforts of my electronic gear to preserve my hearing, the explosion of the drop ship stabs my eardrums. I can feel the shock wave from the detonation radiating through me as it moves away from the source at the speed of sound, and it feels like someone has thrown me to the ground and then jumped on my chest. For a moment I think that the drop ship must have had some low-yield nuclear ordnance on one of its pylons, and I'm convinced that Sergeant Fallon has just blown up half the PRC, and us along with it. I'm vaguely aware that I'm prone on the ground all of a sudden, knocked off my feet by the impulse of the shock wave.

For a while I can see and hear nothing. My polarized visor only slowly returns my vision, and my audio feed remains muted. I'm blind and deaf in my armor cocoon, rendered senseless by the built-in technology to save my hearing and eyesight.

As the world comes back into focus, I see my squad mates scattered on the ground all around me, everyone in a similar state of disorientation. I get to my knees, pick up my rifle, and check its status on my helmet display. I'm so used to seeing the electronic overlay in my field of vision that it's disorienting to see nothing at all, no symbols and numbers listing my active TacLink channels, the loading status of my weapon, our squad's waypoint markers, or even the colored carets marking friendlies and hostiles. All I see is the green-tinged visual feed from my helmet sensor, void of any interpretation by the tactical computer built into my armor. Other than the low-light enhanced vision, I'm no better off technologically than the people who are shooting at us.

Then my computer resets itself, recovering from the massive knock that has upset its digital equilibrium. I see the familiar code sequence of a system initialization flashing on the helmet-mounted screen, and five seconds later I can see and hear properly once more.

I toggle my TacLink into the squad channel and clear my throat.

"First Squad, comms check. Anyone copy?"

"Yeah, we're back," Baker replies. "Boy, that was a bit of a rattle, wasn't it?"

"No shit," Hansen says. "I haven't heard anything this loud since that floor party in my senior year."

"Perimeter, people," Sergeant Fallon admonishes. "Get up, and mind your sectors."

Her order seems a bit pointless for the moment—anyone caught in this stuff without the benefit of battle armor or integrated helmet systems will be blind and deaf for a while. Still, I check my rifle once more, pick up the MARS launcher, and take up position by the side of a trash Dumpster to cover the mouth of the alley.

The entire alley is covered in debris that wasn't there just moments ago. There are shards of polycarbonate everywhere, and as I look up at the buildings that make up one side of this alley, I realize that every single window in the building has been blown out by the pressure wave, dozens of inch-thick polycarb panes shattered like thin ice on a puddle. In the street beyond, I see flaming debris.

"Grayson and Hansen, head over to the end of the alley and sneak a peek," Sergeant Fallon orders.

We dust ourselves off and trot to the mouth of the alley, back to where we stood just a few moments ago.

"Holy shit," Hansen says as we turn the corner.

The street in front of us looks nothing like it did when we ran up to the drop ship a few minutes ago. The intersection where the wounded ship crashed is no longer a tidy, mappable feature in the cityscape. The road ends seventy-five yards in front of us, and a smoldering crater marks the spot where the drop ship blew up. The buildings that flanked the intersection are simply gone. From our spot at the corner of the alley to the ruined houses at the edge of the explosion radius, there's not a single window left intact on the street. There's debris everywhere—bits of building material, shards of polycarb windowpanes, and chunks of pavement. The drop ship has disappeared entirely, and I can't see a single identifiable part of it anywhere.

"What the hell do they stuff into those demolition charges?" I ask.

"Fuel-air explosive," Hansen answers. "Field-improvised. The tanks are rigged so the remaining fuel gets vaporized into the ship. They also light off whatever ordnance is still on the racks."

"Holy hell. This neighborhood is fucked up now."

"It's not like it was a vacation spot before," Hansen chuckles.

I scan the area with my low-light vision. There are hundreds of little fires in my field of view, flaring bright green on my helmet screen. I wonder how many people were blown up with that drop ship, or had their houses come down on top of them. Would anyone have stuck around after the crash, and the firefight? I'm trying to think about what I would have done, back home in the PRC, and I conclude that anyone who decides to stick around when a drop ship falls out of the sky next to their house deserves to get blown sky high.

"Keep a watch," Sergeant Fallon says. "We're coming out. Let's clear the area while the cockroaches are stunned."

CHAPTER 12

— THE BATTLE OF DETROIT —

Sergeant Fallon has elected to take the most direct route back to the civil center. We're walking out of the place the same way we walked in, on the main road that leads straight back to the plaza. The side streets and alleys offer more cover, but that would benefit our opponents more than us.

I am once again on rear guard duty. The two pairs of troopers carrying the pilot and crew chief are shielded by two pairs of unencumbered troopers in the lead and rear. Hansen and I are keeping an eye out on the road behind us, but the street scene is eerily quiet once more. Every once in a while, I see movement in a doorway or alley mouth, but nobody's shooting at us. For my part, I'd gladly call it a night, and as we leapfrog back in the direction of the plaza, I hope that the other side shares that sentiment.

Overhead, Second Platoon's drop ship descends out of the dirty night sky to land on the plaza once more. I hold my breath as they pass over the tall apartment building where one of the heavy machine guns was raining down armor-piercing rounds onto Valkyrie Six-One a little while ago, but the drop ship passes over the roof of the building without incident.

"Third of a klick, people," Sergeant Fallon says. "Almost there. I don't know about you, but I'm good and ready for a shower and a stress fuck."

"Amen to that," Stratton chuckles.

"It's gotten too fucking quiet," Jackson says from the front. "They all pack up and go home, or what?"

I open my mouth to comment on Jackson's entirely too clichéd interjection, when something catches my eye up ahead. There are flashes of light coming from the apartment building in the distance, and I realize the source of those flashes just before the booming reports of heavy gunfire reach the acoustic sensors on my helmet.

"Incoming!" I shout, and dodge to the left, where a doorway offers some cover. My helmet display flashes as the computer updates threat vectors and enemy positions on the tactical map.

"High-rise at twelve o'clock, three or four floors down from the top!"

The tracers reaching out from the building look like laser beams in the darkness—the fake red beams of old science fiction movies, not the invisible high-energy pulses of real laser weapons. The first burst rains down right in front of our squad, skipping red-hot tracers off the asphalt.

In front of me, the squad dashes for cover, but there is precious little to be found on this block, and nothing that will stop a heavy machine-gun round. The gunner must have tracked us for a little while, and opened fire only when we were away from any alleys, with nothing but building walls flanking the road on both sides of us. The nearest alley mouth is a few dozen yards ahead, far enough that it might as well be a mile away.

Sergeant Fallon drops to one knee, sights her rifle, and fires back at the source of the incoming rounds. The high-rise is almost half a kilometer away, which is about as far as our rifles will reach. Her M-66 sounds weak and tinny compared to the thunderous reports of the heavy gun in the distance. Next to the sergeant, Stratton and Jackson follow suit and return fire.

The heavy machine gun stops firing for a moment, and then opens up again. This time the burst is right on target. I watch in horror as the stream of tracers reaches out and touches Stratton, who falls backwards.

I catch movement out of the corner of my eye and turn to see a rifle barrel poking over the edge of a roof to our rear. There's movement on that rooftop, people shuffling into position, and my guts contract as I realize that the locals aren't done fighting after all. It's a crude ambush, but we ambled right into it.

The heavy machine gun in the distance opens up again. The gunner has good fire discipline. He fires his weapon in short bursts. Whoever is working that weapon isn't new to the task. Hansen pushes me into the doorway to my left and then piles in after me, just as the new flight of tracers from the distant machine gun rakes the pavement in front of us. I bump into the entrance door of the building. The impact of my armor-clad bulk rattles its polycarb panes. The MARS launcher slides off my back, and I land on top of it. We scramble away from the curb as the tracer rounds whiz by just a few feet to our right. One of the tracers hits the corner of the doorway and knocks off a chunk of concrete, which rains down on us in bits and pieces.

On my tactical screen, I see two more of our squad icons flash brightly with the icon that shouts "medic needed." Our squad medic, Paterson, is one of the medical emergencies. The rest of the squad is moving forward, toward the mouth of the nearest alley, but the machine gunner has our little group dialed in now. The next burst drops another one of my squad mates, but I can't tell which one.

Hansen is back up on her feet, exchanging fire with someone on a rooftop out of sight.

"Grayson, open that fucking door," she says conversationally, nodding to indicate the entrance door to my left.

I don't have any buckshot grenades left, and using an HE round would mean that we'd have to step out into the road to avoid getting caught by the blast of the explosion. The rubber rounds will just bounce off the inch-thick polycarb door panels. I switch my rifle to manual fire, set the selector to "continuous burst," and aim at the center of the door as I pull the trigger. The muzzle flash illuminates the doorway as my rifle burps out the contents of its magazine at two thousand rounds per minute, thirty-three needle-pointed high-density tungsten fléchettes per second. The storm of fléchettes chews into the polycarbonate with ease, and after two or three seconds the entire upper panel of the door disintegrates in a shower of plastic shards.

With the window panel gone, I can reach through the door-frame and activate the emergency unlock. I shoulder the door open and turn around to see Hansen on her back, pushing herself farther into the doorway with her heels. Her rifle is on the ground next to her. I reach over, grab the back of her helmet, and pull her up into the doorway, out of the line of fire. She weighs close to two hundred pounds with the armor and all her gear, but I am so pumped on adrenaline that I yank her into the dark hallway of the building without ever letting go of my rifle with the other hand.

"You okay?" I ask, and she groans in response. There's a hole in her armor right by the joint between the chest plate and the shoulder pauldrons.

"Get my rifle," she says. "I can still shoot with the other arm."

"Sit tight," I tell her. The magazine in my rifle is nearly empty again, and I eject it and insert a new one from the stash tucked into the side pocket of my leg armor. Then I hand the rifle to Hansen.

"Take this one for a minute."

I step back out into the doorway and pick up the MARS launcher. Out in the street, I hear the hammering of the heavy machine gun again. My tactical screen shows nothing but blinking carets, flashing in alternate shades of blue and red—medical emergencies. Across the street there are a few heads poking over the edge of the roof. I hold the launcher with my left and pull the pistol I had stuffed into my harness back in the drop ship. The sidearm feels odd and unfamiliar in my hand—I've only ever fired one back in Basic, during small-arms familiarization—but the computer in my armor immediately recognizes the weapon, switches sighting modes, and displays the remaining ammo count at the bottom of my screen.

The pistol only holds twenty-five rounds, a tenth of the rifle's magazine capacity, but at short range it beats fighting with bare hands. I draw a bead on one of the heads on the rooftop and squeeze the trigger. The pistol barks a sharp report, and the head underneath my aiming reticle disappears suddenly. There are shouts on the roof, and another head pops up, this one behind the barrel of a rifle. I briefly register that the weapon aimed at me looks a lot like a military-issue M-66. I squeeze off three more rounds in rapid cadence, and the rifleman on the roof disappears. His weapon tumbles from the rooftop ledge onto the street below, where it lands with a hollow clatter. For the moment there are no more heads coming up on that roof.

I stuff the pistol back into the harness and shoulder the MARS. The machine gunner in the distance has switched to very short bursts, two or three shots at a time, undoubtedly to preserve ammo while making us keep our heads down. My TacLink display shows Hansen moving further into the hallway to my left and the rest of the squad huddled in a side alley thirty yards ahead. More than half their number are out of the fight, according to the symbols on my screen.

The operation of the MARS launcher is dead simple. We've drilled the deployment of the MARS a dozen times, and for some odd reason I hear Sergeant Burke's voice in its unforgettable drill-instructor twang as my fingers perform the necessary steps to ready the launcher for action.

I point the center of the reticle at the muzzle flashes of the heavy machine gun in the distance, near the top floor of the high-rise a third of a mile away, and pull the trigger.

The rocket leaps out of its launch canister with shocking speed. The tail end of the rocket glows with the heat of its internal booster, and the whole thing shoots off into the distance only a little slower than a tracer round. I expect to see the rocket leisurely rise skyward like the Sarissas we used back at the embassy a few weeks ago, but the MARS streaks downrange in a blink, covering the distance in just a few seconds.

My aim was a bit off. The rocket hits the building two floors below the machine gun that is still spitting tracers our way. There's a bright flash that cuts through the hazy night sky, and then the thunderclap of the explosion rolls across the PRC.

When I grabbed the rocket launcher, I took a high explosive and a thermobaric warhead out of the rack and loaded one of them into the launcher to be less encumbered. The one I loaded was the thermobaric missile.

The MARS launcher fires ninety-millimeter rockets. It's designed to take out enemy fortifications and reinforced structures. A high-rise tenement is a very light structure. It's a steel skeleton with thin modular concrete sheets for walls.

The missile hit twenty feet below the window with the heavy machine gun, but the bunker-buster warhead is rather forgiving of aiming errors. The front of the floor around the impact point erupts outward, windows and walls turned into millions of bits and shards by the overpressure. The explosion is much more dramatic than the one caused by the thermobaric rifle grenade I fired into the building with the sniper during the embassy evacuation. Over by the high-rise, the sky is filled with flaming debris as the pressure of the explosion radiates outward. Then the entire front of the building above the point of impact collapses with the tortured groan of fatigued metal and concrete. I watch in horror as the four or five floors above the explosion pancake into each other. More concrete slides off the face of the building, this time in bigger chunks. When the rumbling stops, there's a dust cloud above the high-rise that reaches hundreds of feet into the sky. The side of the building that's facing us now has a massive wound in its upper half, a smoking gash that's five floors high and three-quarters of a floor wide.

Part of me realizes that I just blew up twenty apartments, with everything and everyone within. I may have killed the machine-gun crew, but I have snuffed out the lives of lots of other people, too. Men, women, maybe kids. I feel nauseated and light-headed, and almost drop the launcher.

Nearby, the rifle fire picks up again. I get down on one knee and work the fastener for the now empty cartridge husk at the rear of the launcher. As I drop the expended hull and pick up the second cartridge, someone starts shooting from the rooftop across the street again. I feel something hitting the side of my armor right underneath my arm. The impact is hard enough to make me drop the launcher tube in surprise. Hansen's rifle is half a foot to my right, and I scoop it up and work the bolt. The grenade launcher is empty, but the magazine is still half full.

The shooter on the roof is a woman. She's dressed in baggy and shapeless clothes, but I can clearly see her long hair, and her feminine features underneath the bill of the cap she is wearing. She's down on one knee, right by the edge of the roof, and she's holding a rifle with a wooden stock. As I watch, she works a lever at the bottom of her rifle to load another round into the chamber. She performs the motion without taking the weapon off her shoulder, and her eyes never waver from the sights.

I stare at her, this woman that looks like a dozen I've known back home, just a hood rat in too-big clothes, and I want to wave her off, shout a warning, or both—anything to keep her from shooting at me, so I won't have to shoot her in turn. Then she pulls the trigger on her rifle.

The bullet hits me right above the eyebrow, on the ridge that forms the upper edge of the face shield. It feels like being beaned with a well-thrown fastball. I stumble backwards and fall on my ass. My helmet display blanks out momentarily from the shock of the impact.

This was a killing shot that just barely missed. She shot at my armor to get my attention and make me turn around, and the second shot was aimed right at my visor, the weakest point of my battle armor. My sensors restore my low-light vision just in time for me to see the woman on the roof complete another stroke of the loading lever on that antique rifle of hers. My right hand is still wrapped around the grip of Hansen's rifle, and unlike my opponent, I don't have to bring my rifle up into my field of vision to aim it.

We pull our triggers at the same time. Her bullet cracks into my visor, right at the seam between the clear face shield and the reinforced ballistic shell of the outer helmet. It's another near miss, but an improvement over the last one. I feel a sharp jab of pain right underneath my left eye that radiates out to my ear, as if someone had sliced the side of my head with a sharp knife.

My rifle sends not just one, but half a dozen rounds in return. They hit the woman on the roof dead center in the chest, the perfect aim of a computer. She doesn't cry out or flinch. Instead, she just falls forward, and there's nothing between her and the street below to break her fall.

From the way she falls, limbs flailing without any semblance of control or coordination, I know that she is already dead when she hits the ground. Still, I feel the urge to run the twenty yards to where she is now splayed out motionless on the dirty asphalt.

I seize her by the collar of her jacket and turn her around to get a look at her face. Her eyes are open, but unfocused in death. There's no pain in her face, no surprise or distress. She looks about thirty, maybe a few years younger. Her ball cap fell off her head when she fell off the roof, and her hair is held together in a loose ponytail. I can't tell the exact color of it with my augmented night vision, but it's dark hair, brown or auburn. If I had seen her on the street back in my PRC, killing her would have been the last thing on my mind. Even in death, she looks more vital, more substantial than most of the people I know back home. Even though she tried to kill me, I'd take those rifle rounds back now if I could.

"Grayson, if you're still standing, get your ass over here," I hear over the squad channel, the first time someone has used the voice network since the machine gun opened fire. The identifier tag on my helmet screen marks the speaker as Corporal Jackson, but she sounds odd, like she's speaking slowly through clenched teeth.

"Copy," I respond, and check her location on the map. The bullet that pierced the side of my visor missed the monocle of the data computer, and I still have a data feed in my field of vision. The left side of my face feels like it has been worked over with broken glass. I can feel warm blood trickling down my cheek.

The squad is huddled together in the alley ahead and to my left. I reload Hansen's rifle with a fresh magazine.

"Hansen, do you copy?" I ask into the squad channel.

"Yeah, I'm here," Hansen replies. "I'm at the end of the entrance hallway, right before the bend. Mind your trigger finger when you come in."

"How's the boo-boo?"

"Right arm's on vacation," she says. Her voice sounds tired. "I'll be fine. Just give me a second to catch my breath."

"Anyone home in there?"

"If they are, they're smart enough to stay inside. I'm not in a super social mood right now."

The left side of my face hurts as I smile. Our armor is lined with thermal bandage modules that automatically attempt to seal wounds and stop blood loss, but the helmets lack that lining, and the blood streams down my cheek unhindered. I make my way down to the alley where the rest of my squad is holed up. My rifle is pointed at the edge of the roof across the street as I move, ready to put a fléchette into any heads popping up behind rifle sights, but if there's anyone left up on that roof, they have the good sense to keep their heads down.

"Grayson, you got any trauma packs left?" someone asks as I turn the corner to the alley. My squad is hunkered down behind yet another trash container, and several of them are laid out on the ground.

"Yeah, I have two," I respond.

"Bring 'em over here."

Two of my squad mates are tending to Sergeant Fallon, who is sitting with her back to the wall. There's a pool of blood under her right leg, and as I get closer I see that the lower half of her leg is badly mangled. I crouch down next to the troopers who are working on the sergeant, pull the trauma packs out of my right leg pocket, and hand them over.

"She dragged Stratton out of the road and caught a round in the leg," Jackson says next to me. I glance over to the two inert bodies next to the Dumpster and look at Jackson in question.

"Stratton's gone, man. So's Paterson. Right through the fucking armor, both of them."

"Fuck," I say, and Jackson nods in agreement.

"That ain't no welfare riot," she says. "Heavy belt-fed guns? Where the fuck did they get those? That's military hardware."

"I shot a guy who had an M-66," I say. "And I guarantee you

that fucker on the heavy machine gun had magnified night vision. He was right on fucking target with the first round."

"Whoever it is, they fucked us up," Sergeant Fallon says. Her voice is slurred, undoubtedly because of a healthy dose of injected painkillers. I try not to look at the mess that is her lower right leg, but I can't help glancing at it. It looks like someone stuck a small explosive charge into her calf muscle. I can see shattered armor, pulped flesh, and shards of bone.

"What the fuck do we do now, Sarge?" Baker asks.

There's movement on a rooftop overhead, and a moment later a bottle with a flaming rag stuffed into its neck comes sailing down from above. It hits the edge of the trash container and bounces off into the street, unbroken. As it rolls away from the trash container and into the gutter, it leaves a trail of burning fluid. Jackson rushes over, seizes the bottle with a gloved hand, and hurls it down the street, where it finally shatters and ignites. Baker and I get up and rush to the opposite side of the alley to get a bead on our attackers. We don't see anyone, but a moment later two more bottles come sailing over the edge of the roof. One of them falls a little wide and cracks open in the middle of the alley, but the other is dead on. It clears the edge of the roof just barely and then falls straight down into the group huddled behind the garbage container.

"Get out of there!" Jackson yells. The troopers behind the container don't need the invitation—the bottle cracks open and spews burning liquid, and everyone scrambles to get out of the way. Someone drags the motionless forms of Stratton and Paterson away from the container. Behind me, Baker fires his rifle at the edge of the roof above.

"We need to get the fuck out of this alley," Sergeant Fallon says into the squad channel. Her voice sounds detached, which probably has more to do with the chemicals in her bloodstream than her state of mind.

"The building is clear," I say. "Hansen's inside already. Let's hole up and get out of the rain here."

We make our way out of the alley and back to the entrance door where I left Hansen a few minutes ago. Every trooper who's still able to walk is carrying or dragging another who isn't. Jackson and I are dragging Stratton, who has two neatly stenciled half-inch holes in the chest plate of his battle armor—one in the abdomen and one right in the center of his sternum.

"Hansen, we're coming in," I say. "Mind your muzzle."

"Copy," she replies. "Don't slip on the blood."

The building is a low-rise apartment tenement, ten units per floor. There are never any vacancies in a PRC. Even for these shitty shoeboxes made out of paper-thin concrete, there's a long waiting list. The residents are undoubtedly pressing their ears against their doors as our TA squad barges into the ground-floor hallway, and I know that at least a few of them will be on their net boxes in a moment to ring the neighborhood alarm.

Here they are; come and get them.

We lay down the dead in a corner and the wounded in the center hallway, away from the entrance door. Sergeant Fallon is severely mauled and doped up. Stratton and Paterson are dead, and every other member of the squad has at least a minor injury. I finally take a moment to pull off my helmet, and wince when the liner on the left side pulls itself loose from the wound to which it was glued with congealing blood.

"Got yourself a beauty mark there, Grayson," Baker says. "That'll leave a scar, I think."

"Yeah, well, I'll worry about that later," I say.

"They'll have to blow off his head before he's as ugly as you," Hansen says weakly from a few yards away.

"With the way things are going right now, they just might."

"Bravo C2, this is Bravo One-One," Sergeant Fallon says into her helmet mike. C2 is command and control—the people at Company who are calling the shots and relaying orders from the boss down to the platoon and squad leaders.

"First Squad is holed up half a klick from the admin building. We have extracted the pilot and crew chief from Valkyrie Six-One, but we have two KIA, and most of the rest are wounded. Got anything you can send our way here?"

Sergeant Fallon listens for the response from C2, and everybody sort of listens in without being too obvious about it.

"That's a negative, C2. No way can we walk that distance, with half the city on our ass out here. Two of my guys are dead, and three of us can't walk. We barely have enough people to carry all the casualties."

There's another delay, and then Sergeant Fallon lets out a chuckle that sounds genuinely amused.

"Look, guy, I'd love to comply with that order, I really would. My squad is *combat ineffective.* You make us all walk back through Indian country right now, you'll be picking up our pieces in the morning. Send the replacement drop ship our way once they get here, and we'll evac from here. They can land in front of the building, and cover our egress."

The response from C2 makes Sergeant Fallon roll her eyes.

"The machine guns are gone. Six-Four got the first one on their strafing run, and one of my guys blew the hell out of the other one with a MARS. That drop ship can take a whole lot more small-arms fire than we can, chief."

She waits for the reply, and by now we've all given up trying to be subtle about listening in.

"Copy that, Lieutenant. If I lose another trooper on the way, you can be sure that I'll pay you a visit as soon as they stitch me back together. Bravo One-One *out*."

She taps the comm channel button on the inside of her wrist with emphasis.

"We are to exfil to the civic plaza for medevac, on foot. They don't want to risk another bird. ETA on the drop ship is ten minutes."

I look around at the remnants of our squad. We have two dead bodies, Sergeant Fallon and the drop-ship pilot can't walk, and the crew chief is still unconscious. Hansen won't be carrying anyone, either. The five of us who are still on our feet will each need to carry someone. We're in no shape for a fight anymore.

"Well, let's get to it, then," Corporal Jackson says. She shoulders her rifle and bends down to pick up the unconscious crew chief.

"Grayson, you take the sergeant. Let's get going. If we miss this ride, we're well and truly fucked."

I don't want to go back out into the street, but I don't want to stay here, either. Once the PRC comes alive after sunrise, and people start collecting the bodies of their friends, any soldier in the area will be fair game for a public barbecue.

"Ten minutes," Sergeant Fallon says as I help her up and drape her arm over my shoulder. "Don't be stopping to smell the flowers."

"Don't worry about *that*," I say.

Encumbered by Sergeant Fallon's armored bulk, I am out of breath at the end of the first block. We're running down the street that leads straight back to the civic plaza, stopping on every intersection to catch our collective breath and check the cross streets for enemy presence.

The shooting starts again when we're a block and a half away from the building where we had holed up. Up ahead, at the nearest intersection, someone leans around a corner and starts popping off shots at our ragged little column. I'm in the lead with Sergeant Fallon, and her bulk on my right side prevents me from using my rifle to shoot back on the run. I sway to the side and lower the sergeant to the ground in the cover of a doorway, but by the time I have my rifle in my hands, the shooter at the corner has disappeared. Then I hear gunshots behind us, from the intersection we had just cleared a few moments ago.

"Watch the corners," Corporal Jackson shouts.

I sight my rifle and fire back. My fléchettes are kicking up concrete dust, but the shooter disappeared around the corner as soon as I brought my rifle to bear. If we're going to be harassed like this all the way back to the civic plaza, we'll get there in a few hours at best. They know where we are and where we're going, and they're smart enough to avoid a stand-up fight.

"Shoot on the run," Corporal Jackson says. "Switch to full-auto and hose down the corners when they pop their heads out. Monitor your ammo, and reload when we pause to take a breath."

Our progress along the street is painfully slow. Sergeant Fallon is doped up, but conscious, and she's assisting me by using her rifle with her unencumbered right hand. Others in my squad are carrying deadweight. We go from block to block, rushing across intersections as fast as we can, and pausing after every dash to reload our weapons and rest for a few seconds. I parcel out the spare magazines I have left from Lieutenant Weaving's stash to the rest of the squad. Firing bursts makes the enemy keep their heads down, but our ammo stock is dwindling fast.

As we get closer to the civic plaza, the shooting gets more intense. Where before there were individuals taking potshots at us, now there are groups of three and four working together, like infantry fire teams. It seems that everybody with a working firearm is out on the street tonight, and they all know which way we're going.

I'm in the front for a change, stumbling along with Sergeant Fallon by my side. We've turned into a symbiotic organism, a slow-moving creature with three working legs and two rifles. As we come up on the intersections, she covers the right side of our frontal arc, and I cover the left. Without the aiming marker projected onto my helmet display, I wouldn't be hitting anything. As it is, I'm not wildly accurate firing my rifle from the crook of my arm as we're ambling along, but it's enough to make the other guys duck back behind corners. I'm firing three-round bursts, and my rifle is down to a hundred rounds, with two magazines remaining in the pouches on my harness.

"Quarter klick to go," Sergeant Fallon says over the squad channel as we hunker down for a rest after dashing across yet another intersection. Whenever we walk up to the intersection, people shoot at us from alley mouths and building corners, and every time we cross a major street, the fire from our left and right gets twice as dense as we offer the crowd a clear line of fire from four sides. Standard infantry practice is to pop smoke grenades before dashing across, but we popped our last smoke a few hundred yards back. Now we're just relying on the laminate of our battle armor and the knowledge that most black-market small arms can't pierce our suits easily.

In running shoes I can cover 250 meters in well under a minute. Right now it might as well be 250 miles. We're taking fire from every alley and side street along the way. I fire a burst at a building corner up ahead where someone with a rifle just popped off two shots at our column. The shooter pulls back the moment he sees my muzzle swing towards him, and my salvo hits nothing but dirty concrete. Still, I mash the trigger again, and again, sending two more bursts into the space where his head was just a moment ago.

"Grayson, you got any grenades left?" Sergeant Fallon asks. Her voice sounds weak.

"Just two rubber rounds," I say.

"Well, fuck. I'm just about out, too."

As she says this, she aims her rifle at an alley mouth to our right, and pulls the trigger. I didn't even see anyone there, but as her burst tears into the darkness, I hear a cry of pain and a shouted exclamation. Then the bolt of Sergeant Fallon's rifle locks back on an empty magazine.

"Sling it, and take this," I say, and pull the pistol out of my harness. She lets go of the rifle, which remains suspended muzzle-down by her side, and seizes the pistol.

"Where'd you get that cap gun?" she asks.

"Drop-ship armory," I reply. "I'll reload your rifle when we're across the intersection."

"Good man." She hefts the pistol. "Shitload easier to use with one hand."

The next intersection is a major one, two main roads crossing. I stop at the forward edge of the corner building and aim the rifle around the corner with my left hand. The M-66 has a built-in uplink to the TacLink computer, and we can use our rifles as remote cameras to snoop around corners without exposing ourselves to fire. As soon as my muzzle clears the edge of the building, I see a bunch of red carets on my tactical map, advancing on the intersection from the left. There are at least a hundred people coming down the street, and the closest one is less than fifty yards away.

"Hold," I yell into my mike.

"I see them," Jackson says behind me. "If only half of 'em got guns, we'll never make it across."

"I'll stay at the corner with the sarge and cover. You get across, and then cover us."

"You got ammo left?"

"Two mags," I say. "Hurry the fuck up, will you?"

I lower Sergeant Fallon to the ground and replace the partially empty magazine in my rifle with a full one. Sergeant Fallon holds out her hand, and I pass her the other full magazine. I drop to one knee, lean around the corner, and commence firing.

The closest gaggle of people is twenty yards away when I drop them with single shots, one round each. The crowd behind them scatters. Some dash for cover in the nearest alley, some turn around and run the way they came. A few shoot back, and they go down next. I have low-light vision, computer-controlled weaponry, and ballistic armor. They have outdated weapons and battery-powered flashlights. For once, they're caught in the open, and I have no remorse about exacting payback.

Behind me, the rest of the squad rushes across the intersection. Jackson has the crew chief, Phillips has the dead Paterson over his shoulder, Priest is carrying the drop-ship pilot, and Baker and Hansen are both carrying Stratton's body. We're a rifle squad in a combat battalion, with state-of-the-art equipment, and we got reduced to a limping pack of walking wounded—and two dead—in just a few moments of battle, fighting against our own people, in the middle of one of our own cities.

At this range, it's hard to miss. I center the reticle of my gun sight on the silhouettes ahead of me and pull the trigger of the rifle methodically. A scrawny guy with a scoped rifle dashes toward the mouth of the alley, and I aim just ahead of him and nail him with a single shot that sends him sprawling across the concrete. A girl passes him and bends down to pick up the rifle he dropped, and as soon as her fingers touch the rifle stock, I shoot her, two rounds right into the middle of her hunched-over silhouette. Sergeant

Fallon is firing her rifle from the prone position, adding the contents of her magazine to the carnage.

Just as the squad is across the intersection, I hear gunfire from my left. I turn to locate the source of it when something hits the side of my armor. It's a rather unspectacular impact, barely enough to make me sway, but there's a sudden intense pain in my side, and I know that the round has pierced my battle armor. There's another blow, this one lower than the first. It feels like someone sticking a red-hot needle into my side and driving it home with a hammer. Then I find myself on the ground next to Sergeant Fallon. My lungs feel like all the air has been sucked out of them in an instant. I want to shout a warning, but I can't work up the breath for anything beyond a groan.

There's a small group of rioters at the corner of the intersection we just passed a little while ago. One of them is kneeling and aiming a familiar-looking rifle at me. I recognize the twin muzzle arrangement of an M-66, topped with a standard military combination sight. My own rifle is on the ground in front of me. I reach for it, but the whole thing seems to have tripled in weight all of a sudden. The shooter with the M-66 takes aim again, and I know that I won't be able to lift my own gun before he curls his trigger finger and exerts the nine pounds of pressure necessary to launch another fléchette round.

Then I hear a burst of fire from behind me. The shooter falls on his butt with an almost comical look of consternation on his face. For a brief moment, he sits on the street, his legs stretched out in front of him, his rifle still in his hands but aimed at nothing in particular anymore. Then there's a second burst of fire, and the shooter takes all three rounds in his face. He falls back, still holding on to his rifle. His two comrades dash out of the line of fire and disappear behind the corner of the building.

I look over to the right, and see Corporal Jackson on one knee, her rifle aimed at a spot behind me. I raise myself on my hands and knees, and scoop up my own rifle. The ammo counter on my screen shows 159 rounds remaining. I've pulled the trigger almost a hundred times in the last minute or two.

"Grayson, you okay?" Jackson asks over the squad channel.

My left side feels like it has a pair of knives sticking out of it. The pain is so intense that it takes my breath away. I have to force myself to fill my lungs, and every breath makes the pain in my side flare to almost intolerable levels. I try to find the air for a reply, but then I just shake my head.

"Baker, with me," Jackson says. "Whoever's left, give us some covering fire."

Baker and Jackson come dashing back across the intersection. Behind them, Priest and Hansen lean around the corner and start firing their rifles. I want to add my own fléchettes to the covering fire, but I don't have the strength to lift my rifle anymore. Someone grabs me by the harness and starts dragging me across the street. I see Jackson helping Sergeant Fallon to her feet, firing her rifle with one hand as she pulls the sergeant along with her. My computer informs me that I still have a bunch of rounds in my magazine, and it points out the threat vectors to the people down the road who are still standing and shooting at us, but right now I'm just a passenger, no longer able to take advantage of all that superior technology.

Eventually, my bumpy journey across the intersection stops. I don't remember having closed my eyes, but I open them now to see Baker bent over me, his visor raised.

"How bad?" he asks. Behind him, Hansen and Priest are still firing their rifles, exchanging rounds with the newly emboldened rioters that have decided to stick around and nail us down. Now that they've seen our casualties, there's blood in the water, and the sharks are circling. Soon they'll get reinforcements, and our ammo is almost gone.

I lift up my rifle—barely—and pat the magazine well with one hand to let Baker know there's still ammo in my weapon. He nods and takes the M-66 out of my hands.

"Priest, here's another half a mag," he says over his shoulder.

"About time. I'm just about dry." Priest takes my rifle and goes back to his spot at the street corner.

Baker checks the damage to my armor. My left side has gone from searing hot to ice cold. I still have to expend most of my energy forcing air into my lungs, and it feels like something important is broken inside. For the first time in my life, I think that I might be dying. I suppose I should feel dread or panic, knowing that I may slip into unconsciousness at any moment and never wake up again, but I'm too tired and too out of it to care.

"You want me to shoot you up, man?"

Baker has a narcotics injector in his hand, and he makes a motion like clicking a pen in front of my face. I shake my head—I don't want to numb myself and lose the ability to suck air into my lungs.

"C2, this is Bravo One-One," I hear Sergeant Fallon say. "We are down for the count here. We have more wounded than we can carry. Hostiles all over the place, and we're just about out of ammo. Send a ship, or send a recovery detail with body bags. Your call."

There's a reply over the platoon channel, but I can't quite make it out as I am drifting off. It feels like the onset of a really bad flu, that floating feeling you get in your head that makes you all woozy and shaky on your feet as you stumble into the bathroom for some medicine.

I close my eyes and listen to the battle going on around me. The reports from military rifles are sporadic, single rounds here and there, with the occasional short burst. The gunshots from civilian weaponry are getting more frequent, and it seems like they're coming from every direction now.

"I'm hit!" someone yells on the squad channel. I'm too out of it to recognize the voice—Baker? Priest?—but there's nothing I can do anyway. I barely have the energy to keep breathing.

Then there's a new sound, a thunderous roar overhead. I smell the stench of burning fuel, and a hot gust blows across my face. I hear what sounds like a giant zipper being undone, and look up to see the welcome silhouette of a Hornet-class drop ship overhead, gun turret blazing as the hulking machine descends in a graceful hover.

I fade out again for a little while. There's the sensation of floating away from the ground. People are talking right next to my head, but it all sounds like it's coming through a brick wall, and I don't even try to make sense of it. I get jostled against a hard surface, and the pain in my side flares up. I squirm, but there are strong hands holding me down, and I feel the pinprick of an injector against my neck.

Then the world turns quiet around me.

CHAPTER 13

——— GREAT LAKES———

When I was younger, I often dreamed of falling from a great height. The part of the dream that was most terrifying was the moment of weightless feeling just after I stepped out over the abyss—the second when I realized I was going to fall, and my stomach tried to float up inside of me. The dream always felt so real that I took it for the real thing every time, and I was always terrified when I plunged toward the ground, certain that I was experiencing the last moments of my life.

I would always wake up before hitting the ground, but in a way my mind lived through my final moments hundreds of times. I remember feeling regret every single time—for things I had done, or failed to do, and for all the things I would leave unaccomplished. Sometimes I would think of my mother, and the sorrow that would be added to her already joyless life by surviving her only child.

This time, the dream is different. When I step over the precipice, I am in my battle armor, holding my rifle, and I am fully aware that I am merely dreaming. Still, the feeling of weightlessness is real, and so is the fear that grips my mind as my body falls into the darkness below.

This time, I don't wake up before hitting the ground. This time, I crash onto the ground after a fall that seems impossibly long. I don't blink out of existence, which is what should happen after a fall from such a height, a body shattered in a microsecond, just enough time for the brain to register a final shock before getting turned into paste. Instead, I am aware of the impact, the shock it sends through my body, and the way it seems to jar every molecule in me out of alignment. Nobody can survive a fall like that, but here I am, flat on my back, still breathing. Nothing seems to be broken—there is no pain at all, actually—and when I try to sit up, my body obeys instantly. My armor is unscratched, and my rifle still safely cradled in the harness on my chest.

Then there's a bright light in my face, and I flinch. I feel hands on my shoulders, holding my upper body steady, and my brain finally decides to let go of the dream and rejoin the real world.

The bright light is the end of an optical wand, and it's a scant inch away from my eyes. I'm flat on my back, and as I try to emulate the action in my dream and sit up, I make it about half an inch before a pair of hands gently, but firmly pushes me back into the horizontal position.

"Hold up there, soldier. You can't do that yet, 'less you want to undo all the patchwork."

The voice sounds jovial, but professional, someone who's used to giving advice and equally used to having it followed. The person standing over me is a woman in a TA Class B shirt, but I can't make out her rank device, or her collar flashes. I try to speak, but my throat is parched, and all I can manage is a hoarse mumble that sounds nothing like human communication. The woman seems to be able to translate my utterance nonetheless, because she shuts off her wand, reaches past me, and brings a plastic cup into my field of vision.

"Water, cold, three ounces," she declares, describing the item in mock military supply jargon. "Don't drink too much at once. The patchwork in your abdomen is still tender."

She brings the cup to my lips. I take a careful sip, then a bigger one. The water doesn't even feel liquid as it runs down my throat, just a cool sensation coating my tongue and washing past my uvula.

"Better?" she asks. I nod in response.

"Good. Hold off on the speaking for a minute, okay? I have a good idea what you want to ask, so I'll give you the rundown. If you still want to talk after I'm done, you can have at it. Deal?"

I nod.

"You're in Regional Medical Center Great Lakes. You've been wounded in combat, and our doctors have stitched you back together. You'll have to ask the medical officer in charge on details about your injuries, but as far as I know, you had a collapsed lung, and you now have about three feet of small intestine less than you had when you were brought in. You'll be with us for a little while before we can release you back to your unit."

She pauses for a moment and then gives me a curt smile.

"Now, do you have any questions?"

"Where's the rest of my squad?" I ask.

"Not a clue. They brought you in from a different facility via medic flight. We had a bunch of other arrivals that night, but I don't know who or where they are. You're going to have to ask the medical officer in charge. I'm just the nurse."

"How long have I been here?"

"Three days," she says. "Two and a half, actually. They brought you in early Saturday morning, and now it's Monday afternoon."

"Shit," I say. "Missed Monday morning orders. The company sergeant is going to kick my ass."

The nurse laughs softly. She reaches past me again and turns on a light behind her. In the soft glow of the LED bulb she switched on, I can see her name tag and her rank device. She's wearing corporal's chevrons, and the tag above her right shirt pocket identifies her as MILLER C. We're all just a rank, a last name, and an initial. I'd ask her first name, but she outranks me by three pay grades, and I don't want to offend the person in charge of my medications for the next few days.

"You have a bit of stuff in your desk drawer," she says. "Mostly the effects you had on you. See if there's anything that doesn't belong, and I'll get rid of it for you."

"My PDP make it?"

"Yeah," Corporal Miller says. "You can't kill those things, you know."

She gets up from the chair on which she had been sitting and straightens out her uniform shirt.

"I'll leave you alone for a bit. There's a call button right over your head if you need anything. I'll be back with dinner in a little while."

She gives me another curt smile and leaves the room.

The room is entirely devoid of furniture except for the bed I'm in, a little white nightstand beside it, and the display that's hanging on the wall in a corner of the room. It's as sterile an environment as I've ever seen outside a PRC tenement.

I roll onto my side and look at the nightstand next to my bed. It has two drawers, and I reach over and pull open the first one. Inside is my dog tag on its ball chain, my PDP, the set of playing cards we all carry in rubberized trauma pack pouches, and the half-empty pack of breath mints I forgot I had stuffed into the right-leg pocket of my armor before heading out to the drop ship. I reach up and touch the side of my face, where a fresh line of scar tissue leads from the corner of my left eyebrow to the back of my ear.

My PDP turns on at the first press of the button. I had it in my pocket throughout the last mission, and it seems impossible that the electronic gear has survived all the running, falling, and getting shot at, but there's not a scratch on the thing. Even the battery is still at a full charge.

I check the MilNet link, the wireless network that connects all the military's communication systems and that every military PDP can access from anywhere on Earth and Luna. There are smaller MilNet nodes on navy ships and marine outposts as well, but they only synchronize with the rest of the network every few days. On the two inhabited bodies in our own solar system, however, the network is always in sync, and always just a tap on a PDP screen away.

The network is present, but for some reason my PDP can't connect to it. I can bring up everything that's not reliant on the MilNet—my calendar, the technical manuals, the ballistic conversion tables, and the book reader—but every time I try to access something that requires network access, I get an error message, even though the PDP shows full network signal strength.

I want to send a message to the rest of the squad, and another one to Halley, but I'm cut off from the rest of the world, which is a rare experience. The net terminals in the PRC apartments crap out every time a gnat farts in front of the government communications relay, but the MilNet link has been so reliable that the lack of connectivity feels a bit surreal.

There's a remote on the table for the screen in the corner of the room, but I'm not interested in boring myself to tears with some insipid Network show, or the stuff they sell as news reports.

Since I can't get in touch with anyone, I decide to use the opportunity to catch up on some sleep. I toss the PDP back into the drawer and roll over to settle into a more comfortable position. The mattress is better than the one on my bunk at the base, the room is quiet, and whatever drugs I have in my system are making me sleepy.

When the door opens again, I wake up once more. The window in the room shows a starry night sky outside, which makes it a projection—there are few spots left on the continent where you can see stars at night, and I'm pretty sure the Great Lakes isn't one of them, not with Chicago and Detroit nearby.

"How are we doing?" Corporal Miller asks. She's carrying a meal tray in her hands.

"I don't know about you, but I feel like I've been hit by a bus," I reply. "What's for dinner?"

"For you, Liquid Nutritional Package Seventeen. Your choices are vanilla or applesauce flavor. I have to warn you, though. The flavor designations do not accurately reflect the taste experience."

"I'm used to that," I say, eyeing the nondescript white containers on the tray. "Ever tried BNA rations?"

"Yes," she says. "My hometown is PRC Houston-23. Trust me, this stuff here is gourmet food compared to welfare chow. Just pretend it's a milkshake. You're on liquid diet for the next few days, by the way. Doctor's orders."

"I'll try the vanilla. Any idea why my PDP can't get onto the network in here?"

Corporal Miller shrugs.

"Not a clue. I'm not a network tech. The Information Support group at your home battalion is in charge of your access. You may want to check with them when you get out of here. Maybe your toy is broken after all."

I know that it's not the PDP, but I just shrug in return. If Corporal Miller knows why they killed my link, she's not willing to tell me, but I have my own theories.

"Have your dinner, and call me if you need help."

"I'm going to have to hit the head before too long," I say. "I'm guessing you don't want me up and running around."

"No, I don't," she smiles. "There's a relief tube on the right side of your bed. Use it at your convenience. Your bowels are empty, so don't worry about the other thing. That won't be an issue for a while."

"Good to know. Thank you, ma'am."

She leaves the room, and I take a sip from the container in front of me. Liquid Nutritional Package Seventeen tastes as bland as unadorned rice cakes, but there is a vague vanilla aftertaste to it, so I take Corporal Miller's advice and pretend I'm sipping on a milkshake.

Piss tubes, liquid food, solitary room, and no MilNet access, I think. *This will be a long week.*

On the morning of my third day of rehab, I have a visitor. Just as I finish my breakfast—I've graduated to mushy corn cereal—the door opens, and a TA major in full Class A uniform walks in.

"As you were," he says jovially, as if I was going to toss my blanket aside and jump out of bed on the spot at the sight of the golden leaves on his shoulder boards.

"Good morning, Major," I say. At first I guess he's with the Medical Corps, but then I see the branch insignia on his uniform. They're the crossed muskets of the infantry. I scan the fruit salad of ribbons above his left breast pocket automatically and see that he has very few combat-related awards. There's the combat-drop badge, Master rank, but that's something every TA trooper in a line battalion earns within two years of service. He has a marksmanship badge with a rifle and pistol tab, both the lowest rank. Most TA troopers in our company elect to not wear the marksmanship badge unless they have scored Expert, the highest rank. The ribbons and badges on a Class A uniform are a soldier's business card, and this major's card says "pencil pusher."

"Good morning, Private," he replies. He looks around for a chair. Failing to spot one, he walks up to the side of my bed and adopts an awkward position that looks like he's not sure whether to stay formal or relaxed.

"My name is Major Unwerth. I'm the battalion S2."

"Yes, sir." The S2 is the officer in charge of intelligence and security. I've not had dealings with any of the brass that inhabit the Pantheon, which is what the troopers informally call the battalion headquarters building.

"I have a few questions for you, if you don't mind, Private."

"Of course not, sir."

"Do you recall what happened last Saturday?"

"Of course I do. We were sent into a PRC up in Detroit, and they shot the hell out of my squad. Sir," I add.

The major isn't exactly out of shape, but he doesn't have any hard edges, either. He looks soft, and I feel a sudden dislike for him. Maybe it's the way he looks down on me, like I'm a different, inferior species, or maybe a defective piece of machinery.

"Well, that covers the basics of it," the major says. "Let me ask you something specific. Do you remember firing a thermobaric warhead from a MARS launcher in the course of that mission?"

"Yes, sir, I do." I suddenly understand why the major is here, and why my PDP doesn't have access to the MilNet.

"And can you tell me who authorized or ordered you to fire that particular warhead?"

"I did not receive a direct order to fire that launcher," I say. "We were told by the platoon leader on the way to the objective that lethal force was authorized in self-defense. They were shooting at my squad, we had several people down, and I defended myself, sir."

"I guess you did, rather vigorously." Major Unwerth purses his lips briefly.

"The problem is one of proportion, Private Grayson. You used a highly destructive hard-shelter demolition warhead on a civilian target—government property, at that. There were significant civilian casualties in that building due to your self-defense measure." He pronounces the last two words with just a hint of mocking emphasis in his voice. I conclude that I definitely don't like him.

"We're supposed to protect and defend the citizens of the NAC, Private. Blowing the hell out of a civilian high rise isn't exactly the kind of thing that makes us look like we're doing a good job at that."

I feel the heat rising in my face.

"What the hell do you suggest I should have done, Major? You have the telemetry from our computers, don't you? Should I maybe have asked them politely to stop shooting at us from that particular spot?"

"You could have responded in a more proportionate fashion, I think," the major says. "There were other weapons than thermobaric rockets available to you."

"Well, I was sort of in a hurry, and I didn't have time to read labels, sir."

"That's a pity," Major Unwerth says. "I'm the one who has to mop up the mess with the media and the division brass, and believe me when I tell you that I'm not pleased about that."

I couldn't give less of a shit about what you're pleased about, I think. I briefly consider saying that thought out loud, but then decide against it. He's near the top of the battalion food chain, and I'm all the way at the bottom. Whatever they have in store for me, I don't want to compound it with a disciplinary offense.

"I was doing my job, Major. My squad was getting chewed up, and I stopped the threat. That's all I have to say about that."

I feel anger flaring up inside me. This jackass with his crisply ironed Class A uniform and his desk jockey ribbons was probably in C2 back at Shughart when we were getting shot up by the locals in Detroit, and if he witnessed the battle at all, it was from the perspective of the drop-ship cams and the ground telemetry from the squad leaders. He wasn't around when we were chewed up by heavy weapons fire out of the blue, and he wasn't at the receiving end of the thousands of rounds the locals sent our way that night. He didn't have to drag someone half a mile through a contested urban battlefield lousy with pissed-off hostiles. For just a moment, I have the urge to grab him by the lapels of his immaculate uniform and drive my forehead right into the middle of his face.

The major apparently senses my sudden shift in emotions, because he backs off from my bed just a little.

"Well, there'll be time for a thorough review later," he says. "We'll debrief with your squad leader and the rest of your team when you get back to Shughart."

"I'm looking forward to it," I say. "Then we can figure out which genius made us walk back to the civil square with half the squad dead or wounded. That was really fun, getting shot to bits."

Major Unwerth's eyes narrow. My response seems to have triggered some authority reflex in him, because he straightens up and puts his hands behind his back once more, elbows out, like he's standing at parade rest.

"When I last checked the personnel files, Mr. Grayson, you were a private in the First Squad of Bravo Company's First Platoon. I don't recall you being present at any of the staff officer meetings, so I'm going to assume that's still the case."

I don't answer, and just glare at him.

"You're in the Territorial Army, and you're bound and required to follow orders from your superior officers, no matter how much you personally disagree with them. If that's too much of a challenge for you, let me know, and I'll inform the personnel office that you've changed your mind about serving your term of enlistment."

I know that he's full of it—the TA doesn't release anyone from their service contract after the completion of Basic, unless they get shot up enough to make the medical treatment too expensive. For major fuck-ups, they just give court-martials and lock people up instead. I don't have the desire to discuss the Uniform Code of Military Justice with this pencil-pushing asshole, however, so I say nothing. Major Unwerth takes my silence as a sign of acquiescence.

"Now, when you are released from this facility, you will be transferred back to Shughart, where you will report to the company sergeant the instant you're back on base. If you get in after hours, you'll report to the CQ. Is that understood?"

"Yes, sir, it is," I reply.

"Good." He looks around with obvious distaste on his face. I don't know whether he doesn't like the comparative luxury of my single-occupancy room, or whether he feels that he has debased himself for arguing with an enlisted grunt who doesn't even have a rank device on his collar yet.

"That will be all for now, then," he says, and turns to leave the room. "I will be back later to take a full statement from you. As you were, Private."

Some motivational visit, I think as the door closes behind him.

The next two days are filled with meals, physical evaluations, and long stretches of boredom. As the medication levels in my system are reduced, I'm no longer in a constant state of pleasant sleepiness, and the lack of entertainment even has me watch some Network news.

I call up the holoscreen on the far wall of the room, and the Network's interface pops up on the stark white wall. The news channel I pick is one we've not had available on the Network's connection in Mom's PRC apartment. There are commercials for stuff I've never seen and couldn't have afforded anyway: jackets made from weatherproof fiber that changes color and patterns based on the wearer's mood, personal comms slabs that look about a hundred years more advanced than our monochrome PDPs, and snack foods that look like edible jewelry. I've always known that there are two worlds out there, a low-rent one for the PRC rats and an air-conditioned one for the middle-class suburbanites and the rich people, but ever since I joined the military, that other, nicer world is much more visible.

I ask the interface for news items from Detroit for the last week. The computer curator brings up a selection of active tiles for me to choose. I pick one that looks like it begins with an aerial nighttime shot and lie back to watch the feed.

". . . demonstration against the recent changes in the Basic Nutritional Allowance composition. Authorities suspect that unauthorized manufacture of illegal stimulants is to blame for the explosion. Three citizens lost their lives, and seventeen were injured, some severely. Due to the ongoing civil disagreements, rescue crews were not able to respond to the scene until forty-eight hours after the incident. Authorities wish to remind public residence occupants that public services and all BNA deliveries are suspended for the duration of any disturbances that involve physical interference with public safety personnel."

The news segment ends, and I bring up another one, then another. All of them say basically the same thing. Unspecified disturbances at a public gathering, and then an explosion in a PRC residence tower that killed and injured a handful of people. Cause undetermined, but suspected illicit chem trade.

I sit back and cut the audio, then turn off the holoscreen altogether. The wall on the other side of the room reverts to a cheerless and antiseptic white.

Why would they not mention anything about the soldiers that were killed? We lost two in our squad alone, and I know that Third Squad lost a bunch more. They didn't even mention the rioters we killed. I never kept a count, but I know how much firepower we used down there. I know for a fact that we killed hundreds of civilians—armed rioters trying to kill us, but still PRC residents and NAC citizens. It seems that the news report just mentions the minimum number of plausible casualties for the observable damage on the building, wrapped in the most generic explanation. It doesn't mention a word of the military shooting at civilians down there. I don't have any love for the armed bastards that shot us up and forced us to respond with overwhelming force, but the residence tower has been like a poisoned barb in my conscience ever since I saw those floors pancake onto each other. Not everyone in there was a rioter, but I killed them. By accident, sure, but they're still dead, and I'm the one who pressed the launch button. They didn't blow themselves up with an illegal stim lab. I know that the military knows this—hell, it was recorded on high-definition three-dimensional video by our helmet cameras.

So why do they feign ignorance? Why do they suggest the PRC tower blew itself up by accident?

I recall all the news I've ever seen in the PRC, back when I lived with Mom. If they downplay all the bad stuff like this to keep the pot from boiling over, we must be in much worse shape than I thought.

I get a trip out of the room later that day, which lifts my mood. Corporal Miller has procured a powered wheelchair for me, and after a short introduction into the finer points of power chair operations and hospital traffic rules, she accompanies me on my first trip out of the room.

"Where do you want to go?" she asks as we wheel along the corridor. The hospital is as sparsely appointed as my room—stainless steel furniture, white walls without decorations, and carpeting in cheerless slate gray.

"I don't know. Is there anything worth seeing in this place? Some place that has a bit of color to it?"

"There's a rec room on the top floor, and a cafeteria at the ground level. You can try your hand at some solids if you want. The doctor says your intestinal fusing should be up to it by now."

"That sounds awesome," I say. "Do they have anything worth eating?"

"Oh, yeah. There's your regular army variety of breakfast pastries, and three varieties of coffee," she says with a little smile. "We spare no costs to provide our guests with culinary variety."

"Let's go, then. I'm dying to chew something for a change."

The cafeteria is a bit more cheerful than the rest of the facility. There are some baskets with synthetic flowers set up on the sills of the projection windows. The scene outside the windows is a serene lakeshore, which probably doesn't even remotely reflect the true scenery outside. I know that the Great Lakes don't have much in the way of uncluttered shoreline left, and whatever is left will be in the upper-class suburbs, not near a military installation.

There's a meal counter on one side of the cafeteria. The room looks like a smaller, cozier version of the chow hall back at Shughart. There are small tables all over the room, each just big enough for two people. A few patients are milling about, all in the same green two-piece hospital outfit I'm wearing.

As I roll over to the meal counter, Corporal Miller keeping pace by my side, I hear a familiar voice from one of the tables.

"Grayson, always heading straight for the chow."

I turn to see Sergeant Fallon at a nearby table. She's sitting in a powered chair of her own, and there's a cup of coffee and an empty plate in front of her.

"Hey, Sarge!"

I alter course and veer over to her table. She gives me a tired-looking smile as I pull up.

"I thought you were done for, Grayson. When they put you on the stretcher, you didn't look too good."

"I felt like I was going to check out," I confirm. "The doc says I took two fléchettes through my armor. One nicked the left lung, and the other went through my lower intestines."

"Ouch," she says. "That ought to be good for a Purple Heart."

"I doubt that very much," I say. "I just got chewed out by the battalion S2 for putting a MARS round into that high-rise. I doubt they'll give me any medals any time soon."

"Major Unwerth? He's a worthless fat-ass. I punched him in his stupid face once, back when I was platoon sergeant and he was still a captain. I still can't believe they promoted that useless pile of blubber."

She looks up at Corporal Miller, who has followed me to the table.

"You can leave him with me for a little while, Corporal. Go and take a break or something, why don't you?"

"Sounds good to me," Corporal Miller agrees amiably. "I'll be back in twenty minutes or so. Don't try to do any push-ups while I'm gone, okay?"

"Don't worry," I say. "If you go over to the counter, would you mind grabbing something for me?"

"Any preferences?"

"Whatever looks good," I say.

"No problem."

Corporal Miller walks off, and Sergeant Fallon watches her with tired eyes. The sergeant looks diminished somehow, as if she left part of her substance on the street back in Detroit. I look down at her leg, the one that was mangled by machine-gun rounds back in the PRC, and I recoil a little when I see that it's no longer there. Sergeant Fallon's right leg ends just below her knee, and the surplus material of her hospital trouser leg is neatly folded up and pinned to the thigh.

"Yeah, it's gone," she says when she notices my reaction. "The round turned the bones in my lower leg into shrapnel. There wasn't enough left to piece together. They already fitted me for a replacement. I hear titanium alloy is much better than bone and tissue anyway."

"I thought you got an automatic discharge for an injury like that," I say.

"Not if you have that big-ass medal on the blue neck ribbon," she replies. "Then you can get away with shit. I even get to kill two officers per year, no questions asked."

I laugh and shake my head.

"In that case, I have one to get rid of, if you haven't hit your quota yet."

"Next time that asshole stops by, you ask him for a Legal Corps officer in the room, and you don't say a damn thing until they get you one, you hear?"

I should have thought of that myself, I think.

"I will. He wouldn't even tell me what happened to the rest of the squad, and I can't get on MilNet to send messages."

"No shit?" Sergeant Fallon leans forward. "They locked out your PDP?"

I nod, and she shakes her head in disgust.

"Don't say a thing without a legal beagle nearby, Grayson. They're setting you up to take the heat for something. You didn't do a damn thing wrong back in that shithole, so don't let 'em."

"I'd say that's out of my power, Sarge."

"Oh, we'll see about that. Where'd they quarter you in here anyway?"

"Unit 3006," I say. The low-level sense of panic I had been feeling since Major Unwerth's visit is growing suddenly.

"Stratton and Paterson are dead," Sergeant Fallon says, her voice suddenly flat. "Hansen is in rehab with a new shoulder joint. Everyone else is back at Battalion already, but as far as I know, they're keeping our squad confined to quarters for now, like we're some sort of freaking penal unit."

"My fault, I guess," I say. "Shouldn't have used that rocket. Shit, I didn't even realize I had a thermobaric loaded. I just aimed the thing and let fly."

"And you know what, Grayson? I would have done the same fucking thing, and so would anyone else in our squad. Don't even think twice about it. They got some bad press from the Networks, and now the public liaison at Battalion is all in a panic. It'll blow over."

"I don't know, Sarge. The major seemed pretty set on pinning that tail on me."

"We'll see about that," she repeats. "I may just have a word or two with him. We go way back, Major Unwerth and me."

"If they toss me in the brig, just let the rest of the squad know I'm not a fuck-up, will you?"

"Don't worry," she says. "They try to fuck you over, the whole battalion's going to know about it, trust me on that one. We don't throw our own to the wolves to appease some candy-ass civilian brass."

Her words make me feel a little more at ease, but I still feel as if there's a sword hanging over my head. Sergeant Fallon has a lot of pull in the battalion—there aren't many living Medal of Honor winners in the service, and she's a prestige item, like a trophy in the battalion showcase—but she's still just a staff sergeant.

"Is it true that you got to pick your assignment when they gave you that medal?" I ask.

"Yeah," Sergeant Fallon says. "That's part of the package. You get a yearly bonus for the rest of your life. They give you a nice blue flag in a nice wooden case, and even the brass have to salute you. And if you want reassignment, they have to grant it. You can't ask to be a starship captain, of course, but if I had wanted to be a tank driver or drop-ship pilot, they would have sent me off to armor or aviation school."

"And why didn't you?"

"Didn't want to leave my guys," she says, and shrugs. "Different service would just mean different kinds of crap. I like sticking with the crap I know. I guess I didn't want to feel like a recruit all over again. Shit, can you imagine a staff sergeant going to Fleet School? Sit in a classroom with all those green kids just out of Basic?"

I try to imagine battle-hardened Sergeant Fallon sitting in a lecture on interstellar travel or shipboard safety, with all the other students staring at her Medal of Honor ribbon, and I shake my head with a smile.

"Why didn't you pick retirement? Take your bonus and go home?"

Sergeant Fallon looks at me as if I had just suggested she should strip naked and dance on the table.

"Retire to where? You think anyone musters out after sixty months? Do you know the retention rate in the military?"

I shake my head.

"Ninety-one percent, Grayson. Ninety-one out of a hundred service members who make it to month sixty end up reenlisting.

You think you were going to take the money and run after five years?"

"Yeah," I say. "Doesn't everyone?"

"The money they pay out? That'll pay for shit outside in the real world. You get out as an E-3, maybe E-4, that's half a million dollars for five years. That kind of money means you don't qualify for public housing, and it's not enough for anything bigger than a broom closet in the suburbs. It sure as shit isn't anywhere near enough for a slot on a colony ship. And even if you could go back to the PRC, what the hell kind of reception do you think you'll get as former TA?"

"I don't know," I say. "My father was TA, but he got kicked out early. I don't know any other veterans."

"There's a reason for that, Grayson. Shit, we just killed a few hundred welfare rats last Friday night. How do you think they feel about the military right now? The TA gets sent out every time the welfare cities get out of control. What do you think will happen to you if you show up back home with your shit in a duffel bag, and a government bank card with a million Commonwealth dollars on it?"

I chew my lip at that. What she says makes perfect sense, of course, and I feel like an idiot for not having thought about this before. There are no recent veterans in our PRC—people who leave for Basic never come back. I always figured it was because they didn't want to come back, not because they couldn't.

"No, we were all locked in the moment we signed that paperwork in Basic. You can't go back home after five years, and you don't have enough money to do anything else, so you sign for five more, and then five more. Before you know it, you're a lifer. You go for the ten-year bonus, then the fifteen-year bonus, and then you figure you might as well stick it out for twenty."

She looks at me and circles the rim of her coffee cup with one finger.

"They know that most of us are going to keep reenlisting. And seriously, what the hell are we good for in civilian life? I spent the last eleven years as a combat grunt. I know small-unit tactics. I know how to blow up shit and kill people. Can you see me working as a commissary clerk somewhere?"

"No, I can't," I say. "You'd scare the fuck out of the civilians."

"That's no longer our world, Grayson."

I never meant to return to the PRC anyway. There's nothing left for me in that place, and it stopped being my world the second I stepped on that shuttle to Basic. But I had this nebulously pleasant idea in my head about getting out of the military in a decade or so and being able to afford a place in the middle-class 'burbs, where you don't have to worry about people stabbing you for your weekly box of crummy calories. Now I realize that I had no idea just how radical the break with my former life would be.

"Did I screw up, Sarge?" I ask her. "Did I sign myself away for good?"

She doesn't respond right away, but there's a knowing little smirk on her lips.

"It should be a crime," she finally mutters. "Kids your age, you don't know shit about shit yet. They just dangle the mess-hall steak in front of you, and of course you'll sign the fucking papers."

"So what do I do now?"

"What do you want to get out of the military? What would you ask for if the president put that medal around your neck tomorrow?" Sergeant Fallon asks. She studies me with a slight smile, as if she already knows what I'll say.

"Seriously?"

She nods in reply. "Seriously. Private Grayson, Medal of Honor. Sky's the limit. What would you do with that ticket?"

I don't want to answer, because I don't want to sound like I'm not loyal to my unit, but I find it hard to be dishonest with Sergeant Fallon. So I tell her the truth.

"I'd ask for a slot in a space-going service. Navy, marines, whatever, as long as I get to go into space." If I have to break with my old life, I want that break to be complete, as radical as possible. And I know there's at least fresh air out on the colony planets, not a quarter million neighbors sharing your particular square mile of neighborhood.

"No shit?" Sergeant Fallon raises an eyebrow.

"No shit."

"Well, that's the only way people like us are ever going to get off this shitty rock. I should give you a speech about how the other services suck, but truth be told, I don't blame you one fucking bit."

CHAPTER 14
—URGENT OCCUPATIONAL—
NEED

My PDP still won't let me onto MilNet, but the document reader still works. Most troopers in my platoon only use the reader for field manuals and military reference materials, but I figured out a while ago that it works with any form of electronic text. There are plenty of public repositories for literature out there, and it takes me all of two hours to shovel a small library's worth of classic books onto my PDP.

I'm a third of the way through *Heart of Darkness*, and halfway through my second doughnut, when the door opens and Major Unwerth walks into my room.

"As you were, Private," he says as I wipe my mouth and dump doughnut, napkin, and PDP onto my nightstand. I hate the fact that he's in full Class A uniform and I'm in flimsy hospital garb. The difference in dress makes me feel vulnerable, and the fact that I'm in bed only makes it worse. The only way I could feel more uncomfortable would be if he walked in on me in the bathroom while I'm taking a dump.

"Major," I say. "Did you go all the way to Shughart and back since breakfast?"

"Yes," he says. "I had a meeting with the battalion commander over lunch. I see they're feeding you okay in here."

"Yes, sir. All the luxuries of home."

"Well, good. Do you feel up to a debriefing? I need to get your version of events on the official record."

"I'm pretty sure I'm entitled to having a Legal Corps officer in the room, if you're going to do that, sir."

Major Unwerth makes a face as if he just caught a whiff of something unpleasant. His amiable demeanor evaporates in a blink.

"You're entitled to nothing, Private. You're about three nanometers away from a court-martial, and you can be damn glad I didn't bring a pair of MPs with me to park outside your room and escort you every time you leave to take a piss. I'd keep a low profile if I were you. Now, you can give me your version of the events to record, or I can write down that you refused to give a statement. Come to think of it, I'd appreciate it if you just did that and saved me a bunch of paperwork. I'm getting a bit tired of your attitude."

I've changed my mind about the disciplinary offense. I reach out to grab the major by the lapels of his Class A smock, but before I can get a hold of him, someone yanks him backward violently. I see the look of grim satisfaction on his face replaced by one of shocked surprise.

The major left the door open, and neither of us heard Sergeant Fallon come in. She is out of her powered chair, and even with a missing lower leg, she has the strength and leverage to haul Major Unwerth away from my bed as if he's merely a moderately stuffed combat pack. He falls on his ass in a rather ungraceful fashion, and Sergeant Fallon is on top of him in a blink. She seizes him by the collar with one hand and pins him to the floor. With the other hand, she snatches one of the pens the major carries in the breast pocket of his uniform jacket. She uncaps the pen with a flick of her thumb and presses the pointy end right against the major's throat. Then she brings her face close to Major Unwerth's, until their noses almost touch.

"Listen up, fuckhead," she says. Her voice is so infused with anger that it comes out as a hoarse growl. "That man over there is one of *mine*. He dragged me through half a mile of hostile territory. If I ever hear you talking to him again like he's some green recruit who overstayed his weekend leave, I will tear out your trachea and piss down your neck. Is that understood?"

I can see Major Unwerth's throat move under the tip of the pen as he swallows. There's naked fear in his eyes now, and the sight of it gives me intense satisfaction. Part of me wants Sergeant Fallon to drive the barrel of that pen right through his throat.

Finally, he gives an almost imperceptible nod. Sergeant Fallon releases him and drops the pen in front of him. Her face is contorted with disgust, as if she has just cleaned out a latrine with her bare hands.

"You are out of control, Sergeant," Major Unwerth says. He tries to sound assertive, but his voice is unsteady. "Assaulting a superior officer, *again*. That'll get you drummed out, Medal of Honor or not."

"You can go back and report me," Sergeant Fallon says. "They may even manage to lock me up before I get a hold of you again. In fact, you better hope they do. I'll tell you one thing, though: Every last grunt in the battalion is going to know about the stunt you're trying to pull with Grayson, and then your life won't be worth a bucket of warm piss. Have fun checking the shitter for frag grenades."

"You are out of your mind, Fallon," Major Unwerth says. He stands up and straightens his jacket collar and tie. "You can't threaten me like that. The CO is going to throw you into a cell and throw away the access code."

"Yeah," Sergeant Fallon says. "He might. And think about what lovely headlines that would make for the fucking *Army Times*. 'Medal of Honor Winner Tries to Kill Officer.' There's a morale booster for you. I'm sure the civilian press is going to be all over that one."

She steps in front of him again, and he recoils.

"I don't give a shit, Major. You want to turn me in? Fine. We'll see if the CO is willing to deal with the bad press. But you let Grayson take the fall for Detroit, and I'll make sure your ass is in a body bag before the end of the month."

The major straightens out his tie and jacket. He shoots me a scowl, and then makes eye contact with Sergeant Fallon again. I can almost smell his fear, but he's trying to maintain poise in front of a lowly private and his squad leader.

"The brass at Division is throwing fits over Detroit, Sergeant. The civvies are up in arms. They're still putting out the fires, you know. That rocket took out twelve million adjusted dollars of government property, and thirty-seven civilians. You're out of your mind if you think the battalion can sweep that one under the carpet."

"Make it happen," Sergeant Fallon says. "I don't care how you do it. You sock Grayson with so much as a weekend curfew, you might as well just eat your gun."

"And how the hell am I supposed to do that?"

"Get rid of me," I say.

Major Unwerth and Sergeant Fallon both look at me in surprise. My mind is racing, and I recall the conversation I had with the sarge earlier, about the assignment I'd ask for if I could have a pick. I didn't win a Medal of Honor, but maybe I can give Unwerth a way to wash his hands of me and get me what I want in the process.

"Do what now?" the major asks.

"Transfer me," I say. "Send me to a different service. You get to tell the division brass you've kicked me out, and they have something to tell the civvie press."

"Not a chance," Major Unwerth says. "You can't transfer out of TA."

"Sure he can," Sergeant Fallon says. "They do interservice transfers all the time. Get on the comms with your friends in S1 and make it happen."

"The only way we ever do those is through occupational-needs transfers. Shit jobs. Slots they can't find volunteers to fill." He looks at me, and I can tell from his expression that the idea has gained some appeal to him just now.

"Do it," Sergeant Fallon says to the major. "Do it, or I'll make sure the rest of the battalion knows why I slugged you the first time, before they demoted me."

Major Unwerth just glares at Sergeant Fallon. I have no idea what she has on him, but it must be excellent blackmailing currency, because he bends over, snatches his hat off the floor, and then walks out of the room without another word or glance. He pulls the door shut behind him with emphasis.

"He'll come back with a dozen MPs and have us both thrown in the brig," I say.

"No, he won't," Sergeant Fallon replies. "Trust me on that one. He'll call his buddies and shake loose a few favors. You'll get your transfer, you'll see."

"You must have some shit on him," I say.

"You have no idea."

She doesn't share any more details, but I can see that she's completely unconcerned about just having assaulted and blackmailed the battalion's S2 staff officer.

"Let's just say I had a one-time 'Get Out of Jail' card, and I just used it on your behalf. Now finish your food and take a nap. Don't worry about Major Unwerth anymore. The next time he comes to see you, he'll mind his manners."

The next morning, I find that my PDP has network access again. I'm in the middle of breakfast—scrambled eggs and toast, with a bowl of rice cereal on the side—when I hear the faint chirp that indicates waiting messages in my mail queue. I pull the PDP out of the nightstand drawer and check the screen to see eighty-nine messages waiting for me. More than half of them are official company or platoon announcements, schedule changes, and general bulletins, but the rest of my mail queue is personal stuff, messages from platoon mates checking on my well-being. I scan the incoming queue until I find what I had hoped to see—a message from HALLEY D/SBCFS/LUNA/NAVY. The subject line is "Halfway there."

I open the message with the impatience of a pillhead unscrewing the cap on a bottle of black-market painkillers.

Everything OK? Haven't heard from you in days. Did you pull guard duty on the ass end of your base or something? Anyway, drop me a note. We're officially halfway through Flight School. If you think Sergeant Riley was a hard-ass, you should meet my flight instructor. Tomorrow is my first hands-off flight on the right seat. I'd send pictures if they'd let me take some. Check in, will you? That's an order, Private. (I outrank you now. HA!) —D.

I read her message a few times, just to make sure I can recall it from memory at will if my MilNet access gets turned off again for some reason.

I activate the keypad to write a response. I want to tell her about everything: Friday's domestic call, the squad shot up, Stratton and Paterson killed, my injuries, the court-martial hanging over my head. But as my fingers hover over the keys, I find that I can't write it all out after all. No matter how I arrange the words and sentences in my head, the text does not even begin to convey what's on my mind. The MilNet isn't the right vehicle for that kind of conversation, and once again I don't want to burden Halley with bad news.

I start typing out a reply, this one as vague and nonspecific as possible, despite all the stuff swirling in my head that feels like it will blow off the top of my skull if I don't let off some pressure and share my troubles with someone who's on my side. I tell Halley that I've been laid up in sick bay for a few days, but that I'll be back at Battalion soon, that she's a brown-nosing little instructor pet for getting herself promoted ahead of me, and that it won't matter because I'll be a twenty-star general before the navy abandons all judgment and makes her a genuine officer. They will do just that, of course—on graduation from flight school, they'll promote her to ensign and send her to her first fleet assignment. I may not even be in the TA anymore when that happens, and I'll never know about it, since I won't have access to the MilNet anymore. If they kick me out of the military, Halley will never be able to contact me again, even if she wanted to stay in touch with a wash-out who had a dishonorable discharge around his neck for the rest of his life.

The thought of being back in the PRC, forever pondering the opportunity I lost and being cut off from the only friends I've made since getting out of public school, hits me harder than anything else I've experienced in the last week. The thought of my impending death back on the streets of Detroit-7 wasn't half as bothersome. Even the knowledge of Stratton's death, the squad mate I liked best, doesn't quite shake me like the thought of being back in the place I left, and being doomed to stay there forever after getting a taste of life elsewhere. Everything in the PRC is bland and gray and hopeless, but I didn't even know just how bland that life was until I got to be alive for a while. Half the things we do in the military are tedious, boring, or dangerous, but at least we're alive enough to feel boredom or fear. In the PRC, you have no contrast in emotions. You just wake up every day and feel as inert as the bed you woke up in, just a chunk of public property that'll be broken down and recycled once it falls into disrepair.

I send the message into the MilNet, up to the satellite and then across the quarter-million-mile stretch of space between my hospital room and the Spaceborne Combat Flight School on Luna. Then I shut off the PDP and stow it in the nightstand drawer.

I feel like crying for the first time in many years, and there's nobody in the room to witness it, so I give in to the urge and let the tears come freely.

In the afternoon, I go back down to the chow lounge to see if Sergeant Fallon is around. I spot her in a corner by one of the projection windows, flexing her right knee and looking at her lower leg. When she sees me approaching, she smirks and raps her knuckles on her new shin, which has the dull gleam of anodized metal.

"Titanium alloy," she says as I sit down in the chair across the table from her. "Feels weird, but it's much stronger than the old leg. Maybe I should have the other one replaced, too."

"That was fast. Didn't they just fit you for that yesterday?"

"Day before yesterday. They bumped me to the top of the spare-parts queue. I'll have to suffer some dog-and-pony show with a few people from *Army Times* in return. They're having me do a few weeks of rehab before I get to go back. As if I don't know how to walk anymore all of a sudden."

"Thank you for what you did, Sarge. You didn't have to put your ass on the line for me. Shit, I'm just a private with three months in the battalion. You have a whole lot more to lose than I do."

"Don't talk out of your ass, Grayson," she says, and gives me a hard glare. "There's nobody in the squad worth less than anyone else. You pick up a rifle and stand your watch, you're one of us, and it doesn't matter how many stripes you have on your sleeve. Shit, look at Unwerth—he's a major, and any of you grunts are worth ten of his kind."

"Yeah, well, he still has lunch with the battalion commander, and we don't."

Sergeant Fallon laughs out loud.

"Let me tell you something about the boss," she says. "He's an infantry grunt. He was actually a sergeant before he went to officer candidate school. And he can't fucking *stand* Major Unwerth. Thinks he's just a ticket puncher, which is right on the money, of course."

"Ticket puncher?"

"Those are the guys who go up the chain of command and collect promotion points along the way. When they get a field command, they lead from the rear. And when they've gotten just the bare minimum time in a combat command to be eligible for the next promotion, they get themselves transferred out. When I got into the battalion, Major Unwerth was First Lieutenant Unwerth, and he was my platoon leader. Best officer the SRA had at Dalian, I tell you that."

"Is that when you punched him out?" I grin. The story is legend in the battalion, of course, and like all army stories, it exists in a hundred different variants, each one doubtlessly exaggerated. The mildest versions have Sergeant Fallon storming into the company command post and butt-stroking the platoon leader with her rifle in front of the company commander and the battalion XO.

"Well," Sergeant Fallon says. "I'm under orders from the boss not to tell that story to anyone, least of all to the junior enlisted. Let's just say that he made a bunch of bad calls, and he's lucky he's still sucking down air."

Sergeant Fallon folds the leg of her hospital pants back over the metal of her new lower leg. She never wastes a movement. All her actions are always efficient and to the point. I watch as she folds the bottom of the pants leg exactly three times, tugging the completed fold once to make sure there are no wrinkles in it.

How much can one person push their luck? I wonder. She's survived a lot of dangerous missions, collected a Medal of Honor along the way, and never even thought about quitting, even when she had full retirement offered to her on a silver platter. They blow off half her leg, and she shrugs and goes back to work a few weeks later. This is her job, and she will do it until they shoot something off the medics can't replace. I know I'm not cut from the same cloth as Major Unwerth, but I also know that I am not made from the same stuff as Sergeant Fallon.

"I hate to leave the squad short," I say.

She looks up and smiles at me. Sergeant Fallon's smiles are so rare that she looks like a completely different person for a moment.

"Don't even worry about that, Grayson," she says. "They'll send a few new guys fresh out of Basic. If you can get the army by the balls and make them give you what you want, you have to take the opportunity, because that only happens once in a blue moon. The screwing usually goes the other way."

"I just don't want the squad to think I'm bailing on them, Sarge."

"They won't," Sergeant Fallon says. "I'll let them know what went down."

We look at each other across the table. Something strange has happened since Friday. She's still my sergeant, and I'm still her private, but somehow our relationship has changed. We're still as far apart in rank and position as we were before we dropped into Detroit, but on a certain level, we're equals. In a way, I feel closer to her than to anyone else, even Halley.

"I'll miss them," I say. "I'll miss Stratton. He was a trip."

"He was, wasn't he?" Sergeant Fallon smiles again. "Always running that mouth of his, making jokes about everything and everyone. I'll miss the cocky little bastard. He was a good guy."

We sit in silence for a while. Sergeant Fallon studies her

untouched mug of coffee, while I look at the smooth plastic surface of the table and stare at the spot where my coffee would sit,
had I ordered any.

At the end of the week, I am bored to tears. There's only so much
Network watching my brain can endure before I want to stick a fork
into my ear. The only things that keep me sane are my daily chats
with Sergeant Fallon down in the chow lounge and the messages I'm
exchanging with Halley and my squad mates. I learn that Halley
passed her first flight on the right-hand seat with flying colors. The
right seat is where the pilot-in-command of a drop ship sits, an
arrangement that is the opposite of any other ship class in the arsenal. Apparently, she's a natural with a Wasp.

I also learn that Stratton and Paterson are being buried in their
hometowns this weekend. Stratton is from SeaTacVan, Seattle-
Tacoma-Vancouver, and Paterson grew up in some small city on
Michigan's Upper Peninsula. It's TA tradition that the squad mates of
a fallen trooper provide the honor guard, and the squad leader heads
the funeral detail, but Sergeant Fallon is still in rehab, so Battalion is
going to send the platoon leader instead, Lieutenant Weaving, whose
injuries were light enough for the infirmary at Shughart to handle.
Most of the squad is still on light duty, but everybody opted to go
anyway. Stratton was my best friend in the squad, and I would have
liked the chance to tell his folks how well we got along from the start,
and how he had made me feel at ease when I came into the squad. It's
the kind of thing I figure I would want to know if my son went off to
join the service and came home in a coffin two years later.

On Friday, just before lunch, the door to my room opens again,
and Major Unwerth walks in, immaculately dressed in his ironed
Class A smock.

"At ease," he says as he enters the room. I am fit enough to do push-ups once again, but I wouldn't have snapped to attention for him anyway, but he just said the phrase on autopilot anyway, saving both of us a great deal of discomfort.

He walks up next to my bed, hat tucked underneath his arm. I look up at him and pointedly close my PDP. I was in the middle of composing a message to Halley, and I'm mildly irritated at the interruption, but Major Unwerth still has my fate in his hands, so there's a great deal of anxiety mixed in with the irritation. I am, however, determined not to show this prick any more weakness, so I merely meet his disapproving gaze with what I hope is a neutral expression.

"Here's the deal," he says. "I got you an interservice transfer to the navy."

I feel a sudden buoyancy in my stomach, and it's pretty clear that I can't quite keep the sudden relief out of my face, because Major Unwerth gives me a grim smile.

"However, there are some things you won't like. For starters, your time-in-service counter will reset. That means you'll start with the navy as if you had just finished Basic. Your service time with the 365th won't count towards your fifty-seven-month obligation, or promotion eligibility."

He's correct—I don't like that part at all—but he's setting the terms, and I have a strong feeling that those aren't up for negotiation if I want to get out of TA and into space.

"Also, you'll be going into Neural Networks. That specialty is marked 'Urgent Occupational Need,' so once you finish tech school, you'll be locked into that job for the duration of your first enlistment period."

I try to recall my knowledge of the TA Neural Networks guys, and all I can remember is that it involves sitting on a chair in front of a NN admin console. It doesn't sound at all like exciting or challenging work, but I already know that this is my only way into the navy right now, so I just nod my head.

"Finally," Major Unwerth says, "you leave as soon as you get medical clearance, straight from here. You'll report to Great Lakes for your slot in the next Navy Indoc training cycle, just like a recruit fresh out of Basic. Five weeks of Indoc, and then it's off to your tech school. No going back to Shughart once you sign the paperwork."

That condition is much harder to swallow than the previous two. I don't care about losing the few months of service time I had built up in the battalion, and I don't mind learning how to sit in a chair and hold down a computer console for the rest of my service time, but being excised from my squad with such speed and finality feels like I got shot in the gut all over again. Apparently, I can't quite conceal my sudden dismay, because Major Unwerth frowns at me.

"It's a bit too late for you to change your mind now. I called in a lot of favors for this. Don't think I'll go back and undo all the paperwork now."

"I'll sign whatever I need to sign."

Major Unwerth puts his hat and briefcase down on my bed, all the way by the foot end, and extracts a neat stack of forms from his briefcase.

"Now, I can stand here and let you read all the fine print, if you want, or you can just go ahead and sign, so we can both get on with our lives. There's no hidden clause that will have you smashing ore in a refinery ship, I promise."

From what I know about the major so far, I wouldn't trust his promise further than I can pull a Hornet-class drop ship with my teeth, but I know that he's afraid of Sergeant Fallon, and I also know that the sarge would break Major Unwerth's neck if he went back on his promise. I hold out my hand for the forms, and he hands them to me. I briefly skim the stack of paper—dense legalese, just like our enlistment forms back at Orem—and turn to the last page. There's a pen clipped to the document clasp that holds the forms together.

For the third time in my short military career, I sign a bunch of forms and change my status with the stroke of a pen.

"As of this moment, you're no longer in the Territorial Army, Mr. Grayson."

I nod slowly as I hand the stack of forms back to the major. He tucks them into his briefcase and then looks at me expectantly.

"The PDP is TA property," he says when I shrug in response. "You need to turn it in. They'll issue you a new one in the navy."

I take my PDP, with the half-finished message to Halley still on it, and hand it to the major with numb fingers. The PDP won't reveal my personal files to anyone, and the data is stored on the MilNet directly. As soon as I open my new PDP, my half-written message will be on the screen, exactly at the point where I left off, but it still feels as if I'm handing over my diary to a bully. Major Unwerth takes the PDP and slides it into his briefcase without even glancing at it. Then he takes a folded set of forms out of a side pocket and tosses them onto the bed.

"These are your transfer orders, and that concludes our business. Farewell, Mr. Grayson," he says, and turns to walk out.

"Wait a second," I say. "I don't have my personal gear from Shughart."

"I'll have them send your stuff," he says without pausing. He opens the door and walks out without looking back. He doesn't even take the time to close the door behind him, as if I'm no longer worthy of any expenditure of energy on his part. I watch as he briskly walks down the hallway to the elevators.

Deprived of my PDP, I have no entertainment left, no contact with my squad mates or Halley. I lie down on the thin pillow again and stare at the projection window that is selling me the illusion of a windy autumn lakeshore outside.

I got what I had wanted since I walked into the recruiting office—a slot in a space-going service. When the doctor releases me for active duty, I'll take a military shuttle up to Great Lakes, where all new navy recruits get their initial training, and in six weeks I'll go to my tech school on Luna. I'll finally go into space and see the planet from a few hundred thousand miles away. After my training, I'll travel on an interstellar warship that will take me dozens of light years away from this place.

So why do I feel like I've just been kicked to the curb and abandoned?

CHAPTER 15

—— CAREFUL WHAT YOU ——
WISH FOR

My stuff arrives the next day. The battalion doesn't even bother to send out a staff monkey to deliver my few civilian possessions. Instead, they arrive in a standard military-goods mailer, a little plastic tub that's barely bigger than a meal tray. Inside are the two sets of clothes I had with me when I went off to Basic, the clothes I only wore for my trip to Fort Shughart after that.

It feels weird to see my civilian stuff again. It's my last tangible connection to my old life. One of the sets is the ensemble I wore when I went to see my father—a half-sleeved shirt, a pair of jeans made out of synthetic cotton, and a thin hooded jacket in inoffensive gray. This is flimsy stuff that costs just a few dollars to produce, rags for the peasantry. When I try out my old clothes, I suddenly feel inferior, unworthy, out of place. In a way, I'm back to being nobody: no longer a TA trooper, and not yet in the navy.

I change back into my hospital clothes. As drab and simple as they are, they're a uniform of sorts, and they change me back into somebody who has business being in this room at the military medical center. I no longer feel like a hood rat who has managed to sneak into a place where he doesn't belong.

———

When I get down to the chow lounge for the now customary afternoon coffee with Sergeant Fallon, the spot where my PDP used to sit in my waistband feels unnaturally empty. I didn't fully appreciate just how much I relied on it until they took it away.

"Hey, Sarge," I greet Sergeant Fallon as I sit down across the table from her. She's wearing her dark hair down today, and it's the first time I've seen her without her usual helmet-friendly hairstyle. She looks a lot more feminine this way, and the strands of hair framing her face greatly soften her chiseled features. She's an attractive woman, and if she wore a set of glasses, she could pass for a librarian instead of a soldier, if she wore clothes loose enough to conceal her rock-hard warrior build.

"Hey there, navy puke."

I grin at her salutation.

"Not yet. I have to wait until the doc says that I'm back to normal, and then I have to report to Great Lakes straight from here for the next available training cycle."

"Well, good for you," she says. "So I guess I won't see you again after tomorrow."

"What's tomorrow?"

"They're sending me to a different facility for rehab. A few weeks of some Medical Corps therapist showing me how to walk. I'll be totally out of shape by the time I get back to the battalion."

I'd be willing to bet half my discharge bonus that Sergeant Fallon is doing push-ups and pull-ups in her room every day already. She's not the type to sit on her butt, watch Network shows, and eat pastries for a few weeks. I already pity the poor therapist who almost certainly won't be able to keep up with his new patient.

"The major took my PDP when I signed the transfer paperwork," I say. "I can't get in touch with anyone right now. If you make it back to the squad before the navy gives me a fully enabled PDP . . ."

I don't know whether I want her to tell my squad mates that I'm sorry, or that I miss them, or that I'm ashamed I have to leave them without even saying good-bye, so I don't finish the sentence, but Sergeant Fallon merely nods.

Then she reaches across the table and holds out her hand.

"You're not in my squad anymore. You're not even TA anymore, technically speaking, so we can just go by first names now. I'm Briana."

I take her hand and shake it.

"Andrew, but you knew that already."

It's a bit weird to think of her as *Briana* instead of *Sergeant Fallon*. A week ago, addressing her by that name would have been inappropriate chumminess and borderline insubordination. Now we're just two people, no longer bound by the complex rules dictated by military tradition and protocol.

Still, a part of me will never stop thinking of her as my sergeant. She's the toughest, most competent, and most evenhanded soldier I've known, and she runs her squad as a strict meritocracy. If only a tenth of the military consisted of people like Sergeant Fallon, we would have kicked the SRA off of every inhabited celestial body between Earth and Zeta Reticuli fifty years ago already. As things stand, we're weighed down by people like Major Unwerth, who coast through the system doing only the expected minimum. If a military is the reflection of the society it serves, it's amazing that the Commonwealth is still at the top of the food chain on Terra. Even with all the dead wood in our ranks, we have been able to hold the line against the SRA and the dozens of regional powers in the Middle East and the Pacific Rim that are short on resources and long on grievances with their neighbors.

"I hope I'll see you again," I say. "Can I stay in touch through MilNet?"

"Of course," she says. "And when you get to take your leave, and you end up coming back Earthside for a week or two to visit the folks, stop by at Shughart and drop in on the squad, okay?"

"You can count on it," I reply, even though I know that if I come back to Terra on leave, I'll make a very wide berth around the old homestead.

"Space," she says, in a tone that suggests the idea is the dumbest one she's heard in weeks. "You couldn't pay me enough to be a navy puke, that's for sure."

"You've never wanted to get off Earth?"

"Hell, no." She picks up her plastic coffee mug and takes a sip. "Months at a time, in a big-ass titanium cylinder without windows, getting fat on navy chow, and the only combat grunts on board are freakin' jarheads? No, thank you. I'll stay on this overpopulated ball of shit and slug it out with the Chinese and the Indians, thank you very much. There are still some decent patches of ground left on Terra, you know."

"Yeah, I do," I say, remembering the pristine little middle-class town near NACRD Orem, with its manicured trees and lawns, and the clean, snowcapped mountains rising up in the distance. "I just don't think I'll ever get a shot at living on one, not on this planet."

"So you'll try for twenty years and a spot on a colony ship?"

I shrug in response.

"Colony life is hard, Andrew. You think people are only nasty and mean and violent in the PRCs? You take a thousand of our best and finest, put 'em on a colony ship, fly 'em out past the Thirty, and drop 'em on a newly terraformed pebble by themselves, and you'll see all the shit attitudes from Terra popping up in short order. You'll have the slackers, the self-righteous, the social engineers, the power grabbers, the religious fruit bats, and three months of peace before people gang up in tribes again and start messing with each other's shit. You think people like Unwerth only make it in the military?

I've seen dozens of guys just like him in the civilian world. Imagine some jackass like him as your colony administrator, and the next arbitrating body is a few light years away. Some of those outer colonies only get a visit from the navy once or twice a year, and then it's some old frigate dropping off supplies and checking satellites before skipping the hell out of the system again as fast as they can unload their hold. You get your patch of land, but you're truly on your own, at the ass end of the known galaxy."

She pauses and takes another sip before shaking her head once more.

"That kind of isolation fucks with people's heads, knowing that you're so far away from the rest of humanity that your local sun can go nova, and it'll take a generation before someone on Terra can see the event with a telescope. And then there's the environment. You could end up in a place where ten below is considered a heat wave. Other places, you have three-quarters of the local year without a sunrise, or a sunset."

I don't quite know how to answer. Everything she says sounds true. The colonies are not exactly vacation resorts, despite the fact that the government has to hold lotteries for spots on the colony ships. Just like the military, there are always a hundred times more applicants than slots. Still, there are only a handful of colonies whose population has even broken the million mark, and the idea of sharing a whole planet with a tenth of the number of people living in the Greater Boston area is something I can barely wrap my head around. I don't know if I could handle that much elbow room, that much clean air to breathe, but I'd love to find out.

"I'll put up with a few months of darkness if I don't have to wear another bad air mask for the rest of my life," I finally reply.

Sergeant Fallon gives me a smile that looks a lot like the ones my mom used to give me whenever I said something charmingly innocent and utterly ridiculous as a little kid.

"There's no perfect place, you know. You always end up trading one kind of shit for another. Me, I'll stick with the shit I know."

"Well," I say, "I'm sick of this shit, and I want to try a different kind for a change."

We both laugh. I don't want to think about the fact that I won't see her again after today. I've laughed more in the last two months than I did in the two years before joining the service. My squad mates are the closest thing I've ever had to siblings, and if I have one regret about jumping ship and joining the navy, it's giving up my new circle of friends. I'm sure I'll make new friends in the navy, but I'll be the new guy all over again, the one who has to prove himself.

"Well, I hope it works out for you," she says. "Getting what you want is a rare event in the military, especially at our pay grades. Make the most of it."

"I will," I say. "And if I hear some jarhead talking shit about the TA, I promise I'll pick a fight."

Sergeant Fallon chuckles in approval.

"You better," she says. "And just to make sure you don't forget where you're coming from, I'm going to make sure they put you in for the combat-drop badge. You wear that on your navy uniform, you might as well have a tattoo on your forehead that says, 'I am a former TA grunt.' "

The combat-drop badge is awarded to line troopers after their first drop involving hostile fire. What exactly constitutes hostile fire is up to the discretion of the battalion commander. Some unit COs set the bar rather low, and count drops where the lead drop ship may have taken a round or two of small-arms fire, but the commanding officer of the 365th AIB has higher standards. Still, I have no doubt that anyone who can bend the battalion S2 over a barrel like that would also be able to make good on that promise and have the battalion award the CDB to a private with two battle drops.

"I think you've done enough for me, Surge," I say. Even though I wouldn't mind a CDB above my left breast pocket, I don't want Sergeant Fallon to push her luck with the brass. That Medal of Honor can only get her so much credit with the CO before he decides that she would serve the TA better as a recruiter in some forsaken office in northern Manitoba.

"You shut the hell up, and when that badge comes your way in the interservice mail, you pin it on your navy smock, and you show those desk moppers and console jockeys that you are a combat grunt."

"Yes, ma'am," I say.

CHAPTER 16

INDOC

Being a navy trainee is like being back in school. There are no stern drill instructors like Sergeant Burke, and nobody ever raises their voice at us. Our instructors are navy officers dressed in immaculately starched khaki shirts and slacks.

We live in dorms, with separate rooms for every trainee, and my first night in navy training is the first night since PRC Boston-7 I have spent in a room all by myself. The furniture in my room looks like nobody has used it before. There's a brand-new PDP on my desk when I move into my room, the shelves on the wall are lined with reference materials printed on real paper, and my room even has a private bathroom, complete with shower stall.

Navy Indoc training takes five weeks, and nearly all that time is spent in air-conditioned classrooms. There are physical-exercise sessions every day, but most of them are ball games between different training platoons or companies, and none of the PT sessions involve running up and down the roads of the naval station. Our instructors explain to us that outside runs are restricted because of the abysmal air quality so close to the Chicago metroplex, so we just kick and throw balls to each other in the gym of our "ship."

The first week in training, I suffer a bit of a culture shock from my transition. In Basic, I followed the policy of always running with the crowd, and never sticking out. Here in Navy Indoc, I stick out no matter what I do. My responses to instructor orders are too loud, my salutes are too sharp, and my PT scores are too good. The creases in my uniform are too precise, my shoes too spotless, and my classroom answers too prompt. Not a week into Indoc, the entire training company seems to know that I'm a transfer from the TA.

Sticking to yourself is not difficult in Indoc. We have a regular workday, just like in the TA, and the evenings and Sundays are our personal time. I spend my free time working out in the gym, or staying in my room and reading manuals. Our PDPs are fully enabled, unlike the one I had in Basic, and I spend a lot of time exchanging messages with Halley and my old squad mates. The squad gives me a good ribbing over being a navy puke now, and Halley is simply astonished that I managed to make the jump between services. When I send her the first message from my new node, GRAYSON.A/INDOC/RTC/TERRA/NAVY, she accuses me of playing a very elaborate prank on her. It takes two cycles of replies for her to realize that I am, in fact, in the navy now.

I have no clue how you pulled that one off, but congratulations! she writes.

I'm far away from the 365th AIB right now, and well out of Major Unwerth's reach, but for some reason I don't want to tell Halley about Detroit over the MilNet. It's not just that I don't know who else might be reading our exchanges, but I also find that I'm not able to frame the events in written language. I make three attempts at composing a message, but all of them end up in the electronic trash bin of my new navy PDP. I want to tell her in person. I don't want to rely on a MilNet message, where she can't see my face or hear my voice, to explain why I blew up a building with maybe hundreds of people in it just to save my own life. I'm still not entirely sure I can justify it to myself. Instead, I just tell her a slice of the truth—my squad sergeant managed to pull a few strings for me out of sympathy.

You'll go to Luna for tech school in a few weeks. Are you excited?

Hell, yes, I reply. I'll be the first welfare rat from my block to go into space. Do you get to see Earth from your window, or what?

Nope. Our quarters have no windows. There's a clear panorama wall in the mess hall, but it faces the wrong way. All you'll see is a bunch of stars.

I'll deal with it somehow. Maybe we'll bump into each other up there?

I doubt it. Your tech school is in a different complex from Combat Flight School. They don't give us a lot of time off anyway. But hey, we'll be on the same rock together. Maybe we'll get posted to the same ship.

That would be great, I reply, but I think I just used up all my luck last week, so I won't hold my breath.

In week four, we get a break from the classroom. For the Shipboard Safety Training, we move to another building on the base. This one houses a full-sized simulator of a Lancer-class fleet destroyer. It's a complete and utterly convincing replica, a five-hundred-foot-long hull with navigation lights, antenna arrays, missile-silo covers, and armor plating. The whole thing looks like it could be towed into space and added to the fleet if needed.

Shipboard Safety Training is like starship kindergarten. We learn how to properly move in the narrow aisles and gangways of a navy warship. As big as the destroyer hull looks from the outside, there's very little space on the inside.

There's a lively part of Shipboard Safety Training, and that's the firefighting and evacuation-drill portion. We all get to don sealed vacsuits with oxygen tanks, and the shipboard systems do a convincing job of simulating a major fire on board. We take turns connecting flexible hoses to wall-mounted valves and dragging our fellow students to safety through smoke-filled corridors. Outside the quarterdeck hall, this is the first time I actually get to work up a good sweat in Indoc, and I enjoy doing something physical for a change. I have the feeling that the evac drills are largely a feel-good measure to make the enlisted personnel feel like they have some control over their fates when their ship is on fire and adrift in deep space, but I suppose it's better than sitting on your hands and waiting to burn or suffocate. So I learn how to direct fire suppressant, operate the thermal-imaging gear built into the vacsuit, and search smoke-filled spaces for victims.

We spend a whole day doing emergency drills on the simulated destroyer, culminating with a full pod evacuation from low alert status. Navy ships have life-pod systems that are distributed all over the hull, so that no crew member has more than a compartment or two to cross before reaching a pod in an emergency. When your ship breaks, you're supposed to find a pod, launch away, and hope that the expeller motor doesn't fire the pod into the gravitational pull of a gas giant.

The pods on the simulated destroyer don't launch out of the hull, of course. We rush to the nearest escape hatches, slide down into the pods, and activate the hatch controls. The pod gives a little jolt to simulate a successful launch, and then the exercise is over. I notice that everyone's pod makes it off the ship and into space, and I wonder just how often a pod evac results in a 100 percent evacuation rate. The instructor in charge of the exercise just smiles when I ask him that question on the way out of the simulator, and I draw my own conclusions.

At the end of our fifth week in training, we take a battery of skill tests and written exams to verify that we haven't slept through Indoc, and most of us are pronounced fit to join the fleet. On graduation day, we get to dress up in our new navy dress uniforms and pass in review before the training-division commander. Then they hand us ball caps and declare that we're now welcomed into the fleet.

I receive a merit promotion at the ceremony. The navy grants me a bump to E-2, because I had the highest combined test scores of my training company. I should feel good about finally receiving a promotion and getting a rank device pinned to my bare collar, but all I can think about is the fact that I would have been an E-2 in the TA by now as well. I shake the commanding officer's hand and smile when he puts the E-2 chevron on my collar. I carry the platoon guidon as we march out of the review hall, but I don't feel like I've accomplished anything at all in the last five weeks.

Did you feel a bit let down by Indoc after Basic? I ask Halley through MilNet later that evening.

Sort of, she replies. It was a bit of a snooze, wasn't it?

I just don't feel like I've actually earned those chevrons. That was too easy. Nothing like Basic.

I hear you. Don't worry, things will be different in tech school for you. If yours is anything like mine, you won't have much free time most of the week.

I very much doubt that Neural Networks School is anywhere as demanding as Combat Flight School, but I also doubt that it's as relaxed as Indoc. Anything less formal and strenuous would have to involve the trainees spending all day in their beds and eating hand-delivered meals.

―――――――――

The next morning, I haul my new duffel bag onto a shuttle to Luna.

I've never been religious. My mother was raised Catholic, like two-thirds of the people living in our corner of the Greater Boston metroplex, and she tried to raise me in the faith as well, but I never went to church again after my first communion. Seeing the planet from orbit, however, is the closest I've ever come to having a religious experience. The shuttle takes off, climbs through three hundred thousand feet of ever-thinning atmosphere in ten minutes, and then rolls over onto its back, giving its passengers a perfect view of the planet below through the windows along the dorsal ridge of the ship. Small shuttles like this have no artificial gravity system, and we're strapped into our seats with six-point harnesses. When I feel the pull of gravity lessen, I have to resist the temptation to just unbuckle my harness and push off the floor to bounce around the inside of the shuttle.

From this altitude, Earth looks like a lovely place. I take in the vastness of the planet below, the swirling cloud formations that look like they're floating on the shimmering waters, and the gentle arc of the horizon. I can see the thin, bright layer of atmosphere that separates the brilliance of the planet from the blackness of space, an almost insignificant film of air that keeps out the cold darkness beyond. For the first time since I signed my transfer papers, it occurs to me that this may be the last time I get to see my home world. If I get killed somewhere in the expanses of the explored galaxy, my first glimpse of Earth from orbit will also be my last. Still, nobody back home in my neighborhood will ever see what I'm seeing right now, so even if I die next week, I will have come out ahead.

I've seen pictures of Earth taken from space, but a mere image doesn't come close to conveying the sheer size and majesty of the planet. I take in mountain ranges, lakes, and big swaths of ocean through the windows of the shuttle, and I realize that I've spent all my life confined to just a few square miles of all that vast terrain spreading out below. I've never climbed a mountain or crossed an ocean on Terra, and if things go well for me in the navy, I never will.

I tell myself that there are plenty of colonies out there with mountains and oceans and clean air, and that all those familiar continents below are merely random collections of carbon, but as the shuttle speeds along its path along the curvature of the planet, I admit to myself for the first time that I'll miss the place just a little—not the place where I grew up, the smelly urban mess that is my home city, but the concept of Earth itself, all the places that may have kept me from wanting to go into space, if only I'd had the chance to see them with my own eyes.

CHAPTER 17

——NEURAL NETWORKS——

Neural Networks School is my fourth duty station in eight months. Once again, I am getting used to a new building, a new duty schedule, and a new group of instructors and fellow students. The school curriculum is devoid of anything that doesn't have to do with networking. There's no PT, no firearms instruction, no drilling, and no memorization of rank structures or military history. Instead, we spend eight hours a day learning the functions of a typical shipboard network, and how to manage and control it with our admin decks. Every week, we start a new subject, and every weekend, we have a skill test that covers the material from the week before. I haven't spent this much time in a classroom since public school. With the artificial gravity and the lack of windows, it's easy to forget that we're actually on Luna, and I occasionally have to remind myself when I feel like going for an evening run in fresh air that there's a hard vacuum outside.

The week before graduation, I receive a mail container.

I check for the coded label on the sealed container, and see that it came from the Territorial Army's 365th AIB—my old unit. I remember Sergeant Fallon's promise to send me a combat-drop badge, and I open the seal of the container.

In the box is not just a single award case, but three. I open the first one to find a shiny new combat-drop badge, Basic level. In the second box is a Purple Heart, and the third box contains a Bronze Star.

Underneath the medal boxes, there's a neatly folded message form. I open it and see that it's a handwritten note, penned in Sergeant Fallon's precise block script.

> Andrew,
> Here are some things of yours from the battalion. They're legit, and by the time you read this, they will be reflected in your navy personnel file. Every member of the squad got the same set except for Priest, who missed out on the Purple Heart because he had the misfortune to come out of it without a scratch. I sent Stratton's and Paterson's medals to their folks last week.
> Wear them—you've earned them. The squad sends their greetings.
>
> Best,
> Briana Fallon, SFC, TA

I look at her signature twice before I notice the new rank after her name—SFC, sergeant first class. It looks like they restored her old rank after Detroit.

I take the medals out of their velvet-lined cases and weigh them in my hand. The Bronze Star has a red and blue ribbon with a small, bronze-colored letter V on it, to signify an award for valor. The Purple Heart is the military award for receiving wounds in combat. It's my reward token for a pierced lung and three boring weeks in a military medical center.

The two medals have smaller ribbons in their cases, for wearing on the jacket or shirt of a dress uniform. I take the ribbons out of their spots and walk over to my locker. I pin the ribbons onto the jacket of my Class A uniform, right above the top edge of the left breast pocket. The combat-drop badge, a little silver drop ship in frontal profile flanked by a set of curved wings, goes on top of the ribbons. When all the decorations are in place, I smooth out the front of my Class A jacket with my hand and look at the arrangement for a few minutes, the two ribbons from Basic and Navy Indoc joined by the one for the Purple Heart, and topped with the Bronze Star ribbon and the CDB wings. The ribbons are just thin brass strips covered with a bit of colored fabric, and the badge is merely a piece of chrome-plated alloy. They hold no honor or achievement by themselves.

It feels good to have tangible, official proof that we did our jobs well on the ground in Detroit, but I would trade a whole warehouse full of ribbons and badges for an opportunity to go to the chow hall with Stratton one last time and shoot the bull for an hour over sandwiches and coffee. My old squad mates were the first people my age who seemed to like me—not for the stuff I could get them, or the things I could do for them, like the kids my own age back home. In the PRC, everyone looks out for themselves. On the street in Detroit with my squad, we looked out for each other.

Halley completes her Combat Flight School training three days before I take my final Neural Networks exam. She sends me a message the morning after her graduation to let me know that she passed, and that she's now wearing a brand-new pair of pilot wings.

91% score on the final flight exam, she writes. I am the fucking Mistress of the Wasp.

Congratulations, I reply. When are you getting into the fleet?

Tomorrow. We got our assignments last night. I'll be on the Versailles.

I check my PDP for information on the NACS *Versailles*, and it looks like she's a fleet frigate from an older class. She was commissioned almost thirty years ago, which means that she's just a few years away from the scrapyard.

I didn't even know they had marines on those little frigates.

Just one platoon. One drop ship, and one in reserve. I'll be one of four pilots on that tub.

Well, good for you. Any leave before you ship out?

I had five days, but they cancelled my leave for some reason. They're letting me take it after the next deployment instead. Hey—maybe you'll get some leave by then, too!

That would be nice, I reply, even though I have no idea what I would do with a week or two off.

We could go to some military resort somewhere, and do nothing but eat and screw for a week or two, what do you think?

Halley's reply makes it look as if she had read my mind, and I chuckle at the screen.

That sounds tolerable, I send back. Pencil me in.

Our final exam is a grueling eight-hour marathon session of computer tests and practical problems. We have to use our admin decks to serve requests from fictitious ship officers, and fix a series of ever-more-complex simulated network problems. The final test is the solving of a total environmental control failure in fifteen minutes, before the crew suffocates. Most of us figure out the source of the problem—sabotage by virus—but a few of the trainees don't find the solution in time and fail the exam, to be recycled into the next training flight.

At the end of the day, there's the obligatory graduation ceremony, and I'm glad to see that it doesn't involve parading in front of a flag officer in dress uniform. Instead, our section commander pins

Neural Networks admin badges on our shirts, shakes our hands, and orders us down into the chow hall for a graduation party.

We all gather in the building's galley, mingle with instructors, and drink crappy alcohol-free beer. Everybody is anxious to learn their assignment, and our instructors don't keep us in suspense for long. One of the petty officers brings in a large plastic tub, and as we crowd around it, we can see a bunch of little white cylinders at the bottom.

"Each of those has the name of a ship on it," our commanding officer explains. "We will call roll, and each of you will step up and pull a name out of the bowl. We do it this way so everybody gets the same chance to get on one of those luxury cruise ships you all want to serve on."

The ships in need of new Neural Networks personnel range in size from small escort corvettes to giant assault carriers, and every-thing in between: frigates, destroyers, supply ships, space control cruisers, and deep-space reconnaissance ships. When it's my turn to draw a ship, I mask my nervousness by quickly reaching into the tub and popping the cap off the cylinder before giving myself time to think about the process. I shake out the slip of paper and read the name of my new ship out loud to the assembled crowd.

"NACS *Polaris.*"

There are whistles and hoots all over the room as soon as I say the name of the ship.

"Damn, Grayson," the petty officer in charge of the tub says with a grin. "Pulled the jackpot ticket."

I raise an eyebrow and reach for my PDP, but the trainee standing to my right supplies the information eagerly.

"She's a brand-new assault carrier. Newest and biggest ship in the navy, one of the new Navigator class. That's the most advanced ship in the fleet, Grayson."

I tuck the slip of paper into my shirt pocket and take another swig of my drink as the next trainee is called to the lottery bowl to draw his assignment.

We're almost at the end of the lotto when one of the students pulls a ticket out of her cylinder and announces her new assignment to the rest of us, and I feel a jolt of surprised shock when I hear the name of her ship.

"NACS *Versailles*."

There's general groaning as our classmates consult their PDPs and find out that the *Versailles* is a tired little frigate from a now obsolete class that has long been superseded by more capable designs.

"That's a rust bucket," someone chuckles, but I don't feel like laughing. Instead, I walk up to her as she steps away from the table, a dejected look on her face.

"Trade with me," I tell her, and she looks at me in wide-eyed surprise.

"Are you joking?" she says. "Didn't you pull the *Polaris*?"

I pull the slip of paper out of my pocket and hold it up for her to see.

"I did. What do you say? I'll trade you my assignment for yours."

"Are you serious? Why would you trade that ship for a frigate?"

"I have a friend on the *Versailles*," I reply.

"Oh." She looks at the nearest instructor, her expression a mix of incredulity and sudden excitement. "Can we just do that, trade off assignments?"

"I don't see why not. They're not finalizing our orders until tomorrow anyway. Ask one of the petty officers."

She walks over to one of our instructors and exchanges a few quiet words with him. When she comes back to where I'm standing, I can tell the instructor's response by the excitement in her face.

"He says it's no problem, as long as we both agree."

"Well, I agree. How about you?"

"Are you kidding? Hell, yeah, I agree."

I hold out my hand, and she gives me her paper slip. I hand her mine, the ticket to the most advanced warship in the navy. She takes the slip gingerly, as if she suspects a last-minute hoax on my part. Then she walks off, looking over her shoulder with an expression that clearly implies I must have lost my marbles. Maybe I have, but thinking about being close to Halley again, smelling her scent and hearing her laugh, gives me a kind of excitement that I don't want to trade for the vague promise of better rec facilities and cleaner mess halls.

The next morning sees me packing up my things and stuffing them into a duffel bag again. The staff office has our final orders ready, and we all file in one by one to pick up our official printouts. We're all dressed in our Class A uniforms, because that's the required smock for reporting to a new unit, and I notice a few of my fellow trainees glancing furtively at the small collection of ribbons above my left breast pocket.

All of us have assignments on navy ships, so we board shuttles to Gateway Station.

The *Versailles* is docked in a far corner of the Gateway fleet yard. I have to traverse what seems like miles of increasingly narrow and dirty corridors before I finally reach the docking collar that says NACS *Versailles* FF-472 on the sign above it. There are two marines guarding the airlock, both wearing the marine corps version of ICU battle dress and carrying sidearms in thigh holsters.

"I'm new to the ship," I say, and hand my orders form to one of the marines. "Where can I find the XO?"

The marine looks at my order printout and looks at my breast pocket.

"Uh, try the CIC. You the new Networks guy?"

"Yes, sir."

"Go through the lock, follow the gangway to the central fore-and-aft corridor, and turn right. You'll get to an elevator bank. Ride down to Deck Five. CIC will be straight ahead as you step out of the elevator."

"Thank you, sir."

I take my orders form back, pick up the duffel bag I had rested on my foot, and render a sharp salute in textbook TA fashion. The marine corporal salutes back, and I step past him into the airlock to set foot onto my new ship for the first time.

The *Versailles* is showing her age. She has a patina of wear almost everywhere. The flooring in the gangways is smoothed out from decades of constant foot traffic, and the markings on the bulkheads and walls look like they have been refreshed and painted over many times. The interior of this ship is a little more cramped and a lot more worn than the fleet-destroyer simulator back at Great Lakes. As old as the ship is, however, every deck and gangway is neat and clean. The floors are worn, but there are no supply crates and broken equipment piles in the corridors like at Gateway.

I take the elevator down to Deck Five. CIC, the combat information center, is hard to miss. It's a big, circular room that takes up a big chunk of the deck. The hatches and windows are armored, and I can see the telltale synthetic gasket of an autonomous environmental system on the edges of the open entry hatch. This is the battle station for the ship's captain and the senior staff officers, one of the best-protected parts of the ship.

I hand my orders form to the marine guarding the CIC hatch. He studies it briefly and waves me on.

"Leave your gear out here," he says, and nods at my duffel bag. "The skipper hates it when people drag their kit into CIC just to report in."

"No problem." I take the duffel bag off my shoulder and slide it up against the wall, away from the hatch.

There are enlisted crewmen sitting at consoles all along the periphery of the room. The center of the CIC is a sunken floor space with a large holotable in the middle. There are three officers standing in a small group on one side of the holotable, holding a discussion in low voices. One of them looks up when I step into the center of the CIC. He's a tall man with the sharp and angular features of an infantry grunt just out of some hard training regimen. He's wearing the gold leaves of a lieutenant commander on the collars of his khaki shirt, which makes him the highest-ranking officer of the small bunch. I walk up to him and render a snappy salute across the holotable.

"NN2 Andrew Grayson, reporting for duty, sir."

The lieutenant commander returns the salute with an expression that's not quite a frown. His name tag says "CAMPBELL T," and he's wearing no decorations on his shirt other than the space-warfare badge in gold.

"Mr. Grayson," he says when I finish my salute and lower my hand. "You supposed to be our new Networks guy?"

"Yes, sir. Just finished Networks School yesterday."

Lieutenant Commander Campbell shares a pointed look with the lieutenant standing next to him. "Well, Mr. Grayson. Welcome aboard, I suppose. I'm your new executive officer. Would you walk with me for a second?"

"Of course, sir."

I follow the lieutenant commander out into the corridor.

227

When we are far enough to be out of earshot of the CIC, he stops and turns to face me.

"Every deployment cycle, I get a few crew members who decide to spruce up their smocks a little to impress the boys or girls at the rec facility on Gateway. Now, before we start off on the wrong foot here, would you mind telling me what you're doing, coming fresh out of tech school with a valor award, a drop badge, and a freakin' *Purple Heart*? And if you don't have a good explanation, I'm willing to give you exactly five seconds to pull those things off your jacket before the command master chief sees them and has the master-at-arms toss you into the brig for wearing unearned awards."

I feel my face flush with embarrassment, and a moment later I chide myself for feeling shame at the XO's accusation.

"That's a negative, sir. Those are legit. I'm an interservice transfer, from the Territorial Army. Have the chief check my personnel file."

Lieutenant Commander Campbell looks at me with a raised eyebrow.

"No shit?"

He pulls his issue PDP out of his pocket and starts tapping on the screen.

"No need to ask the chief. I can pull up your file right here and now."

I wait as he digs through a few layers of menus on his screen. He studies the screen for a few moments, and lets out a low chuckle.

"Well, I'll be dipped in shit."

He turns off his PDP and stows it. Then he extends his hand to me.

"I do apologize, Mr. Grayson. I've been the XO on this boat for two years, and I've never had a transfer from TA before."

"Not a problem, sir," I say. "No apology required."

I shake his hand, the discomfort at having put my new XO on the spot mixing with the sense of vindication I feel.

"Grab your gear, and I'll unlock your new office for you."

The Neural Networks Center is a secured room in the aft section of the ship. It's located on Foxtrot Deck, near the engineering section and well away from the CIC and the crew quarters. Lieutenant Commander Campbell unlocks the armored hatch of the NNC, and I step into the room behind him. There's an admin console and a pair of chairs near the front of the room, and the rest of it is taken up by banks of neural-processing units and data-storage modules.

"This is all yours now," the lieutenant commander says. "We are supposed to have three Networks admins—ideally. You were going to be number two, but my Networks petty officer came down with something on our last cruise. We've been without a Networks admin for a few weeks now."

"I won't have a petty officer at the top of the department? Who's going to be my supervisor?"

"You'll be reporting directly to me," Lieutenant Commander Campbell says. "I could put you under the engineering chief, but he knows about as little about neural networks as I do, so we might as well streamline the chain a bit. You're now your own department head. Don't get too excited, though—if something breaks, you're the one who will get the blame."

"I'll manage, sir."

"The good news is that your job is technically an NCO billet. Impress me, and you'll have a good shot at some petty-officer chevrons as soon as you have the time in service."

"Understood, sir," I reply.

"Very good. Now let me set you up with your access credentials, and then we'll have the command master chief find you a place to sleep."

––––––––––

The single cabin I'm assigned is nowhere near as spacious and well appointed as my room at Networks School, but it beats the three-to-a-cabin arrangements most other junior enlisted ratings have to share. I have a cot that folds out of the way, a bathroom nook with a toilet, and a desk and chair that are bolted to the floor, just like the furniture in my room back at the PRC on Earth. Out here, the practice has a different reason, of course—rather than preventing theft, the navy wants to minimize damage by untethered heavy objects if the ship gets jostled hard. I fill up my new locker with my belongings and then change from my Class A dress uniform into the far more comfortable black-and-blue working uniform all the enlisted crew members are wearing for everyday duty. Then I sit down at my desk to do what I've been itching to do ever since the lieutenant commander enabled my network access—I check the ship's personnel-movement roster for Ensign HALLEY D.

Halley is assigned to the *Versailles*'s combat-aviation section, a grand title for a pair of drop ships and a spare ship in storage. The ship's personnel-movement system tracks everybody on the *Versailles* through the low-power RF chip embedded in their dog tags, and the computer tells me that Halley is in a briefing room on Foxtrot Deck right now.

By the time I find my way around the ship and down to the right corridor, the briefing in F5103 is over. I pass the room's open hatch and try to look casual as I sneak a peek inside, only to see rows of empty chairs. I keep walking, not wanting to stop on the spot to pull out my admin deck and check on Halley's new whereabouts.

As I walk around a bend in the corridor, I almost collide with a group of pilots in dark-green flight suits standing in front of a bulletin board on the corridor wall right past the bend.

"Whoops. Excuse me," I say as I stop on my heels, a millisecond before I see that Halley is part of the little group. She stops her conversation with the pilot standing next to her and looks at me in sudden, wide-eyed surprise. This is not exactly the way I had planned to reveal my presence on the *Versailles* to her, but she's only three feet away from me now, and there's no chance to rehearse and do this over.

For a moment, I am sure that she'll simply give me a nod and a low-key "hello," so her fellow officers won't know that she's socializing with an enlisted crew member, but Halley quickly disavows me of that notion.

"Huh," she says, sounding like someone who has just found a lost and forgotten commissary note in her pocket.

Then she crosses the distance between us in one step, grabs me by the front of my shirt, and shoves me back against the corridor wall before kissing me on the lips. Behind her, the other pilots stare and chuckle.

"Holy fuck, Andrew, what are you doing here?" she says when she finally lets go of me. My lips are now pleasantly tingly with the sensation of the unexpected contact.

"I got transferred," I say. "I'm your new Networks admin."

"Huh," she says again, and pulls me close for another kiss.

I don't resist.

"I'm off my watch in fifteen minutes," she says. "Are you free?"

"I'll be getting settled in the NNC," I say. "You know where that is?"

She shakes her head in response.

"This deck, Foxtrot 7700."

"Fifteen minutes," she says. "Hope you're rested."

"Yes, ma'am," I reply.

CHAPTER 18

VERSAILLES

Our ship leaves Gateway Station two days after I join the crew. By the time we clear our moorings, I'm tapped into the vitals of the *Versailles* enough that I don't have to ask where we're going, or what we're going to be doing. The *Versailles* is tasked with a supply-and-mail run to the NAC colony on the planet Willoughby. It's a recently terraformed planet that's orbiting one of the stars in the Auriga constellation. Its astronomical notation is Capella Ac. The marine designation is "dirt speck at the ass end of the known galaxy." Halley, who got top grades in astronomy and astrophysics back in Fleet School, asserts that this is not quite true, since the Capella system is only forty-two light years from Earth—well past the thirty-light-year line that separates the inner from the outer colonies, but well short of the settled fringe, which is sixty-one light years away. Capella Ac—Willoughby—is not the ass end of settled space, but it's definitely located well below the neck.

It doesn't make much of a difference to me, of course. I'm about to leave the solar system for the first time, and even though the *Versailles* has no windows in its hull, I have a great time sight-seeing through the sensors and optical feeds of the ship. As old as the ship is, her network hardware is in great shape, and I have very little to do other than monitoring the shipboard systems and running self-checks on occasion. Traveling on a spaceship is not at all

233

like I imagined it. The lack of outside visual references combined with the artificial gravity of the ship itself makes for smooth travel, and if I didn't know I was on a space-going vessel, it would feel no different from sitting in a classroom on Luna or Earth. The first few days of our journey, I tap into the external feeds from the hull cameras, but after we leave Gateway Station, there's nothing to see out there other than blackness and the occasional distant star.

Halley spends her watches with briefings, simulator training, and other pilot business. I spend my watches in the NNC, ready to take complaints and fix things in case the galley dispensers fail to communicate their need for resupply to the ship's supply clerk. That leaves seven and three-quarters of an eight-hour watch to poke around in the ship's data banks, or see if I can get a glimpse of my girlfriend through one of the security vid feeds.

Halley seems to be flattered rather than offended when I tell her that I've been stalking her through the ship's security system.

"You must be bored as hell in this office, you poor thing," she says. "Too bad we don't have security cameras in the officer showers on Deck Three, or I'd give you something better to look at than me walking the corridors with my ass looking all unflattering in that green flight suit."

"Nothing wrong with the way it looks in that flight suit," I say. We're in the NNC, where Halley has started to seek refuge whenever she needs a quiet place to do paperwork, or talk about something other than drop ships, approach vectors, and docking procedures.

"Oh, you think so? Lieutenant Foster agrees with you, I think. He's been a bit grabby lately."

"Any of your officer buddies say anything about the fact that you're poaching among the enlisted crew?"

"Fuck, yeah," she says. "But it's not like they have a leg to stand on. Foster and Rickman are both doing the same. Foster's screwing some petty officer from Propulsion, and Rickman has the hots for one of the purple shirts from the flight deck."

"Purple—what's that, refueling?"

"Yeah, gas monkey. Red is ordnance, yellow is wrench spinners."

"How elitist. What do you fancy pilots call the Networks admins?"

"No idea what they call the other ones, but you're 'that lucky fucker,' according to Lieutenant Rickman."

"Well, good to know I get to best him at one thing, at least," I say.

Halley's PDP vibrates on the tabletop in front of her, and she picks it up with a sigh to read the message on the screen.

"Speak of the devil. I'm being summoned to the pilot briefing room. I'll see you tonight after your watch?"

"You bet," I say. We can't do dinner together because we eat in different galleys—they'd kick me out of the officer galley, and give her strange looks for eating in the enlisted mess—but I have a private cabin, a rare luxury on a warship, and we spend a lot of our free time in there.

"Later, computer jock," she says, and gives me a quick kiss.

"Later, pilot babe," I reply.

I watch as she walks through the hatch and into the hallway beyond. There's definitely nothing wrong with the way her backside looks in a flight suit.

I'm on the way to the enlisted galley when I hear my job title on an overheard 1MC announcement.

"Neural Networks admin, report to XO in CIC. Neural Networks admin, report to XO in CIC."

I reverse course and head to the staircase that leads down to Deck Five.

The CIC is busier than it was when I set foot into it for the first time. The XO is once again standing by the holotable, looking over a stack of printouts. I walk up to the table and render a salute.

"NN2 Grayson reporting as ordered, sir."

The lieutenant commander looks up from his printout.

"Ah, Mr. Grayson."

He puts the stack of paper aside and waves me closer.

"At ease. Mr. Grayson, how far away is this ship from the nearest communications relay at present?"

"Three and a half light minutes, sir—the orbital relay above Mars."

"Very good," he says. I'm pretty sure that he knew the answer to his question already, and that he just wants to check whether his new Networks admin is on the ball.

"We'll be entering the Alcubierre chute to Capella shortly," he says. "Please make sure you check your pre-FTL procedures, and that all the data banks are fully synchronized with the main network before we go FTL."

"Yes, sir," I say. "I'll get right on it."

"Very good. Report network readiness to me directly by 1800 hours, please."

"Aye-aye, sir."

I don't know much about our drive systems for interstellar travel. I do know they're called Alcubierre drives, and that a ship traveling in an Alcubierre bubble can't send or receive any messages, because it outruns even the near-light-speed data traffic. Before an Alcubierre trip, every navy ship synchronizes all its onboard data with the in-system network. I learned to run the process in Networks School, and it's just a matter of telling the computer to do it, but navy regs still require the results of the sync to be double-checked twice by the Networks admin on duty, and verified by the next senior department head up the command chain. I find that most of my daily duties consist of babysitting an automated process and standing ready to get my head bitten off if I fail to catch any errors.

Back in the NNC, I open my admin deck, tap into the system, and start the automated protocol for pre Alcubierre preparation. While the data banks synchronize with the nearest navy communications relay to make sure we're not going to deliver last month's mail by accident, I go through the manual to make sure everything is going right. I suppose I should feel a little intimidated or overwhelmed by the fact that I'm running a department that should be staffed by two enlisted admins and a petty officer, but the truth is that everything is so automated that anyone with the ability to read a few checklists could run the NNC from their rack. Still, I don't want to give the XO a reason to start disliking me, so I go by the book and hand-check every data-bank-replication time stamp when the computer indicates that the process is finished. Then I hit the communications switch on the console next to the desk.

"CIC, Networks."

"Networks, CIC. Go ahead," comes the reply.

"Networks reporting ready for Alcubierre transition. All data banks synchronized and verified."

"CIC copies Networks ready for Alcubierre transition."

With the level of computer integration on the ship, I have no doubt that CIC was aware of the network status the moment the update finished, but this is the military, and everything has to have its proper procedure and ritual, like a kabuki theater with uniforms. There are the right gestures, phrases, and movements to be observed, and everybody plays along because that's just the way it's done.

I tell the admin deck to locate the RFID signature belonging to the dog tags of Ensign HALLEY D. The system finds her RF chip in the officers' mess, and I tap into the camera feed to see her at a table with her officer pilot friends, eating sandwiches and discussing something. I take out my PDP and dash off a message to her.

Mind sitting on the other side of that table, so I can get a better view of your ass? This camera angle is kind of crummy.

I send the message and watch the camera feed with a grin. Halley sits up slightly and removes her PDP from the leg pocket of her flight suit without interrupting the conversation with the lieutenant sitting next to her. I watch as she reads the message on her screen. Then she looks up, searches for the lens of the camera on the ceiling, and scratches her nose with her middle finger.

I smile and send another message her way.

You'll have to wait until my watch ends, I'm afraid.

I don't like the transition to Alcubierre. When the ship enters the chute and turns on its Alcubierre drive, every bone and muscle in my body suddenly develops a low-level discomfort—not exactly an ache, but a disjointed feeling, as if some gentle, yet irresistible force is trying to pull every molecule in my body into all directions at once. My joints and teeth feel loose in their sockets, and my skin prickles with an unpleasant sensitivity. A few hours of discomfort are probably much easier to suffer than the boredom of spending a few years on an interstellar journey, but I can already tell that Alcubierre transitions are going to be my least favorite part of traveling on a starship.

Navy ships are at combat stations when they go in and out of Alcubierre chutes because their entry and exit points are fixed in space. The location of the navy's transit points is a secret, of course, lest the Sino-Russians simply mine our exit points to ambush our ships when they finish their Alcubierre trips, but every military has its intelligence service, so there's always a chance of a welcome committee of SRA destroyers waiting for us as we transition back into normal space. Thirty minutes before the end of our Alcubierre run, the *Versailles* goes to combat stations once again.

"Stand by for transition," the all-hands announcement comes from the CIC. "Transition in *ten . . . nine . . . eight . . . seven . . .*"

We transition back into normal space a mere twenty light minutes from Capella A, and forty-two light years away from Terra. There's no welcoming committee of SRA warships waiting to blow us out of space. I feel the moment the Alcubierre drive shuts down because the low-level discomfort I've been feeling for the last twelve hours is suddenly gone. The screen of the admin deck in front of me shows that the ship's neural network has already started its battery of post-transition integrity checks. I divert a tiny bit of system time to show me the feed from the ship's optical arrays on the outside of the hull, but there's not much to see out there. Capella A looks a lot like our own sun—a tiny, washed-out yellow orb in the distance—and I can't make out any other celestial bodies at all. The Capella A system doesn't look very different from our home system—vast stretches of nothing, punctuated by the glimmer of distant stars.

Out of curiosity, I check the navigational plot. The exit point of the Alcubierre chute into Capella A is much closer to our destination than the chute's entry point from Earth. We are just fifteen light minutes from Capella Ac—Willoughby—and we will be in orbit in just a few hours. The ship's long-range sensor grid shows a whole lot of nothing between us and Willoughby. It looks like we're the only starship around, NAC or otherwise.

"All hands, secure from combat stations. The watch schedule will now resume," the XO announces overhead. "Welcome to the Capella system."

We start our orbital approach to Willoughby right at the end of my watch. I'm tired and hungry, but I decide to stay in the NNC for a few more minutes to witness our approach to the first extrasolar planet I've ever seen.

I'm looking at the feed from the dorsal array when the hatch buzzer sounds. I walk over to the hatch and peek through the viewport to see Halley's face.

"Hey, you," she says as I unlock the hatch for her. "Mind if I duck in for a few minutes? I want to fill out this flight log without Lieutenant Rickman chewing my ear off."

"Sure thing," I say, and wave her in. She steps through the hatch and lets herself drop onto one of the chairs in front of the admin console.

"Isn't your watch over?" she asks. "It's 2230."

"Yeah, I'm off. I just wanted to hang around to watch us go into orbit. Here, check it out."

I point to the screen of my admin deck. She leans forward to look at it, and puts her flight log aside.

"Wow. That's Willoughby? I didn't realize we were already this close."

"We'll be in orbit soon. Aren't you supposed to play taxi with those drop ships of yours?"

"Yeah, but not until 0600 tomorrow morning. I guess they're not set up for nighttime deliveries down there."

We look at the globe of azure and brown that's slowly shifting around underneath the ship. It looks a lot like Earth, but there's also something profoundly different about Willoughby. I've seen the familiar picture of Terra from orbit often enough that looking at a planet with completely different continent shapes feels a bit disorienting.

"Look at that," Halley says. "Continents, and oceans, and everything. Looks a lot like Earth, doesn't it? Do you think they have wildlife down there?"

"I have no idea," I reply. "I don't know how that terraforming thing works. Did they get to bring livestock from Earth when they set up the colony?"

"Maybe in a tube, as genetic samples or embryos. I doubt they would have wasted the cargo space on that colony ship for a herd of live cattle. Do you have any idea how much it would cost to transport a whole cow forty-two light years across the galaxy?"

The ship lurches to the side so hard that I lose my footing and stumble against one of the data bank racks. Halley lets out a surprised shout.

"What the fuck was that?" I ask when I regain my balance.

The overhead lights flicker, and switch to the red-orange combat-lighting scheme. The overhead starts to announce combat stations, but whoever's doing the announcement in CIC only makes it halfway through "combat . . ." before the audio cuts out with a squelch. Then there's the sound of explosive decompression coming from the deck below us. The ship lurches again, much more violently than before, and the sudden jolt throws me into another rack of equipment. The side of my head collides with the unyielding edge of a data storage cabinet, and then I'm prone on the rubberized deck and rapidly slipping into unconsciousness. I hear Halley screaming, and I register the thumping of the emergency locks on the NNC hatch, and then my brain turns off the lights.

CHAPTER 19

————GETTING OUT————

I wake up to the sensation of cool air hitting my face. The right side of my head feels wet and sticky, and when I touch my fingers to my forehead, I feel a deep, bloody gash over my right eyebrow. It's dark, and eerily quiet. All I can hear is the familiar soft humming of the data storage racks. I look up to see Halley standing above me.

"On your feet, sailor. We're in deep shit."

She looks at the gash on the side of my face and winces sympathetically.

"That looks awful. You okay?"

"Yeah," I say. "I'll live."

My admin deck is on the floor over by the rear bulkhead. I walk over to it and pick it up to find that the deck is still running, none worse for the wear. I put it back onto the desk in front of the admin console. Then I lean over to press the button on the priority voice link to CIC.

"CIC, Networks."

There is no reply, and Halley shakes her head.

"Already tried that. The circuit's fried. I haven't heard shit over the 1MC, either. Place is quiet as a tomb."

I tap into the system with the admin deck, and it doesn't take long for me to realize that the *Versailles* is profoundly broken.

Virtually every vital subsystem shows a long string of emergency alerts and error messages.

"Holy shit," I say. Halley steps next to me to look at my admin deck's screen.

"What is it?"

"Power circuits are out—everything down to the tertiary. That's not supposed to happen, ever. We're running off our backup power cells."

"What about the reactor?" she asks. I check the engineering section, and an unwelcome feeling of dread gives my stomach a little twist.

"It's out. We're dead in space. This is not good."

"Yeah, I kind of figured we're in deep shit."

I scroll down the list of priority system messages, and my feeling of dread turns into borderline panic.

"The 'abandon ship' order came twenty fucking minutes ago."

"Holy shit," Halley says again. "How long were we out?"

"Almost an hour, it looks like."

Halley walks over to the hatch and pounds on the control box with her fist.

"We got a red light," she says. "Not enough breathable air on the other side. It won't let us open."

"Well, how the fuck are we going to get out of here? I'd rather not suffocate on this can, you know?"

"Chill out, Andrew. Check your toy, and let's figure out how to get out of this room before the air runs out."

I check the system for the location of the nearest unused escape pod, only to unearth more bad news.

"Fuck. They're all gone."

"What's all gone?"

"The pods. They all launched. There's not a single escape pod left in the hull. The last one launched seven minutes ago."

Halley throws her hands up in an exasperated gesture that looks almost comically understated, considering our circumstances.

"Well, isn't that just fucking awesome."

"I can blow the lock on that hatch remotely with the admin deck, I think, but we won't have any air to breathe."

"Or any way off the damn ship." She pauses for a moment, and then snaps her fingers.

"Can you see if the drop ship is still on the flight deck?"

"Yeah, hang on."

I flick through a dozen status pages and submenus until I reach the optical feed from the flight deck camera. The feed shows an empty set of docking clamps over a sealed drop hatch. The flight deck is empty and dark.

"It's gone. Looks like your pals left without you."

"Well," Halley says. "Then that's that."

"Don't you guys have more than one drop ship on this tub?"

I see excitement in her face, which is a lot better than the fear that was there just a moment ago.

"Yeah, the spare. It's in the far corner of the flight deck, in a berth. Can you see that on the camera feed?"

I cycle through all the visual feeds from the flight deck. Finally, one of the overhead camera lenses gives me a perfect oblique view of a Wasp-class drop ship.

"There it is. Looks like they didn't want to take the time to fire that one up, too."

Halley leans over my shoulder and studies the screen.

"That bird is dry and bare—no fuel, no ordnance. Even if we can lock it into the clamps and drop it out of the hatch, we'll go in ballistic. We're too close to that planet."

"Well," I say, "isn't the refueler automated?"

"Yeah. The ordnance monkeys have to load the ammo by hand, but the computer does the refueling. I have no idea how to work it, though. They usually have it filled up and ready by the time they hand me the keys, you know."

"Well, I don't know how to do it, either, but I bet the computer does."

For a minute or two, I dig through the systems that are still talking to the neural network, expecting the automated flight deck modules to be offline, or the system objecting to my poking around with a security lockout. Luckily, neither event comes to pass. The refueling module on the flight deck is active and idle, waiting for human input. I log into the refueling console remotely, and point to the screen of my admin deck to draw Halley's attention to the menus.

"That's gotta be the one," she says, tapping the screen over the menu item that says "READY FIVE LAUNCH PREP."

"Good thing they label their stuff clearly," I say, and activate the sequence. The menu status changes to "INITIATED/IN PROGRESS," and I switch back to the optical feed to make sure that something is really happening down on the flight deck. Near the drop ship, a warning strobe starts flashing. As we watch, the robotic arm of the refueling module comes into view and swivels around the Wasp to dock with the refueling port in the top of the hull.

"That takes care of the gas," I say. "How long does it take for the tanks to fill up?"

"Ten minutes," she replies. "Another five to fire up the avionics and do the preflight self-checks, and two to move the whole thing over to the drop hatch."

There's a low rumble going through the hull that makes the floor shake slightly underneath our feet. Over by the data storage modules, something starts to beep, and all the lights in the room go out briefly. When they come back on, all the storage banks in the NNC fall silent at once. I've never been in this room without hearing the drone of the cooling elements for the storage banks, and the lack of background noise is ominous.

"I think your shit just broke," Halley says flatly.

"Yeah, no kidding," I reply.

My admin deck is still running, and the local telemetry is still up, but the link to the hangar bay systems is gone. The neural network of a warship is terrifically resilient, backup data links on top of backup links, but now I can't see anything beyond the local telemetry range, half a deck in either direction. Something big just broke, and the *Versailles* is dying. If the link had gone down twenty seconds earlier, I wouldn't have been able to verify the presence of the drop ship on the flight deck, much less activate the refueling sequence.

"Let's get out of here while we still can," I say.

"No argument," Halley replies tersely. "Let's."

I can't see much through the viewport of the NNC's hatch. The corridor outside is dark, and I can't tell whether there's smoke outside, or hard vacuum. The system only knows that opening the door would be dangerous, so the safety lock keeps the hatch closed.

"Can you unlock that with your toy?" Halley asks, pointing to my admin deck.

"Yeah, I can override the safety. There's no air on the other side, though. It'll blow all the air out of this room, and then we'll suffocate."

"What about the NIFTIs? We got a ton of those on every deck."

"Of course." I grin, and feel like slapping my forehead for overlooking the obvious. The NIFTIs—navy infrared thermal imagers—

are stored in emergency lockers on every deck on the ship. They're little masks with infrared goggles and a small oxygen supply, designed to let a crew member see and breathe in the event of a major fire on the ship. I open the admin deck and check the emergency chart for the nearest NIFTI locker.

"There are three right on the bulkhead just before the aft staircase," I say. "Twenty yards to the left. Think you can hold your breath that long?"

"I guess we'll find out. If I faint, you'll just have to drag me, you fierce combat grunt."

"Like I have a choice," I say. "I can't fly a drop ship for shit."

We both laugh, even though we're scared almost witless.

"Where are we going after we get the NIFTIs on?"

I consult the admin deck again.

"Staircase, and down to Deck Seven. This thing doesn't show any fires. We should be okay with the infrared from the NIFTIs. Just watch your step."

"Let's hope your toy is right about that," Halley says as she zips up the collar of her flight suit. "I'd hate to open a hatch and get baked."

"Check the hatches with your hand before you open them," I say, recalling the firefighting lessons from Navy Indoc.

"Right. Let's get the hell out of here."

I don't really want to trade the relative safety of the NNC and its autonomous oxygen supply for the air-deprived corridors on the other side of that access hatch, but there's no way of knowing how much longer the *Versailles* is going to hold together. I open the admin deck and find my way to the emergency override for the fireproof hatch in front of us. Once again, I expect the system to refuse my request, but the light on the door panel switches from red to green without complaint. I close the lid of the admin deck and stow the device in its carry pouch.

"Ready?" Halley asks, her hand on the door release.

"Left turn, twenty yards. Ready," I say. "Go."

Halley slaps the hatch release with her palm, and the locking bolts on the hatch retract with a loud clacking sound. Then she pulls the hatch open, and the room immediately starts filling with smoke. We step over the threshold of the hatch and rush out into the passageway.

The air outside smells toxic and acrid, like smoldering insulation. My eyes start burning as soon as we step out into the dark corridor. There's no light anywhere, not even the emergency strobes that should be running until the ship's battery banks are depleted. I stretch out my right arm and use the walls of the passageway to guide myself along. In front of me, Halley lets out a series of rasping coughs, and after a few moments, I follow suit. The air out here burns in my lungs, and I have no doubt that we'll be dead soon if we don't find the NIFTI lockers.

The distance from the NNC hatch to the nearest row of NIFTI lockers is only twenty yards, but in the smoke-filled darkness, it feels like much more. I'm holding my breath to keep the toxic-smelling fumes out of my lungs, and by the time we reach the lockers, my system is screaming for fresh air. Halley pulls the locker doors open, and fumbles around in the dark before handing me one of the NIFTIs. I put the mask on in a hurry, and bite down on the mouthpiece to activate the unit. A moment later, I have clean, oxygen-infused air streaming into my lungs. The air in the little NIFTI tank tastes like old socks, but it beats the hell out of the noxious blend of fumes that's now permeating this section of the *Versailles*. The goggles of the NIFTI turn on automatically, and I can once again see my surroundings, albeit in the alien red tinge of the infrared imager.

Halley takes the lead as we take the staircase down to the lower decks. When she reaches the landing of Deck Seven, she puts her hand on the access hatch to the corridor, and I reach out and tap her shoulder. She turns around, and I point to the admin deck over my shoulder, and then to the hatch in turn. Halley nods, and I take the bag off my shoulder to pull out the deck and turn it on to check what's in store for us on the other side.

There's no fire in the passageway beyond, but there's no breathable air, either. I wave Halley closer and type a message to that effect. She looks at the screen and nods, giving me a thumbs-up for good measure. Then she flips the latch and throws open the hatch.

There are a few bodies in this section of corridors. Somebody in enlisted work blues lies crumpled up against a bulkhead, a dark pool of blood spread underneath his head. Halley turns him on his back, but even through the fuzzy, red-tinged image of the NIFTI goggles, it's pretty clear that this sailor is beyond help. There's blood all over his face, thick streams of it coagulating underneath his nostrils and around his mouth, and his eyes are half open. Halley lowers his upper body back to the deck.

The next section of the ship has emergency power. The red ceiling lights are on, and the orange floor markers designating the escape pod hatches are blinking in an urgent rhythm. Every time we pass a pod hatch, I check it just to make sure the computer didn't feed me any misinformation, but every single pod on the deck is gone, and its hatch sealed.

The flight deck is in the center of Deck Seven. It takes up the middle of the deck between the main port and starboard passageways. Halley walks up to the control box for the hatch and enters her credentials. The light on the panel flicks from amber to green, the locking bolts of the hatch retract obediently, and the hatch opens with a sigh of expelled air.

Inside, in the darkness, the drop ship is still in its berth by the wall, with the refueling hose still pumping fuel into the tanks. The only light in here is the flashing warning beacon on the ceiling that's painting the inside of the hangar in dim, orange light. Halley closes the flight deck hatch behind us, and the little air safety indicator on the lower edge of my NIFTI's thermal imager goes from red to orange, and then green. There's still breathable air in the hangar bay. I pull the NIFTI off my head and take a very small breath to test the computer's assessment. The air in here smells like fuel, but it's fine otherwise. I give Halley a thumbs-up, and she follows my example.

"I wish those things had voice comms built in," she says as she pulls the NIFTI's hood off her head.

"Yeah, I know. Shouldn't that bird be fueled up by now?" I nod at the drop ship, still secure in its berth.

"It should," Halley says. "Go and grab a flight helmet out of that locker over there. I'll go check on the ship."

Just as I take a helmet out of the locker she pointed out, the ceiling lights all come alive, bathing the flight deck in bright light that hurts my eyes after stumbling through NIFTI-enhanced darkness for ten minutes. I open my mouth to say something to Halley, but then the lights go out again, and this time the orange warning strobe on the ceiling goes out with them, leaving the hangar in complete darkness. The low droning sound from the refueling unit stops as well.

"Shit," Halley says into the darkness. "There goes the battery power."

I pull the NIFTI over my head again to turn on the infrared imager. Over by the drop ship, Halley opens an access hatch. She waves me over with a hurried gesture, and then climbs into the Wasp. As I follow her into the drop ship, the interior lights turn on, and I can once again see without the infrared goggles.

"Ship's got its own power cell," Halley says. "That won't get us over to the drop hatch, though."

"So now what?"

"Open up your handy little toy there, and see if you can kick loose some power for the flight deck, or we're stuck for good. I have no clue whether we slowed down enough to make proper orbit, and I'd rather not burn up in atmo with this shit bucket."

I sit down on the nonslip flooring and open my admin deck. The local network is completely dead—I can't even connect to the wireless cloud. I scan through all the local nodes, and none of them are transmitting or receiving.

"Nothing," I shout into the cockpit, where Halley is strapping herself into the right-hand seat. "Network's down. I can't see shit."

The lights in the hangar come on again suddenly. I hear the soft whirring of the refueling module as it resumes its task. I look at my admin deck's screen and see that the local network is once again coming to life.

"What'd you do?" Halley shouts.

"Not a damn thing. It came back on all by itself."

"Can you get into the refueling subsystem?"

"Hang on, I'm already on it," I reply.

I go back down the menu tree from memory to get to the hangar bay systems. The access is mercifully quick, since I am directly at the destination node without having to go through a quarter mile of damaged neural pathways. The active menu still says "READY FIVE LAUNCH PREP," and the progress bar underneath is only three-quarters complete.

"System says five more minutes," I tell Halley.

"Cut it short," she says. "Power goes out again before we're clamped and ready to drop, and we're fucked."

"I'll try."

Thankfully, the fuel systems are labeled very predictably, presumably simple enough for enlisted personnel to figure out. I delete the fueling process from the task queue, and tell the system to shift the Wasp to READY/LAUNCH status. A moment later, the noise from the refueler stops, and the fuel hose retracts away from the ship. Then a warning klaxon blares, and there's a low rumbling sound overhead as the docking clamps roll into position above the Wasp.

"Outstanding," Halley says, relief in her voice. "Now get your ass into the chair over here, and strap in."

I feel out of place in the left seat of a drop ship. The automatic clamp lowers itself onto the Wasp, locks onto the hardpoints, and then lifts the ship off its landing skids. Next to me, Halley is powering up avionics and going through on-screen checklists at a rapid, focused pace, her fingers doing a quick dance on the various screens. I strap myself in with shaky hands and watch as the docking clamp moves the drop ship across the hangar bay at infuriatingly slow speed.

"Plug in your helmet," Halley says. "If we get a hull breach out there, you'll want to be hooked up to the oxygen feed."

I slip the flight helmet over my head and attach the hose coming from the mask to its receptacle on the side of the cockpit wall. The helmet is made for someone with a smaller head than mine, and the helmet liner squeezes my head uncomfortably. I connect the voice circuit and toggle the intercom channel.

"If there's a Chinese destroyer out there, this will be a short flight," I say.

"If there's a Chinese destroyer out there, they would have boarded us already, or blown us into tiny little bits," Halley answers without taking her gaze off her screens. "Besides, there's precisely fuck-all we can do about that, unless you want to wait for the rescue ship on this busted tub."

"No, thank you," I say. "I'm not a huge fan of suffocation."

The lateral movement of the docking clamp stops, and then the ship moves down into the drop hatch. We're just a few moments from getting off this ship, and I hold my breath and pray to the entire Terran pantheon of deities for the ship's power to stay on until we release from the docking clamp.

"Turning One," Halley says as she reaches overhead and flips a succession of switches. Behind us, one of the drop ship's engines comes to life with a loud and steady whine. When the engine has spooled up to Halley's satisfaction, she moves her hand to a different bank of switches.

"Turning Two."

The noise outside doubles as the second engine starts up. I feel a low vibration going through the hull.

"I feel like I'm taking my parents' hydrocar for a joyride without permission," Halley says. "Never had one of these to myself before."

"Did we fill up enough to get us down?"

She checks a display with a few taps of her gloved finger, and shrugs.

"We're half full. Enough to get us to the surface, and then some."

Underneath us, the floor drops. The drop hatch is a huge airlock in the bottom of the hull. Normally, the ship would be oriented with its belly facing the surface of the planet below, but all I can see outside is the nothingness of space. Despite Halley's assessment, I imagine a Chinese cruiser right next to the *Versailles*, point-defense armament standing by to shred any escapees that manage to get clear of the hull.

The drop hatch finishes its downward-and-outward travel arc, leaving nothing between space and us but ten feet of drop through a hole in the ship's armor plating.

"Here goes," Halley says. "Dropping in three. Two. One. *Drop.*"

She thumbs a button on her throttle lever, and the Wasp drops out of the belly of the ship, sixty tons of spacecraft in free fall. I feel my stomach lurching upward sharply. Then we are clear of the hull, and the artificial gravity field of the *Versailles*, and the feeling of falling from a great height is replaced by a sudden weightlessness that pulls me out of my seat and against the straps of my harness. The floating feeling doesn't last long. Halley guns the engines and whips the Wasp into a steep turn as soon as we're out of the *Versailles*'s gravity field. She turns left, then right, and the countermeasures dispensers underneath the engine pods kick out a burst of decoy cartridges.

"I think we're good," she announces after a few moments of hard turns, and reverts to a less stomach-churning flight profile. She brings the Wasp around to get the *Versailles* into view.

"Holy fuck," I say, and Halley merely exhales sharply into her helmet mike.

The *Versailles* looks like someone blasted her flank with a giant shotgun. Gray smoke is pouring from hundreds of holes in her outer hull. The planet below looks much closer than it should be for a proper orbit, and the battered frigate is drifting without propulsion, pointing nose-first at the green and brown planet surface below.

"I hope we were the last ones on there," Halley says. "That thing's going to come down in a million glowing pieces."

We make a slow pass along the hull. The smooth and streamlined cigar shape of the ship is peppered with holes from bow to stern. Each hole is no bigger than a foot or two across.

"That wasn't done by antiship ordnance," Halley says. "What the hell kind of weapon makes holes like that?"

"Whatever it was, it did the job," I reply. "I bet there's not an airtight compartment left on this side of the hull."

The *Versailles* is trailing debris on her aimless trajectory. There are bits of armor plating, frozen bubbles of leaked fluids, and random bits of junk from the compartments that were vented into space. As we make our way along the hull, Halley has to bob and weave to avoid hitting larger chunks of debris head-on. We see a few bodies, too—shipmates, asphyxiated and frozen, drifting away from the ship in head-over-heel tumbles. There are body parts as well—arms, legs, and heads, torn from the bodies of their owners either by the impact of whatever tore through the hull, or by the shock of the sudden decompression that ejected everything in the compartment into space in the fraction of a second. I recall that the berthing spaces for the enlisted engineering crew are close to the outer starboard hull, and I wonder whether Halley and I would be floating out there as well if I had left the NNC on time at the end of my watch. Of all the possible ways to die, gasping for air in hard vacuum is one of the least pleasant ones I can imagine.

"Let's see who else made it off this wreck," Halley says. She toggles the comm channel over to the navy emergency frequency.

"NACS *Versailles* personnel, this is Stinger Six-Two," she says into her helmet mike. "Anyone listening in on shipboard or escape pod comms, please acknowledge."

There's only static in response. Halley repeats the broadcast twice, but there's no reply, not even the click of a toggled send button.

"I'm going to get us clear of this hull, and closer to the planet," she says, and pulls the Wasp into a roll. I look at the *Versailles* through the side window of the cockpit until the battered frigate disappears from view.

"*Versailles* personnel, this is Stinger Six-Two," Halley transmits again when we are clear of the *Versailles*'s bulk. "Anyone copy down there?"

This time, there's a garbled response on the emergency channel. Halley looks at me and exhales with emphasis.

"Thank goodness. I was starting to think we're all alone out here," she says to me. "*Versailles* personnel, stand by. I'm going into a lower orbit to improve reception. Next transmission in five."

We coast away from the *Versailles* and toward the planet below. Under other circumstances, the ride would be a spectacular sightseeing tour. There's nothing between us and the blue-green planet but a few avionics consoles and an inch of armored glass. The planet spread out in front of us is a pristine world of clean oceans, snowcapped mountain ranges, and wild and empty continents. The NAC colony is the only human presence on Willoughby, twelve hundred colonists on a planet two-thirds the size of Terra.

As we dip into a lower orbit, Halley rolls the ship around its dorsal axis to give us a better view of the outside. She has a very light hand on the controls, and the Wasp follows her input like a powerful, well-trained animal. I remember how difficult it was for me to simply get the nose of the simulated drop ship pointing the right way in Basic, and Halley says that the real thing is about five times more difficult to fly than the simulator.

"Pretty, isn't it?" she says to me, and I nod in response.

"Look at all that land down there, and it's all unsettled," Halley says. "We could set this ship down in the middle of one of those continents, and live on the supplies in the back of the Wasp for years. You'd get your wish early, about that patch of land on a colony planet."

I laugh in response, but the thought of being marooned on a far-off world with Halley is almost indecently exciting for a moment.

"The navy would come looking for us," I say. "They'd want their drop ship back, and I doubt they'd be willing to forgive us the rest of our contract."

"The hell they would. The *Versailles* is going to break up in atmo. Far as the navy would know, we burned up in that hull, and the second drop ship never made it out of the flight deck."

For a moment, I can't tell whether she's kidding, and the possibility hangs in the air between us almost like a physical thing.

Then there's another garbled transmission on the emergency channel, and the ear-grating sound of the mutilated broadcast serves to snap us both back into reality.

"I guess we shouldn't have advertised that we're up here with a working Wasp," she says. "Makes it kind of hard to skip town unnoticed."

"Stinger Six-Two, do you read, over?"

The voice on the emergency channel is suddenly perfectly clear, as if the broadcast is coming from our own cargo hold.

"Affirmative," Halley replies. "Stinger Six-Two copies five by five. Broadcasting party, please identify."

"Stinger Six-Two, this is the XO. What's your status and location?"

"Stinger Six-Two is in orbit. We're clear of the ship, and heading for the deck, sir."

"Six-Two, do you have any ordnance loaded?"

Halley exchanges a glance with me.

"Uh, that's a negative, sir. This is the spare drop ship. We just have gas in the tank, but the racks are bare."

"Copy that, Six-Two. That's too bad."

Halley taps a few buttons on the tactical console before toggling back a reply.

"Sir, my TacLink node shows your pod four hundred klicks north of my position. I can be on top of you in twenty minutes."

"Sooner would be better. Six-Two, do you have any weapons on board at all?"

"That's affirmative, sir. We have a full weapons locker with standard tactical loadout."

"Outstanding," the XO says, and the relief in his voice is unsettling. "Expedite your descent as much as safely possible. Don't break your ship, because you're the only hardware we have in the system right now."

"What the hell is he talking about?" Halley asks me. "What about the other drop ship? That one's fully armed with air-to-ground ordnance."

I can only shrug in response.

"Sir, didn't Six-One make it down to the surface with you?"

"If they did, they're not talking to us. You can try to raise them on the way down. Now hurry up—we need you down here yesterday."

"Affirmative, sir. We're on our way."

Halley cuts the comms and starts tapping buttons on her tactical console again.

"Flight profile for descent says we'll be down on the deck in twenty-two minutes," she says. "I'll be goosing it all the way, so make sure you're buckled in tight. It's gonna be a bit bumpy."

"What the hell is going on down there? He sounded like he's scared shitless. You think the SRA's trying to take the place?"

"I have no idea," Halley replies as she adjusts our trajectory and points the nose of the Wasp below the far-off horizon. "I guess we'll find out in twenty minutes," she says. "Now hold on and shut up."

CHAPTER 20

—EMERGENCY DESCENT—

If the combat landings in the TA were a high-speed descent in an express elevator, the ride into Willoughby's atmosphere from high orbit is like a rocket-assisted free fall down the elevator shaft. As we enter the upper layers of the planet's atmosphere, Halley pulls up the nose to expose the ceramic belly armor of the Wasp to the friction heat generated by our high-speed entry. For a good ten minutes, I can't see anything on the other side of the cockpit window but superheated gases streaming past in bright flares. Halley makes control inputs on her stick and throttle to keep the ship on the right angle and trajectory, but the results of her corrections are too subtle for me to feel. To me, it feels like we're just falling into the atmosphere belly-first, and only Halley's calm and focused demeanor keeps me from full-blown panic. When the fireworks outside the cockpit finally subside, the blackness of space has given way to the bright, pale blue of a clear sky.

"Altitude one hundred thousand," Halley announces, more to herself than for my benefit.

"Ever done this all by yourself?" I ask.

"Not without Lieutenant Rickman riding shotgun in the left seat. Relax, Andrew. I know what I'm doing here."

"Never doubted it," I say, and claw the molded armrests of my seat as she increases thrust and pulls the Wasp into a banking turn.

"They got some shitty weather down there," Halley says when we pass through twenty thousand feet. "All I see is storms. I thought this place was terraformed."

I look outside at the top of the cloud cover, a roiling mass of gray and black that extends from one end of the horizon to the other.

"Just because it's terraformed doesn't mean it's like Earth in springtime," I say, remembering Sergeant Fallon's words back at the medical center.

"Well, if this is what it looks like after they had the atmo exchangers running for a decade, I don't want to know what it looked like when the survey ship got here. Hang on—this is going to be a bit bumpy."

Halley has a gift for understatement. As we enter the cloud cover above Willoughby's surface, the ship gets whipped around like a plastic bag on a windswept sidewalk. We're in the clouds just a few moments before rain starts hammering the thick glass of the cockpit, fat drops that sound like heavy-caliber small-arms fire hitting the window panels. I shoot Halley a worried glance, but she's focused on her instruments and flight controls. There's nothing I can do to help get us down on the ground in one piece, so I do my best to merge with the thin padding on my armored seat.

"This weather is fucked up," Halley says after a while. "We're at five thousand, and it's twenty-five degrees Celsius out there. It's like fucking Florida in late spring."

"Too warm?"

"For this rock? Hell, yes. Weather briefing yesterday said they're just above freezing this time of year."

We finally break out of the cloud cover over muddy-brown terrain that looks entirely too close for comfort. Halley levels out the ship and banks slightly to the right to get a good look at the planet surface below.

"Wow, that mess went almost all the way down," she says. "We're fifteen hundred feet above the deck." She toggles the transmit button on her control stick. "*Versailles* personnel, this is Stinger Six-Two," Halley broadcasts. "I'm a hundred and ten klicks out from your position. ETA five minutes. Can you find me a nice flat spot and pop some IR smokers?"

"Copy, Six-Two," a voice replies on the emergency channel. "Uh, negative on the smokers. We have hostiles in the neighborhood. Just home in on the pod and set down as close as you can. And have that ramp down, 'cause we need to evac in a hurry."

"Six-Two, copy," Halley replies, and then gives me a bewildered look. "Hostiles? What the hell is he talking about? My threat board is blank."

"Native wildlife?" I offer, and Halley shakes her head.

"Ain't nothing living down there except what came in on the colony ship, except for some algae."

"Chinese or Russians? Think they have troops on the ground?"

"I don't fucking know, Andrew," Halley replies. "All I know is that I wish we actually had some ordnance on those pylons, 'cause if we bump into someone who needs shooting, all we can do is flip 'em the bird."

———

The escape pod looks like a projectile from a giant cannon. It's lying on its side on a gently sloping hillside, lines from the retardation parachute draped all over it like bright-orange vines. Halley makes a low pass over the site, and I can see several people down by the pod, waving at us with urgent gestures.

"Well, that looks flat enough," she says. "Hang on, I'm putting down in that spot over there."

We coast in at a low angle and touch down on the surface less than a hundred yards from the stranded escape pod. As soon as the Wasp comes to a rest on all three skids, Halley cuts the throttle and punches a button on her console. Behind us, I hear the familiar whine of an opening cargo hatch. A few moments later, we hear several pairs of boots running up the ramp and into the cargo bay.

"Don't bother unstrapping, pilot," an out-of-breath voice says over the emergency channel. "You get airborne and close that hatch as soon as I say, you hear?"

"Copy that," Halley replies.

There's more tromping behind us as more crew members thunder up the cargo ramp.

"Dust off!" the breathless voice shouts into the comms. "Get us the hell off the ground, now."

Halley hits the cargo door switch with her palm, seizes the stick and throttle again, and gooses the engines. "Hang on to something back there," she shouts into the intercom, and pulls the Wasp into a vertical climb. She swings the tail of the ship around and points the nose back the way we came. Then we pick up speed again and climb back into the cloud cover. Not even thirty seconds have elapsed since our ship's skids touched down on the planet's surface.

Back in the cargo hold, the XO claims the jump seat of the crew chief and plugs himself into the ship's intercom circuit. The armored hatch between the cockpit and the cargo hold is open, and I can see crew members opening the arms locker and distributing small arms, even though the drop ship is once again getting bounced around by turbulence.

"Talk to me, sir," Halley says. "What's going on down there?"

"We have a nonnative species down there, that's what," the XO replies.

Halley and I share an incredulous look. The spacefaring nations of Earth have a few hundred colony planets and moons as far out as Zeta Reticuli, and nobody has ever encountered any life on those that could be observed without a microscope.

"Nonnative species?" Halley repeats. "What, like fucking *aliens*?"

"Yes, like fucking aliens," the XO says. "Unless the colonists brought along livestock that's eighty fucking feet tall. Now find us some better weather, and stay the hell away from the ground, you copy?"

Halley takes the ship back up through the clouds. The ride up isn't quite as bone-jarring as the descent had been, but I still breathe a sigh of relief when we break through the cloud ceiling and the skies are blue once more.

"We're clear of the chop," Halley tells the XO over the intercom. "Where do you want me to take this thing? I have forty-five minutes of fuel left."

Behind us, Commander Campbell unbuckles from the crew chief's jump seat and walks up to the cockpit, where he crouches between our high-backed pilot seats.

"Ensign, how far is the nearest colony settlement from our current datum?" he asks Halley. She checks her nav screen and shrugs her shoulders.

"I have no idea, sir. This is the spare bird, remember? All the data banks are blank. We didn't get to upload any nav data before we left. I can get a satellite fix and tell you our coordinates, but I have nothing else on my map."

"I can probably pull that off the admin deck," I say. The commander looks at me, and I raise the eye shield of my flight helmet to show my face.

"Mr. Grayson," he says. "Glad to see you made it off the ship. Get back here and fire up your toy, please."

"Aye-aye, sir." I unbuckle my seat harness and climb over the armored sidewall of my chair.

I am still in a state of shocked disbelief. Since the invention of the Alcubierre drive, we've been expanding into other star systems, but nobody's ever picked up so much as a stray radio signal from another civilization. I remember the ongoing debates on the science channels in school, the Rare Earthers arguing that we're probably the only sentient species in the galaxy, and the Saganites and Copernicans arguing that the universe is probably chock-full of spacefaring species like ourselves. Until now, that particular discussion wasn't settled. We're only forty-two light years from home, which means that we're still playing in our front yard, astronomically speaking. If we've already bumped into another species capable of space travel, the galaxy must be lousy with them.

"What do they look like?" I ask the XO. "Are they hostile?"

"Are they hostile? Shit, I hope not. The one we saw was fucking huge. Passed our pod in the rain, a few hundred yards off. Shook the fucking ground."

"I'm picking up beacons from two more pods," Halley says from the right seat. "They're both down in the soup. You guys got scattered all over this rock."

"Can you get there with the fuel you have?" the XO asks her. Halley considers his question briefly and shrugs.

"Sure, but we won't be flying anywhere else. One's three hundred fifty klicks east, the other's three hundred northwest. Plus, I won't be able to see shit all the way down."

"Forget it, then," the XO says. "Let's just take a look at the map, and we'll try to get them on the comms later."

"Aye-aye, sir," Halley replies.

There are three of the *Versailles*'s officers in the cargo bay, all junior watch officers from CIC, and four anxious-looking marines in fatigues.

"Where's the skipper, sir? Wasn't he in CIC when we got hit?"

"The skipper took a different pod," Lieutenant Commander Campbell replies. "As per regs. One of the pods burns up or crashes, it won't take out both senior officers at once. Now crack that thing open, and let's see if we can figure out where the hell we are."

My admin deck holds the other half of the location puzzle. I can bring up the complete data set for Willoughby, including the locations of every structure on the planet, and the trajectories of every satellite in orbit, but I have no way of telling where we are.

"Halley, can you give me a nav fix?" I ask her over the intercom.

"Sure thing. Stand by."

She consults her screen and then rattles off a string of coordinates. I plug the numbers into the satellite map of Willoughby, and my admin deck pinpoints our position with a neat crosshair that looks disturbingly like an aiming reticle.

"Here we are," I say to the XO, and turn the screen toward him. He studies the display for a few moments, and frowns.

"Figures. We're in the wrong fucking place. Main settlement's on the other hemisphere."

He hands the admin deck back to me, and rubs the bridge of his nose with thumb and forefinger.

"Well, that's just special. Our ride's got no ordnance and almost no fuel, we're three thousand klicks from the only refueler on this rock, and the place is under new management, from the looks of it."

I pan and zoom the satellite map to check the radius Halley estimated earlier as the maximum range of the ship with the remaining fuel. We're on a peninsula that's hundreds of miles long and wide, and most of it is absolutely barren, but there's a base marker directly south of us. I check the range to find that it's less than two hundred miles away.

"Here's something, but I have no idea what that map symbol means."

I fold the display over and hand the deck to the commander. He looks at the map for a moment, and pokes a finger at the symbol.

"That's one of the terraforming units. Big-ass atmospheric exchanger, with a fusion reactor underneath."

"They got any food and water?"

"Yes," he says. "They have maintenance crews on site. Chow, hot water, showers, and cots to sleep on. They even have comms gear. Hell, they may even have fuel. Good find, Mr. Grayson."

He gives the admin deck back to me, and claps his hands.

"We found a rest stop, people. Let's go see if anyone's home."

The terraforming station is a huge, square building that looks like the factory box for a fleet frigate. It's made of unpainted concrete that has weathered a lot since the terraforming network was set up over a decade ago. There are rows of smaller box-shaped structures all along the long edges of the main building, each of them crowned by giant, square exhaust nozzles that look large enough to land a drop ship in them with room to spare.

"Ugly, ain't it?" Commander Campbell says behind us, giving voice to my thoughts. "Class Three atmospheric exchanger. They have sixty three more of those on this rock. Takes a lot of money to terraform a planet like this."

I look at the ugly, hulking mountain of concrete below us as Halley circles the complex at low altitude, and try to imagine over five dozen of these things lined up side by side. The sheer material cost of that network must be staggering, but it's probably dwarfed by the amount of money it took to truck the machinery inside those atmospheric exchangers across forty light years of space. Suddenly I understand why the Commonwealth is always short on cash, and why the welfare cities only get protein patties and recycled shit to eat.

"Anyone awake down there, keep your heads low. Navy flight Stinger Six-Two is coming in for a landing," Halley broadcasts.

There's a cluster of prefabricated buildings at one end of the massive main structure, and a gravel landing pad marked crudely with white spray paint. We descend over the landing spot, Halley putting the seventy-ton war machine down on the gravel so gently that I can't even feel the skids touching the ground. The buildings of the outpost are undamaged, and I can see lights inside. Halley cuts the throttle and hits the switch for the rear hatch with the outside of her fist. Then she reaches overhead and throws a few important-looking switches, and the engines shut down with a prolonged whining sound.

"Let's see who's home," she says.

Behind us, the marines file out of the cargo bay, weapons at the ready. The navy officers follow, looking a lot less martial in their work uniforms.

"Well, we might as well join in," Halley says to me. "Unless they have a few tons of drop-ship juice stashed away somewhere, this bird's staying put."

We unbuckle our seat harnesses and take off our flight helmets. Halley leaves hers on her seat, and I follow suit. On the way out of the cockpit, she pauses for a moment and pats the frame of the bulkhead briefly, as if she's thanking a loyal steed for getting her to her destination safely.

I open the hatch to the weapons locker and take a rifle off the rack. Halley steps in next to me and takes a rifle as well. She checks the chamber of her weapon, opens a munitions drawer, and starts handing me magazines.

"You remember how to use one of those, don't you?" I say, and she flips me the bird without pausing her task. I stuff a magazine into each of my leg pockets, and insert another one into the rifle. Being armed with a proper battle rifle again gives me a small bit of comfort.

With Halley charging her rifle next to me, I have a sudden flash of déjà vu, remembering the times before urban-combat training back in Basic, when we got ready to do mock battles against each other, like a game of tag with armor and pretend rifles. Every piece of gear in this arms locker is designed for humans in battle armor to fight other humans in battle armor, and it occurs to me that we're not prepared to stick our collective toes into the galaxy beyond our own little backwater star system.

"Eighty feet tall," Halley mutters next to me as she's slipping a load-bearing harness over her flight suit. "Makes you wish those MARS rockets came with nuclear warheads, doesn't it?"

By the time we leave the drop ship to join the rest of the crew, there's a welcoming committee waiting for us outside. A full squad of marines has come out of one of the buildings to greet us. They're all in partial armor, chest and leg plates but no helmets or web gear, evidence that our arrival has taken them by surprise. As Halley and I walk up to join the group, the leader of the marine squad lowers his rifle and salutes our XO.

"Sergeant Becker, sir. We're the garrison squad. Glad to see the navy's finally in town."

"Lieutenant Commander Campbell, NACS *Versailles*. Care to fill me in on what the hell is going on here on this rock, Sergeant?"

The sergeant exchanges unsure glances with his squad.

"We were hoping you'd tell us, sir. We haven't heard anything from Willoughby City in almost a month."

The terraforming station is staffed by a squad of marines and twelve civilian colony techs. Even with our five navy officers and four *Versailles* marines added, everyone on the facility fits into the station's mess hall with room to spare. Commander Campbell is the highest-ranking officer of the group by far, and he slips into his XO function seamlessly.

"You've had no comms with the main settlement in over three weeks?" he asks.

"No, sir. One morning, we were talking to them, swapping status reports—and then the feed dropped, just like that. We have run diagnostics on all the gear all the way up to the satellite uplink. It's all working as it should."

"Sergeant Becker," the XO says.

"Sir?"

"Take your marines and mine, and give me a perimeter guard around this place. Corporal Harrison is going to tell you what to look for. You see anything at all coming this way, you ring the alarm."

"Aye-aye, sir," Sergeant Becker says. "You heard the man. Let's get busy, marines."

The marines gather their weapons and file out of the room.

"What's going on, Commander?" one of the civilians asks the XO. "Are we under attack by the SRA?"

"Well," he replies, "the good news is that there's not a single SRA unit within five light years of this place, as far as we know."

"I'm guessing there's bad news, too," the civilian says. "Since you just sent out all the marines to stand guard outside."

"Oh, you have no idea," Commander Campbell replies.

The revelation that humanity just encountered its first alien species shocks the techs visibly, but they seem rather more upset about discovering that we're not here to evacuate them to a waiting navy fleet unit, and that the ship that brought us here is probably dispersed all over the continent by now.

"Well, that caps a lousy month," the supervisor of the station says after the XO finishes briefing the civilians on the events since we dropped out of the Alcubierre chute a few hours ago.

"Tell me about it," the XO chuckles.

"When we lost contact with Willoughby City, the weather went all weird on us. We've been keeping tabs on the atmospheric data ever since we set up shop in this place, and I've never seen anything like it."

"We noticed it's awfully warm out there," Halley says. "I thought this place was just above freezing right now."

"We've been at five degrees Celsius this time of year for the last five years running, ever since the terraforming team handed us the keys," the supervisor says. "Right now, it's twenty degrees above normal, and the temperature has gone up by five degrees per week for three weeks now."

"There's a bitch of a storm system a few hundred klicks south of here," Halley says. "Eighty-knot winds, and rain from ten thousand feet all the way down to the deck."

"We got more rainfall just last week than we got in the three months before that. Lots of storms. But let me show you something a little more troubling."

He opens the portable data terminal he had been carrying in his hand, and sits down at one of the mess tables. The XO and the junior officers gather behind him to get a look at the screen.

"We have all the terraforming stations on this planet networked, so we can share data and keep things in sync. Not too long after we lost contact with Willoughby City, the stations have been dropping out of the network. We synchronize our data over the satellite every morning and evening, and right now we only have forty-nine live nodes left. Every day, another station or two drops off the network. But that's not even the really bad news."

He types away at the keypad briefly and points to the display.

"When they turned over the place to colonize, the atmosphere was pretty close to Earth's own. We were at eighty point three percent nitrogen, eighteen percent oxygen, point eight percent argon, and one hundredth of a percent of carbon dioxide."

He calls up another screen and points at a data table.

"Ever since we've lost contact with Central, the oxygen content of the atmosphere has dropped, and the carbon dioxide level has increased. Right now, we're at fifteen percent oxygen, seventy-three percent nitrogen, and three percent carbon dioxide. The oxygen level is dropping by a percentage point every week, and the carbon dioxide is increasing by a percentage point. At this rate, we'll have a hard time breathing in a few weeks. With the temperature increase thrown in, you're looking at reversal of ten years of terraforming in a month. Even with our terraformers turning off one by one, the atmosphere shouldn't flip like that. All these stations are in maintenance mode now, and the terraforming is pretty much done. *Was* pretty much done," he corrects himself.

"You think it's something they did, sir?" one of the *Versailles*'s lieutenants asks the XO. He looks at his subordinate in disbelief for a moment, and then lets out a barking laugh that makes me flinch.

"No, Lieutenant Benning. I think someone accidentally nudged the thermostat on the main atmospheric exchanger."

He looks around at the mixed group of civilians and navy personnel watching him, and shrugs his shoulders.

"Well, folks, it looks like someone else grabbed the deed to this place, and we just got our eviction notice."

CHAPTER 21

—THE FATE OF THE COLONY—

The XO sends us out in teams to take stock of the station's supplies. Even with the personnel we brought, there's enough food and water to last for months. Between their stores and the small-arms locker on the drop ship, we can arm everyone in our group to the teeth and keep them fed and sheltered until the relief ship gets to Willoughby. One thing we didn't bring, however, is enough oxygen to keep everyone breathing once the air on this planet goes bad.

"What do we have for transportation?" the XO asks when we gather in the mess hall again to compile the inventory.

"There's a half dozen cargo mules in the shed outside, and two ultralights," Halley reports.

"How do you get to the main base and back?" Commander Campbell asks the administrator, a lanky, gray-haired man named Hayward who looks like he spends most of his time working outside with his hands.

"Puddle jumper," he replies. "Atmospheric shuttle from Willoughby City. Comes out twice a month, or by request if there's a medical issue our doc can't fix."

"That's a long ride," Halley says. "That place is, what, three thousand klicks south?"

"Twenty-eight hundred. Six hours each way, if the weather's good."

"Take us two weeks to drive with these mules, even if we could carry enough fuel to make the trip," the XO says.

Mr. Hayward shakes his head. "You'd never get there. There's a mountain range and an ocean strait between here and there."

"Well, shit," the XO says. "Looks like we're waiting out the cavalry right here, then."

"You got any fuel stores at all?" Halley asks Mr. Hayward. "I mean, other than the juice for the mules and those ultralights."

"There's a tank buried by the landing pad. That one's full of JP-101AA. It's for the puddle jumpers. They usually carry enough for a round trip, but we have some anyway, just in case. Five thousand gallons."

"JP-101AA," Halley repeats.

"Yeah. Atmospheric aviation. Can your ride use that stuff?"

"Those are multifuel engines," she replies. "We'll have less thrust, and we'll need to stay in atmo, but yeah, they'll burn 101."

"We don't have a refueler," Mr. Hayward says. "Just a portable manual pump. It'll take forever to fill that monster." He looks out of the window, where the drop ship is visible a few hundred feet away. "How much fuel does one of those hold anyway?"

"Twenty-one thousand eight hundred and forty-four pounds," Halley replies without missing a beat.

One of the techs lets out a low whistle.

"That's damn near seventeen thousand liters," he says to Mr. Hayward. "Looks like we're getting cleaned out with one fill-up."

"Oh, that's okay," Mr. Hayward replies and turns off the portable terminal in front of him. "I have a feeling there'll be little demand for that stuff around here by the end of the month."

The refueling takes four hours, even with a dozen people working on the process. Trying to fuel a Wasp-class drop ship with a manual pump and fuel hoses with nonstandard coupling is like trying to fill a bathtub by wringing out wet towels over it. We all take turns holding open the fuel ports on the upper hull of the Wasp by hand, and feeding the wrist-thin hoses of the little emergency hand pump system directly into the sealed tanks. By the time the tanks are full, we all smell like aviation fuel, even the XO.

"So, the bird is full," Commander Campbell declares when we gather in the mess hall again. "We'll be going down to see what's going on at Willoughby City. I'd rather not take everyone along for this, just in case we run into trouble."

"No argument," Mr. Hayward says. "We're not military. We'd just be baggage to you guys."

"I suggest we go light," Halley says. "I've never flown this thing with atmo fuel in it, so I have no idea how much she'll lift anyway."

"What if you run into trouble, sir?" Corporal Schaefer asks. "You may want some rifles on the ground when you get there."

Commander Campbell shakes his head.

"Not likely, Corporal. Let's be realistic—if that colony's gone, the bad guys have more firepower than we can handle, and the four of you aren't going to make any difference. I'd rather be able to make a quick exit without having to worry about getting your guys down safely, too."

"Understood, sir," the corporal says.

"Lieutenant Adams, you're in charge while I'm gone. If we lose comms, and we're not back in twelve hours at the most, you are to stay holed up and wait for the rescue ship to arrive. Is that clear?"

"Aye-aye, sir," the lieutenant replies. "Stay put and wait for the cavalry."

"Corporal Schaefer, you and your men will unload the drop ship's armory and supply lockers while Ensign Halley does her preflight. Just leave us three rifles and a launcher, in case we end up having to put down in the boonies. I don't want all that hardware going to waste if they blot us out of the sky."

"Copy that, sir. We'll get right on it."

"Very well." The commander claps his hands again. "Let's get this show on the road, people."

"Here we go again," Halley says as we strap into our seats in the cockpit once again. The engines are warming up, but their drone sounds different now, lower and rougher than before.

"Make sure those straps are tight," she advises. "If we have to bail out, you don't want to slip out of your harness on eject."

"That would be bad," I agree. "Now would you stop talking about ejecting out of this thing? I'm not too keen on adding a parachute ride to my list of new experiences today."

"Oh, those are kind of fun," Halley says. "In a white-knuckled terror sort of way."

I watch as she goes through her preflight checklists, at a more leisurely pace than back in the *Versailles*'s hangar a few hours ago.

"Okay, board's green. We're looking good. Are you strapped in back there, Commander?"

"That's affirmative," the XO replies over the intercom. "Take us up whenever you're ready."

Halley seizes her throttle and stick, and a few moments later we are hovering above the landing pad. She waggles the tail of the ship left and right cautiously to test the control surfaces.

Once again, I am amazed at how agile such a huge, ugly machine can be.

"Here we go," she says, and increases thrust. "Stinger Six-Two is back in business."

Soon, we are once again cruising twenty thousand feet above the rocky surface of the peninsula.

"Give me the bearing for the settlement again," Halley says. I check the satellite map on the admin deck.

"Willoughby City is at bearing one-seven-niner from the terraforming station, distance two-eight-two-one nautical miles."

"Give me the coordinates, please."

I read off the satellite coordinates, and she plugs them into her navigation console.

"There. Now the computer in this bird knows where we're headed. Makes me feel a little better about going back into *that*."

She points at the windshield and the huge storm cell that's blanketing the continent ahead.

Without the ability to go into space, the drop ship is merely a huge, inefficient aircraft. Halley is not happy with the way the ship behaves with the inferior fuel in its tanks.

"This thing feels like someone put in a governor," she says when we are crossing the mountain range mentioned by Mr. Hayward earlier. "I'm having trouble just getting up to twenty thousand feet, and I'm getting four hundred knots airspeed. We should be almost twice as fast."

"Better than walking, though," I say.

"Barely. I feel like I'm transporting a hold full of rocks."

On the way to the central settlement, Halley picks up more emergency locator beacons from stranded escape pods. By now, we're back above severe weather, and even though Halley broadcasts our presence every few minutes on the emergency channel, nobody on the ground is answering. Halley reads out the coordinates of the downed pods as they pop up on her TacLink screen, and I enter them into the satellite map on my admin deck. None of the pods are closer than a hundred miles from our flight path, and the XO tells Halley not to divert the ship when she asks him over the intercom.

"They have supplies and commo gear," he says. "I don't want to fill this bird up with hitchhikers and end up killing everyone. Besides, we don't have the fuel. They'll be okay until the rescue ship gets here."

"Aye-aye, sir," Halley replies.

The storm clouds cover the planet like a funeral shroud, denying us a view of whatever is roaming the surface. Some species is taking over the planet, transforming it to fit their needs, and we won't find out what we're facing until we descend into the dark maelstrom below to put our fragile selves right among them. I feel like a little kid who has just been tasked by his parents to venture into the monster-filled basement for an unimportant errand.

I've lost track of our time aloft when Halley finally points the nose of the ship at the angry-looking clouds below.

"Get ready for some bounce," she tells us. "We're fifty miles out. I'm going lower to see if I can get a fix on the AILS beam."

"AILS beam?"

"Automated Instrument Landing System," she replies. "Lets me land the bird in zero visibility without even touching the controls."

I watch with dread as we descend toward the clouds, where sporadic flashes of lightning illuminate the dark sky. As soon as we enter the clouds, the ship gets buffeted again, but this turbulence doesn't feel as severe as the violent winds we encountered on our first descent through the storm.

"Willoughby Control, this is navy flight Stinger Six-Two," Halley transmits. "We're four-niner miles north, inbound for AILS landing."

There's nothing but static in return, and Halley repeats the broadcast twice before giving up with a shrug.

"All their nav gear is up and running. I can see the radio beacon and the AILS beam. Whatever happened down there, they still have juice."

When we break through the cloud cover, the ground isn't quite as close as it was when we picked up the XO earlier. The rain has slacked off to a drizzle. When Halley levels off the ship, we're two thousand feet above the ground, and I can see half a mile into the distance.

"Weather's getting better," Halley says. "Looks like we may not even need the AILS."

I crane my neck to look at the ground below, trying to spot the alien beings that ought to be easy to see even from this altitude, but there's nothing moving down there. The landscape looks as boringly monotone as the rocky plateaus and hills back by the outpost.

"Thirty miles out," Halley declares. "Nothing going on down there. I have zip on radar and infrared." All I see ahead is the radio beacon.

"Stay sharp," the XO says over the intercom. "First sign of trouble, you get us back up above the soup."

"Oh, don't you fucking worry about *that*," Halley mutters under her breath without toggling the transmit button on her stick.

The town that pops out of the misty haze half a mile in front of us looks untouched. As we get closer, I can see rows of prefabricated buildings, boxy steel-and-concrete modules with thick polycarb windows. The houses are lined up on a neat grid of concrete mesh roads. The administrator back at the terraforming station called this settlement Willoughby City, but that title seems grandiose. The local soil is a pale shade of ochre. I can see where the colonists have set up patches of grass to introduce our own vegetation to the place, but from up here it doesn't look like Willoughby is very accommodating of Earth grass.

Halley makes a high pass above the settlement, banking the Wasp into a tight spiral turn to get a look at the ground. I peer past her through the thick armored glass of the starboard canopy, but I see nothing out of the ordinary. The houses and roads look undamaged. I can see lights on many of the buildings.

"Looks fine to me," Halley says. "Let's go a little lower and take a closer look."

We make another pass over the city, this time much lower and slower than before. This time, I notice something else down below, something that wasn't obvious from almost two thousand feet up. There are people down there after all, but they're not reacting to the drop ship overflying the settlement at low altitude. They're lying on the concrete latticework of the road grid, slumped up against the walls of the buildings, or facedown on the ochre-colored dust of the ground between the houses. Most of them are lying on the ground alone or in pairs, prone on their stomachs or flat on their backs, as if the entire colony decided to take a collective nap at the same time. My mouth is suddenly very dry, and I can feel my heart hammering in my chest. When I look at Halley, I see that she is biting her lower lip as she's watching the scene below.

"Commander, you better come up front and take a look at this yourself," she says into the intercom.

A few moments later, Commander Campbell appears in the cockpit hatch behind us. He grabs hold of both our seats to steady himself, and leans over to my side of the ship to look at the ground below. Without a word of explanation, Halley merely puts the ship into a gentle portside turn to give him a better view of the grave-yard the colony has become.

"My God," the XO says in a toneless voice.

"All the buildings are intact," I say. "I don't see any damage at all. What the hell did they do to them?"

"Fucked if I know," Halley replies. "But if you don't mind, Com-mander, I'd rather not land this thing and risk contamination."

I hadn't even considered a ChemWar attack, but now that Halley voices her concern, I feel very uneasy about our low flight level. I know it's just my overactive, terrified brain playing tricks on me, but I imagine a cloud of lethal contaminant getting stirred up by the downdraft of the ship's engines. Back in ChemWar class, we were shown videos of chemical and biological attacks from the last major tiff with the Chinese and Koreans back on Earth, and the close-ups of hapless NAC troopers who died by choking on their bloody vomit left a lasting impression in my memory.

"Let's not," the XO agrees. "I don't feel like puking out my lungs today. Take her back up, and let's get on the radio, see if anyone's made it out of there. Maybe their marines had their suits on."

We circle above the settlement at high altitude for a while, trying to contact the marines that may have made it out of the city. Halley sends challenges on the marine field frequency for twenty minutes while flying a holding pattern, but once again there's no reply.

"If they're within fifty miles, they should hear us," she says. "I can't do this much longer if we want to make it back to the terra-former on what's left in the tank."

"Understood," the XO says. "Make another loop south, and then let's head back to the barn."

"That's a whole lot of flying done for nothing," I say to Halley in a low voice, careful to keep my finger away from the transmit button. She merely shrugs in response.

"Beats sitting on our asses and waiting for the next navy boat to come pick us up."

There's a soft chirp on her TacLink console, and she turns her attention to it. She taps the screen, reads the display for a moment, and then sits up straight with a jolt.

"What is it?" I ask, dreading more bad news heading our way.

"Emergency transponder," she says. "It's the other drop ship from the *Versailles*. Stinger Six-One."

Her fingers do a rapid little dance on the comms console as she goes to a different frequency.

"Stinger Six-One, this is Halley in Six-Two. I'm picking up your beacon two-niner miles to my south. If anyone down there can hear me, please respond."

Again, we get no reply. Halley repeats the broadcast two more times, and then lets out an exasperated little snort.

"I swear, this is the Planet of Broken Fucking Radios, or something. I'm getting tired of talking to myself out here."

She toggles her intercom button.

"Commander, I'm picking up the emergency beacon from our other drop ship. I'm going to try and eyeball the site, check if anyone's made it out."

"Go ahead," the XO says.

When we're back in the weather, Halley runs a radar sweep of the ground ahead of us. I look over at her sensor screen as the display shows a wedge-shaped segment of the planet surface below and in front of us, swept from side to side in short intervals by the focused beam from the drop ship's radar transmitter.

"We don't usually run continuous ground sweeps like that," Halley says when she notices that I'm watching the screen. "That radar lights up threat-warning receivers like a Christmas tree. If we had SRA down there, it would be like turning on a huge billboard that says 'Shoot Me.' "

"You know what? I almost wish those were just SRA troopers down there," I say, and she smiles.

"Yeah. Who would have thought we'd ever wish for that, huh?"

Suddenly, the ship transitions out of the heavy cloud cover and into clear weather with startling abruptness. One moment we're flying among drifting bands of rain in zero visibility; the next moment we're in calm skies. I look out of the port cockpit window in surprise, and see a wall of clouds receding behind the ship. I can see the ground a few thousand feet below us. It looks like we just crossed into the eye of a hurricane. We're in a huge bowl of calm weather that looks like it's twenty miles or more across.

"Holy living fuck," Halley says next to me, in a tone of profound awe and astonishment.

In front of the ship, right in the center of this clear patch of sky, there's an enormous spire reaching into the sky. It's the color of dirty snow, and so tall that I can't see the top of it even after craning my neck and peering through the top panel of the drop ship's windshield. In relation to its height, the structure seems impossibly thin, but even at this distance it's obvious that the trunk is a few hundred yards in diameter. It flares out at the bottom, like the lower section of a tree.

"What the hell is that?"

"You want to come up here and take a look at this, sir," Halley tells the XO, who promptly unstraps from his jump seat once more and steps forward into the cockpit.

"Jesus," he says when he sees the spire rising into the dark clouds ahead of us.

"I have nothing on radar," Halley says in astonishment.

"Come again?"

"It's not showing on radar," she replies, and cycles through display modes on her screen. "Ground radar, air-to-air mode, millimeter wave—not a damn thing. If the weather hadn't cleared up back there all of a sudden, we could have flown right into that thing without ever seeing it."

"Looks like they've been busy," the XO says. "They've built that thing in less than a month?"

To me, the structure rising from the surface of the planet doesn't look *built* at all. There are no visible supports, no protrusions or seams. The surface of the spire looks smooth and uninterrupted. It looks like an enormous tree stripped of its bark.

"The emergency beacon is five degrees off our bow, four miles ahead," Halley says. "Right near the base of *that*."

"Just fly around it for now," the XO orders. "Keep your distance. I don't want to add another crash beacon to the first one."

The patch of calm weather seems to be perfectly circular, and the tall, white structure is right in the center of it. Halley turns the Wasp to the left, putting us on a course that's parallel to the outer walls of this strange eye in the storm.

"It shows up on infrared," she says. "It's not like a furnace or anything, but it's definitely throwing out some heat."

"Yeah, but what the hell *is* it?"

I lean forward to look up through the top windshield panel again. The clouded sky overhead is a little lighter in color than the wall of clouds towering to the left of the ship in the distance, and as I look at the cloud cover directly above the Wasp, I get a sense of swift movement, like a front of storm clouds rushing across the sky in a high wind. The flood of lead-gray clouds is pouring straight out from the center of the storm's eye, and flowing toward the walls.

"It's a terraformer," I say. "Atmospheric exchanger, whatever *they* call it. Look at that."

Halley follows my gaze with her own, and the XO leans forward over the center console to get a glimpse of what we're looking at.

"I think you may be right, Mr. Grayson," he says. "And if that's the case, I think we're off this rock for good."

He retreats from his uncomfortably stretched position and settles in a crouch between the pilot seats.

"It took us fifteen fucking years to build a terraforming network on this rock and get it fit for people to live on. If these things can waltz in here and set up a working network of their own in three weeks . . ."

He leaves the sentence unfinished, but I get the sentiment. If this is a working atmospheric exchanger, the alien species is so much more advanced that trying to compete with them for the same real estate would be like showing up at an architecture competition with a child's erector set and a few rolls of polymer sheets.

"Let's get a little closer to that beacon, but be careful."

"Aye-aye, sir," Halley replies. "You may want to buckle in again back there, just in case."

We make a wide turn to the right, until the enormous white spire is right in the center of the Wasp's windshield. Halley does a quick measurement with the optical-targeting system of the Wasp, and declares that the structure ahead measures twenty-eight hundred feet from its base to the point where the stem disappears in the clouds overhead.

"I'm getting the faintest return on radar now," she says. "I'm going to stop painting it with the beam. Don't want to piss off the locals."

From our position, the spot where the beacon is sending out its regular, mindless electronic wails is on the opposite side of the huge stem. Halley decreases altitude while taking the ship around the trunk in a left-hand turn that gives me a perfect view of the structure. By now, we're less than a quarter mile away from it, and I can see small imperfections in the surface I hadn't noticed before, irregular bumps and knots that reinforce the grown look of the spire.

"Five hundred feet up," Halley says. "That's about as low as I care to go, I think."

The place where the other drop ship crashed into the planet's surface is easy to spot. There's an impact mark on the ground, just a few hundred feet from the base of the spire, and a scorched furrow leading away from the initial mark. At the end of the blackened scar in the rocky soil, there's a debris field, and the shattered wreck of what was once Stinger Six-One. The remains of the drop ship are mangled so badly that I wouldn't recognize it if I didn't know what a Wasp looks like in undamaged condition. Halley makes a low pass over the crash site, and I can see that parts of the wreckage are still burning.

"See any chutes?" Halley asks.

"I don't know. What am I looking for?"

"The outside of the canopy is camo, and the inside orange. You can use 'em as signal markers for the search-and-rescue birds."

I look around the crash site as we circle overhead, but I don't see anything other than broken and twisted bits of drop ship. When I glance over to the base of the alien structure, I notice something else, however—there are scorch marks and impact splatters marring the surface of the spire.

"Looks like your buddies tried to take a chunk out of it," I say to Halley, and point to the damage. She looks over to the stem and observes the impact marks for a moment.

"Well, shit. So they did. The dumbass Rickman thinks with his balls most of the time. Figures he'd make an attack run on that thing."

"Wonder how they brought that ship down. Think they got weapons?"

"I'm not too interested in finding out," Halley says. "Let's get out of here before we do."

CHAPTER 22

—WILLOUGHBY FOUR-SEVEN—

"Attention, all *Versailles* personnel. This is the XO. Remain at your location, and do not attempt to reach any colony settlements. We have hostile invaders on this planet, and you are ordered to lie low and avoid contact until our rescue ship arrives. I repeat, do not attempt to contact or reach any colony settlements, and do not engage unless attacked."

We're cruising at high altitude, far above the weather, and the XO is broadcasting the same message every few minutes. We have received a few replies from our people stranded below, but the XO has denied all requests for pickups, much to my relief. I don't want to leave our people stranded, of course, but they'd be no better off in the hold of the drop ship than they are near their escape pods on the ground, and I don't want to go back into the mess below and discover more bad news. In any case, our remaining fuel is barely enough to get us safely back to the terraforming station where we left the rest of our crew.

"Talk about a one-sided ass-kicking," Halley says to me while the XO keeps himself busy with the ship's radio suite back in the crew chief's seat. "Our ship's gone, our colony's wiped out, and now they're just setting up shop down there."

"I don't think they even tried to kick our asses," I say, and shudder at the fresh memory of hundreds of colonists lying dead in the streets of the main settlement, with no apparent injuries, or damage to the buildings. "That place back there wasn't wiped out. Just fumigated. Like you'd smoke out a bunch of ants in your kitchen cabinet, you know? Toss in a pest stick, come back to mop up the dead stuff later."

"That's a cheery thought," she says. "Like we don't even rate real weapons."

To our left, the local sun, Capella A, is just about to touch the horizon. The sun looks bigger and more washed out than our sun back on Earth, but the display is still spectacular, like a hydrogen bomb going off in the distance. The sky on the horizon is a brilliant palette of orange, red, and dark purple. I watch my first extrasolar sunset for a while, and it occurs to me that I can't remember ever having sat down just to watch a sunset back on Earth.

"Well," Halley says. "I do hope the navy's going to send something bigger than an old frigate to check on us, or there'll be a bunch more crash pods raining down soon."

The night on Capella Ac is black as pitch. There's no local moon overhead to serve as a planetary night-light. As soon as the last sliver of the local sun sinks below the horizon, the world outside disappears. I can't even make out the ragged line of the horizon ahead of us anymore, and the lack of external visual references makes me disoriented.

"Put your visor down, and tap the switch on the brow ridge," Halley tells me when I voice my discomfort. "You got infrared and low-light magnification built into that brain bucket there."

As we slowly cross the mountain range, the engines of our ship laboring to keep a few thousand feet between us and the highest peaks, Halley tries to contact the terraforming station that still lies a few hundred miles to our north.

"Terraformer Willoughby Four-Seven, this is Stinger Six-Two. Do you read, over?"

I expect another long period of silence in my headset, but the reply from the station comes almost instantly.

"Stinger Six-Two, I read you. Glad to see you back."

"Four-Seven, we are two-niner-zero miles south of you, inbound to land. What's the weather like down there?"

"Lousy," the reply comes. "Heavy rain, visibility less than a quarter mile, winds at three-zero knots from bearing one-eighty. You sure you want to try landing your bird in this mess?"

"We have nowhere else to go," Halley replies. "I have thirty minutes of fuel left. It's either that, or putting down in the sticks. Just turn on all the lights for me down there. I'll find the complex with ground radar, and do the last bit by sight."

"Copy that, Six-Two. We'll keep the lights on for you. Good luck, and be careful."

Halley looks at me and chuckles.

"'Be careful'? We're in an unarmed ship, low on gas, on a planet crawling with giant things that aren't friendly, and about to make a landing in the soup with no AILS, and he tells me to 'be careful.'"

"I'm having second thoughts about this navy career," I tell Halley. "We make it off this rock, I'll put in for office duty, or laundry folding. Something low-stress on a quiet space station somewhere."

"Fat chance, son," the XO says from behind our seats. I'm so tired that I didn't hear him coming through the cockpit door. "Hate to break it to you, but we just bumped into the first alien species ever encountered by humanity. We make it off this rock, you'll be one of the most popular guys in the entire fleet. Once the Intel guys are done with us, that is."

By the time we're over the terraforming station again, I'm definitely ready for a new career in the custodial services, far away from drop ships and emergency crash pods. As we descend through the weather, it feels like the ship is getting shoved around at random in all directions, but Halley is icy calm on the controls, so I once again shut up and try to meld with my seat. Even with the infrared feed from my helmet, I don't see the lights of the station's buildings until we're just a few hundred feet above the landing pad. Then we're on the ground, before I have a chance to become concerned with our rate of descent. As soon as the drop ship settles on its skids on the gravel of the landing pad, Halley cuts the throttle and exhales sharply.

"Remind me to log this flight when we get back," she says. "I'll put it under 'Shit Weather Flying.' Thirty-knot winds, my ass."

The dash from the landing pad to the nearest building is less than a hundred yards, but by the time we've made it into the building, we're soaked to our bones.

"I'm wiped out," Halley says to me as we shake the rainwater out of our hair inside the admin building, leaving puddles on the rubberized floor. "I love flying and all, but holding that stick for ten hours straight is a bit of a bear."

"How long has it been since you've slept?" the XO asks her.

Halley shrugs. "No idea, sir. I was just getting off watch when the ship got hit. Twenty-four hours, maybe?"

"You go find some dry clothes somewhere," the XO orders. "I'm sure the marines have some spare fatigues stashed away somewhere. Find yourself some chow and a cot, and crash for a while. That goes for you, too, Mr. Grayson," he adds.

The terraforming station has living quarters for the techs and the garrisoned marine squad, but we don't want to claim someone else's bed, so Halley and I set up a pair of folding cots in one of the many storage rooms. I've been on a steady dose of adrenaline and fear since the *Versailles* got hit, and I haven't much felt like sleeping until now, but the relative safety of the warm storage room suddenly makes me feel my fatigue. We lean our rifles against the nearby wall and exchange our soaked navy clothes for dry marine ICUs before lying down on the creaky cots.

"I'm scared shitless," Halley says as we listen to the low humming of the environmental system. The cots are short, and far less comfortable than our bunks back on the ship. The blankets are scratchy and smell like they've been in a dusty storage locker for the last five years.

"Gee, I can't imagine why," I reply. "Lush planet, friendly locals . . ."

"Do you ever stop being a smart-ass, Andrew?"

"No, I don't. You see, it's my defense mechanism, to cover up the fact that I'm scared shitless, too."

"I see," she smiles. "Glad I'm not the only one. Aren't we just the biggest shit magnets?"

"You have no idea," I say.

With the cots pushed together, we lie close enough to each other that our bodies are almost touching. I reach over to wrap my arm around her shoulder, and she scoots over a little to nestle herself against my side, as if she had just waited for me to raise my arm.

"Thanks for saving our asses today," I whisper. She looks up and leans in to kiss me.

"Thanks for not dying on me today," she murmurs.

Sometime later, someone runs past the door of the storage room, and I jerk awake. It feels like I've been dozing only for a few minutes, but when I check the time, I find that we've been asleep for over six hours.

There's a rumbling in the air that's so low I can feel it more than I can hear it. The floor under our cots vibrates almost imperceptibly. Then the tremor is gone, only to return a few seconds later, just a little more noticeable than before. It sounds like a very faint earthquake, or artillery shells exploding at a great distance. Something about the low and steady vibrations makes me feel a great swell of unease.

Next to me, Halley stirs on her cot, and I reach over to shake her awake.

"Get up and get your boots on. Come on."

The low-frequency vibrations beneath our feet return every few seconds, each time just a little stronger. Each tremor is accompanied by a low rumbling in the air, slow and regular, like the beating of a giant heart.

"What the hell is that?" Halley asks, her voice still thick with sleep.

"I think we're in deep shit," I reply.

Overhead, the base alarm starts bleating.

We put on our boots and grab our rifles. My admin deck in its shockproof case is leaning against the wall on my side of the cot, and I grab it and sling it over my shoulder. Then we dash over to the mess hall, where the rest of our little crew is already busy charging weapons and fastening harness straps.

"Everyone grab a commo kit," the XO says as we come into the room.

"What's the story, sir?" I ask.

"The marines up on the roof say we have incoming. They can't see what it is yet, but it's coming through the soup from the north. I'm going to go ahead and guess it's pretty fucking big."

Underneath our feet, the floor of the station shakes again slightly, as if to emphasize his statement.

"Marines," Corporal Harrison shouts. "Grab some launchers, and let's get up on that roof."

Our *Versailles* marines are now wearing partial battle-armor helmets, chest plates, and leg armor, undoubtedly borrowed from the local garrison supplies. They each take a MARS launcher off the tables where the drop ship's armory is spread out, and then file out of the door at a run. We're left in the mess hall with a few navy console jockeys and a small group of worried-looking civilian techs.

"Anyone knows how to use a rifle, you best grab one now," the XO tells the civilians.

I have the rifle from the drop ship, but I still walk up to the tables with the remnants of the drop-ship armory, to see what the marines have left for us. All the MARS launchers and rocket cartridges are gone, but there are plenty of rifle grenades left. I slip a spare harness over my clean marine ICUs, and start filling the loops and pouches with rifle magazines and forty-millimeter grenades. Next to me, Halley is doing the same. The civvie techs are just milling about anxiously, eyeing the two of us and studying the rifles left on the table like some vaguely interesting, but scary artifacts.

"Where do you want us, sir?" Halley asks the commander when we have finished gearing up.

"Hell, I don't know," he says. "Find a good spot to use those rifles, I suppose. The jarheads are all up on the roof of the main building. Someone needs to stay here and work the comms."

"We have a shelter," the civilian administrator says. "It's in the main unit, down in the basement level. It's got its own air supply and comms gear."

"Outstanding," the commander says. "You civilians go and hole up there. Lieutenant Benning, go with them and make sure someone answers the phone if the navy shows up and starts calling. The rest of you, let's go topside and add a few more rifles to the squad. Let's go, people, before our guests get here."

The rain has slacked off in the hours since we landed the drop ship. The roof of the atmospheric-processing station is a flat, rubber-coated surface the size of a city block. The wet rubber squishes under our boots as we rush from the access door to the edge of the roof, where the marines have spread out in fighting positions. Even the short side of the building is at least a hundred yards wide, and the three fire teams spread out along the edge of the roof have an awful lot of empty space between them. The fire team on the right corner is setting up a crew-served automatic weapon, a large-bore machine gun that's mounted on a tripod and fed from large, translucent ammunition canisters.

"Friendlies to the rear," the XO shouts as we come up behind the marines in the middle of the roof. "We brought you a few more trigger pullers, Sergeant."

"Can't hurt, sir," Sergeant Becker says. "The more, the merrier."

"Where do you want us, son? I'll let you run your own show here, 'cause I'm worthless as a ground pounder. You just tell me where to stand and when to shoot."

"Yes, sir," the sergeant replies. "If you wouldn't mind, just split up your people and pad my three teams."

"No problem," the XO says. "Ensign Halley and Mr. Grayson, you go over to Corporal Harrison. Lieutenant Davis and Lieutenant Grazio, you go over to Corporal Schaefer, and do whatever he tells you to do. I'll stay here with the sergeant and do the same."

By the time Halley and I reach the corner of the roof where Corporal Harrison's fire team has set up shop, the impact tremors coming our way are strong enough to rattle the prefabricated wall sections of the admin building fifty feet below us. Something very large is coming through the rainy haze in front of the terraforming station. I notice Halley looking over to the landing pad, where the drop ship sits on the gravel like a huge insect at rest. On the whole, I'd rather be twenty thousand feet above the ground right now, and I can tell by Halley's expression that she feels the same way.

"Here it comes," one of the marines from another fire team shouts. "One o'clock, four hundred."

We look over to the spot he indicates and see the outline of a massive shape in the haze a few hundred yards ahead. It's still mostly obscured by mist and fog, but the general shape and size of it is terrifyingly large, like a fleet destroyer coming at us through the rainsqualls. Then our visitor steps out of the obscuring mists with slow, giant steps that feel like small earthquakes under our feet.

"Holy shit," Corporal Harrison says. All over our thin battle line, I hear marines shouting in surprise.

There's no doubt about the alien origin of the creature that's now coming across the rocky plateau toward us. My mind tries to come up with a comparable example of terrestrial biology, and draws a blank. It somehow looks reptilian, avian, and mammalian all at the same time. I see a huge, eyeless head that slowly swings from side to side, and what seems like acres of rain-slick skin the color of eggshells. Its front limbs are much longer than its hind limbs, and joined at the center in a way that seems structurally

Impossible. It walks hunched over on its forelimbs, like a giant fruit bat walking on its wings. Even with its stooped posture, it's probably fifty or sixty feet tall, and it looks like it could unfold itself to twice that height if it stood up straight on its hind legs. Its overall appearance is familiar and unsettlingly strange at the same time.

"Autocannon," Sergeant Becker shouts. "Hose it down!"

On the opposite corner of the roof, the autocannon crew opens fire. The squad automatic weapon sounds like a giant jackhammer. It pours out three hundred rounds per minute in a slow, authoritative staccato. I watch as the rounds from the autocannon swarm out to meet the towering form coming out of the mist, and then bounce off in brilliant little explosions, sending sparks in every direction.

The alien creature lets out a piercing scream that is earsplitting even at this distance. It sounds like nothing I've ever heard before—a high-pitched, trilling wail that sends shivers down my spine and makes me want to find a hole to crawl into. A quarter mile away, the creature staggers and sways to one side. Then it regains its footing and continues on its path. Its sheer size makes it look like it's moving in ponderous slow motion, but it's covering the distance between the mist line and the terraforming station at alarming speed.

"You have got to be shitting me," Corporal Harrison says next to us.

"Rocket launchers," Sergeant Becker shouts from the central position. "Ready, aim, and fire on my mark."

The autocannon is still hammering out its streams of tracers in long, steady bursts. The alien is walking right into the incoming barrage, tracers bouncing off its hide as if the creature is wearing ceramic composite armor. The marine gunners are raking its torso, trying to probe for a weak spot, but there doesn't seem to be one.

The autocannon's standard round is a dual-purpose shell, an armor-piercing penetrator with a piggybacked high-explosive fragmentation warhead, and those rounds pack enough of a punch to take out an armored vehicle at a thousand yards. Against the tough hide of this creature, the shells burst in a shower of sparks, like oversized fireworks. The creature is clearly annoyed, screeching its earth-shaking wail, but it's still coming at us.

Along the edge of the roof, marines shoulder the stubby tubes of their MARS launchers, and draw a bead on the approaching creature. I only have the rifle and its low-pressure grenade launcher, which will barely reach out this far, but I open the launcher's breech and feed it a fragmentation grenade anyway.

"In three, two, one. *Fire!*"

Half a dozen rocket launchers boom at the same instant, and half a dozen missiles leap out of their launcher tubes. They streak toward the alien creature, their exhaust nozzles glowing like a swarm of very large and angry fireflies. One of the missiles lands short, hitting the ground in front of the creature and throwing up a geyser of dirt and rocks. Another one streaks past the alien, missing its left side by a few feet. Then the other three warheads explode against its torso in huge fireballs that light up the night in the distance.

The simultaneous impact of three MARS rockets manages what the fire from the autocannon failed to accomplish. The alien creature is knocked off its feet. It tumbles to the muddy ground, screeching its nerve-racking scream. The marines start shouting and cheering in triumph.

The autocannon ceases its relentless fire. I look through the optical sight of my rifle and switch to maximum magnification. The creature is flailing on the ground just three hundred yards away. There's smoke rising from its hide where the MARS rockets slammed into it. The limbs of the alien throw up mud and dirt as it thrashes around. Then it manages to steady itself, and slowly rises back to its feet. It takes a step as if to make sure its legs are still working and then continues its march toward the terraformer, albeit a little less steady than before.

"Fuck me," Halley says in astonishment. I can only shake my head in agreement. The creature just absorbed enough explosives to tear a drop ship into fine shrapnel, and now it's back on its feet, looking only a little worse for the wear.

"Launchers, reload!" Sergeant Becker shouts into the common circuit. "Load the armor-piercing shit. On the double!"

The MARS gunners load new cartridges into their launchers, shoulder the rocket tubes once more, and aim their weapons. I would grab one of those launchers myself, but our reinforced squad only has six of them, with three rockets each, and they're all in the hands of marines right now. All I have is my rifle, whose grenade launcher shoots wet firecrackers in comparison, but I bring up my rifle anyway, and put the ladder of the launcher's aiming reticle over the creature that's now again approaching with thundering steps.

"On three, two, one, *fire!*"

Again, half a dozen launchers send their payloads downrange with a muffled bang. This salvo is a little more precise than the last one. Only one of the rockets goes wide, and the rest connect with the bulk of the alien's torso. One of the missiles clips the shield-like protrusion at the back of its head, and I can see chunks tearing off as the high-speed penetrator of the armor-piercing rocket tears into it. The other three rockets slam into the center of its torso, with far less pyrotechnic drama than before.

This time, the creature falls forward with a wail, carried by its own momentum. I only realize how close the alien has come to our position when I see its head digging a furrow into the ground a mere fifty yards at most from the landing pad where our drop ship crouches like a resting insect. The roof under our feet shakes with the force of the creature's impact. The alien wails again, and starts flailing, this time less vigorous than before. Something about it reminds me of a bird twitching on the ground with a broken wing—panicked, frenzied, mindless desperation.

"Fire at will!" the sergeant shouts, and the space in front of the administration building turns into the Seventh Circle of Hell as a dozen marines start firing their weapons at the same time.

To our right, the autocannon opens up again. All along the edge of the roof, fléchette rifles start chattering their hoarse reports. I aim at the downed creature, and start firing grenades. Next to me, Halley follows suit. Our little reinforced squad is firing every weapon on the roof at the downed alien, and the noise is deafening. I go through the few grenades in my harness one by one, firing them as fast as I can stuff them into the breech of the launcher and then adding the contents of my rifle magazine when I'm out of grenades. At this range, the huge form is impossible to miss. I fire one magazine after another, two hundred and fifty rounds at a time in three-second bursts, pumping out needle-tipped tungsten darts as fast as the technology will let me.

Then there's no movement from the figure below, and all we're doing is shooting at dead matter. Still, I keep my finger on the trigger and my aiming reticule on the target until the bolt of my rifle locks back on an empty magazine.

"Cease fire, cease fire," someone calls over the common channel, and the gunfire gradually ebbs. For a few moments, there are no sounds other than the rain falling on the rooftop all around us. Down below, the alien creature lies motionless, sprawled out in the mud just a few dozen yards in front of the admin building. I eject the magazine from my rifle and search for a new one in the pouches on my harness, only to find that I've burned through my entire supply of rifle ammunition and grenades.

A whooping cheer rises from the ranks of the marine squad.

"*Nailed* the motherfucker," Corporal Harrison shouts, and I hear similar exclamations from all sides. Halley merely exchanges a wary glance with me as the marines celebrate our victory by slapping each other on the armor and pumping their fists into the air. I look down at the alien creature, lying still in the dirt. Its skin is still smoking in a few spots where the grenades and cannon shells have spent their explosive payloads against the alien's incredibly tough hide. We brought it down, but we had to throw just about every piece of ordnance in the armory at it, and the thing made it to within a hundred yards of our rooftop position.

Next to me, Halley squints down at the creature, and gives me another weary look.

"That was too damn close," she says, echoing my thoughts.

Underneath our feet, the roof of the terraforming station vibrates faintly, and there's a familiar rumbling in the air that's making my stomach clench once again. I look up, and by the expression on Halley's face, I can tell that she felt it as well. All around us, the laughter and cheering ebbs as the marines notice the new tremors as well. This time, the vibrations are strangely dissonant and out of phase, not steady and rhythmic like before.

"Oh, shit," Halley says.

"Reload those weapons," Sergeant Becker shouts from his position fifty yards to our right. "Get those launchers back up, right the hell now."

There are small ammunition stashes at each fighting position. I open a box of rifle magazines and find it half empty, twenty out of forty magazines already used up. I take out a magazine, slap it into my rifle, and stuff two more into the pouches on my harness. One of the marines puts down a MARS launcher next to me and grabs a rocket cartridge from a very small stack of them.

"That's all we have left?" I ask.

"We had three per launcher," he says. "I used up two just now, and the rest ain't even armor piercing."

I hear shouts of alarm, and turn around to see not one, but four more of the huge alien creatures ambling out of the fog a few hundred yards away.

"Oh, *shit*," Halley says again.

CHAPTER 23

LIGHTS OUT

The newcomers don't simply follow the path of the previous visitor. Instead, they pause at the very edge of the mist line and then fan out in a widely spaced line abreast, as if they are aware of the fate of their fellow traveler and the limitations of our handheld weapons. When they finally start to cross the rocky terrain toward the station, they fan out even more, until there are several hundred yards between each of the approaching creatures. Their battle line now takes up half a mile, and they advance in a more urgent stride than the one that came before them. With only fourteen troops split up into three teams, and three-quarters of our ammunition already expended, I know at once that we don't have a chance of stopping this new assault.

On the right side of the roof, the autocannon crew opens fire again. The big ammunition canister attached to the gun is made of see-through polymer, and even from a hundred yards away, I can see that the level of remaining shells is very low.

"Left flank!" Corporal Harrison shouts. "Shoot the one all the way to the left. Fire at will!"

With the newcomers spread out, our teams are forced to split up their fire. Our fire team around Corporal Harrison starts pouring rounds into the creature on the left flank of the approaching line. Like before, I switch my rifle to fully automatic mode, and start dumping my magazines into the advancing alien.

"Don't you fucking miss with that rocket," Corporal Harrison tells his MARS gunner. "Wait until he gets closer. Cohen, grab that last rocket and reload for him as soon as that tube's empty. Make 'em count."

To our right, a cheer rises from the location of the autocannon team. We look over to the right flank and see that the cannon crew is aiming at the legs and feet of their target, instead of trying to score a hit on the torso like before. Their effort seems to be working. The creature's sure and steady gait falters as the tracer rounds start slamming into its lower extremities. Some of the tracers deflect off its hide and career into the darkness like embers in a breeze, but some clearly punch through. The creature lets out an awful, eardrum-shattering wail, and stumbles. Then it crashes to the ground with all the grace of a collapsing building.

"Shoot the legs," the call goes out over the common channel. "Aim low and shoot the legs!"

We shift our fire and aim at the legs of the alien that's striding across the plateau toward our corner of the building. Through my optical sight, I can see our fléchettes and grenades churning up the dirt in front of the creature's huge, three-toed feet. What worked with the high-velocity cannon rounds doesn't seem to work with our pitiful arsenal of small-bore weapons, however. I know that most of my bursts are finding their target, but the alien strides on, undeterred. Then our MARS gunner launches one of his two remaining rockets. I hear the familiar popping of the launcher tube's caps and raise my head over the sights of my rifle to observe the flight path of the rocket. It strikes a glancing blow to the outside of the creature's upper leg and then bounces off to explode in the mud behind the alien.

"Fuck!" the gunner exclaims. Another marine lifts up the last rocket cartridge and shoves it into the back of the launcher, performing the fastest MARS reload I've ever seen. He pops the locking latches shut, and pats the gunner's shoulder.

"Up!"

The gunner takes aim once more. By this time, the creature is so close that I could hit it with a well-thrown rock. The launcher booms again, and the rocket leaps out of the tube. A fraction of a second later, the explosive warhead strikes the left upper leg of the alien dead center between what looks like knee joint and hip. At this range, the pressure from the blast is enough to make me stumble back a step or two. The alien falters, and goes down on its injured leg with a shriek. It hits the corner of the building with its shoulder as it falls, and I get knocked off my feet. The surface of the roof is lined with mercifully soft rubber, but my head still hits it hard enough to make me see stars. When I regain my senses a moment later, my rifle is gone from my hands.

"Get the fuck back," one of the marines shouts. "It's getting back up."

The marines scramble back from the edge of the roof. A pair of hands grabs the collar of my borrowed marine fatigues, and I turn my head to see Halley crouching over me.

"Let's go, Mister," she shouts.

To our right, the two other fire teams failed to duplicate even our modest and temporary little victory. The two creatures that made up the center of the alien line have reached the building. The shield-like tops of their heads just barely clear the edge of the roof, but their long forelimbs can reach way beyond it. I see a three-fingered hand coming over the rooftop ledge and clawing into the rubber coating of the roof, the structure underneath yielding to the grasp of the enormous hand like the metal foil cover on a meal tray. The other creature doesn't even bother with such a probing approach. It merely brings down a huge arm on top of the roof, where it lands with a bang that sounds like an exploding artillery shell. This time, everyone left standing on the roof is knocked to the ground. Over to our right, there's suddenly a trench in the roof between us and the spot where Commander Campbell and Sergeant Becker's fire team took up position.

I scramble to my feet and pull Halley along with me. The surface of the roof is now slanted toward the spot where the alien creature tore a gash into the rooftop. My rifle lies on the ground a few yards away, but when I start toward it, the creature we downed just a few moments ago reaches over the edge of the roof and buries its three fingers in the rubber of the rooftop in front of me, clawing for a hold.

"Screw the gun," Halley shouts, and pulls me away. "We need to leave, right now."

I can't see if the commander and Sergeant Becker are still alive, but I don't want to wait around for instructions while the alien behemoths are taking apart the building under our feet.

The run back to the access door seems to take a lot longer than the dash out when we arrived up here, even though it feels like I'm running about twice as fast. Behind us, it sounds like someone is dropping frigates onto the hard ground from high orbit.

When we get to the door, there's a momentary traffic jam as ten of us are trying to squeeze through the hatch at the same time.

"Where's the damn shelter?" Halley yells through the din.

"Down the stairs, basement level," one of the marines shouts back as we duck through the door and run down the first flight of stairs. "Bottom of the stairs, take a right."

We thunder down the stairs like a herd of spooked animals. I have a brief flashback to our countdown lineups in front of the building back in Basic, and find that mortal danger is an even better motivator for a speedy descent than a pissed-off senior drill instructor.

Just as I reach the landing at the top floor, a huge jolt shakes the building, and most of us are knocked off our feet once again. I manage to hold on to the handrail with both arms, and avoid cracking my head on the metal latticework of the access staircase. Overhead, the lights flicker once and then go out altogether.

"The fuck?" someone demands. "How can they cut the power? This place is a fucking fusion plant."

"Keep moving, moron," another marine replies. "Don't fucking matter right now."

We rush down the stairs to the basement level. The building above our heads is shuddering with every new impact. With the power gone, the basement hallway is only lit by red emergency lights, which paint the scene in an eerie glow. On one of the levels above, something big crashes to the floor with a thundering racket that makes the walls shake. I feel like one of the little pigs in the storybook, running away from the big, bad wolf that has come to blow the house down.

The door of the emergency shelter is a small armored hatch set into a recessed section of the hallway. The traffic jam from before repeats itself down here in the semidarkness as a dozen people converge on the little alcove all at once. The marines at the front of the pack start pounding on the hatch with fists and rifle butts.

"Lieutenant Benning, open the fucking hatch," Halley shouts into the headset of her comms unit.

"Affirmative," comes the lieutenant's muffled reply over the common channel. "Stand back—that hatch opens out."

The marines clear the area in front of the hatch, and someone inside unlatches it and swings it open. The hatch itself is almost a foot thick, and the concrete walls of the shelter are at least twice as thick, but after the display I witnessed on the roof, I have my doubts about crawling in there and letting our visitors stomp around on top of us. Part of me wants to run off, find an exit door, and make for the hills. Then the marines behind us push me along, and we file through the narrow doorway and into the shelter.

The emergency bunker is a small room that's already crowded with all the civilian techs working at the station. The sudden and rapid influx of another dozen people in bulky battle armor turns the room into tight quarters worthy of an enlisted berth on a navy ship. Someone behind me closes the hatch, and the awful crashing and rumbling sounds coming from above diminish a little.

"Everyone make it down okay?" a voice asks, and I recognize Commander Campbell's gruff baritone.

"Headcount!" Sergeant Becker shouts.

"Rivers and Okuda are still topside," someone replies. "They were over by the autocannon. Can't raise 'em on comms anymore."

"Well, shit." Sergeant Becker checks the loading status of his rifle and shoulders his way through the crowd. "Two of you come with me. McMurtry, Gonzales, you're it."

"Belay that order," Commander Campbell says. "You keep that hatch shut right now."

Sergeant Becker turns around and glares at the commander, who is standing at the other side of the room.

"We don't leave marines behind, sir. If I still have men out there, I need to go and get them."

"You'd get turned into paste for nothing. That whole corner of the roof is gone. I saw them rip it right off, cannon mount and all. Your guys are KIA, Sarge. Stand down."

There's a general grumbling in the ranks of the garrison marines, but the XO is by far the highest-ranking person in the room, and McMurtry and Gonzales seem rather relieved by the commander's order. Halley and I make our way through the cluster of armored marines by the access hatch and join the commander and Lieutenant Benning at the far corner of the room.

All around me there's a sudden swell of conversation as the civilians want to know what happened on the roof, and the marines are more than willing to share. Commander Campbell fills in the details for Lieutenant Benning, who only got a very sketchy view of the short battle through our sporadic radio messages.

There's a sudden, massive jolt, much stronger than the ones before it, and the emergency lights in the room flicker briefly. I can hear an eerie groaning sound, and deduce that a good part of the building structure overhead is collapsing on top of us. Then the first jolt is followed by another, this one even more bone rattling, and it sounds like the Chinese just dropped a thermobaric artillery shell into the hallway just outside the shelter's hatch. Most of the marines hit the deck, shouting and cursing. Halley and I crouch down and look up at the ceiling.

The shelter is a square room, maybe thirty by thirty feet, and largely devoid of furniture. There's a comms console on a table in the back of the room, and the walls are lined with metal benches that are bolted to the concrete floor. There's another door near the comms station, this one fitted with a privacy partition rather than a steel hatch. I walk over to the second doorway and move the partition aside to find a smaller room, taken up mostly by a chemical toilet and a stuffed supply rack. There's nothing in this shelter solid enough to crawl under if our visitors manage to crush the roof over our heads.

Overhead, the sounds of tortured and groaning metal creates a terrifying crescendo. I can feel the floor of the shelter shaking with every major jolt and crash. With the hatch closed, we're like a bunch of rats in a box, no place to run or hide if whatever makes up the ceiling of the bunker proves inadequate to hold the weight of an eighty-foot-tall creature stepping on it. I briefly wonder how much they must weigh, but then decide that I'd rather not do that particular estimate while several of those things are trashing the terraforming station upstairs.

"What's going to happen if they crack open the fusion reactor?" I ask nobody in particular.

"Then the magnetic containment field fails and the plant shuts down," one of the civilian techs says. The name tag on her dirty overalls says "BARMORE."

"Is it going to kill those *giant* things if it does?"

"Nope," Technician Barmore replies. "You shut down the juice to the mag coils all of a sudden, they may burst. The size of those things, it probably won't do much."

Another jolt shakes the room. This one sends concrete dust raining from the ceiling.

"Shit," Halley says. I follow her gaze and see a crack in the wall of the shelter, no more than a few millimeters wide, but spanning the wall from ceiling to floor. Overhead, the lights flicker again, then go out. This time, they don't come back on.

"Emergency power's gone," one of the techs says.

"No shit," a marine mutters.

All around us, armor-suit taclights come on, illuminating the room in an eerie red hue. The fans of the ventilation unit whir listlessly as the system comes to a stop.

"Now what?" Halley asks.

"There's a battery bank for tertiary power," Technician Barmore says. She walks over to the small supply room with the toilet. "Can I get a light here?"

One of the marines obliges and steps closer. Barmore removes the cover from a wall-mounted panel and reveals a row of old-fashioned mechanical switches with safety covers. She flips a few of them, and the overhead lights come back on silently. A few moments later the fans of the environmental system spin back to life, coughing out a small amount of concrete dust in the process.

"How long is that going to last?" Commander Campbell asks.

"Hour, maybe two," Barmore says. "A bit longer if we can all take turns holding our breaths."

"Check ammo and gear," Sergeant Becker tells his marines. "Air goes out, we exfil. Giant fucking monsters outside or not."

I look at the marines, who don't look exactly enthusiastic about the idea. We have a handful of M-66 rifles and pistols, but nobody managed to salvage a rocket launcher in the chaos, and I know that we don't have the firepower to stop one of those things. But suffocating is not high up on my list of desirable ways to go, so I resolve to go out with them when they go through that hatch.

Just to my left, the comms console suddenly starts squawking. Whoever used the comms suite last left the volume cranked up to maximum level, and the sudden noise right beside me makes me flinch.

"*NAC personnel, NAC personnel. This is NACS* Manitoba, *on the emergency channel. Any NAC personnel reading this transmission, please acknowledge.*"

The talking in the shelter ceases at once, as three dozen pairs of eyes turn to the comms table. There is a moment of absolute, shell-shocked silence in the room. Then Commander Campbell dashes to the console and sits down in front of it.

"*Manitoba*, this is the XO, *Versailles*. Do you read?"

There's no reply, just the faint hiss of static. Then the *Manitoba*'s message repeats.

"*NAC personnel, NAC personnel. This is NACS* Manitoba . . ."

Commander Campbell tries to reply again, but the *Manitoba* doesn't acknowledge. He pounds his fist on the side of the console in frustration.

"Someone check this goddamn comms rack, please. If we can't call help down, we're done for."

"The disaster buoy must have made Alcubierre," Halley says. "And the fleet sent backup. This place wasn't on the roster for any resupplies this month other than *Versailles*."

"And a fat lot of good it's going to do us if that comms kit is Tango Uniform," Commander Campbell says. Behind us, the marines and civilian techs are murmuring among each other in excitement. Overhead, our visitors continue to tear the place down, but the crashing and banging has moved away a little, toward the back of the complex.

"The gear is fine," one of the techs says as he checks it out. "We're receiving, obviously. Far as I can tell, we're sending, but the link to the topside dish must be fucked."

"Can one of us run out to the surface with armor comms?" Halley asks. Sergeant Becker shakes his head.

"You could, but the suit comms don't have the juice to reach a ship in orbit. Drop ship less than, say, two hundred klicks away, maybe. Not all the way up into orbit, even if they're right overhead."

"What about your Wasp?" I ask Halley. "If they didn't wreck it, that is."

Halley and Commander Campbell look at me in surprise.

"Oh, sure," she says. "If we could get off the ground. But preflight from cold and dark takes ten minutes. Five if you say 'fuck it' to the regs and safety manuals. I don't think we'll have that much time, Andrew."

She looks at the closed hatch. I can tell from her expression that she's not wild about the idea of trying to get to her Wasp with what's milling around topside. I find that I'm not too crazy about it, either. In fact, now that I've said it, I almost wish I could reel it back in, just to make the look of anxiety on her face disappear again.

"But you don't have to be in the bird to preflight it," I say. "How did we refill that Wasp on the *Versailles*? We were nowhere near it at the time."

"Don't you remember? You did it through the neural-networks link. But we don't have a shipboard network around, do we?"

I'm suddenly very aware of the minor weight of my admin deck in its shockproof case slung over my shoulder.

"No, we don't," I say, a rush of adrenaline flooding my brain. "But I have a pretty good portable one."

I pat the case hanging by my side. She looks at it for a moment, uncomprehending. Then her eyes widen.

"Andrew," she says. "Just for that, I'd climb into your bunk in boot camp all over again."

"All I need is line of sight to the ship. The wireless maintenance network has a hundred-and-fifty-feet range." I look at Halley. "Please tell me you have the master access code for your bird's network interface."

She hesitates for a moment, then pulls her dog tags out from underneath her flight suit. She flips the bottom tag around. It has a laminated strip of polymer bearing handwritten numbers on it.

"Couldn't ever remember that long-ass code, so my crew chief wrote it down for me."

"Can we do the transmission from the ground, from cover?" I ask.

"Comms put out five megawatts," Halley says. "But with these mountains around, and in this soup? They may not hear us at all until they're directly overhead in orbit. If we want to be sure, I'll need to take off and get above the weather and clear those mountaintops. From twenty thousand feet, they can hear me over most of the hemisphere."

"Take your marines and have them cover for Mr. Grayson and

the ensign," Commander Campbell says. "If one of those things comes back that way, you'll just have to distract it long enough for Ensign Halley to make her ride."

Sergeant Becker looks around at his ragged group of tired marines. Then he nods and lifts his rifle again.

"On your feet, marines. Let's play linebacker for the ensign."

The crawl up to the surface through the debris-strewn basement access ramp takes a good ten minutes of sweaty, dirty climbing and squeezing through barriers of fallen concrete and steel. When we finally reach the doors to the outside, Halley and I have to sit down for a quick breather. My heart is pounding, and my anxiety feels like a clamp around my chest.

Then Sergeant Becker slowly opens one of the double doors and squeezes through quietly to scout out the outside again.

"Come on out," he says after a few moments. In the distance, there is crashing and rumbling, but it's less frantic and violent now.

We file out of the basement door and follow Sergeant Becker. He signals for his marines to take up covering positions, and they fan out, rifles at the ready. I feel very exposed out here, with no weapon in my hands.

The destruction on the surface is shockingly extensive. I turn around at the top of the steps to look back at the building, only to find that there's no structure left on this end of the station. There are steel girders and chunks of concrete strewn as far as I can see. What was once the front third of the terraforming station Willoughby Four-Seven is just a pile of rubble now. A hundred yards away, part of the remaining building has collapsed, the floors pancaked into each other like the layers in a sloppily made sandwich. I can see through the hole in the building toward the landing pad where Halley's Wasp is parked, and I can barely see the tops of the vertical stabilizers on the tail.

The rain is coming down in cold, steel-gray sheets. Within a few moments of being outside, my marine fatigues are drenched. The vital admin deck hanging on its ballistic strap by my side is cocooned in a case that's waterproof and resistant to small-arms fire, which makes it far more durable than its wearer. Halley hugs the wall to my left and rushes toward the corner of the building, a good seventy meters from the basement ramp's double doors. If one of those giant things turns that corner right now, there won't be any time for her to run back to the shelter. After a moment, I gather myself and trot after her.

We have to climb over debris piles and weave between mangled girders and ferroconcrete mesh as we make our way to the corner of the building. The sounds of demolition have moved into the center and back of the complex. With the rain falling like this, it's impossible to see much farther than sixty or seventy yards without the comforting sensory augmentation of a battle armor's helmet.

Halley reaches the corner and crouches before peeking around it. Then she turns back to me with a grin.

"It's still there. Do your thing, Andrew. Hurry up."

I don't need the encouragement. I kneel down in the mud next to her and unfasten the cover of my admin deck. Halley's Wasp is maybe a hundred meters from what's left of the front of the building, which is the upper limit of a drop ship's built-in wireless short-range network interface. I turn on my admin deck and scan for nearby virtual service jacks.

"Fuck," I say when nothing shows up on my screen.

"What's wrong?" Halley asks. There's a thunderous crash in the distance, and she looks over her shoulder with wide eyes, then back to me.

"Can't find the jack. Too far away, probably. Or it's the rain, or both. I need to get closer."

I look around again and run out into the open toward Halley's cold and dark drop ship. Fifty meters away, there's a large, ragged sheet of roof lining crumpled on the ground like a mangled tent, and I crawl underneath it to have some cover. After a few moments, there's splashing behind me as Halley joins me.

"Tell me you're getting a signal."

I check the screen of my admin deck and re-scan for open network ports. This time I see an available node popping up.

"I'm getting a signal. Passcode, please."

Halley pulls her dog tag chain over her head and tosses it to me. I wipe the dog tag on my soaked fatigues and read off the code as I enter it on my admin deck.

"I'm in. Come over here and help me with the preflight stuff."

Halley crawls closer until our bodies are wedged against each other side by side.

"Skip the nonessentials. I need avionics, flight controls, and the engines turning. Everything else I can turn on once I'm off the ground."

I go through the control panel and turn on the systems she indicates one by one.

"Electrical systems on."

In front of us, the lights in the cockpit of the Wasp come on. On the wingtips, the position lights start blinking, red and green.

"Main data bus on. Avionics on."

"When you turn the engines, do one at a time," Halley says. "Without auxiliary power, you're working off the batteries. They don't have enough juice to start both mills at the same time."

"Got it." I let her look at the controls for the fuel systems, and she points at the screen.

"Those right there. Turn on crossfeed and the aux fuel pumps. Wait with the engines until everything else is running. Those'll make a racket."

"How long do they need before they're up to where you need them for takeoff?"

"Minute, minute and a half."

All the tests they ever gave us at Neural Networks School didn't even come close to duplicating the pressure I feel right now as I prep Halley's Wasp for an emergency takeoff from a hostile world. I don't allow myself time to think about what will happen if I screw up and we blow our one good chance at getting that drop ship off the ground.

"Say the word and I'll light 'em," I tell Halley. She draws a shaky breath and peers out to where her Wasp's position lights are now painting the rainy night with green and red streaks.

"Do it," she says.

I press the part of the rain-splashed screen that says "ENGINE #1 START SEQUENCE INITIATE/ABORT."

Fifty meters ahead, the port engine of the Wasp comes alive with a soft whine that increases in volume by the second. Ten seconds later, the whine has grown into a throaty howl.

"Twenty percent. Twenty-five. Thirty."

"Light the other one when number one hits forty."

"Got it." I let my finger hover over the field labeled "ENGINE #2 START SEQUENCE INITIATE/ABORT."

Behind us in the distance, the sporadic demolition sounds have stopped.

"Uh-oh," Halley says.

A few moments later, there's a familiar low vibration that makes the ground underneath our bodies shake ever so slightly.

"Navy, get the hell out of there," Sergeant Becker's voice comes over my headset. "We're about to have contact back here. One bogey, coming out from the southern wall."

A few moments later, there's gunfire on the southern side of the ruined complex, the high-pitched rattling of fléchette rifles on maximum-cadence automatic fire. I look at my screen.

Forty percent.

I push the screen hard enough to leave a mark on the polyplast cover. In front of our skimpy cover, the second engine turns on, its low start-up whine mostly swallowed by the racket the first engine is making now.

"Open that side hatch," Halley shouts. "And then fucking *run.*"

I do as she ordered as she scrambles to her feet. It takes a few seconds to find the menu for the hatch controls, and by the time I have it activated, Halley is already halfway to her bird. I get up and run after her.

Behind us, all hell is breaking loose. Some of the marines still have grenades for their launchers, and I can hear the *whoomp* sounds from the launcher tubes, followed by the low but authoritative explosions from the grenades. Then there's an ear-shattering wail. I look over my shoulder and immediately wish I hadn't. One of the giant aliens is coming out of the rain, towering over the remnants of the southeastern corner of the terraforming station. It's still partly obscured by the squall and the darkness, but the flashes from the muzzles and grenade explosions lend enough illumination for me to see that it's moving fast. I'm caught between the building and the Wasp, and the way this thing is moving, there's only one way out of this. I'll never make it back to the basement ramp doors where the marines have taken up their blocking position.

"Get out of here," Sergeant Becker shouts again over the din. "We're getting under cover in ten seconds."

I turn back toward Halley's ship and run the fastest fifty-meter sprint of my life. The hatch is on the opposite side of the ship, so I skid underneath the Wasp's belly to avoid the exhaust of the engines, and jump to my feet before throwing myself into the open side hatch.

Up in the cockpit, Halley is already in her seat. Behind us, now in the dead spot of the drop ship's tail, there's another shrieking wail that's so loud that it drowns out the Wasp's engines.

"Sit down, hang on," she shouts. I throw myself into the armored copilot seat just as she seizes the controls. There's no time for me to even strap in as the Wasp lurches up and forward. Outside, beyond the thick polycarb panes of the cockpit window, the remains of the alien we killed from the rooftop earlier block the path in front of us, and Halley curses as she pulls up the nose of the Wasp and only barely manages not to ram her ship into the bulk of the dead creature. Beyond, darkness and rain shroud everything, and we're hurling through the night at full throttle. Halley is going for speed over altitude. I glance over to see that she has no helmet on—no night vision, no infrared, flying blind and deaf. I recall how many steep hills and mountains surround the terraforming station, and I open my mouth to shout something to Halley, but one look at her face tells me that she's quite aware of the problem. She banks the Wasp hard right and pulls up the nose to gain altitude.

When a minute has passed without a mountain coming out of the darkness and smacking into us, I allow myself to breathe again. Halley arrests our upward spiral, straightens out the ship, and toggles some controls on her console. The ship's bank angle becomes less severe, and we level out. Then she lets go of her controls and straps herself in. I follow her lead and put on the helmet I knocked off the seat in my haste.

"That's better," she says when she turns on her helmet and lowers the visor. When I activate my own helmet, the world outside becomes visible again, albeit in various shades of green. We're clear of the hilltops around the terraformer, in a gentle right-hand ascent into the clouds.

"That plan almost went straight down the shitter," Halley says. "I think that was the fastest takeoff anyone has ever done with a Wasp."

She brings more systems online while the ship flies itself on autopilot. I allow myself a few moments to check whether I'll need a change of uniform pants, which is thankfully not the case.

"Now what?" I ask.

"Now we turn on the radio, get above the soup, and call down our friends in space," Halley replies. "And then I'm going to land this ship somewhere safe and have a heart attack."

"*Manitoba*, this is Stinger Six-Two, the Charlie drop ship from NACS *Versailles*. Do you copy, over?"

"Stinger Six-Two, I read you five by five. What's your status and position, over?"

The reply from orbit is crystal clear. We're cruising in a loop above Willoughby Four-Seven, twenty thousand feet up and only about a thousand feet above the cloud blanket that now covers most of the continent as far as we can see.

"*Manitoba*, we have friendly personnel in need of SAR and close-air support at terraforming station Willoughby Four-Seven. We have hostile life-forms attacking the station. Personnel count is three-eight personnel, all holed up in the emergency bunker."

"Copy, Six-Two. Stand by."

The navy comms guy sounds remarkably businesslike for someone who has just been informed that there are aliens on the planet.

A few minutes later, the *Manitoba* sends again.

"Six-Two, *Manitoba*. We have a Shrike flight and a pair of drop ships inbound to your datum right now. ETA for close-air support is seven minutes. Their call sign is Hades, and they'll check in with you for target verification when they're close. The SAR flight will come in once the Shrikes have cleaned up."

"Copy that, *Manitoba*," Halley says, grinning at me. "I'm going back below the ceiling to spot for you. Visibility is shit down there. I'll mark the bad guys with the designator on the Wasp. You can't miss 'em—they're eighty feet tall."

"Uh . . . copy that, Six-Two."

Halley takes the Wasp back down through the cloud cover. The descent is much less terrifying than our blind ascent, but it's still a white-knuckle experience for me as the winds bounce the sixty-ton drop ship around like a cork in a rain-swollen creek.

When the cloud cover breaks, we're less than five hundred feet above the ground. Halley heads back toward the terraforming station, which now stands dark. Even from a kilometer away, I can see the hulking creatures on the perimeter of the ruined building. They've resumed their slow and methodical destruction of the station. I zoom in the optical feed and marvel at the complete wrongness of their physiology. They look like someone took the creepiest aspects of bats, lizards, birds, and humanoids, and mashed them all up in an impossibly tall, lanky package.

Halley brings the ship to an unsteady hover and fires up her targeting suite.

"God, I wish I had some missiles on these racks. Or just a hundred rounds for that autocannon." She puts targeting reticules on all four creatures and strokes the "LIVE/FIRE" button on her flight stick with a grim expression.

"Stinger Six-Two, this is Hades Three-Zero, inbound with air-to-ground. Tell me who's who down there."

"Hades Three-Zero, the good guys are holed up in the basement shelter of the station," Halley replies. "I am in a hover one klick to the southeast of the station, and I'm painting your hostiles. Repeat, all the good guys are in the shelter. Launch on my designators when you're in range."

"Copy that, Six-Two. Stand by, and you may want to plug your ears down there."

There's no warning, no engine noise to herald the arrival of the assault ships. The first indicator of the CAS flight's presence is the low, rumbling roar of a large autocannon spitting out shells at an incredibly high rate of fire. One kilometer in front of us, one of the alien creatures disappears in a shower of large-caliber grenade hits. A moment later, a Shrike assault ship streaks past us at full throttle, and our drop ship shakes in its wake. The Shrike pilot hoses the alien down for another second, then peels off to the right and disappears in the clouds again. When the dust has settled, the alien is on the ground, flailing.

From another direction, half a dozen very fast rocket-exhaust streaks come tearing through the cloud cover. They converge on the terraforming station, each following Halley's targeting beams and heading for one of the hulking aliens. The fireball that follows is so bright that my helmet filters kick in and turn the visor black briefly. When my sight returns, none of the aliens are standing anymore.

Halley lets out a shaky breath.

"Turns out you can be too worn out to cheer," she says.

———

The Wasp lands on a clear stretch of ground well away from the terraformer. Halley shuts down the engines and pats the flight console in front of her. Overhead, the Shrikes are flying cover at low altitude in case of additional visitors.

"Eight minutes of fuel left," she says. "Thanks for holding together, Six-Two."

We step out of the ship just as the engines come to a final, shuddering stop. I walk over to a large chunk of concrete, sit down on it, and feel a sudden urge to just lie in the wet dirt altogether. Halley walks up and drops on the ground next to me with a grunt, not even bothering to use something solid as a makeshift seat. A few hundred meters in front of us, the terraforming station is little more than a pile of mangled steel and concrete rubble.

"I have had my fucking fill of near-death experiences today," she says.

"I hope this counts as a defeat," I say to Halley, "because if this is a victory, I'd really hate to see what it looks like when we get our asses kicked."

CHAPTER 24

———— THE END OF THE ————
BEGINNING

The navy comes prepared for once. The next flight of drop ships that descend out of the rain-heavy clouds thirty minutes later are loaded to the wingtips with air-to-ground ordnance pods. The Shrikes continue to circle overhead as the drop ships land on the ground in front of the ruins of Willoughby Four-Seven. When the tail ramps of the drop ships lower onto the muddy ground, each ship disgorges a full squad of marines in sealed battle armor.

"Glad to see you people," Commander Campbell tells the lead marine when they reach our ragged and tired group of survivors. "It's getting a little unfriendly down here."

"So we've heard," the marine says. Because his suit is sealed, his voice is projected through the speaker in his helmet, and he sounds disconcertingly artificial as a result. "Had a bit of trouble with the new neighbors, I see."

We trot to the waiting drop ships while the newly arrived marines bring up the rear. When I walk up the ramp of the closest Wasp, I see that the hatch to the cockpit is closed, and that the crew chief standing by the ramp controls is in full sealed Chem-War gear as well.

The pilots of the drop ships do not waste any time with sight-seeing. As soon as our ragtag mix of civilians, marines, and navy stragglers is distributed onto the two Wasps, the pilots gun the engines and get the ships airborne before the rear cargo hatches have closed all the way.

"You pick up any more of my people?" the commander asks the marine team leader seated on the bench across the aisle from him. The marine shakes his head.

"Not us, sir. But there's SAR flights in the air all over this place. They sent down just about every drop ship in the battle group, I think."

"What do we have up in orbit?"

"Carrier Battle Group Sixty-Three, sir. The *Manitoba*, two cruisers, two destroyers, and a frigate."

"Hot damn," the commander says. "That's a lot of tonnage to send our way."

"We were in the neighborhood, I guess. Live-fire exercise out by Deimos. We were supposed to practice zero-g assaults, but then your buoy popped out of Alcubierre and started wailing."

"Sorry about spoiling your exercise," the commander says, and the marine chuckles.

"Not at all, sir. A combat drop beats exercise every time. Three more drops, and I get to pin on the master drop badge."

Now it's the commander's turn to chuckle.

"The way things are going right now, I think you marines are going to get your fill of combat drops soon enough, son."

The Wasp has no windows back in the cargo hold, but I can tell we've left the atmosphere of Willoughby when my body pulls against the lap belt of my seat. We hear the engine noises changing as the drop ship transitions to spaceflight and climbs into orbit to meet up with the carrier.

The sensations of forward motion and weight return when we enter the artificial gravity field of the assault carrier. I've never been in a drop ship that docked with something floating in space, and I expect something similar to the shuttle-docking procedure when I arrived for Fleet School on Luna, but the skids of the drop ship simply touch down on a hard surface. Then we're in motion again, this time being lowered on the platform of a large elevator.

When the cargo ramp lowers, there's a welcoming committee waiting for us. The flight deck of the assault carrier is cavernous compared to the two-ship affair on the *Versailles*. I see rows of drop ships and Shrikes, and the flight deck is abuzz with activity, crews in color-coded shirts fueling and arming the craft parked on the deck. The section where our ships set down is walled off from the rest of the flight deck with a transparent barrier of flexible polymer, and there's a decontamination tent set up not too far away.

"Well, I *was* looking forward to a good shower," Halley says dryly when she sees the ChemWar team in full protective gear waving us toward the decontamination tent. "Just not in the middle of the damn flight deck, with half the carrier watching."

We get scrubbed, rinsed, and doused with what seems like a dozen different chemical agents before the ChemWar team lets us put on some fresh uniforms. Even after the decontamination session, the *Manitoba*'s armed marine guards keep us segregated from the rest of the crew. We are led into a large room that looks like a hastily cleared storage area, and a dozen medical officers and nurses descend upon us to treat our minor scratches and bruises. When they're finally convinced that none of us will suddenly grow tentacles and devour the rest of the crew, we're led into yet another room, this one a briefing lounge big enough to hold a platoon of troops with room to spare. In front of the briefing lectern, there are rolling tables loaded with sandwich trays and beverage pitchers.

As we stand around the food tables, wolfing down sandwiches and draining pitchers of navy bug juice, a group of officers enters the room. They split us up and take us away for debriefings in smaller rooms. I hate to be separated from Halley after all we've been through, and for a moment I have to fight an impulse to punch the navy ensign who takes her out of the room and away from me. I end up at a table in a corner of one of the hangar's maintenance sections, with two officers sitting across the table from me. One of them is a lieutenant commander with a space-warfare badge, and the other is a lieutenant with Military Intelligence. Despite his lower rank, he's in charge of the conversation.

I know the military's dim view on lost and broken equipment, and considering the fact that we just lost a warship worth more than a billion Commonwealth dollars along with all the gear on board, I expect a rather hostile grilling from the MI officer. Instead, the debriefing is almost amiable, without a word of accusation. The officers listen to my version of the events, starting with our drop out of Alcubierre, and ending with the arrival of the rescue drop ships less than an hour ago.

"I can tell you we got shot out of orbit, but I have no idea how it happened. When we got out with the spare drop ship, there was no other ship around, just the *Versailles*."

"Wasn't a ship," the lieutenant commander says. "We came in with all the curb feelers out. Our new friends did some upgrades to the place, and that's all I can tell you right now."

"What, like we ran into something? Like an orbital minefield?"

The fleet officer looks at his MI counterpart.

"Yes," the lieutenant says. "Some sort of pods. You get close to one, they just kind of pop open and spray the neighborhood with penetrators. We didn't catch 'em at first, because they don't show on radar, but the Linebacker cruisers took care of the problem."

I know that under normal circumstances, the two officers wouldn't give me the time of day, much less explain enemy dispositions, but I can tell they're excited about being on the pulse of the action for this momentous event in human history, and their excitement makes them disregard the social and professional gulf between staff officers and junior enlisted for a little while. I don't share their excitement. I'm tired and worried, and I just want to find a bunk and sleep. I answer their questions, fill in the details they request, and repeat the sequence of events a few more times. Finally, the officers are satisfied with the amount of information they managed to squeeze from my brain, and I am dismissed to rejoin the rest of the crew.

Back in the briefing room, we continue our meals and exchange data to piece together the big picture. Carrier Battle Group Sixty-Three dropped out of Alcubierre roughly four hours ago, and approached our last-known location above Willoughby at combat stations, ready to do battle with the Sino-Russians. What they found instead was an orbital field of proximity mines that wouldn't show on radar, and looked like nothing listed in the spaceborne-weapons-recognition manuals. The drop ships of the *Manitoba* are still shuttling stranded *Versailles* sailors up from the surface, and rumor has it that the Shrikes have been emptying their ordnance racks at the alien terraforming structures, only to come back for bigger warheads.

"What's going to happen now?" I ask the commander later, when we're finishing the last of the food and waiting for the rest of our marooned crew to trickle in.

"Well, they're going to take care of business down there. I expect we'll see half the freakin' navy in orbit around this rock before too long. Then I guess we'll head back to Gateway. We'll all end up in the Transient Personnel Unit until the navy figures out what the hell to do with us. You may yet get your wish about that laundry-folding job, Mr. Grayson," he adds.

"Any chance for some leave, you think?" I ask, and he barks a laugh.

"We just had a run-in with a sentient alien species," he says. "If you think they're going to let us back to Earth, you're in for some disappointment. They're going to keep a lid on this until they've figured out how to break the news to the folks back home."

He stuffs the rest of his sandwich into his mouth and washes it down with the last of the juice in his cup.

"You know, it's kind of funny, in a weird sort of way," he continues. "Back at Staff Officer School, they have all these war games and scenarios they throw at you, to see how people deal with command pressure. We used to call the scenarios for alien encounters 'bug levels.' "

He puts his plastic dishes on the floor next to his chair, and leans back in his seat with a sigh.

"Now here we are, in our first real bug war, and *we're* the bugs."

When Halley comes back from her debriefing, she waves me toward her as soon as she spots me in the back of the room. I walk up to join her, and we claim a pair of chairs in a quiet corner of the room. By now, everyone in the room is stretched out in a briefing chair or two, dozing or talking.

"They're loading fucking nukes on those attack birds," she says to me when we're sitting down. "We cut across the corner of the flight deck when we got back from the debriefing, and I got a good look. Mark Sixty-Five guided nuclear missiles, fifteen kilotons."

"Holy crap," I say. The last time a military used nuclear arms in battle was forty years before I was born, during the last global fracas with the Sino-Russians that left half a million dead and led to the signing of the Svalbard Accords that put an end to direct Earthside conflicts between the two blocs.

"Guess they couldn't crack the stuff down there with the rack-grade stuff."

"That's going to mess up the real estate down there," Halley says. "If those things set up half the number of atmo exchangers we did, there's going to be close to a hundred nukes raining down soon. Nobody's going to farm down there for a few decades at least."

The idea of rendering a planet uninhabitable just to pry off a competing species seems ludicrous, but after my experience in Detroit, I know the military is going to do precisely that.

We're assigned a few empty enlisted berthing sections far away from the flight deck to get some rest. At this point, I've slept only six hours out of the last thirty-six, and I'm starting to have auditory hallucinations. There's a pair of medics outside the berthing section, handing out pilot-grade no-go pills to anyone who wants them, but Halley and I pass on the sleep aids, since we're both tired enough to sleep standing up if needed.

The *Manitoba* is a much newer ship than the *Versailles* was, and everything is far more modern, but the enlisted bunks aren't any bigger. Halley and I try to occupy one of the bunks together, but we conclude that the space is barely enough for one person. I let her have the bunk to herself, and take the one directly below hers. I close the privacy curtain and get under the thin blanket without bothering to take off my clothes. All around us, the sounds of a warship under way are ringing through the hull—announcements, tromping boots on metal gangways, humming machinery—but at this point in my short navy career, I am used to falling asleep to that particular soundtrack.

There are no daytimes on a warship, just watch cycles. The powers in charge let us sleep through a watch and a half before sending in some petty officers to shake us out of our cots. When I climb out of my coffin-like cot, I have no idea whether we're on first, second, or third watch, because my internal clock has lost the careful calibration it achieved just before the *Versailles* slipped into the Alcubierre chute to Capella A.

While we were asleep, the *Manitoba*'s drop-ship crews managed to pry another few dozen of our stranded crew members off the planet's surface. When we file back into the briefing room we used before, several rows of seats are already taken by other *Versailles* enlisted and officers. There's a general commotion as people rush to meet up with friends and berth mates. I don't know too many people on the crew yet, so I stick with Halley. She looks around to find some of her fellow pilots, but frowns when she comes up empty.

"Looks like I'm the entire aviation section now," she says. "Rickman and the other pilots are all on the KIA list."

I do a cursory headcount and come up with roughly sixty people, less than a third of the *Versailles*'s standard crew complement. Even allowing for a bunch of injured people in sick bay, our crew received a terrible drubbing.

"Attention, all hands," the XO says to the assembled crew after the first general buzz of excited conversation has dimmed a little. Everyone stops talking and faces the commander.

"We're done here," he continues. "The *Manitoba* will remain on station and continue combat operations on the surface. Some of you will be hitching a ride back home on the *Bunker Hill*. The lieutenant here will read off a list in a minute."

He pauses for a moment to look over the assembled remnants of the *Versailles* crew.

"You can all look forward to more debriefings and new assignments to God knows where. That's for the navy to decide. I wish they could give us a new frigate, so we could paint 'FF-472' onto the side and get back to business, but that's not in the cards."

Some of the sailors chuckle quietly and murmur their assent.

"For those of you going to Gateway for reassignment: Until you report to a new XO or commanding officer, you're still crew members of the NACS *Versailles*, and if I hear that any of you don't act the part while you're waiting around in the Transient Personnel Unit, I'll personally stop by and recalibrate your skulls. Do you understand?"

"Yes, sir," we shout back, loud enough to make the XO recoil just a little.

"Well, good," he says. "Glad that's out of the way."

"Sir," one of the petty officers says. "Any word from the skipper?"

"Captain Hill's pod was recovered last night," the commander says matter-of-factly. "Their chute either didn't deploy, or got ripped off the crash pod on descent for some reason."

The room turns deathly quiet in an instant.

"There were no survivors," the XO continues. "In the pod with the skipper were Lieutenant Commander Schiller, Lieutenant Munoz, Chief Petty Officer Ellis, and Marine Lieutenant Connelly."

For a few seconds, you could hear a piece of lint falling on the ground.

"Spare a thought for the old man and the rest of the CIC crew when you're on the way back to Gateway. You'll have plenty of time for that in Alcubierre. The skipper was a good man, and a fine commanding officer."

He looks at the lieutenant next to him, who carries a clipboard with a bunch of printouts stuffed into the document clasp.

"Mr. Benning will now read off the list of personnel who will hitch a ride on the *Bunker Hill* in an hour. If your name's not on the list, you're staying with me. If it is, I wish you good luck and safe passage. I am proud to have served with each and every one of you, and I'll gladly stand the watch with any of you again."

My name is on the list for the *Bunker Hill*, but Halley's isn't.

I was hoping for some more time with Halley, time that doesn't involve trying to get out of peril or flying around a desolate planet with an unarmed drop ship. As things stand right now, all I get is a quick good-bye in a busy gangway outside the hangar deck.

"Isn't that just fucking fabulous?" Halley says to me as we embrace for our third attempt at letting go of each other. "You pull all these strings to get transferred to my shit bucket, and then they blow it up from underneath us."

"I think the universe might hate me," I say.

"I don't think that's quite true, Andrew," she says, and kisses me on the corner of my mouth. "You managed to get on the right ship, after all. And we didn't crash or get sucked into space. I'm pretty sure I'd be a charred spot on the ground down there if I hadn't ditched Rickman after my watch and come to hang out with you."

"Well, there is that," I concede.

"We'll just do the distance thing again. Who knows, though? It's not that big of a navy. Try to get yourself posted to some big bird farm, one with lots of drop ships, okay?"

"I will."

We embrace one last time, ignoring the looks from passing crew members. Halley kisses me, and then gently pushes me away with the palm of her hand against my chest.

"Go, before one of us goes unauthorized absence and ends up in the brig for missing deployment."

"Stay safe," I tell her, and she laughs her cheerful, dark laugh.

"You've been there, Andrew. You can't be careful in the left seat of a Wasp, don't you know?"

"Later, pilot babe," I say.

"Later, computer jock," she replies.

"Last one," the crew chief of the shuttle Wasp tells me when I walk up the ramp without much enthusiasm. "Get strapped in— we're running behind already."

"Aye-aye, sir," I reply, and take a seat near the tail hatch. The crew chief steps back into the ship and pushes the control button for the cargo ramp. I fish for the worn safety straps on my seat and slip into the harness.

"Sorry to hear about your ship," the crew chief says against the noise of the rising ramp. I merely nod in acknowledgment.

"Well, you'll be at Gateway in a week. This one's over for you guys."

The ship's engines come to life, and I sit back and close my eyes, forcing myself to look away from the ever-narrowing gap of the rear hatch, toward the spot where Halley disappeared into the corridor a few moments ago.

I doubt that very much, I think. *This one's just begun.*

—— ACKNOWLEDGMENTS ——

When you work on a novel for a few years, you have a long list of people to thank in the event of your success. If you have worked on a novel for years and don't have such a list, you're either super-human or doing it ALL WRONG.

This novel had its genesis as an application piece for the Viable Paradise SF/F Writers' workshop. As such, I owe thanks to all my VP XII friends for their critiques, suggestions, and encouragement, especially Tiffani Angus, Claire Humphrey, Katrina Archer, Sarah Brandel, Madge Miller, Jeff Macfee, Chang Terhune, Steve Kopka, and Curtis Chen, my current VP XII Twitter posse and occasional critique partners. I also owe much to my instructors: Patrick Nielsen Hayden, Steven Gould, Laura Mixon, Uncle Jim and Dr. Doyle, Elizabeth Bear, and John Scalzi, who kindly shoehorned an unscheduled personal critique into his schedule for me. You have all been instrumental to the success of that little Space Kablooie novel you critiqued at Viable Paradise XII.

Thanks to my friends and family who had the courtesy not to roll their eyes whenever they heard I was still "working on my writing."

Thanks to my agent, Evan Gregory at Ethan Ellenberg Literary Agency, who makes sure I don't sign away my stuff for a shiny bauble and a handful of cool magic beans.

And lastly, thanks to my readers—the ones who just discovered me, and especially the ones who have been following my scribblings on the blog over the years. I put the little Space Kablooie novel out there, you bought it and liked it, and awesome things started to happen. Thank you all for your support and your kind words.

─── ABOUT THE AUTHOR ───

Photo by Robin Kloos, 2013

Marko Kloos is a novelist, freelance writer, and unpaid manservant to two small children. He is a graduate of the Viable Paradise SF/F Writers' Workshop.

Marko writes primarily science fiction and fantasy because he is a huge nerd and has been getting his genre fix at the library ever since he was old enough for his first library card. In the past, he has been a soldier, a bookseller, a freight dock worker, a tech support drone, and a corporate IT administrator.

A former native of Germany, Marko lives in New Hampshire with his wife and two children. Their compound, Castle Frostbite, is patrolled by a roving pack of dachshunds.